Winter's Awakening

Ravena's Prophecy

J. D. VICTERY

Winter's Awakening

© 2025 Jennie Victery

All rights reserved.

No part of this book may be reproduced, stored in a retrieval system, or transmitted in any form or by any means— electronic, mechanical, photocopying, recording, or otherwise— without prior written permission of the author, except for brief quotations used in reviews or critical articles. This is a work of fiction. Names, characters, places, and incidents either are products of the author's imagination or are used fictitiously. Any resemblance to actual persons, living or dead, or actual events is purely coincidental.

Cover design by Achlys Book Cover Designs

Paperback ISBN: 979-8218788742

Hardcover ISBN: 979-826596886

Printed in the United States of America

Dedication

Firstly, to my husband for always putting up with my never-ending hobbies, and most importantly for believing in me every step of the way and not letting me quit. You've shown me that anything is possible if I don't give up even if some days just suck. I love you for infinity!

Secondly, I want to thank all my new friends I have met on this journey, you all have inspired, supported, and read my unfinished book. You have all become family, and I'm forever grateful.

Pronunciation Guide

This story blends Greek and Norse mythology. Here's a quick reference for names, places, and terms.

Agnar —(AHG-nahr)
Eirik —(EYE-rik)
Runar —(ROO-nahr)
Chione —(kee-OH-nay)
Thyraheim —(THEE-rah-hyme)
Dionysus —(dye-oh-NYE-sus), god of wine
Agora —(AH-go-rah), marketplace
Korinthos —(koh-REEN-thos), city
Kalos —(kah-LOHS)-my beautiful one
Kapeleion —(kah-PEH-lee-on), tavern
Kapelos —(KAH-peh-loss), wine-seller / tavern host
Pandokeion —(pahn-do-KAY-on), inn / lodging house
Pandokeus —(pahn-do-KYOOS), innkeeper / host

Table of Contents

Chapter One

The forests of Nordmarka were a place that felt like time stood still, buried beneath endless snow and towering pines just outside of Oslo. My life revolved around ancient texts and relics, dedicating my early adulthood to uncovering the secrets of time. But even in the quiet of my research, I felt a pull I couldn't explain–a connection to something far older than history itself. For most, the silence out here would be stifling, but for me, I loved it. After a childhood of being excluded, I'd almost grown to prefer it.

My routine was simple. Ever since I arrived on my work visa, my days were spent between the university museum and long hikes out to the nearby historical site, my satchel always stuffed with sketches and notes. At the museum, they called me Ravena–sometimes *Miss Ravena* in a tone that felt half-respectful, half-dismissive, as if I was still too young to be taken seriously. They refused to use my last name, and I never corrected them. To be honest, I was too tired, and used to being background noise. I was only here to complete my work and bury myself in history.

Nights were spent tucked away in my assigned cabin, the fire chasing away the chill while stacks of books on the desk kept me company. Here, I didn't have to answer to anyone.

Sometimes I reminded myself this was only temporary. A work visa had an expiration date, after all. Eventually I'd pack up, return home, and try to pretend this life in the snow and solitude hadn't meant something. But every night, staring at the northern lights, restlessness twisted in my chest. I always felt like something was coming—like my real life hadn't even started yet.

But tonight felt different. The northern lights danced across the sky, their iridescent hues reflecting off the snow-covered trees. I let out a sigh, my breath forming a white fog in the cold air. I should have felt at peace here, but tension coiled in my stomach—a strange, crawling anticipation, as if something just out of reach was waiting for me.

I tossed and turned, unable to shake the sense that something was stirring. When sleep finally came, it wasn't the restful escape I'd hoped for.

I was no longer in my cabin but in a dark forest. Snow-covered mountains rose against the starry sky, their jagged peaks stark and imposing. The air was thick with an oppressive weight that made my chest feel tight. Breathing felt difficult as a biting wind howled through the trees.

In the distance, a figure stumbled forward–a woman, pale and weakened. Her breath came ragged as she trudged through the knee-deep snow. Long white hair, damp with sweat, clung to her face, parts of her hair were staining ominously red. She clutched her side before collapsing into the snow.

An invisible force yanked me toward her. I tried to dig my heels into the snow, but my body moved without my permission—my pulse pounding, breath caught. I knelt beside her, staring at the side of her face, which struck me as eerily familiar. Her lips trembled as she spoke, her voice no louder than a whisper.

"Odin, All-Father, hear my plea," she begged. "Fates... anyone, please help. Send me somewhere safe, where I can heal and return to stop this titan's madness."

The words reverberated through me. My breath hitched—I reached for her hand and then—darkness slammed into me.

I shot upright, gasping for air. My heart hammered in my chest, each beat echoing in my ears. The dream clung to me; I still felt like I was standing in that forest, the snow biting against my skin. My hands trembled as I swung my legs over the side of the bed, sitting there until the dizziness eased. I needed air...

My hands shook as I dragged my coat on, desperate for air—anything to shake off the icy panic clinging to my skin.

I noticed it immediately–the forest around me was eerily still. No wind stirred the trees. No nocturnal animals moved through the underbrush. Even the faint crackle of the fire pit's embers seemed muted.

I tilted my head back, letting my gaze drift to the northern lights. Their glow rippled across the snow like spilled ink, painting the world in soft, shifting hues.

Then, a whisper broke through the night, sharp and sudden. I flinched, heart hammering.

It is time.

Before I could even begin to look around, a flash of light engulfed me. The world twisted—and when it righted itself, I was no longer standing outside my cabin, that much I could tell.

I bent forward, hands braced on my knees, gasping for breath as my dark braid fell over my shoulder. When I straightened, my stomach dropped and I had to steady myself, swallowing down a wave of dizziness.

Before me, nestled among snow-capped mountains, a village stretched hidden in the trees. And when I turned to my right, distant rooftops of homes protruded, near the coast the water shimmered beneath the early morning light.

But this wasn't the world I knew. There were no modern buildings, no cars. Only trees for miles, dirt roads, and untainted air. I could faintly smell the smoke from the fires of the villages, and the distant bray of livestock and the singing of birds.

Then, from the corner of my eye something moved. I spun towards it–a shadow, cloaked figure, darting between the trees. For a split second, the air shifted; it smelled faintly of smoke and herbs, like incense, before it was gone.

My pulse raced, breath clouding the air. Every part of me screamed to turn back, but my feet kept moving, drawn by something I couldn't explain. Swallowing hard, and like every moment in a horror movie, I followed the flickering shadow into the snow-laden forest, the crunch of my boots echoing in the silence.

With each step, the realization settled deeper into my chest. I wasn't in Norway anymore. And I was starting to believe I wasn't even in my own time.

As I followed the cloaked figure, I could only wonder how. How had I somehow been transported to another time?

The shadow figure disappeared, and the forest thinned ahead. I halted, out of breath and lightly shivering. Cautiously, I stepped forward, the murmurs of that same village reaching my ears. The shadow had directly led me here.

Through the trees, I glimpsed modest houses—mudbrick walls, exposed wooden beams, and steep, terracotta-tiled roofs. The chimneys were little more than holes at the peaks, thin smoke trailing up into the cold air. Courtyards and porches hugged each home, stacked firewood piled neatly against the walls. A few goats picked their way between the open gates, while villagers bustled about: some carrying baskets of goods, others tending fires or conversing in hushed voices. Children ran after one another, their laughter ringing through the morning.

At the village's center stood a larger building—wider, taller, with painted columns at the entrance and brighter tiles along the roofline. It looked like a meeting hall, or maybe a place for the village elders. I hesitated, my heart pounding, hands fidgeting at my sides. Should I reveal myself?

Before I could decide, a villager spotted me and hurried off.

Murmurs spread quickly. Children darted behind their parents, wide-eyed as they pointed at my strange clothes. A few men reached for weapons, their expressions wary.

Then, what appeared to be an elder stepped out of the meeting hall. His gaze locked onto mine, and for a moment, his face betrayed shock—or was it recognition?

"Elder Theron," someone whispered. "She doesn't look normal."

I flushed, suddenly aware of my own awkwardness. "Rude," I muttered under my breath.

But then my stomach dipped. *Wait—how did I understand that?* The murmurs swelled, villagers speaking too quickly, their words slipping over each other. At first, I only caught fragments, bits of phrasing I recognized from my studies... but the meaning threaded itself together in my head, smooth and seamless, as if it had always been there.

Theron's gaze never wavered as he stepped closer. "It can't be... You've come."

A chill ran down my spine. The whispers faded as all eyes turned to me, waiting, expectant. My mouth went dry. My hands toying with my sleeves, desperate to distract my nerves. "I... I think I'm lost."

The man Theron didn't answer right away, but an understanding look softened his eyes. He turned to the murmuring villagers and raised a hand, silencing them. "Let's not linger outside. You must be cold." He gestured toward the main hall. "Follow me. We have much to discuss."

With no better options, because honestly, I was out here in sweats and a jacket. I stepped forward, following him into the warmth of the village's main hall.

Inside, the scent of burning wood and incense filled the air. The hall was modest, yet well-kept, flat stone floors polished smooth, walls lined with woven tapestries. A fire crackled in the hearth, casting flickering light across the long table where several plates of food were being placed.

"Sit, Lady Ravena," Theron said, motioning to a chair. "Eat. Warm up. Once Lydia returns from the temple, all will be explained."

I balked at the title, sinking into the chair, my hands clasped tight in my lap as my eyes drifted over the steaming food. My stomach twisted with hunger, but questions swirled too fast to ignore.

Before I could open my mouth to ask, or before I could even think about eating, the doors swung open with force.

A woman entered—tall, regal, her striking pale green eyes locking onto mine immediately. She moved with purpose, her expression reflecting mixed emotions. Then, without hesitation, she dropped to both knees.

"Lady Ravena," she whispered, awe lacing her voice. "The prophecy was true. You have come."

The hall fell utterly silent. Even the fire in the hearth seemed to dim, its crackle fading beneath the affliction of her words. Theron's eyes stayed fixed on me, his expression indecipherable, while Lydia remained bowed low, as if waiting for me to confirm what she already believed.

I gripped the edge of the table, nails digging into the wood, as my head spun from the gesture and her words.

A prophecy? What?

My pulse spiked, the word clawing at my chest. Their eyes were on me, expectant, certain I was someone they had waited for. My throat went dry, my mind scrambling for anything that made sense.

This had to be a mistake. A dream. A trick. Even so, the seriousness in their eyes, the way the air felt heavy... it wasn't something I could laugh off.

I'd never fit anywhere before, never belonged the way others seemed to without trying. But here, hearing those words, the world tilted beneath me. For the first time, I wondered if the reason I'd always felt out of place was because I wasn't meant to stay in my own time at all.

Faintness swept through me, my grip tightening on the table. Had I really left my world behind? Was I truly standing in Ancient Greece?

I looked at the poor woman still kneeling before me, her eyes filled with awe as though I were something other than... me. My mouth opened before my thoughts could catch up, the only words that fit the chaos in my head spilling out.

"I'm sorry—what?" I blurted in broken Ancient Greek.

Chapter Two

It was mid-day after my conversation with Elder Theron and High Priestess Lydia, I found myself standing in a small, dimly lit bedroom. The space was simple yet comforting, the mudbrick walls adorned with beautiful tapestries and a narrow wooden bed pressed against the far wall. A small fireplace crackled in the corner, casting a flickering glow that made the whole place feel older than anything I'd ever known.

I slipped off my boots and set them neatly by the door, glancing at the bundle of clothes left for me on the bed—a set of traditional Greek clothing, a sharp distinction to the modern attire I still wore. My jacket and sweatpants felt out of place here, a reminder to me that my world no longer existed for me. I ran my fingers over the tunic, the fabric soft and heavy, the blue so rich it almost looked royal. Next to it sat leather bracers, a belt with gold accents, and—at the foot of the bed—knee-high boots with gleaming armor. Even as curiosity tugged at me, I left them untouched, not ready to give up the last reminder of my old world.

I let out a slow breath, pressing my hands against my face. My body ached, my mind racing with thoughts I couldn't settle. A part of me still clung to the idea that this was some elaborate dream. But deep down, I knew better. The air here felt lighter, these people spoke of a prophecy, and I had seen Korinthos sprawled out in the far distance, far different than its modern-day counterpart. This was real.

When I said I wanted an adventure... this isn't what I meant. My fingers curled into the fabric of my borrowed clothes as I fought against the sting of emotion rising within me. I never let myself cry—not when I was lost, not when I was afraid. Strength has always been my armor. But for the first time, I wasn't sure if it would be enough.

The room felt too quiet, too unfamiliar. For a split second, I thought about stepping into the hall, maybe finding Lydia or someone else, but the idea of facing another conversation today just made me anxious. So I stayed put. Time seemed to stretch out as sunlight drifted across the tapestries, and every little sound in the hall seemed magnified—distant voices, footsteps, the soft clatter of dishes from somewhere deeper in the building. Once or twice, I heard someone pause just outside my door, but no one knocked.

A tray of food appeared on a small table—a round loaf of bread, slices of cheese, a bowl of olives, and something that might have been roasted lamb. I was too hungry not to eat, but also too nervous to do more than pick at it, every bite settling heavily on my stomach. The afternoon passed in a blur. I drifted between pacing the room, curling up on the bed, and staring out the narrow window at the village. A few villagers moved through the courtyards, carrying baskets or tending to their animals, always glancing up every so often as if checking on me. I wondered what they thought of all this.

By the time dusk fell, I felt even more exhausted than when I'd arrived. My head throbbed, starting at my temples and slowly working its way across my forehead. So, I did the only thing I could do I curled up on the bed, blanket pulled around my shoulders and stared at the fire until the room blurred. Sleep found me quickly, but it did not comfort.

※ ⁂ ※

In my dreams, I found myself once again in the dark forest that had haunted me during a previous sleep. The oppressive energy hung thick in the air, but this time, instead of the woman who had fallen to the ground with injuries, there was a shadowy figure, as though it couldn't quite manifest itself.

"Finally, we are here," the figure said, its voice both familiar and strange—the same voice from my first nightmare.

My heart pounded with fear, and I stepped back, but the figure raised a pale hand to calm me. "You have nothing to fear, Ravena. We are one and the same."

Before the figure could finish speaking, the scene began to change. To my horror, the snow beneath our feet turned red, as if stained by blood. Panic surged through me as the dream world started to fade, and I watched the figure fall. The last thing I heard was that feminine voice echoing in my mind:

"Find your guardian...uncover the truths... the threat has returned."

I awoke with a start, my heart racing, covered in a cold sweat that felt like ice. The room was shrouded in darkness, the only light coming from the dim moonlight filtering through the window. I sat up in bed, trying to shake off the remnants of the dream that clung to me. My breathing was heavy, each breath visible in the cold air.

What in the world was that? My mind raced as I tried to piece together the fragments of the dream. The words—*Find your guardian... uncover the truths... the threat has returned.* —echoed through my head, along with flashes of red snow.

I glanced around the room, my eyes settling on the fireplace. It had long since lost its embers, leaving the room cold and dim. The fire that had once provided warmth and comfort was now just a pile of ash. I wrapped my blanket tighter around myself, seeking comfort in its warmth—or maybe just the feeling of it. Strangely, the cold didn't bite as much as I expected. I should have been shivering, but instead, I only felt a faint chill.

This can't be real. Gods? Any of this! My life had turned into some mythological tale. How was I supposed to uncover truths? How was I supposed to fight a battle I didn't even understand yet? The questions swirled in my mind, building into another headache.

I rose from the bed, my feet touching the cold floor, sending a shiver up my spine. I walked over to the fireplace, stirring the ashes with a poker, hoping to coax some flames from the dying embers. But it was no use. The fire was long gone, leaving me to face the chill and darkness.

Wrapping the blanket tighter around myself, I sat down near the window, staring out at the moonlit village below. The scene was oddly serene, a sharp contrast to the turmoil churning within me.

The figure in my dream said we were one and the same. How could I possibly be connected to such a seemingly otherworldly being?

I felt the weight of anxiety pressing down on me. *Am I really meant for this?* That was my final thought as I laid my head against the windowsill. This time, no dreams came to me as I slept.

Chapter Three

The first rays of dawn filtered through the window, casting a faint glow over the room. A dull ache settled in my neck and shoulders as I stirred, curled against the hard surface of the windowsill. My body protested as I shifted, wincing at the stiffness in my limbs. I barely had time to register my surroundings before a firm, but gentle knock echoed through the quiet room.

The door creaked open, and soft footsteps crossed the wooden floor. A voice, warm yet touched with concern, broke the silence. "Lady Ravena, why do you rest in such a place? The bed is far more comfortable than a chair."

The sound startled me fully awake, and I blinked blearily as I sat up, my muscles aching from the awkward sleeping position. A woman stood nearby, her presence filling the room with an air of care and authority. She crossed the space swiftly, her hands reaching out as if to help before thinking better of it.

"I—I didn't sleep well," I admitted, rubbing the sleep from my eyes. My voice was hoarse from disuse, and I shifted to stretch out the stiffness in my back. "I must have drifted off here."

The woman let out a soft tsk, though her expression held no reprimand—only kindness. "There is no need for an apology, milady. I only wished to see you well." She offered a gentle smile. "I am Cora, a keeper of this home."

I managed a small smile in return. "Thank you, Cora," I said, testing the name on my tongue. "I'm not used to being fussed over like this."

Cora chuckled, her eyes twinkling. "It is only right that you are, Lady Ravena. You hold a place among us." She gave me a slight bow of her head before stepping toward the bed, picking up the rest of the neatly folded garments I hadn't touched. "Please dress. Elder Theron and Lydia will be expecting you soon."

I hesitated before reaching for them, still feeling out of place with the attention. "Thank you. I really do appreciate all this... it's all very overwhelming." I admitted.

Cora nodded knowingly. "A weight placed upon shoulders unready will always feel heavy, but in time, you shall stand firm beneath it." She turned toward the door, politely facing away to allow me privacy as I changed.

I skimmed my fingers over the fabric of my new clothes once more, reality settled in. I wasn't waking up from this. This was real, and I had a role to play in it, whether I liked it or not.

When I finished dressing, Cora hummed thoughtfully. "I imagine it is as strange to you as it is to us," she said, leading the way toward the dining area.

I let out a small. dry laugh. "That is an understatement," I replied, following her through the space.

As we walked, I glanced through the open courtyard at villagers starting their day. Some swept porches, others chased off their chickens, and a couple of kids chased each other around a well.

Curious, I asked, "So, Cora, have you always lived here?"

"Oh yes, I was born within these walls," she said, a soft smile tugging at her mouth. "My family has tended to the temple for generations. It is a life of quiet purpose."

I hummed. "Could you tell me about the village? It is unlike anything I have seen."

Cora's smile grew. "Our village has stood longer than many great cities, its roots deep in the old ways. The gods have watched over us, and in turn, we have honored them. Few outsiders step upon this mountain—the path is treacherous. But our warriors travel far, bringing what is needed from Korinthos and beyond."

I raised an eyebrow at that. "That is unusual. Maybe it's the gods' will that you stay untouched by war."

"Yes, perhaps," she agreed. "We offer prayers and rites to shield us from such misfortune. It is our way."

When we reached the dining area, Cora showed me to a seat at the set table. "Eat, milady. It will serve you well."

I sat down, taking in the food before me. As I ate, I watched the workers bustling about—quiet, efficient, and weirdly purposeful. They didn't act like servants, just... people who actually liked what they were doing. They stood back, gave me space, but were always there if I so much as looked around. It made me feel out of place—definitely not the kind of girl who gets waited on.

With each bite, I tried to make sense of everything: the prophecy, my strange dreams, and the people now surrounding me. Mostly, I was trying to ignore how unsettling it all was. I was living a new life I wasn't sure I could ever adjust to.

Once I finished eating, the workers moved quickly to clean up my area. It felt strange to be waited on, but I realized until I found more answers, I'd have to accept that this was just how things worked here. Standing from the table, I approached Cora and a few other workers bustling about in the small kitchen.

"Is there anything I can do to help?" I asked, desperate to feel useful, to have a sense of normalcy.

The workers exchanged startled glances before Cora quickly stepped forward. "Oh no, Lady Ravena! A lady such as yourself shouldn't be doing chores. We're here to take care of you."

I felt a bit put off but decided not to argue. "I see. Well, if there's anything I *can* do, just let me know. I really don't mind—it would actually make me feel more normal," I said, crossing my arms.

Cora smiled warmly, the wrinkles at the corners of her eyes becoming more prominent. "Your kindness is noted, Lady Ravena, yet your focus should be upon your rest and purpose..." She trailed off, expression brightening as if a sudden idea came to her. "Would you like to visit the temple?"

I perked up at her suggestion. I nodded eagerly. "I'd love that."

"This way, then," Cora said, reaching for a heavy wool cloak from a peg by the door. She handed me another—thicker than I expected, and it nearly draped to my boots.

"You'll need this. It's colder at the temple." she said, fastening her own cloak at her shoulders before gesturing me outside.

The crisp morning air greeted us, carrying the scent of dew and fresh earth. As we walked through the village, I took in the sights of the villagers already busy with their morning chores. The air was filled with the hum of chatter and the clatter of tools.

After climbing what felt like an endless number of steps, I was starting to question if all ancient temples required a personal test of endurance to reach. My legs burned, my breath came quicker, and just as I considered asking Cora if gods preferred their followers in shape, we finally crested the last step.

My breath caught—not from exhaustion this time, but from the sight before me. The temple was stunning: intricate stonework and adorned with vibrant tapestries that depicted various deities. The faint scent of incense drifted through the air, mingling with the earthy aroma of the village below.

This is a remarkable temple for such a small village. I thought, barely resisting the urge to gape.

Cora led me inside. The walls were lined with flickering torches. Their soft glow illuminated detailed artwork, casting dancing shadows that added to the mystical ambiance.

I looked around in awe. The interior of the temple was even more magnificent than I had imagined. The high ceilings were painted with celestial scenes, their beauty breathtaking. The polished stone floor reflected the light from the torches and the rising sun, which cast a warm glow around the room.

"It's beautiful," I whispered, unable to tear my eyes away from the scene before me.

As we walked deeper inside, we found Lydia preparing for the day's prayers. She looked up and smiled warmly when her gaze landed on me.

"Lady Ravena," Lydia greeted, her tone measured. "It gladdens me to see you among us. How does the morning find you?"

I nodded, still taking it all in. "Better than last night. This place... it beyond words."

Lydia's smile widened. "I am pleased it brings you comfort. The temple has long stood as a place of wisdom and strength. Many have sought its guidance." She regarded me with a keen eye. "Shall I show you its halls, Lady Ravena? There is much to see, and much to speak of."

Comfort? I wasn't sure I'd go that far. Awe, maybe.

My face lit up with excitement anyway. "Yes, please!"

Lydia inclined her head. "Come, then. We shall walk and speak," She turned to Cora. "You have done well in tending to her needs. Your care is seen."

Cora smiled warmly and nodded. "I shall see you later, Lady Ravena. The midday meal awaits my hands." She headed back toward the main house.

One random and completely unnecessary thought crossed my mind as I watched her go: *I'd hate to climb those stairs every day.*

Chapter Four

As we walked toward the right wing of the temple, I couldn't help but stare at everything. *Holy shit... this is really happening.* My heart thudded a little harder, anxiety creeping up the back of my neck—then, weirdly, a thin layer of calm smoothed it over. Maybe it was shock, maybe just adrenaline.

When we reached the back side of the temple, Lydia led me through an open doorway to the outside. I froze. The view in front of me... even after all my travels, nothing compared. I'd seen some wild places on digs, and in the field, but this? This was something else.

An altar stood ahead, ringed by stone columns arching gracefully around it. Benches, weathered but clearly well-cared for, lined the clearing. But it was what lay behind the altar that took my breath away—a vast, snow-blanketed field, pines and firs hemming it in, and beyond, a mountain crater so enormous it made the whole scene look ethereal. Jagged peaks rose like sentinels against the sky.

Lydia pointed to the altar, her voice even. "This here is where it all began. I was forty winters old, when a strange event took place." She gestured towards the mountain's highest peak.

I looked up—and as I did, a sudden, hair-raising sensation hit me, so strong my knees nearly buckled. Lydia's voice faded as the scene in front of me changed. I wasn't just *seeing* it; I was *there*:

It was a clear winter night two years ago. The sky above the mountain was filled with brilliant stars, not a cloud in sight. At the altar stood Lydia, surrounded by villagers seated on the ground in prayer. Suddenly, a white light pierced the sky, striking the mountaintop. Energy rippled down its slopes in a wave, leaving everyone in a hushed awe.

The light faded as quickly as it had come. Rainbow hues danced across the sky, reflected on the snow's shimmering surface. Lydia stepped forward, heart pounding, unsure if it was awe or fear.

Then, voices—not just one, but many echoing in unison:

"Fear not, mortals. We are not here to harm. We send a message: an ice giant by the name of Agnar will come in the future to disrupt the world and its balance, by trying to tear down the divine barriers. A young woman will come, born from a realm and time different from your own. Her fate is written in the stars. She is the reincarnation of the Norse Goddess of Winter Skadi and will bring an end to the evil that threatens our worlds for his own gain. Be warned, he will build an army and gain an ally who betrays their pantheon for the freedom they seek"

The voices paused as a burning sigil appeared on the upper portion of the mountain.

"The woman you seek bears the name Ravena. Protect this information and trust none with it. This place has been marked. Here, the sigil of the Goddess of Winter has been burned, a sign of her rebirth. This will be the place where she rises, where the balance shall be restored."

The vision snapped away, and I found myself back beside the altar, on my knees, breathing shallow and uneven. The sheer realness of what I'd just seen, what I'd just learned about myself, this prophecy and my apparent fate, nearly threatened to send me into a spiral.

A gentle hand landed on my shoulder startling me, relaxing only when I heard Lydia's voice. "Are you all right, Lady Ravena?"

I exhaled sharply, my hands pressing against my thighs as I tried to steady myself. "I think so. But I just... saw everything so clearly. The prophecy. The past. It hit me all at once." My voice wavered, the panic bubbling up whether I wanted to show it or not. "I just need a moment to make sense of it." I glanced at Lydia, forcing a weak smile. "And please, just call me Ravena. No need for formalities."

Lydia raised an eyebrow, clearly unused to dropping formal titles. "Just... Ravena?" She sounded it out, as if testing the word. "Are you sure? It feels... strange."

I let out a small, shaky laugh—part nerves, part habit. "Yes, just Ravena. I mean, it's not like 'Lady' adds any extra powers, right?"

Lydia chuckled, a smile tugging at her lips. "I suppose not. All right, Ravena, let's go eat lunch, and we can discuss everything with Theron."

As we walked away from the altar, Lydia couldn't resist one last tease. "But if you suddenly start controlling the elements, I reserve the right to call you Lady Ravena again."

I laughed, shaking my head. "Deal."

❦ ❦

Unknown to me, a figure stood hidden in the cover of the trees, half-shadowed by the forest. They blended into the landscape so well, I never even glanced in their direction. But their eyes were fixed on me.

They had waited since the prophecy was spoken, counting winters until the day her soul crossed into this realm. Now, at last, they saw the one they were meant to watch over.

A quiet exhale left their lips, a flicker of relief breaking through their usual piercing gaze. Their time of waiting was over. Soon, our paths would cross, and their real duty would begin.

With one last look, the figure slipped into the shadows, vanishing into the trees. I remained—blissfully unaware. For now.

Chapter Five

Back at the village, I found myself seriously wondering how Lydia climbed these stairs every day, especially at her age. Maybe she was just built differently—everyone here seemed a little tougher than they looked. It was a welcome distraction from the whirlwind in my head: the vision, the voices, the fact that apparently, I'm the reincarnation of a goddess. *Which one is even the goddess of winter? Skadi... The name echoed in my head, both familiar and foreign at the same time. Was I supposed to just... become her now? Think, Ravena. You're supposed to know these things. No, don't get ahead of yourself—wait for Theron. Maybe he'll explain everything, or maybe he'll just look at me the same way the others do.*

The scent of smoke and fresh food hit me as we stepped back inside. Cora hurried over, moving with a kind of energy that somehow made me feel even more tired. She smiled wide and held out her hands for my cloak.

"Welcome back! How was the tour?" she asked, her bright smile radiating warmth. It was the kind of greeting you gave family, not a random girl dumped in your village by fate.

"It was... enlightening," I managed, giving her a smile that probably looked more tired than grateful. "I learned a lot, but I think I need some time to process everything."

Lydia set a gentle hand on my shoulder, the gesture grounding me a little. "Take all the time you need. It's a lot to take in."

I nodded, grateful for the out. The last thing I wanted was more explaining right now. We moved into the dining room, and my stomach rumbled at the sight—there was bread, yes, but not the bland, store-bought kind. This was rustic, dark-crusted, still steaming, with a bowl of soup that smelled amazing. And next to it, an assortment of cheeses, olives, and a little dish of what looked like honey and herbs, all set out with care by people who actually enjoyed eating together.

As we ate, I kept waiting for the awkwardness to hit—for more questions, the sense that I didn't belong at this table. But instead, there was just...quiet hospitality. Lydia and Cora chatted easily about the village's history and customs, clearly trying to keep the conversation light.

"You know, we're not all about prophecies and gods," she teased, a sly smile tugging at her lips. "We have our share of festivals and celebrations, too. You should see the dance competitions; they're quite something. Cora once beat another village elder and the blacksmith."

Cora laughed, waving her off. "He twisted his ankle, and you know it. I just managed to survive and not fall over my own feet."

I managed a real laugh, the kind that sneaks out before you can catch it. "Maybe I'll even join in. Though I warn you, I have two left feet—and a habit of stepping on feet."

Lydia's grin was genuine. "Now that's something I'd like to see."

Despite the easy flow of our conversation, a prickling unease crawled up my spine. I found myself glancing at the window, half-expecting to catch someone watching, or maybe just hoping for some sign that all this was normal.

Lydia caught the shift in my expression. "Everything alright, Ravena?"

I hesitated, forcing a small smile. "I'll be fine. I just need a minute to breathe, that's all."

"Understandable." Her tone was gentle, but her eyes searched mine a second longer than necessary. "If you'd like to rest, you're welcome to. We can talk more later, if you need."

Grateful for the excuse, I nodded. After lunch, I brushed breadcrumbs from my lap and I ventured back to my room, hoping maybe a little solitude would clear my head. Instead, the silence made the feeling worse.

No matter how many times I changed positions on the bed, I couldn't get comfortable. My mind spun in circles, and every small creak of the house made me tense.

Eventually, I gave up. Staying inside felt like being trapped, so I pulled on my cloak and headed outside. The crisp air bit at my cheeks, but I welcomed the distraction. The villagers moved about without a care in the world—they hauled wood, tended to their animals, and some chatted in small groups. They didn't look nervous, but their eyes sometimes flicked my way—a split-second too long before darting away.

Wandering toward the outskirts, the hush of the forest pulled at me, almost like a beckoning whisper calling me closer. I could almost convince myself it was just the quiet, but something about the shadows between the trees made my skin prickle. Each step away from the village felt both freeing and reckless, but I needed air. My thoughts churned: prophecy, goddess, expectations that felt so far from anything I recognized as myself.

I paused at a narrow stream, its water sparkling under the soft afternoon light. Kneeling down, I dipped my fingers into the cool water, letting out a deep sigh. *What was I even supposed to do?* Was I really meant to be someone's savior—or was I just the wrong person in the wrong place, as usual?

A faint rustle behind me snapped me out of my thoughts, I whipped around, pulse stuttering. Nothing. Probably just an animal, I told myself, though I didn't quite believe it. The uneasy feeling wasn't leaving. It trailed me as I made my way back, every twig snap and gust of wind making my nerves buzz.

The sun was already slipping lower, throwing long shadows across the village. I pulled my cloak tighter, walking faster. But something shifted when I reached the main path—the stares felt colder now.

Now it wasn't just my nerves. It was them.

The usual hum of conversation dipped slightly as I passed a small gathering near a well. A group of villagers, mostly men and women my age, spoke in hushed tones, their eyes flickering toward me before quickly looking away. I slowed my steps, adjusting my cloak as if merely shifting the fabric, while their words carried through the air.

"She does not appear as one touched by the gods," a man scoffed, his voice thick with doubt. "The prophecy speaks of a warrior, a goddess reborn, but I see no divinity in her."

A woman murmured in response, more hesitant. "Lydia and Theron believe her to be the one. They would not dare misinterpret the gods' will."

A younger voice, edged with frustration, cut in. "That doesn't mean they're right. The gods don't always send champions the way we expect." A pause. "But look at her—she's just standing there, lost. How is she supposed to save anyone?"

I felt heat creep up my neck but kept my face blank. No use arguing. They weren't saying anything I hadn't already thought of a hundred times.

"She is an outsider," another voice said grimly. "And outsiders bring change. Change brings unrest."

I almost stopped, almost turned around to tell them I agreed. But what purpose would that serve? Instead, I kept walking, letting their doubts settle in beside my own.

But their words lingered long after I returned to my room.

Chapter Six

The next morning, I stirred with the first light of dawn, the words of the villagers still echoing in my head. A lingering unease clung to me, as if unseen eyes had followed me into my dreams, refusing to release their grip. I exhaled slowly, rubbing my hands over my face—sleep had done little to chase away the creeping sensation in my bones. My heart beat a little too fast, my limbs tense—like I'd been running in my dreams and hadn't quite stopped.

I wanted nothing more than to be alone, but I knew that wasn't possible here. Cora had been doting over me since my arrival, making sure I was never left unattended for too long. If I wanted even a moment of solitude, I had to take it now before she arrived with a warm meal and more well-meaning fussing.

Deciding I needed a distraction, I figured the hot springs would be perfect—the ones Lydia had pointed out on my first day. Maybe a nice soak could wash away my restless thoughts.

After picking through the clothes Lydia left out, I spotted what had to be ancient Greek underwear—a simple strip of linen, nothing like what I was used to. I stared at it, then glanced at my own underwear, which had survived one more day. I'd just bring mine to wash in the spring. No way was I braving this world in something that felt like a glorified dish towel. Tucking my old clothes and the fresh tunic under my arm, I pulled on my cloak and quietly slipped out of the house.

I followed the narrow path Lydia had described winding through the snow-covered forest. The crisp air carried the sharp scent of pine, each breath a reminder of just how far removed I was from the modern world. There was no faint pollution from distant cars or factories—no subtle reminders of civilization. Even coming from the wilderness back home, the absence felt profound.

When I reached the alcove of trees encircling the spring, the sight struck me with its dreamlike quality. Steam curled up from the water in delicate swirls, mingling with the frigid air and creating a shifting veil of mist. The contrast between the biting cold and the inviting warmth of the spring sent a shiver through me—an odd mix of comfort and anticipation settling over me. I undressed quickly, shivering lightly, and slipped into the hot water with a quiet sigh. The heat seeped into my muscles, loosening the ever-present knots of tension that had settled there. For a blissful moment, I let myself relax, sinking into silence the woods offered me. Eyes closed, I tried to let my thoughts drift away.

But that peace didn't last long.

A soft crunch of snow echoed nearby—too deliberate, too firm to be an animal. My breath hitched, heart jumping as I opened my eyes just in time to see a figure emerge through the mist.

Tall and broad-shouldered, he moved with a quiet intensity that sent every nerve in my body into high alert. The swirling steam obscured him at first, but as he stepped closer, the details sharpened—and honestly, it only got weirder. His jet-black hair spilled down his back, the top section braided in an intricate style straight out of a Viking movie. His face was all sharp angles and a strong jaw, framed by a beard that lent him a wild, untamed look. But god, his piercing gray eyes—they peered out from beneath streaks of dark war paint slashed across his face, the markings casting shadows that made his presence a contradiction—imposing, dangerous, yet strangely protective.

The worn leather armor clung to his powerful frame, molded to his broad shoulders and sculpted chest as if it had been crafted for him alone. Black tattoos wove intricate patterns down his muscular arms, their meanings a mystery to me. He carried himself like a seasoned warrior—one who had seen countless battles and walked away from every single one.

And then he stopped. His whole posture went rigid, those piercing eyes scanning the spring before him, and I swear I saw a flash of horror as he realized his own bad timing.

For a long, tense moment, neither of us moved.

Oh, great. This was awkward.

My heart pounded in my chest as I met his gaze. The uneasy quiet between us was almost louder than words. I arched an eyebrow, crossing my arms beneath the water. "Can I help you?" I tried for false bravado, but my heart was thumping so hard I wondered if he could hear it. Why did my mouth always work faster than my brain when I was actually nervous?

The man's gaze flicked away for the first time, his expression shifting between horror and discomfort. He cleared his throat, shifting his weight. "I... intrude," he admitted, his deep voice tinged with a thick Norse accent. "For that, I ask forgiveness." He paused, pressing a fist to his chest briefly in what looked like an old warrior's gesture of respect. "I am Eirik. I am sent to guard you—to guide you. This is my oath."

I blinked at him, struggling to process his words. "A guardian," I echoed. "And you decided to show up... *right now?* While I'm in a hot spring?"

Eirik exhaled sharply through his nose, running a hand through his thick, dark hair as if just now fully grasping how poor his timing was. "I may have been... impatient," he muttered. His lips twitched in what could have been the start of a smirk, though he quickly smothered it. "I have waited long for your arrival. It did not seem right to wait longer. But... I see now this was poor judgment."

I stared at him. "You think? Next time, maybe wait until I'm not... you know, naked?" My voice all bite, but I was mostly just mortified.

A muscle ticked in his jaw, his light tan skin reddening beneath his face tattoos. "A fair thing to ask," he admitted, inclining his head. "I assure you; this was not meant as...what is the word? *Disrespect.*"

The absurdity of it almost made me laugh. Here was this giant Viking-warrior, probably capable of crushing skulls, looking like he'd rather be anywhere but here.

I sighed, sinking deeper into the water until my chin just barely skimmed the surface. "Well... thanks for the introduction, I guess. Even if your timing is absolutely horrible."

He gave a stiff nod, voice steady despite the situation. "Lesson learned. Next time, I'll wait until you're done, and I will check my surroundings."

For a moment, we remained locked in an awkward silence, the steam swirling between us like a barrier neither of us knew how to cross. Eirik shifted his weight again, his gaze flicking toward the snow-dusted pines surrounding the spring as if searching for an escape route.

"Right," he muttered, clearing his throat. "I... should not be here." His voice, normally deep and even, had a noticeable edge of regret. He gestured vaguely toward the water, clearly reevaluating every decision that had led him to this exact moment. "I'll leave you to your bath. We can talk... later, maybe. In the village."

Without another word, he turned on his heel, his boots crunching through the snow as he strode away with forced determination. His usual strong, commanding presence was undercut by the stiff, awkward way he carried himself.

I ducked my head, cheeks burning. "Good plan. Next time, just... don't walk in on a woman bathing." My voice was smaller than I meant it to be.

Eirik hesitated for half a second before giving another stiff nod, his ears visibly reddening beneath his dark hair. He didn't look back as he disappeared into the trees.

Once I was sure he was gone, I let out a shaky breath. So much for privacy. I leaned back against the edge of the spring, letting the warmth seep into my muscles. My thoughts, however, kept drifting back to him. There was something about Eirik I couldn't quite place. Despite the Viking look, there'd been an almost endearing awkwardness to him—like he was better at breaking things than apologizing for them.

Maybe it was the way his ears had turned red beneath all that dark hair, or the way his shoulders stiffened when he realized his mistake. Whatever it was, it made me feel... lighter. Like I wasn't entirely alone anymore.

I lingered in the hot waters for a moment longer. The steam curled around me, wrapping me in a cocoon of warmth that momentarily dulled the heaviness in my chest. I flexed my fingers beneath the surface, letting the heat work its magic.

A *guardian*. Someone meant to protect me. The idea felt absurd—something out of the mythology books I used to study, not something I'd have to contend with firsthand. But then again, nothing about my life had made sense since I arrived.

I stared at the rising steam, letting the surreal reality settle over me. *Ancient Greece—or some version of it.* If someone had told me a year ago that I'd be living in the kind of world I had spent years researching, I would've laughed. But here I was, stuck in a time and place that wasn't my own, surrounded by prophecies, warriors, and a hot spring that, under different circumstances, I might have actually enjoyed.

I sighed, the sound swallowed by the mist curling into the cold air. *How had I even ended up here?* That question looped endlessly in my mind. One moment, I was outside getting fresh air after that dream then the voice came. A flash of light, a sensation of being pulled through something unseen... and then I was here.

I rubbed my face, frustration creeping in at the haziness of it all. As much as I tried to piece it together, nothing quite fit.

And now there was Eirik.

The last thing I needed—another question in an already impossible situation. And yet, I couldn't shake the thought of him. He was like something pulled straight from a Viking saga: black hair, piercing gray eyes, war paint that made him look both feral and focused. He should have unsettled me. Should have triggered some kind of fight-or-flight instinct.

Instead, he just left me... annoyed, confused and if I was honest, a little too curious for my own good.

"Nope. Don't go there," I muttered to myself, shaking off the lingering thoughts. Curiosity had a way of getting me into trouble, and I didn't need more of that right now. My first thought should have been: Can *I even trust this man?* Trust wasn't something I handed out easily, and I wasn't about to start now. I'd lived alone for too long to feel comfortable relying on anyone else.

That thought sent a flare of unease rushing through me. Someone sent him to protect and guide me... The prophecy hadn't mentioned anything about a guardian—at least, not from what I'd learned so far. The stubborn part of me bristled at the idea of being watched over, like I was some fragile thing in need of constant supervision. I hated the thought.

"Get a grip," I muttered again, dragging my hands down my face. All I wanted was to wake up in my bed back home, where I could hide until my thoughts stopped pestering me.

The cold bit at my skin as I stepped out of the water, forcing me back to the present. I cast a quick look over my shoulder, making sure Eirik wasn't about to reappear for an encore. The trees stayed mercifully empty. I dried off fast and dug through my bundle for the fresh tunic Lydia had left out for me. The Greek underwear was still there, looking just as ridiculous as before. I tried to make sense of how to wear it, twisting the linen strip in my hands, but after one failed attempt and nearly falling over, I gave up. Absolutely not. My own underwear, slightly damp but a thousand times more comfortable, would have to do.

Pulling the clean tunic over my head and belting it tight, I bundled up in my fur-lined cloak. I headed back towards the village, bracing myself for whatever came next—Cora's inevitable scolding, Eirik's reappearance, or just another round of my own existential crisis.

The walk back was quiet, broken only by the crunch of snow beneath my boots. The forest was breathtaking, the towering trees and frost-laden branches giving the world an untouched stillness. It wasn't home—*not yet*—but something about this place felt deeper, more *rooted* than my home ever did.

As the village came into view, the familiar scent of woodsmoke and roasting meat wrapped around me, and my stomach let out a loud, undignified growl. Right. I hadn't eaten yet. I picked up my pace, hoping to slip inside unnoticed.

I made it exactly two steps down the hall before a voice, warm but *dangerously* firm, stopped me cold.

"*Lady Ravena,* where have you been!?"

I turned to find Cora standing near the hearth, arms crossed, her expression caught between relief and exasperation. Her dark curls framed her face, and her brown eyes gleamed with worry. "You nearly sent Lydia and Elder Theon to their graves when we couldn't find you!"

I rubbed the back of my neck, feeling sheepish. "I'm sorry. I couldn't sleep, so I thought a bath might help." I shrugged off my cloak, hoping she'd let it go.

Cora let out a long breath, her posture easing just a bit. "It is good you are safe, *Lady Ravena.*" She said the title with a little smile, but her concern was real. "Though I must say, you have a peculiar way of settling in."

I tilted my head, frowning slightly. "What do you mean?"

Her lips quirked into a knowing smile. "You are meant to rest, to prepare for what lies ahead, yet you slip away into the woods without a thought for the dangers lurking beyond these walls." She shook her head, a fond sort of exasperation coloring her voice. "Every day, I learn something new about you."

I found myself shaking my head, trying to piece the words together. "I tend to bottle things up—my feelings, my thoughts. When it all gets to be too much, I go outside. It helps clear my mind. I didn't want to bother anyone, so sneaking out felt like the easiest way."

Cora sighed, but the gentle shake of her head wasn't reprimanding—just understanding. "There is no need to apologize. I may not fully understand where you came from, but I know what it is to feel overwhelmed." Her expression softened as she motioned toward the table, where a simple meal had been laid out. "Come, eat. And if you are willing, tell me what weighs so heavily on your mind. Sometimes, speaking your worries aloud lessens their burden."

Grateful for her patience, I made my way to the table and sat down, throwing a quick thank-you to the workers as I reached for the bread. I drizzled it with honey, my movements slowing as thoughts crowded in again. "It just feels... too big. Too much to grasp. Like I've been thrown into a role I never rehearsed for." I let out a quiet laugh, but there was no humor in it. "I was a historian, you know. I studied things like this. Ancient temples, rituals, prophecies... but I never thought I'd actually *live* it."

Cora watched me with that same patient, unwavering presence—the kind that encouraged me to keep going.

She leaned forward, her gaze unwavering but kind. "That is because you still think it is a story." She tilted her head slightly. "But it is not. This is your life now."

Her words struck me harder than I expected. I sat in silence, chewing slowly as her statement echoed in my mind. *This is your life now.* The thought rattled me, but at the same time, there was an odd comfort in her bluntness.

"You always seem to know the right thing to say, huh?" I muttered, shaking my head slightly. Then, after a pause, I added, "Do you think I will get used to this? To... all of it?" I gestured vaguely toward the outside, where the ancient world stretched far beyond the village.

Cora chuckled, "It is a gift, I suppose. But yes, I do. I believe you will surprise yourself. You did not come all this way—however strange the path—to wallow in uncertainty. You are here for a purpose, even if your story has yet to unfold."

She straightened, her tone shifting slightly. "Now, finish eating. Lydia will wish to meet with you soon, and I suspect Theron will want words about yesterday."

I nodded and focused on my plate, realizing just how hungry I was. It wasn't much, but after the events of the morning, eating and talking with Cora made things feel almost normal—almost. One step at a time, I reminded myself as I continued eating.

A short while later, Cora returned to clear the table. "Come now, let us do something about that hair of yours. Then you can head to the temple," she said, motioning for me to follow.

I stood and walked behind her, grateful for the distraction.

She led me back to my room at an easy pace, her steps unhurried, as if she knew I needed the calm. Just as I thought we were done, she glanced over her shoulder with a smirk. "I will say this, should you sneak out again without a word, I will drag you back by your ear myself. Lady or not."

I snorted, a grin tugging at my lips despite myself. "Fair enough."

Chapter Seven

An hour or so later, I adjusted my cloak against the cool breeze as I made my way toward the temple. The winding path up the hill felt familiar now, but those stairs still weren't my friend. By the time I reached the entrance, I had to pause, inhaling the crisp air and trying to calm my thoughts. Anxiety wouldn't help me now.

Cora had managed to tame most of my unruly hair, though a few stubborn strands still fought for freedom in the morning breeze.

My footsteps echoed faintly in the cool stone hall as I entered, the faint light of the temple casting long shadows. Lydia stood near the altar, the flickering light from a brazier softening her sharp features. Theron, his weathered face marked by years of wisdom, greeted me with a kind but expectant gaze.

"You're here," Lydia said softly. "Did you find clarity in the spring?"

I scratched my cheek awkwardly, giving a small shrug. "I wouldn't call it clarity, exactly." My gaze dropped to the intricate patterns carved into the temple floor. "It was... definitely an experience."

Lydia exchanged a glance with Theron before stepping aside. "Tell Theron what you saw earlier," she said gently, her voice encouraging.

I shifted on my feet, clasping my hands together as the memory of the vision crept in. "It was... two years ago," I began hesitantly. "A cold, clear night on this very mountain. The villagers were gathered in prayer, and Lydia—you—stood at the altar." I paused, glancing between them, uncertainty creeping in. Would they believe me? The details felt too vivid to be anything but real, yet I had no way to prove what I'd seen.

But neither Lydia nor Theron spoke. Their expectant silence, their unwavering gazes, urged me to continue.

"Then, a light appeared," I said, my voice gaining a little steadiness. "It wasn't just bright—it rippled, cascading down the mountain like a wave of energy. And just as suddenly as it came, it was gone." I swallowed, my throat dry as the memory of rainbow-hued snow flickered through my mind. "That's when the voices spoke. Not just one, but many, all at once. They told you all that an evil would rise—one that threatens the balance of time and the world itself."

Theron's brows furrowed, deep lines forming across his weathered face, but he didn't interrupt. His assessing gaze weighed my words, silently urging me to continue.

"They said..." I hesitated, the words catching in my throat. It sounded ridiculous, but I forced myself to keep going. "A woman would come—from another realm, another time. She's the reincarnation of the Norse goddess of winter and supposed to stop an ice giant... Agnar, from unbalancing the realms barriers."

I hesitated, the enormity of it all making my pulse hammer against my ribs. Saying it aloud made it feel even more real, even more impossible.

Lydia finished for me, her voice quiet but sure. "And that woman... is you." Her gaze had a certainty that made my stomach twist.

I folded my arms across my chest, trying to process the words. "Yeah. That's what they said. I'm..." It still sounded crazy, even in my own head. "I'm the reincarnation of Skadi. Not just named for her, but actually her, somehow born again, and brought to this world."

Theron stroked his beard, looking thoughtful. "A prophecy bridging both Greek and Norse realms..."

I nodded, the memory of the voices echoing in my ears. "Yes, they said he'll gather an army, and..." I hesitated, feeling the tension spike in the room. "He'll have an ally. Someone willing to betray their own for the freedom they want."

Lydia's expression darkened, her mouth tightening at the mention of betrayal. For a long moment, she just stood there, silent. Then she let out a slow breath, smoothing her features before managing a small, reassuring smile. "You did well to remember all of this."

I exhaled slowly, dragging my hand through my hair in frustration. "I just don't get why me. I'm not a warrior."

"Whether you understand it or not, the Fates chose you," Theron said, his voice calm and reassuring. "There's more strength in you than you know. You may not see it yet, but it'll come when you need it most."

Lydia's brows knit together, her voice lowering. "This Agnar... he wants more than power. If he succeeds, the balance between worlds won't hold." She paused, unwilling— or perhaps unable— to finish the thought.

A dry laugh slipped out, brittle and laced with doubt. "No pressure, right?" I rubbed the back of my neck, nerves skittering beneath my skin. "Look, I studied history. I wasn't exactly preparing for end-of-the-world scenarios."

Theron's gaze was unreadable. "You're more prepared than you realize," he said, his words measured. "Your connection to Skadi is no accident—it's the design of destiny itself."

Their words washed over me. I wanted to argue, to deny the whole thing—but deep down, I knew they were right. Fate had brought me here, and my life had become something bigger than I'd ever imagined. There was no turning back now.

I bit my lip, uncertainty gnawing at my nerves. Some days, I struggled just to keep myself together, let alone picture myself as anyone's chosen warrior. Yet the vision was so vivid, so impossible to deny. The voices had spoken my name like I already belonged here, as if this was always meant to happen.

"This was not mere happenstance, Ravena," Lydia said, her voice gentle. "You carry her legacy now—her strength, her will, and perhaps even her magic."

Before I could respond, the air behind me shifted—a presence. I turned toward the doorway and found Eirik emerging from the shadows as if they belonged to him. Snow clung to his dark hair, dampening the braids along the sides of his head, and his piercing gray eyes gleamed beneath the war paint etched across his face. He looked as fierce as ever, a force meant for battle, though his stare was impossible to read—either we were a puzzle, or he was just sizing us up.

"I see I am not too late," Eirik said, inclining his head to Lydia and Theron in a gesture of respect. His words were smooth, but his presence didn't do much to ease the tension. Lydia's gaze flickered with unease and Theron's expression remained unreadable; his silence spoke volumes.

Eirik's attention settled back to me, his storm-gray eyes curious.

"Hmm... barely," I muttered, the corner of my mouth betrayed me with the slightest twitch upward. At least his timing had improved from the first time.

Lydia and Theron exchanged a wary look. Lydia stepped forward, shoulders squared, brow drawn with in caution.

"And who," she asked carefully, her tone cool as steel, "might you be?"

Eirik straightened, his stance measured, almost formal. He placed a fist over his chest in a subtle bow, acknowledging their authority without lowering himself. When he spoke, his voice was steady, and deep.

"I am Eirik," he said. "At your service. I'm Ravena's guardian."

Lydia's eyes narrowed, suspicion blooming beneath her otherwise composed expression. Theron folded his arms, his weathered face thoughtful as he looked at me. He didn't speak, but the question was clear: *Do you know what this is about?*

I sighed and rolled my eyes, unable to hide the faint amusement tugging at my lips. "Yeah... it's a long story," I admitted, glancing at Eirik.

He, on the other hand, didn't seem fazed. If anything, his expression flickered with the faintest trace of amusement, as if the story wasn't long at all.

Lydia tilted her head slightly, her gaze lingering on Eirik as though he were a puzzle. "I was not aware Skadi's reincarnation came with... an escort."

Eirik's amused look remained, though it softened at the edges. "It has long been foretold that a guardian would be chosen to protect her," he replied smoothly. "I was chosen long ago and have trained ever since."

Theron grunted, arms still folded, skepticism deepening the lines on his face. "And what, exactly, does this role of yours entail?"

Eirik stood straighter, words certain. "To guide her, protect her, and ensure she fulfills what was set in motion. Whatever dangers arise, I will stand between her and harm."

Theron's gaze flicked to me, assessing. "And do you trust this arrangement, Ravena?"

I hesitated, feeling the weight of the question settle over me. Trust was not something I gave freely. Yet something about Eirik—his confidence, his ability to be amused, even when faced with suspicion—stirred something in me. He was certain in a way I wasn't. That was... something right?

"I think..." I began slowly, my eyes shifting between Theron and Eirik. "I think I'll have to see how it goes."

Eirik's lips twitched—no real smile, but enough to be annoying already. "I'm honored for the opportunity. I'll do my best to keep her alive."

I shot him a look, torn between exasperation and irritation. "Oh, great," I muttered under my breath. "A babysitter."

Lydia's lips pressed into a thin line, her gaze moving between Eirik and me. I could practically hear her thoughts—measuring, calculating, deciding if any of this made sense. She didn't trust him—not yet.

"Well," Lydia said at last, her voice firm, "if you are to stay, then there is much to discuss."

Eirik inclined his head, still looking unbothered by the scrutiny. But for a moment, his eyes met mine—a surprising warmth, quick, before he masked it again behind his same cool expression.

I exhaled slowly, as a dull ache settled behind my temples. This all kept stacking up, new things happening so quick, but pretending it wasn't real would get me nowhere. Squaring my shoulders, I forced down the tide of uncertainty. "Let's get started," I said, pushing down my nerves. One step at a time.

Eirik nodded and we followed Lydia and Theron deeper into the temple, descending into the archives.

It felt like hours as we combed through texts and scrolls, searching for anything that matched what I'd seen—old prophecies, accounts of omens, any mention of Skadi, Agnar, or the kind of forces we might be up against. The only sounds were the rustle of parchment and the occasional mutter whenever someone found a half-relevant passage.

But it wasn't just the lack of answers that made the air so thick.

Lydia kept glancing between Eirik and me as we hovered over an old scroll, her jaw set in quiet determination. Theron stayed nearby, arms crossed, watching all of us with that impossible-to-read look. The tension in the room was obvious—an undercurrent of doubt and suspicion running beneath every silent exchange.

Eirik, naturally, wasn't oblivious. He met Lydia's gaze head-on, his own expression nonchalant, a hint of amusement in his eyes, as if he was already used to being scrutinized.

Straightening, Eirik turned to me, a glint of humor present in his eyes. "Walk with me a moment?" His voice was pitched low meant only for me. There was no real demand in it, but it didn't feel like a suggestion either. "There are things we need to discuss."

I barely had time to consider before Lydia stepped forward, her posture shifting—protective. "Anything you wish to say to her can be said here," she said, voice polite but with a definite edge.

Eirik met her gaze without a hint of hesitation, cool as ever. "Yes, it could," he agreed. "But it shouldn't be."

Lydia's eyes narrowed, her protectiveness turning cold. "Ravena is under the temple's care. We are responsible for her well-being. I know not who you are, nor what claims you make, but—"

"Relax, priestess," Eirik interrupted, his tone smooth but not mocking. "I've been bound to watch her back long before either of you knew she existed."

I sighed, pressing my fingers against my temples as the tension ramped up again. "Alright, enough of the pissing contest." My voice was sharp, my patience thinning. "I'll be fine."

Lydia's frown deepened, uncertainty flashing in her eyes. I could tell she was weighing trust against caution. "Are you certain this is wise?" she murmured, low enough for only me. "We know not who he truly is."

I shrugged, trying to sound more certain than I felt. "Neither do I, honestly. But it looks like we're stuck with each other, whether we like it or not."

She hesitated but finally stepped aside with a reluctant sigh. "Stay close to the temple. And do not stray far."

Eirik, ever the opportunist, flashed a lopsided grin. "I shall see her returned in one piece," he promised, throwing in an exaggerated wink.

Lydia's expression only soured, unimpressed. Theron muttered, "See that you do," his eyes fixed on Eirik.

Eirik turned to me, offering his hand in a mockingly formal gesture. "Shall we?"

I rolled my eyes, refusing the gesture. "Let's just get this over with." Ignoring his hand, I brushed past him, catching the faint flicker of amusement in his eyes as he fell into step beside me.

The silence between us stretched as we walked, broken only by the steady crunch of our boots against the stone path. The midday sun bathed the mountaintop in golden light, its warmth brushing my skin as the city of Korinthos sprawled in the far distance below. The sight was breathtaking, but my mind was too crowded to fully appreciate it.

Eirik's presence beside me was unhurried—like he was waiting for the right moment to speak. When we reached the edge of the path overlooking the valley, he finally slowed to a stop, leaning against a low stone wall with effortless ease.

"You're handling this better than I thought you would," he said, his voice light, though his gray eyes flicked toward me, searching.

I snorted, crossing my arms as I shifted my weight. "Oh, totally. I'm thrilled to be thrown into an ancient prophecy to save the world from some power-hungry giant. No big deal. And let's not forget the stranger who decided to make his grand entrance while I was naked in a hot spring."

Eirik let out a low chuckle, deep and almost reluctant. "Sarcasm suits you," he remarked, deliberately ignoring the last part, probably for his own dignity.

"It's the only weapon I'm good at," I muttered, glancing toward the horizon. The valley stretched endlessly before us, but all I could feel was this pressure building in my chest. "But seriously. What's your angle in all this?"

Eirik straightened, the amusement fading from his features. "There isn't one. I was given a job—see you through what's coming. I take it seriously."

I shot him a skeptical glance, arching a brow. "That's it? You've been training your whole life just to—what, babysit me?"

Eirik's lips twitched, as if he was holding back a smile. "If that's how you wish to see it, I won't argue." He rested his forearms on the wall, gaze steady. "But it's not just about guarding you. You matter to more than just this prophecy, Ravena. Whether you believe that or not."

I let out a breath, running a hand through my hair. "Great. No pressure."

His grin returned, softer this time—less teasing. "One step at a time, right?"

I almost laughed, realizing he'd echoed my own words from earlier. "Right," I murmured.

A beat of silence passed before I faced him, arms crossed. "So... what exactly do you want to talk about, Eirik?" His name felt oddly natural now, slipping off my tongue before I even thought about it.

Eirik's expression shifted, the playful mask falling away. His gaze grew serious, the lines around his eyes tightening. "The prophecy," he said quietly. "And Agnar."

I shot him a sidelong glance, unsure if I was ready for what was coming. "What do you actually know about Agnar?"

"Enough to say you're not ready for him yet—not as you are now." His voice was calm, but there was an edge of concern that made my chest tighten.

I clenched my jaw, his bluntness hitting harder than I cared to admit. "You think I don't know that? How long do you think it'll take before I'm... actually ready?

Eirik shrugged, his tone calm but direct. "That depends on you. The Norns don't weave fates without reason, but becoming who you're meant to be—coming into your power—takes time. And honestly, time's the one thing we're short on."

I chewed the inside of my cheek, doubt gnawing at me. "And what if I can't do it? What if they made a mistake?"

He shook his head, his eyes locking onto mine. "The Norns don't make mistakes." Then, softer, "Nor do I."

His certainty caught me off guard. No hesitation, no wavering—just stubborn belief. In me. I wasn't sure how to respond, so I held his gaze a beat longer than I meant to, searching for any crack in that confidence.

He broke the silence, his voice gentler now. "You don't have to have all the answers today. We focus on what's right in front of us for now."

I let out a breath, some of the anxiety easing. "Yeah. I can do that."

Eirik nodded, a faint smile tugging at his lips. "Good. That's all anyone can do."

Chapter Eight

"Come on," Eirik said, brushing snow from his sleeve as he pushed away from the wall. "Best we get back before Lydia sends out a search party. I doubt she's the patient sort."

I offered a smile, falling into step beside him. "You noticed that, huh? She practically burned a hole through you with that scowl."

Eirik huffed a laugh. "I've faced worse."

"Oh? Like what?" I teased, arching an eyebrow. "An angry Jarl? A bear, maybe?"

He shot me a sidelong look, his mouth lifting at one corner. "Once fought a pack of wolves."

I snorted. "Sure, you did. And I bet you wrestled a kraken on the way here, too."

Eirik tilted his head, pretending to consider. "Not yet," he mused, his smile deepening. "Suppose there's still time."

I tried to stifle a laugh. "I'm not sure if I should be impressed or worried."

The silence that followed was comfortable. Our boots crunched softly against the frost-covered path, the crisp air biting at my cheeks. As the temple's entrance loomed ahead, I shot him a mischievous glance. "So... did this morning's events make you late, or is being late just your specialty?"

Eirik let out a low chuckle, his ears turning red as he cleared his throat. "It is called making an entrance, young warrior."

"Is that what you tell yourself?" I quipped, brushing snow from my sleeve. "Next time, you might want to make your grand arrival *before* the meeting actually starts."

He gave a short, amused snort. "I'll keep that in mind. But admit it—my timing was *perfect*."

I scoffed. "Sure. If by *perfect*, you mean just in time to look suspicious."

As we reached the temple steps, the cold wind tugged at our cloaks, swirling snowflakes around us. Eirik shot me a knowing look, mischief glinting in his storm-gray eyes. "Suspicious, yes. But memorable."

I rolled my eyes, but a small smile tugged at my lips. "You keep telling yourself that, warrior."

Eirik chuckled as we climbed the steps together, it warmed the cold air around us.

When we stepped inside the temple, the easy banter between Eirik and me dissolved because the moment we entered the archive room, the tension was unmistakable.

Lydia straightened immediately, folding her arms across her chest, her gaze locking onto Eirik. Theron, meanwhile, kept his focus on the scrolls and maps scattered across the table.

"You two took your time," Lydia said, suspicion threading her words. "I was beginning to wonder if our new guardian had already failed his duty."

I sighed. Lydia had a way of being... relentless. "Lydia, please," I said, trying to keep my voice soft. "We need to at least give him a chance. I was new to this world also. Isn't it possible he really is meant to be my guardian?"

Eirik stepped forward. "I understand your doubt, High Priestess," he said, his voice firm. "I meant no insult earlier—nor would I ever bring harm to Ravena. My oath is clear: I protect, I teach, and I guide her. I won't fail her." He inclined his head in respect, but Lydia's expression didn't budge. For a moment, I thought she might challenge him outright, but instead she let out a slow, reluctant sigh and turned back to the table her focus shifting to the maps and scrolls.

"Very well, Ravena," Lydia said at last, though skepticism lingered in her tone. "I will trust your judgment—for now. But know this young man, I'll be watching you closely." she threw a pointed look at Eirik.

The tension in the room didn't vanish, but Lydia's words were probably as close to approval as we'd get. Eirik and I stepped closer to the table, taking it as permission to move forward. Lydia picked up a small map of Greece, carefully unfolding it before passing it to Eirik.

"This land is vast," she said. "If you're to guide Ravena, you must know it well. There are answers hidden among the temples and cities—if you know where to look." She hesitated before adding, "The gods walk among us, but they do not answer to just anyone. Hermes is the only one who may listen. He's aided mortals before, and if he wills it, he can carry word to the higher gods."

I blinked; certain I'd misheard. *Walk among us?* I stared at her, then at Eirik—waiting for someone to crack a smile and admit this was a joke. Nobody did.

"Wait, hold on," I said, shaking my head. "You mean the gods are... literally here? Not just in temples or stories, but actually walking around?"

Lydia arched an eyebrow, as if surprised by my question. "Of course. Some pass among mortals openly; others keep to the shadows."

My brain scrambled to process that. I mean, I knew I was dealing with prophecies, reincarnation, and Norse giants, but the idea of actual gods just... hanging around Greece? That was a whole new level of absurdity.

Eirik shot me a sideways glance, lips twitching with amusement. "You'll get used to it," he said like this was just another day.

I let out a short laugh, more disbelief than humor. "Sure. Just another thing to add to the list of impossible things I'm supposed to accept," I said, sarcasm evident.

Still, with Lydia and Eirik looking at me like I should already know this, I had to keep it together. I bent over the map; the parchment was slightly worn, its edges curled, but the markings remained clear. My attention shifted toward Theron, who stood over a larger, more intricate map spread across the table. His brow furrowed, deep in thought, as his fingers traced an unseen path across the land.

"What do you make of it, Elder?" Eirik asked, his tone curious, and thankfully shifting the attention off of me.

Theron remained focused, his expression pensive. "Hermes will do" he muttered at last, tapping a finger lightly against the map. "If any among the gods would listen, it is him. But gods do not give aid freely. If you seek him, be prepared to offer something in return."

I swallowed, uncertainty creeping in. "I might have an idea," I admitted, my voice quieter now. "But I'm not sure."

Theron looked up, a small, wrinkled smile softening his features. "What course do you propose, dear one?"

I stepped closer to the table, drawn in by the maps and scrolls spread across its surface. Eirik moved beside me. My gaze swept across the parchment, tracing the ridges of mountains and winding roads inked across it.

"I've studied Greece extensively," I began, choosing my words carefully. "Back in my world, I spent years on expeditions—learning the terrain, the people, the histories. I don't know how much of that holds true here, but I suspect some things never changed." I exhaled, steadying my thoughts before continuing.

"I think we should send scouts into the mountains. If he's hiding out there, we might find a clue. And someone should check the villages for anything strange—if Agnar's preparing for anything, he'll leave a trail."

Lydia and Theron exchanged a look, their expressions hard to read, but it wasn't dismissive.

Theron paced the table in thought before settling. "A wise approach," he admitted. "We'll send two teams—one to the mountains, the other to the villages and roads. If this giant stirs, we will hear of it."

Eirik let out a low chuckle, his grin flashing as he clapped a firm hand on my shoulder. "Who would've thought our lady here has the mind of a Jarl?"

I rolled my eyes and shoved his hand off, unable to fully suppress a shy smile. "I'm not an idiot, Norseman." I shot back. "I may not know much about war, but if this land is anything like the Greece I studied, I won't be completely lost—unlike you."

Eirik arched an eyebrow, feigning offense. "Norseman?" he echoed, placing a hand over his heart as if wounded. "And here I thought we were making progress as friends." His tone was light and teasing.

Theron let out a hearty laugh. "Strange times, when the old gods of Greece find themselves tangled up with Norse prophecies and giants," he said, shaking his head. " Never thought I'd live to see such a day."

I ran my fingers through my hair, all humor draining out of me. Anxiety swelled in my chest like a rising tide, threatening to pull me under. *Gods, will I ever be strong enough to stop feeling this way?* A deep sigh escaped before I could stop it, doubt creeping in, unwelcome as ever. *They definitely chose the wrong mortal for this.*

Shoving the thought aside, I focused on the map again and forced myself to speak "The vision said Agnar would gather an army," I managed, my voice steadier than I felt. "It also mentioned an ally—someone willing to betray their own kind for freedom. What if... it's a Greek deity?"

The room went still. The silence was all that permeated the room.

Lydia's fingers curled against the edge of the table, her knuckles turning white. She drew a shaky breath. "As much as I wish to deny it," she said, her voice thin and raw, "it is unsettling to think one of our own could fall to such treachery. But with your arrival, Ravena, and the warnings we received... I cannot ignore the possibility."

Beside her, Theron placed a hand on her shoulder, in comfort. "We'll make sense of this," he said. "We must send scouts first, prepare for potential conflict—and seek our own allies, mortal and divine." His eyes cut to Eirik, the look of a man who had already made a decision. "And you," he added, "will train Ravena. She knows nothing of combat."

Eirik posture tensed, determination sharpening his features. "Yes, we spoke of it. She's not a warrior—not yet. But she will be. I'll see to it."

I arched my brow, trying to mask the unease crawling up my spine. "Hope you've got a plan, Eirik, because I have no clue what I'm doing."

Eirik met my gaze—no smirk, just a flicker of understanding. For a moment, I saw it in his eyes: he noticed the way my hands curled into fists, and the quickness of my breath. He knew.

"I feel we do not have much time," Lydia said, her voice edged with worry.

Eirik exhaled sharply, rolling his shoulders, jaw set. "Then we train quickly and safely, but we will push past limits."

My head snapped up, alarm prickling along my skin. "Push past limits?" The words tasted strange, and I wasn't sure if I was ready.

He held my gaze, no hesitation present, his look alone had me slumping forward. I let out a long breath, muttering, "Didn't expect this to be easy... why would anything be simple?"

At that movement in the room continued. Lydia and Theron dove back into strategy, their voices weaving through plans and preparations. I tried to listen. I really did. But the words blurred, swallowed by the pressure in my chest. The air grew thick, the walls suddenly too close. My heartbeat thundered in my ears, relentless as a war drum.

Cold sweat broke over my skin.

The archive room warped and wavered—maps and scrolls swimming in and out of focus. The people, the plans, it was all too much. I stumbled back a step, the ground tilting beneath me.

Eirik's voice cut through the haze, worried. Lydia and Theron's concerned faces flickered at the edge of my vision; their words drowned out by the roaring in my ears.

"I—I need some air…" The words barely scraped past my throat. I could barely recognize my own voice. "Excuse me." I turned abruptly, missing Lydia's gasp and the edge in Eirik's voice as he called my name.

The cold slapped me the instant I crossed the temple threshold, hitting like a shock to the system. My breath came in uneven gasps as I stumbled forward, the tightness in my chest refusing to ease. The icy wind bit into my skin, but I barely felt it. My legs carried me away from the open colonnade, away from the stifling walls and gazes.

I wasn't just running from the conversation. I was running from the weight of it all. From the expectations. From the crushing certainty that I was horrifically unprepared for any of this.

Breathe, Ravena. Gods, just breathe.

Villagers cast curious glances my way, their murmurs lost beneath the pounding in my skull. I kept to the shadows, slipping past the watchful eyes and toward the trees, where the world felt quieter, where I could finally pull in a full breath.

My feet kept moving, almost on autopilot, like they were searching for something familiar and safe. My breath came in ragged gasps as I stumbled to the familiar overlook where I had first arrived. The cold air stung my lungs, each inhale sharp and unsteady. My legs burned from the strain, but it was nothing compared to the pressure tightening my chest.

Reaching the nearest tree I collapsed against it, the rough bark digging into my back as I slid down to the frozen earth. My body trembled, whether from the cold or the overwhelming surge of emotions, I wasn't sure.

To my surprise, hot tears began to slip down my cheeks. *Why? Why me?* The bitter thought twisted in my mind, cruelly. I wasn't a warrior. I wasn't strong. I had no special skills or abilities—nothing that made me worthy of this prophecy. I was just an ordinary woman thrown into something far bigger than myself, expected to carry the legacy of a goddess I barely understood.

Angrily, I wiped at my tears, frustrated by how quickly control was slipping through my fingers. The familiar surge of anxiety gnawed at my chest, refusing to let go. *Gods, will I break down every time something happens?*

I bit my lip hard, the sting pulling me to the present. The snow thickened, swirling around me in soft, silent descent, but I barely noticed. My eyes remained locked on the distant cities below, where the coast stretched out in the golden light of the late afternoon sun.

"I don't know if I can do this," I whispered, my voice barely audible against the wind. "I just hope I don't screw it all up."

Suddenly, a warmth spread through my chest, unfamiliar yet strangely comforting. A flicker of energy pulsed through me—it wasn't physical, but something deeper. I gasped, pressing a hand over my heart as a voice—cool and strong—whispered into my mind.

You are more capable than you know, young one.

My breath hitched, my entire body locking in place. I whipped my head around, scanning the empty overlook. "W-who?" I stammered, barely able to form the word.

A soft, knowing laugh rippled through my thoughts, a sound that carried both wisdom and amusement.

I am what remains of Skadi—the goddess of winter, the last whisper of what I once was.

I froze, my pulse hammering wildly. *S-Skadi?* My thoughts tangled into knots, my mind scrambling for reason. *This isn't real. It can't be.*

It is real, she answered. *My body has long since faded, my power spent, but my essence remains...waiting. Preparing. Until the day comes when you rise in my place.*

A cold shiver ran down my spine. *You mean... I really am your reincarnation?*

Yes. The Fates saw it long ago. When my time ended, they wove the threads of destiny to ensure another would rise. Another who could finish what I could not. Her voice continued to drift quietly in my head.

I squeezed my eyes shut, my stomach twisting. *Why me? Why someone like me? I'm not a goddess; I'm not a warrior—*

Not yet, Skadi interjected. *But the potential has always been within you, even when you could not see it yourself. You felt it, did you not? The pull toward a past that was never truly yours? The sense that you did not belong in your world?*

I swallowed hard. She wasn't wrong. I'd always felt out of place, drawn to history in a way that went beyond mere fascination. *But that doesn't mean I'm ready for this.*

No one ever is, Skadi murmured. *I was not ready either, even though I was born into it. But we do not choose destiny—it chooses us.*

My hands curled into fists at my sides. *I must be losing my mind. First the prophecy, then Eirik, and now I have you in my head?*

You are not mad, child, she reassured me gently. *It is a great deal to bear, but you do not walk this path alone. Your guardian will stand beside you. And when needed... I will be here. My essence lingers until you are ready to ascend. Until then, you must learn. You must survive.*

Her presence began to fade, slipping away like mist in the wind. I felt the emptiness almost immediately.

Rest, young one. We will speak again. Those were her last words before silence fell. The warmth she'd left behind faded, replaced once more by the bite of mountain air and the sound of my own ragged breathing.

I pressed my forehead against my knees, my body trembling—not from the cold, but from the chaos swirling in my mind. The quiet broke with the soft crunch of footsteps behind me, making me tense.

"Ravena?"

I turned, blinking back tears as the rays of the lowering sun caught my eyes. Eirik stood a few paces away, his expression uncertain, concern etched in every line.

"What are you doing here?" I managed, my voice raw and shaky. The last thing I wanted was for him to see me like this—vulnerable, falling apart and ugly crying.

"I could not leave you alone out here," he said simply, his tone softer than usual. "I wanted to be sure you were alright."

My first instinct was to push him away—keep everyone at arm's length, that's what I do best. But the look in his eyes stopped me. He wasn't judging, just quietly present with understanding.

I exhaled, crossing my arms over my knees, my gaze dropping to the ground. "It just...," I trailed off, resting my head against my arms. "Honestly, I don't feel ready for any of this."

Eirik moved closer, settling beside me. He leaned back against the tree, arms folded behind his head like he hadn't a care in the world. "No one expects you to have all the answers or be ready right now," he said, his voice low and calm. "But you're not alone. We'll face this together."

His words sank in, easing some of the tightness in my chest. I gave him a small, hesitant smile. A wave of appreciation washed over me. This poor guy got thrown into being my guardian, yet here he was, still willing to help.

"Thank you, Eirik," I murmured, barely above a whisper. "I promise to try my hardest during training."

We sat quietly as the sun dipped lower, painting the mountains in streaks of orange and pink. After a while, Eirik got to his feet and brushed the snow from his cloak. He turned toward me and offered his hand.

"Let's get you back. It's getting late, and you need to eat."

I stared at his outstretched hand for a moment, then let a small smile tug at my lips. Wrapping my fingers around his calloused palm, I let him help me up.

Chapter Nine

The walk back was quiet, the woods around us blanketed in silence. The setting sun cast long shadows, its fading light the only source of illumination as we entered the village. A few villagers still lingered outside, offering me small nods and a few wary looks, before their eyes darted toward Eirik. He didn't seem to notice, or perhaps he just didn't care as he kept his pace toward the main house.

I hugged my arms tighter around myself, trying to chase off the chill. It wasn't unbearable, but I'd stayed out in the cold longer than I should have. My gaze drifted to Eirik as we climbed the short incline to the door. *The cold doesn't seem to touch him,* I realized, watching how easily he moved—bare arms exposed, no sign of discomfort.

Eirik reached the door first, pulling it open and holding it for me.

"Thanks," I muttered, stepping into the warm hallway. The sudden rush of heat was a welcome relief, and I exhaled quietly as warmth seeped back into my skin.

A flurry of footsteps echoed down the hall. Cora appeared, her expression drawn with worry. The moment she saw me, her features eased, relief in her eyes.

"By the gods, you're alright," she breathed, hurrying closer. "When you did not return with Lydia and Theron, I grew worried. Come, let's get you warm, and find something for you to eat, yes?" Her hand reached for my arm, but she paused, her gaze snapping past me to Eirik.

Instantly, her demeanor shifted—replaced by wary curiosity. Her brows pulled together, and her tone held the firm edge of protectiveness. "And who is this?"

I sighed in exhaustion. "He's ok Cora," I said. "Let's get to the table. Lydia and Theron can explain more."

Her dark eyes lingered on Eirik for a moment longer before she finally nodded, the tension in her shoulders remained. "Of course, Lady Ravena," she said, her voice low. "They told me some of it, and I am deeply sorry this is all so much at once."

As we entered the room, the warm glow of the roaring flames greeted us, along with the rich aroma of freshly prepared food. My stomach gave a quiet, involuntary growl, and I couldn't help but glance toward the table with tired anticipation.

Cora, ever the caretaker, pulled out a chair for me. "Sit, sit, child. You must eat before you make yourself sick," she fussed, shaking her head as if I had been neglecting myself.

I sank into the seat gratefully. My eyes flicked to the empty chair beside me, silently inviting Eirik to sit.

Lydia's voice broke the silence. "Please, join us, Eirik," she said, nodding her appreciation. "We thank you for bringing her back safely."

Eirik moved toward the chair, his broad frame looking out of place in the room. "It is my duty as her guardian to see her safe," he said, voice carrying the faint lilt of a Norse accent. "And with time, perhaps we may stand as comrades." His gaze flicked toward Cora, and he dipped his head in a polite bow.

The gesture seemed to catch her off guard as she set a plate down in front of me.

"I am Eirik," he continued. "It was foretold that Ravena would have a guardian, and I was chosen to stand at her side. It is my honor to meet you, madam."

Cora blinked, clearly flustered by his respectful tone. "Ah... well, it is very nice to meet you, Eirik," she said, her voice softening, though her keen eyes still studied him with scrutiny. "You have no need to bow, child. But I am glad our Ravena has someone to watch over her." She folded her arms, giving him a stern look "I am placing my trust in you. Do not make me regret it."

Eirik's lips curled into the barest hint of a smile. "I do not take such trust lightly," he assured her. "An' I shall not fail in my task."

The tension in the room eased slightly, and the conversation began to shift toward lighter topics, as if some of the ice had finally cracked. Lydia turned to me after a moment; her expression clouded with concern.

"Are you alright?" she asked gently, her voice laced with worry. "We did not take into consideration how you might feel about all this when we jumped in headfirst. For that, I am sorry."

I let out a conflicted sigh, trying to sound more confident than I felt. "There's no need to apologize, Lydia. You're all only doing what's expected of you. I'll have to adjust one way or another." I hesitated before adding, "In time, I'll get better—better at handling my actions when my emotions get to be too much." I offered her a small smile, though my thoughts were far from reassuring. *Gods, I hope that's true.*

My gaze flickered toward Eirik. "His presence was a big help," I admitted lightly. "He's not so bad after all."

Eirik let out a surprised grunt at my comment, earning a curious glance from Lydia and Theron. The two exchanged looks, their expressions softening slightly toward him, as if reevaluating the man, they had been so wary of.

I turned toward Eirik, tilting my head. "I do have a question for you. Maybe two, if you're up for it." My voice coming out a bit hesitant.

Eirik's raised a brow, curiosity lighting in his eyes. "Go on."

I took a moment to gather my thoughts, trying to piece my words together coherently. "I assume you come from Norway... a uh real-life

Viking, right?" I began, my voice uncertain as I worked through my thoughts. "And you said the Greek and Norse gods decided you were to be my guardian. Do the Norse gods also reside in this realm? And... you seemed very curious about the map of Greece. Have you never traveled here before?" The questions tumbled out in a jumbled mess, but I hoped they made sense.

Eirik let out a soft chuckle, his posture relaxing slightly. "Viking, huh? Is that what they call us in your realm?" He shook his head amused. "Back home, we call it going *a-viking*—its more of a pastime than a title." He leaned back in his chair, arms crossing. "But I figured these questions would come up eventually. Yes, I hail from Norway—but not of *this* realm, if that makes sense."

That made me pause and the room felt suddenly way too quiet.

He went on, "My realm is called Midgard. One of the nine realms. The Greek world and mine run alongside each other, separated by portals. Only those with permission may travel back and forth, even the gods have rules."

I blinked, trying to absorb what he was saying. "So... your realm is like this one, but different?"

Eirik set his fork down, leaning forward. "Correct. Midgard has its own gods, its own rules. While beings from different realms can cross over, most prefer to stay in their own. It's... deeply frowned upon to interfere in another realm's affairs. So, the Norse gods stay in Midgard or Asgard, and the Greek gods remain here, and so on. And no mortals are allowed travel through these portals."

The explanation fascinated me, sending a spark of curiosity through my exhaustion. I leaned in slightly, my mind racing with possibilities. "So, it's true then. Other universes, realms, and timelines exist? I studied theories about this in my time, but there was never any proof—only speculation."

Eirik nodded, thoughtful. "That's correct. Your realm is different from ours. It does not run parallel to ours—it exists in its own space, from what I was told."

He hesitated, his gaze dropping slightly as if weighing his next words carefully. "The Norse gods granted me passage to this realm when they felt your arrival here in Greece. Odin knew my role in helping you."

Theron was the one to finally break the silence, setting his fork down with deliberate care. His eyes fixed on Eirik, his voice curious. "You said no mortals could travel through the portals... what makes you different from them?"

The question lingered in the air. The fire in the hearth seemed to flicker, its glow casting shifting shadows across the room. Across from me, Eirik went completely still. His jaw clenched, his fist curling tightly against his lap, as though holding something back.

Before he could answer, I reached out instinctively, my fingers brushing against his upper arm. He tensed beneath my touch startling slightly, his rigid posture easing just enough for him to glance at me.

"Hey," I said softly, meeting his gaze. "It's alright. You don't have to explain anything you don't want to. Your business is your own, you don't owe us any answers about your life."

Theron parted his lips, about to protest, but I shot him a look—one that silently urged him to *drop it*. A heavy pause followed before he exhaled slowly, leaning back in his chair with reluctant acceptance.

Eirik's tension eased further, and after a beat, he gave me a small, almost imperceptible nod. But then he straightened, his expression more composed. "Nay," he murmured, his deep voice carrying a quiet resolve. "It is alright." He met my eyes briefly before looking toward Theron. "I do not go 'round speaking of my heritage, that's all." His hand uncurled from its tight grip, and for the first time since the conversation started, he *chose* to answer. "I am *part* mortal, yes," he admitted. "My mother was a shield-maiden of our clan back home. A fierce warrior." His voice softened, respect clear in his tone. "My father... is a *Jotun*—one of the few who chose to work with Odin rather than against him. He was granted the All-Father's blessing to take my mother as his wife, and so I was born." Eirik continued, his voice hesitant. "I was presented with the title of *demi-god* by Odin himself. It was written in fate that a *half-blood* would be born to protect a future prophecy... and guide her to where she was destined to be."

For a moment, I just stared at him, my mouth was hanging open. *An actual demi-god is sitting right next to me.* The thought was almost surreal. Out of all the things I expected to learn tonight, *that* hadn't even crossed my mind. But then, a slow smirk crept onto my lips, and before I could stop myself, I muttered, "Well... for a demi-god, you do seem to have a *horrible* sense of timing."

Eirik's head snapped toward me, his brows drawing together as a faint flush crept up his neck. He closed his eyes for a beat, exhaling through his nose. "I *said* I'd work on that," he muttered, clearly trying not to rise to my bait.

"Let's hope you're not *late* to training," I shot back smugly.

Theron, who had been observing the exchange in amused silence, suddenly sat up straighter. "Ah, yes. Training," he mused, the corners of his mouth twitching. He turned his gaze toward me as if asking for permission to speak.

I gave him a small nod, offering a reassuring smile. "Go on, Theron. I *promise* I won't bolt this time."

With a slight nod of acknowledgment, he leaned back in his chair, folding his hands over his lap. "When do you plan to begin? And what exactly do you intend to teach her?" His question directed to Eirik of course.

Eirik crossed his arms, his expression darkening in thought. "Tomorrow morning, *if* she's ready," he answered. "We'll start with the basics, stances, footwork, and balance. She needs to learn *how* to hold herself in a fight before she ever wields a weapon. Self-defense first, how to throw a proper punch, how to block, and how to move."

I raised an eyebrow. "So... you *do* have a plan, then?"

Eirik shot me a dry look, his lips twitching. "Yes, *skeptical one*, I do."

I nodded slowly, feeling a strange mix of nerves and curiosity bubbling inside me. *Training.* It wasn't something I had ever seriously considered before, even though I'd always *wanted* to learn self-defense. Living alone, I knew it would have been useful but work, exhaustion, and, if I was honest, my own laziness had always gotten in the way.

I rested my chin on my hand and groaned internally. *Great. I can already feel my lazy side waking up. I hate running.*

As if sensing my thoughts, a faint warmth spread through me, catching me off guard. I barely had time to react before a familiar voice echoed in my mind.

You sound like me when I was but a young one, Skadi mused, her tone carrying a note of wry amusement.

Glad I could bring you some humor, I thought back dryly, a faint smile tugged at my lips.

By the hearth, Cora, who had remained silent until now, finally spoke, her brow furrowed. "And if she gets overwhelmed? If she needs a break?"

Eirik turned toward her, his expression softening slightly, but keeping his voice serious. "We'll stop when she reaches her limits. I won't push her beyond what she can handle—but she *will* need to push past fear. Combat is as much mental as it is physical."

Cora studied him for a moment before nodding, clearly satisfied with his answer, a thoughtful look still lingered on her face. "I don't mean to intrude," she began carefully, "but do you have a place to sleep? We have another room—it would be easier for you to rest and prepare for training."

Her question caught me off guard, and I turned to Eirik with a curious glance. *Where exactly had he been staying?*

Eirik shook his head, offering a polite smile. "I appreciate the offer, madam but I've already set up camp nearby. I prefer keeping' my own space—but I'll be close if needed."

I let out a quiet laugh, shaking my head. "You are not a people person, are you?"

His grin was faint but undeniably genuine. "It's kept me alive this long, *Lady Ravena*," he drawled, teasing.

That seemed to signal the end of dinner. We all stood, preparing to head our separate ways for the night. As Cora led me toward my room, I hesitated in the hallway, glancing over my shoulder.

My eyes followed Eirik as he stepped outside, his broad frame silhouetted against the dim firelight before he disappeared into the darkness. He moved with such quiet confidence, like someone who had never once doubted his place in the world. Or maybe he had and he was just good at hiding it. A twinge of jealousy stirred in my chest. *Would I ever feel that certain—so sure of who I was and what I was meant to do?*

The thought lingered as I turned back down the hallway, exhaustion creeping over me like a thick fog. There was *more* to Eirik's story—of that, I had no doubt. But for now, my questions would have to wait.

With a quiet sigh, I stepped into my room and let the door close softly behind me.

Maybe one day, I'll know more about him. But not tonight.

Chapter Ten

The early morning air was crisp, the ground blanketed in fresh snow that crunched beneath my boots as Eirik and I stepped into a secluded clearing. Towering trees surrounded us, their snow-covered branches framing the quiet space. The stillness was almost unnerving, broken only by the soft sound of our footsteps and the occasional call of a distant bird.

My nerves were already on edge. I'd never been in a fight—let alone trained for one. My gaze darted between the snow underfoot and Eirik, who looked utterly calm, as if this were just another morning for him. His confidence—no doubt from years of experience—only made me more aware of how out of my depth I really was. Anxiety twisted in my stomach, tightening with every step.

Eirik stopped in the middle of the clearing and turned to face me, a slight grin tugging at the corner of his mouth. "You look like you're about to face a beast, not your first lesson," he teased lightly. "Relax. We're starting slow."

I rolled my eyes, pulling my cloak tighter—for a sense of security. "Right, relax," I muttered, heavy on the sarcasm. "Should we also go flower-picking while we're at it?"

Eirik threw his head back and let out a hearty laugh. "Alright, maybe not *relax,* but don't overthink it. I'm not about to throw you to the wolves." He bent down, grabbing two wooden poles from the ground.

Without warning, he spun and tossed one of the poles toward me. I reached for it, determined not to make a fool of myself—but fate had other plans. My foot slipped on the snow as I lunged, and I landed flat on my back with a loud *thud* and a muffled grunt.

Eirik's grin only widened, his amusement painfully clear. "Well, not exactly the most graceful start to training," he teased, holding out a hand to help me up. "Good thing we're starting with the basics." pulling me up swiftly.

I scowled, brushing snow off my cloak, trying to ignore the heat creeping up my neck. "I meant to do that," I muttered.

"Right... of course," he said, raising an eyebrow in mock seriousness. "Such an invaluable skill for any warrior."

I huffed and adjusted my grip on the wooden pole, forcing myself to stand a little taller. My cheeks still burned, but I focused on not letting my embarrassment show any more than it already had.

"All right," Eirik began, stepping into a wide stance and holding his pole like a sword. "First lesson—stance. It all starts from the ground up: balance and strong footing." He nodded at my feet. "If you're not rooted, you'll end up..." He gestured at the ground, with a playful smirk. "...flat on your back. Sound familiar?"

I narrowed my eyes at him but shifted my feet as he instructed, trying to mimic his posture. The wind tugged at my cloak as I planted my feet more firmly in the snow, gripping the pole even tighter. I fought the urge to look away, determined to focus.

"That's better," he said, nodding his approval. "Now, I'll come at you slowly—don't worry. I want you to block. Don't flinch, don't stumble back. Just block." He adjusted his stance and raised his pole, stepping forward.

I swallowed hard, gripping the pole so tightly my knuckles went white. My heart pounded as I watched him swing in a slow arc. Bracing myself, I lifted mine to meet his strike. The impact sent a jolt up my arms, and I stumbled back a step, cursing under my breath.

Eirik chuckled. "Not bad. But you'll need more than sheer willpower to keep your footing."

I frowned, repositioning myself. "Easy for you to say, Eirik. You were probably born with a sword in your hand."

His grin softened, his tone more encouraging. "And you'll learn, just the same." He settled back into his position, tilting his head slightly. "Ready to try again?"

We trained for what felt like hours. Every strike Eirik threw at me sent fire coursing through my muscles, and my body protested with every movement. *My gods, this man has to be joking if he says he's taking it easy,* I winced as I barely managed to block another swing. But as the minutes passed, my initial anxiety melted into something closer to concentration.

The ache in my arms and the rawness of my hands faded to the background as I focused on keeping up with him. It wasn't easy—far from it—but every now and then, I caught an encouraging look from Eirik, and it spurred me to push a little harder.

Finally, as he swung for my shoulder, something clicked. I blocked the strike firmly, surprising myself. A triumphant grin tugged at my lips as I shot him a look, and Eirik nodded in approval, stepping back to let me catch my breath. By midday, we paused for a break. I all but collapsed onto the snow, spreading my cloak beneath me as a makeshift seat. My arms felt like they might fall off, every muscle in my body screamed in protest.

Eirik tossed me a waterskin, and I nearly fumbled it, my hands trembling from exhaustion. "Not bad for a first day," he remarked, amusement dancing in his eyes.

I shot him a glare, trying not to dwell on how unfair it was that he didn't even look tired. *He didn't even break a sweat! Ugh, I swear.* But beneath the exhaustion, I couldn't deny a flicker of pride. I'd made it through the morning, and that was something. I leaned forward, resting my head on my knees as I focused on breathing deeply, willing my muscles to relax.

The cold air filled my lungs, as I closed my eyes. *I just realized I'm severely out of shape... this is embarrassing.* The thought made me groan internally, but I tried to push it away. Around us, the clearing was quiet, save for the wind weaving through the trees and the steady rhythm of our breathing. Peeking one eye open, I glanced over at Eirik, who was leaning casually against a tree with his arms crossed. He looked so at ease, like the hours we'd spent training hadn't affected him at all.

I studied him quietly, hoping he wouldn't notice. Every movement he performed was sharp and precise while every strike it seemed was planned. It was clear he had countless hours of training.

He's built for this. Fighting must have been a way of life for him, I thought, vaguely recalling something about Viking traditions. *His expectations for me will probably be high.* A faint weight settled over me at the thought. *I don't want to let him down, but I know I'll make mistakes.*

I let my eyes drift shut again, trying to chase away the growing doubt. Suddenly, a familiar warmth washed over me, and I tensed instinctively.

You did well, Ravena. Learning the basics is the first step, and I know you will exceed everyone's expectations, came Skadi's cool, reassuring voice.

I let out a quiet sigh, relaxing if only a little. *I'm trying... if only I could get my anxiety to go away, I might do better. The doubt is a struggle, but maybe one day that'll go away also.*

Her hum of agreement was soft, comforting. *Anxiety and doubt are something we all face; they're part of growth. You're doing what you once thought impossible, so your feelings are expected. I'll be more present in your training from now on, though the demi-god here may eventually notice that you're getting... extra guidance.* Her words trailed off, and I felt a flicker of hesitation from her, as if she wanted to say more but was holding back.

What is it, Skadi? My brows knitting in concern.

She sighed softly in my mind, the sound carrying a feeling I hadn't felt before. *I was going to wait, young Ravena, but I fear time is something we don't have. My abilities will awaken in you as you continue training; they will become your own. As you work on your strength and endurance, you'll find them becoming enhanced. You won't tire as easily as you are now.*

There was a brief pause before she added, *other abilities will come in time, but we'll discuss those as you progress.*

My eyes popped open, blinking against the light. I stared up at the sky, as if it held the answers. *So, would this explain why the cold doesn't seem to you know bother me?* I was still struggling to fully believe what I was hearing.

A confirming hum resonated in my mind, and I let out a small snort, the absurdity of it all catching me off guard. *That's... cool,* I thought wryly before muttering under my breath, "I'm not sure why I'm so surprised. Nothing has been exactly normal since I got here."

Skadi's laugh rippled through my thoughts, soothing the racing anxiety that had begun to creep in. *I'll guide you as best I can, Ravena. You're my successor. Now, tell your guardian you're finished for now. You need to eat and rest; you'll be of no use if you can't even feel your arms.* Her presence faded, leaving me with the lingering warmth of her encouragement.

I flexed my fingers, suddenly aware of the numbness in my arms and the deep ache settling in once more. Skadi was right—I couldn't even lift my arms without them protesting. When I turned toward Eirik, I caught him watching me intently, head tilted as if puzzling something out.

I let out a nervous laugh. "Uh—can I help you?" My voice shaky.

Eirik stood up and stepped forward, a faint grin tugging at the corner of his mouth. "Are you alright? You looked like you were having quite the conversation with yourself."

Heat rushed to my face. "Uh—no, I mean, yes! I'm fine. Just... in my head again." I tried to push myself up, but my arms gave out almost immediately. Before I could brace for an ungraceful face-plant, strong arms caught me.

I gasped, my breath hitching as I realized I was now in Eirik's hold. His bare arms were warm against my chilled skin—completely at odds with the icy air. For a moment, my brain stuttered over why he wasn't freezing, but that thought vanished when I felt my cheeks burning. *Oh no, I'm still in his arms.*

I shifted awkwardly, pulse racing as I tried to regain my footing. "Um... thanks," I mumbled, eyes dropping to the ground. I wasn't used to being this close to anyone, let alone someone like Eirik. It made me feel very awkward right then.

He offered a faint smile, his hands lingering just a moment longer to steady me. As I straightened, a strange sensation rippled through me—a subtle faint tug, almost like an invisible thread pulling me away. The feeling was unsettling, like something important was hovering just out of reach.

The warmth of Eirik's arms no longer felt comforting, and an instinct I couldn't name urged me to pull back. I took a quick step away, breaking the contact, my legs finally steady beneath me.

Eirik's brow creased slightly as he noticed my abrupt retreat. "Are you alright?" he asked quietly, searching my face for answers.

"Yeah, just... lost my balance," I replied quickly, my voice betraying the nerves I was trying to hide. "I should've remembered my arms were numb." I bent to pick up my cloak, trying to shake off the strange feeling. But the odd tug—left behind a hollow emptiness, as though I'd left something unfinished.

I forced a laugh, shaking out my cloak to buy time. "Should we call it for now? I'm no good with numb arms. We won't make any progress if we keep going," I said, eager to move past the awkward moment.

Eirik studied me a moment longer before nodding. "You're probably right. Go eat and rest. We'll try again before dinner—if we wait until after, you might end up losing your meal." His teasing smile softened the mood.

Still distracted by the odd sensations, I barely heard his reply. "Thanks—see you later!" I called, practically running off without waiting for him to answer. Behind me, I could almost feel his confusion as I darted through the trees.

"That was an interesting exit. You left that poor man thoroughly baffled," Skadi's voice chimed in my mind, her tone warm and teasing.

I flushed, pulling my cloak tighter around me. "You heard that?!"

"Yes, and it was quite amusing," she replied with a soft chuckle. *"I've always found your awkwardness endearing. I was like that myself when I was younger."*

"Glad I could entertain you, Skadi," I muttered as I reached the edge of the village. "I have a feeling you're going to get endless amusement from me."

"Don't be so hard on yourself. We all have to start somewhere, and none of us were born with fighting skills. You're stronger than you will ever admit. I would know—I've been with you all your life."

I stopped short at the door, her words sinking in. "My whole life? You mean... you've seen everything that's ever happened to me?" I asked my stomach churning a bit at the idea.

"I've been with you from the moment you were born," Skadi said, her voice turning wistful. *"I could see and hear the moments that shaped you, but I chose not to interfere. Your life, your choices... they were always yours to make. I watched and understood, but I retreated to the far reaches of your soul to give you privacy. You needed to find your own path."*

Her admission left me quiet as I opened the door and stepped inside, hanging up my cloak. The house welcomed me with a rush of warmth, but Skadi's words lingered in my mind. "That's... something to think about," I murmured. "I'm not sure if that's comforting or unsettling."

Before I could dwell on it, Cora bustled in, the carrying a steaming tray. Her worried gaze locked on me at once. "Lady Ravena, you look exhausted! What did that man do to you?" she fretted, setting the food down and eyeing me up and down.

I offered her a tired smile. "Cora, you worry too much. Eirik was actually easy on me—I'm just out of shape. I can't remember the last time I exercised." I stretched my arms, grimacing at the soreness.

Cora huffed, shaking her head. "Well, promise me you'll take it easy on yourself. No need to injure yourself before you can even help the world." She uncovered a bowl of hot stew and fresh bread.

I nodded and sat down at the table. "I'll try, Cora, but if I don't push myself, I won't get better. And we can't afford that," I said, folding my hands, already thinking of the challenges ahead.

"I suppose you're right," she admitted, still looking displeased. "I don't like it, but that's just me being overprotective. I take it Eirik wants to train again later?"

Humming in agreement, I picked up the spoon. "Before dinner, I think, was the last thing I heard." I took a bite of stew, savoring the heat and flavor. Food here was so much fresher, more flavorful than anything back in my time. Each bite felt like a small luxury.

"Well, eat up, dear. Then go relax," Cora said, settling by the fire with a book. "You could visit the springs, though I doubt it'll help much if you're going right back to training."

I swallowed another mouthful of stew and glanced over. "Thank you for the meal, Cora. I really do appreciate you all taking care of me," I said sincerely, a smile tugging at my lips.

Cora looked up from her book, her expression soft. "No need to thank me, dear. It's my honor to do so. I will treat you as my own."

I gave her one last smile and a small nod before returning to my meal, my mind buzzing with everything that had happened. The curiosity that had been building finally won out. *Say, Skadi?* I reached for her presence, tentatively.

Yes, young one? Skadi's cool, familiar voice returned.

I glanced toward the fire, hesitating. *There are so many questions I have. I'd feel bad dropping them all on you at once, but you're the only one who knows what's happening...*

It's alright, Ravena. I knew the moment I made my presence known there would be questions, Skadi reassured me.

I bit my lip, gathering my thoughts. *What happened with this Agnar? What's his story?*

There was a pause before Skadi answered. *You all already know he is a frost giant; he hails from Jotunheim. Agnar was imprisoned by the All-Father for attempting to overthrow him and causing destruction in Asgard, injuring many in his wake. He was placed in my ice prison, wounded from battle, and I was tasked with guarding him.* Her voice softened, regret lacing every word. *But I failed... someone, or something, freed him. I fought him as best as I could, but the Fates were not on my side. He was stronger than I anticipated, and he struck me with a near-fatal blow.*

My grip tightened around the spoon. *I... I'm sorry, Skadi. I feel like anything I say would sound foolish. You've been trapped inside some random mortal for years, but I know from the dreams I've had that you fought with everything you had.*

No need for apologies, Skadi replied, warmth returning to her voice. *You've always had a way with words, even if you tend to keep to yourself. I admire that about you. Though I should apologize—I never meant for those memories to surface in you so soon. But as you grew older, our souls began to bond, and I grew stronger.*

I nodded absently, staring at the flickering flames. *That makes sense. I've read about reincarnation, the sources vary, and most people never know who they were in past lives. But I guess I just got lucky huh?*

It would seem so, our connection is unique in many ways. But for now, your caretaker seems concerned with you staring into nothing.

I blinked, startled, and quickly grabbed a piece of bread to dip into my stew to not seem suspicious. "I'll have to practice communicating with you without getting so distracted," I muttered under my breath. Skadi's soft laughter echoed in my mind as her presence faded.

Chapter Eleven

Once I finished eating, a sense of contentment settled over me. But I knew that if I gave in to the temptation of sleep now, I'd never wake up in time for training. Noticing Cora lowering her book by the fire, I spoke up. "Cora, you know I can clean up after myself. You don't have to stop reading."

She waved a dismissive hand as she rose to her feet. "Nonsense, dear. As I've told you, it is my duty. And here, you're far too important to be doing such tasks." She gathered my empty bowl and began tidying up.

I sighed, deciding not to argue. "Well, um, do you have a place I could read? I've only seen the temple archives."

Cora's face brightened immediately. "Of course! I'll take you to our bibliotheca. You may find some texts there that interest you."

My spirits lifted. Finally, I'd have access to books I'd never seen before—and a chance to brush up on their ancient language.

Handing the rest of the cleaning to someone else, Cora turned back to me with a warm smile. "It's only a short walk, but well worth it. Our bibliotheca may not be as grand as others in Greece, but it's a fine place for learning. Many here have worked hard to preserve and add to it over the years."

She passed me my cloak, guiding me out the door and down the path. Her tone softened as she glanced at me. "I imagine this place will be a refuge for you, Lady Ravena. It's good to have a bit of rest between training sessions. Eirik may say he's going to be easy on you, but I don't think that man knows what that is."

I nudged her playfully. "You don't say?" I chuckled. "But thank you for the warning."

"Just my way of looking after you," Cora replied with a smile. "Now go on and enjoy yourself. I'll send Eirik this way if he comes looking."

I shifted in excitement. "Thank you, Cora. You know me well enough already—I'll be spending a lot of time here."

She smiled as I stepped into the bibliotheca. "Then I'm glad it brings you joy, milady,"

The moment I entered, the aged scent of parchment and ink washed over me, mingling with the faint aroma of olive oil lamps and the crisp winter air that drifted through the narrow windows. Light filtered in, casting intricate patterns on the stone floor. I had to stop myself from grinning. I could already imagine losing hours here, surrounded by so much history.

These mortals have quite the collection, Skadi murmured in my mind, her voice thoughtful. *I wonder if any Norse sagas or eddas might be here. Considering their encounter with our gods all those years ago.*

I walked slowly along the shelves, my fingers skimming the spines of books bound in worn leather and scrolls wrapped in faded cloth. "I'll look. It'd be interesting to see how they remember the events," I replied. A faint tug of curiosity stirred in me as I wondered what tales might lie hidden here.

My gaze fell on a leather-bound book embossed with swirling designs that reminded me of Norse motifs. Intrigued, I carefully pulled it from the shelf and read the title: *The Northern Legends: Tales of Ice and Gods of Other Realms.* Curiosity flared. I opened the book, my fingers tracing the ink on the aged pages as I began reading about the Norse gods from a Greek perspective. The Greeks described the Norse gods and their icy lands with awe and a touch of fear. Their words carried a reverence for beings so different from their own Olympians. The text spoke of Asgard, Midgard, and the Nine Realms, describing the Norse gods as powerful figures who rivaled the Olympians, though their knowledge came secondhand, shared in tales after that fateful night two years ago. The Greeks viewed the Norse gods as distant rulers of harsh lands and hard lives, their accounts respectful but clearly filtered through the lens of their own understanding. I found myself both proud and strangely homesick for a place I'd never lived.

Turning a page, I paused at a passage about *The Goddess of Winter*—a powerful warrior, tasked with guarding a dangerous ice titan imprisoned by Odin himself. The description was respectful, almost mythic, describing her powers over ice and snow, her strength drawn from the heart of winter storms. The words painted a vivid picture of her, someone who was a force to be respected, maybe even feared.

It's strange, isn't it, seeing how others remember us? Skadi's voice drifted. *To them, we're legends—maybe even myths. They believe in their gods, but we must seem like distant stories. And yet, in the end, we're all bound by fate.*

I closed my eyes, picturing The Goddess of Winter as the text described her—fierce, resilient, embodying the harsh beauty of a frozen land. A quiet awe settled over me as I realized this legacy, this strength, was something I might be destined to inherit. The thought left me both terrified and humbled.

Can you tell me more about your realm, Skadi? I asked, curiosity deepening with every word I read.

There is much to learn, young one. You know some already, Skadi said, her voice proud and patient. *There is Yggdrasil, the Tree of Life, connecting all nine realms. Its roots lead to Asgard, Niflheim, and Jotunheim, my homeland. The tree is a symbol of life, growth, and connection, tended by the three Norns—the Fates—who water it from the Well of Urd.*

I nodded, picturing the vastness of her world. "And... you?" I asked aloud, glancing down at the book. "I only know you as a giantess and goddess of winter."

Skadi chuckled softly. *I preferred solitude in the mountains—that's where I found peace. Some myths in your time say I was married to Odin, which is amusing. In truth, I was married to Njord before we parted ways, and later to Ullr. But when my life ended, so did that union.* Her tone grew wistful, the memory distant but still poignant.

A pang of empathy hit me, sensing the hidden sadness in her words. "I'm sorry. Would you ever want to find him again, just to let him know you've found peace or something?"

No. It's best for him to move on. I'm nothing more than an essence now, tied to you. My story was meant to end there. She paused, her voice growing softer. *I was simply a being who loved the cold, and the quiet of the mountains.*

I found myself nodding in understanding. "I think we're alike. I never could stand my trips to Egypt—the heat was unbearable." I tried to steer the conversation away from her past.

Skadi's laugh was a quiet hum of agreement. *Oh, I remember. I wanted to hide from the heat as much as you did. But I admit, I was fascinated by their culture and their gods.*

I snorted at the memory. "I learned what I needed and left as quickly as I could. No amount of money would convince me to stay there." Glancing down at the book in my lap, an idea began to form. "I wonder if I could add my own experiences to this book..."

I'm sure Elder Theron and the scribes would welcome it. Knowledge of the Norse isn't a secret.

I wore a thoughtful expression, already imagining the stories I could add. Only then did I notice how much the light had faded. The room was dim, shadows stretching long across the floor. I'd lost all track of time. A soft cough startled me. I looked up—and found Eirik standing in the doorway.

"You were lost in thought again," he teased, his eyes gleaming with amusement. "I do wonder what goes on in that head of yours."

Heat rushed to my face, and I rolled my eyes to mask my embarrassment. "Wouldn't you like to know? My mind is a complex place," I replied, tapping my temple with mock seriousness.

Eirik laughed, his gaze dropping to the book in my lap. "I see you've been busy. That's an interesting find for a place like this."

I shrugged, stretching out my muscle as I stood. "I love to read, and I was curious about the records of the events from two years ago."

Eirik cocked an eyebrow. "And did you find anything?"

"Just a few Greek retellings of Norse mythology. Their take is... unique," I said, letting out a small sigh as I met his gaze knowing why he was here. "I guess it's time for more training?"

A mischievous grin flashed across Eirik's face. "Indeed, milady," he replied, dragging out the title just to get a rise out of me.

I shot him a sidelong look, pretending to consider my options. Tapping my finger against my chin, I tried to look deeply contemplative. The idea of turning the tables on him was tempting.

Come on, Ravena, Skadi's chimed in, her voice harboring a playful tone. *Soon enough, your guardian will think twice before teasing you.*

A hint of mischief crept into my expression as I faced Eirik. "Very well, Eirik," I said, my words laced with dramatic resignation as I adjusted my cloak. "Let's get this over with."

He chuckled, shaking his head, and stepped aside to let me pass. "That's the spirit, milady."

As we stepped out of the bibliotheca, the crisp air hit my face—invigorating and a little sobering. Snow crunched beneath our boots as we headed back toward the clearing where we'd trained that morning. I sneaked a look at Eirik from the corner of my eye. He seemed completely at ease, his strides confident, gaze sweeping the path ahead out of habit.

He's good at what he does, Skadi remarked, her tone shifting from playful to almost contemplative. *But don't let him intimidate you. You have strengths he hasn't seen yet—even if you don't realize it yourself.*

Easy for you to say, I thought back. *You're not the one about to be whacked with a stick.*

Her laughter warmed me from the inside. *You'll see. There's more to you than you think.*

I drew a slow breath, letting the icy air heighten my focus as we reached the clearing. The snow was still gouged with lines from our earlier training. Eirik stopped, turning to face me, his expression softening just for a second as his eyes found mine.

"Ready for round two?" he asked, a playful glint lighting his eyes.

I nodded, peeling off my cloak and draping it over a low-hanging branch. My arms ached, but I wasn't about to let that show. "Ready as I'll ever be," I said, doing my best to square my shoulders and channel at least a fraction of Skadi's confidence

Eirik's grin widened, and he bent to retrieve the wooden poles. This time, he tossed one to me gently—maybe a silent apology for earlier. He settled into a fighting stance, every movement second nature. "Let's start with reviewing what you learned. Show me your stance."

I adjusted my feet, rolling my shoulders back, doing my best to remember what he'd taught me before. Eirik circled slowly, studying every adjustment with a critical eye. "Better," he said at last, approval threading into his words. "You're learning fast."

A small surge of pride rose in my chest, but I forced myself not to get cocky. I leveled the pole, meeting his gaze and bracing myself for his first strike.

Chapter Twelve

I stirred as the first light of morning crept through the window, warming my face. Groaning, I yanked the thin blanket over my head, desperate to shield myself from the new day a bit longer. Every muscle in my body screamed with protest at the smallest movement—a not-so-gentle reminder of yesterday's training with Eirik. After a brief, silent battle with myself, I finally gave in.

With a defeated sigh, I shoved the blanket aside and stretched, wincing as my bruised shoulder throbbed in protest. *At this rate, the ground will become my closest friend,* I thought wryly, recalling the latest in a series of not-so-graceful tumbles—after an overzealous attempt to swing at Eirik's shoulder. Rolling my stiff shoulders, I swung my legs out of bed and let memories of last night's training play through my mind: clumsy blocks, wild swings, and muscles that simply refused to cooperate. Still, beneath the soreness and embarrassment, I found a small flicker of pride I couldn't ignore. I'd stuck with it—every awkward step, every new bruise, every bit of discomfort.

As I reached for my clothes, my mind wandered back to the bath I'd taken after training. The scent of those herbal oils still lingered on my skin. They'd worked wonders on my sore muscles, but what truly surprised me was how the soreness wasn't nearly bad as I'd expected.

"Noticing the quick healing, are we?" Skadi's voice hummed softly in my mind, tinged with pride. "As your strength grows, even in these early days, so too will your resilience."

My hand paused mid-motion as I draped my cloak over my shoulders. The soft morning light filtered through the window, painting long shadows across the floor. "It's strange," I admitted, gazing out at the snow-draped trees. "But I guess I shouldn't be surprised anymore."

A gentle laugh echoed in my thoughts. "You may always feel that way, young one. Even welcome change takes time to become familiar."

"I suppose you're right," I muttered, fastening the clasp of my cloak. "I wish I could hurry it up, though. Patience has never been my strong suit—and my anxiety loves to remind me of every single shortcoming."

Skadi hummed, thoughtful. "Hmm, that may be something I can help you with. I've been with you long enough to know how we can train you to manage it better. Go to the overlook, and we will meditate there."

Her suggestion pulled me out of my spiral, and I gave a slight nod to no one in particular as I left my room. I waved to Cora on my way out, letting her know I'd be gone for a while. Instead of heading to the training area, I turned down the path toward the overlook—figuring I had time before anyone would miss me.

The walk was quiet, almost nostalgic. Just a couple days ago, I'd arrived here for the first time, walking this very path. The snow had picked up since then, coating the trees and piling thick on the ground. I could admit it was nice not to have any pollution here—nothing to taint the sharp, clean smell of snow and pine.

Stepping into the clearing, I drifted toward the same spot where I'd first landed in this strange new realm. My eyes swept over the distant villages far below, everything still startlingly real. The winter wind caught loose strands of my hair, whipping them across my face as the gusts rose off the side of the mountain. Behind me, the village was blanketed in thick snow, but the city below looked untouched—perhaps cold but not buried.

On the outskirts, I could see faint traces of white just starting to gather.

I sighed, scanning the area until I spotted a couple of snow-covered rocks that looked like decent makeshift seats. After brushing them off, I settled down, the coolness of the stone seeping through my cloak.

"Just so you know," I murmured aloud, "I've only ever tried meditating once. And that was in college."

I am aware, Skadi replied with a faint chuckle. *You came close to connecting with me once. But as you said, your patience back then was even worse than it is now.*

I rolled my eyes, almost able to sense her smirking at me. Closing my eyes, I took a slow deep breath, letting it fill my lungs before releasing it slowly. I worked to clear my mind, remembering that one failed attempt years ago. This time, instead of frustration, I tried to picture a place of peace, somewhere safe.

The world around me faded. Even the sounds of the wind died away as I sank deeper into my subconscious. When I opened my eyes, I was somewhere else—a breathtaking field framed by snow-capped mountains, the horizon glowing beneath a midnight sky. Stars glittered above, scattered across the darkness, and a full moon hung high, drenching the world in silvery light. The ground stretched out, endless and untouched, snow glinting faintly wherever the moonlight fell. Somewhere nearby, I caught the gentle rush of a river.

"Wow..." I breathed, the word slipping out before I could stop it. Slowly, I rose to my feet, marveling at the surreal beauty around me. A gentle chill crept along my spine. Then I heard her.

"So... we finally meet, young one," said a familiar feminine voice.

I spun around, my heart racing. From the tree line stepped a woman, radiant and unnervingly familiar. Her white hair shimmered in the moonlight, cascading like a waterfall down her back. Her eyes, cold and impossibly blue, watched me with a wisdom I couldn't comprehend. She moved closer, and as I stood there staring, it struck me like a jolt—she looked just like me. Or rather, like someone I could become. Ethereal, otherworldly, every inch a legend from mythology.

"You... You're—?" I started, my voice barely above a whisper.

She nodded, now standing only a few feet away. "That I am. You've finally reached the place where we can truly connect," she said, her tone cool but calm. She was regarding me with a gaze that was both reassuring and assessing, as if sizing me up as her reincarnation.

Shock kept me frozen, questions swirling so fast I couldn't grab one long enough to ask. At last, I blurted out the only thing that really mattered. "Why me?" My voice cracked, desperate and unsure. "I'm just... ordinary. I don't feel like someone who could carry the power of a goddess."

Skadi's expression softened. "I may not have all the answers. The Fates decided this long before those events happened—this was always meant to be my fate. But from all the years I've spent with you, I know this: strength isn't just about power, nor is it bound to any realm of gods or mortals. It lies within the spirit, in resilience, and in the will to face the challenges ahead. I've seen that in you, even when you couldn't see it in yourself. That's why our souls were woven together—and I believe that with everything I am."

I swallowed hard, a lump forming in my throat as I tried to process her words. "I—I'm not sure I can live up to that. To be...you." The words tumbled out, my hands gesturing helplessly in the cold air.

She stepped closer, her gaze full of understanding. "I don't expect you to be me, Ravena. I want you to be you—to find your own way. My essence is here to guide you, to lend you my strength when you need it, but this path is yours to walk. In time, you'll see that the power within you is both mine and uniquely yours"

It was quiet for a moment, the air thick with my anxiety. I watched her, weighing my next words before finally blurting out, "Will you help train me? I'm not even sure what all I can do."

Skadi nodded, a small smile present. "We'll practice here when you meditate. And when you're training with Eirik, I can guide you also." She paused, her expression turning serious as she met my gaze.

"I believe you should talk to that guardian of yours. He can help more than you realize. I have a feeling Eirik may understand your situation better than you think."

I arched a brow, more confused than ever. This just left me with more questions than I wanted to deal with right now.

"I—what? What does that even mean?" I asked, my frustration slipping through.

She just gave me a knowing look and turned, gliding over to a patch of grass to sit.

"Just talk to him. Now, before it gets any later. I want to teach you how to summon the most basic of your abilities," she said, already settling down cross-legged.

I let out a sigh at her cryptic answer, but curiosity about my powers won out over my need for clarity. So, I dropped down beside her. I gazed at Skadi, taking in every detail. This essence of her didn't carry weapons, but that didn't make her any less intimidating. Her armor was striking—dark blue steel that gleamed like a midnight sky, every piece crafted to fit her perfectly. The helmet was etched with intricate designs and crowned with a pair of carved deer; on either side, wolves howled at a moon engraved into the metal. My eyes lingered on the breastplate, sturdy yet elegant, runes and symbols shimmering like fresh snowfall against the dark metal.

The rest of her armor was just as impressive—flexible gauntlets, bracers, and leg plates designed for both combat and moving through rugged mountain terrain. Every piece was accented with pale, snow-colored details that gave her a touch of ethereal beauty.

A sudden clearing of her throat jolted me out of my gawking. Heat crept up my cheeks—I must've looked like a total idiot staring at her like that.

"It is well, ungr einn, to wonder. Rare it must be, to see one like yourself," she said. Her accent was rougher than before, and I just now recognizing it.

I tilted my head, catching the familiar phrase with furrowed brows. "Ungr einn... young one, right?"

She nodded, and I could see the hint of pride in her eyes. "Yes. I'm pleased you remembered your studies."

I shrugged. "I did graduate with a degree, you know. I'm not entirely clueless."

That got a real laugh out of her. "I wouldn't expect anything less from you," she said, straightening before her tone lost its playful edge.

"Your powers," she began, "aren't something separate from you—they're an extension of what's already inside. You now hold the abilities of winter—its stillness, its fury, and its power to create beauty or bring destruction."

Her words hit me harder than I expected. "How am I supposed to control something I didn't even know existed?" I asked, my voice barely above a whisper.

She gave me a patient look, one that carried centuries of wisdom. "Control is not the goal, ungr einn—even if your guardian or the others think it is. Mastery comes from understanding, not domination. Winter's power can't be tamed, nor should it be. For now, you must learn to simply summon its essence.

I swallowed, hoping my uneasiness didn't show. "Okay, I'll try. How do I even start?"

Skadi extended her hand, gesturing for me to mirror her. Her movements were fluid, and I observed carefully to copy her, resting my hands on my knees, palm up.

"Close your eyes," she instructed. "Feel the air around you and breathe. Focus on the cold—not as something to fear, but as something familiar."

I sighed, nerves rattling in my chest, but tried to gather myself. Inhaling deeply, I let my shoulders relax. It was strange in my mind... there was no real feeling of the cold, but there was an energy humming under my skin. At first, all I felt and heard was the silence and my slow breathing. But as I focused, something began to stir—a tingling at the tips of my fingers spread.

"Good," Skadi murmured, approval in her tone. "Now, picture the frost spreading, growing stronger. Imagine it as a thread, connecting you to the earth around you."

I nodded, my focus deepening, determined not to fail. The tingling sharpened; I could actually feel the cold building. A faint blue glow flickered at the edge of my closed eyelids. A soft gasp escaped me as a chill spread upward, traveling up my arms like a river of icy energy. When I dared open my eyes, tiny tendrils of frost were snaking their way across the ground in front of me.

Skadi's lips curved into a rare smile. "You see, ungr einn? It was always there, waiting for you to call it."

Awe mixed with disbelief as I stared at the frost. "That's...I did that?"

She chuckled softly. "Yes, and that is only the beginning. The abilities of winter and the hunt are vast and multifaceted, much like yourself. You will learn to wield their gifts in time—but first, you must respect them. They can overwhelm you if you're careless."

I nodded looking up, still in disbelief that I actually did something like that. "You said it could overwhelm me... is there the chance, if I get upset or scared, that the magic might act on its own?" The question tumbled out anxiously.

She hummed, tilting her head as she studied my face. "It is possible, Ravena. Mortals do not come by these abilities naturally; it can be a lot for the body and spirit to handle. I was born with this magic, so I learned early to keep myself in check for the safety of others. But for you, the journey will be different. You'll need to learn your boundaries, and what trigger the magic."

"Well, that's just great...something else to add to my already bizarre situation. I'm officially a weirdo," I huffed, exasperated.

"Nonsense, ungr einn. You are not," Skadi said firmly. "You are Ravena—the reincarnation of myself. And you are a demi-goddess." There was no room for argument in her tone. "It's time you to stop doubting yourself," she continued, stepping closer. "You've let those doubts shape you for too long. That ends now."

I drew a long breath; her words echoing around the clearing. With tired clarity I realized I wasn't ever going to be the same woman who'd first stumbled into this world. I had to at least try to accept what I was becoming. For once, the usual flood of self-doubt was silent. Skadi watched me, almost as if expecting an argument, but I only nodded.

"I understand," I said, my voice way more confident than I expected. "So, what do I do now?"

Her expression flickered with approval, maybe... but just for a moment. "You listen. You learn. And you stop holding yourself back."

I found myself nodding, "I'll try," I said quietly, "but I'm terrified of failing."

She tilted her head, her icy gaze softening. "Courage does not mean the absence of fear, Ravena. It means facing it and moving forward despite it. You've already taken the first step by calling your magic to you. That is no small feat."

I looked down at the frost weaving across the ground; it had started to slowly fade back into the ground. "It feels...alive?" I said softly, the awe never leaving my voice. "Like it's really part of me."

"It is," Skadi replied simply. "And it always has been. Now, return to your world, ungr einn. You have much to learn, and the day awaits."

As her form began to fade, the silvery light of the moon dissolving her figure into the snowy landscape. I reached out instinctively. "Wait," I called out. But she was gone, and the serene field of my subconscious dissolved back to my new harsh reality.

I opened my eyes to find the overlook bathed in the pale light of morning. The frost I'd summoned was still there—a delicate web of icy tendrils etched into the snow around me. My breath caught in my throat as I stared. That actually happened. I rose slowly, brushing the snow off my cloak, my mind racing with everything Skadi had said: demi-goddess, powers tied to winter, the importance of controlling my emotions. It was all overwhelming, but there was no escaping it. Not anymore.

The crunch of footsteps on snow pulled me from my thoughts. I turned quickly, my heart skipping a beat. Eirik was making his way up the trail, his expression one of concern. "You've been gone a while," he said, stopping a few paces away. "Lydia sent me to check on you."

I wrapped my arms around myself. "I needed time to think," I said simply—though the understatement was almost laughable.

Eirik's gaze flicked to the frost still etched into the snow, his brows furrowing in surprise. "That's new," he said, nodding towards it.

I glanced down, unsure how to explain. "I... may have awakened my magic?" I muttered; my voice tinged with uncertainty. "I—she said I need to talk to you. That you might understand... this."

He raised an eyebrow, folding his arms across his chest. "Who is this 'she'?"

I blushed, suddenly feeling stupid for what I was about to say. "Skadi, she's been able to talk to me. For a couple days now." I hesitated, her cryptic words hanging between us. "What did she mean?"

The air between us grew heavy. I caught a flicker of something in Eirik's eyes—reluctance, maybe even guilt. But why?

His jaw tightened and he looked off to the side. "Ravena, I—" A sudden noise from the direction of the village startled us both.

"What was that?" I breathed.

He rested his hand on his axe, every muscle going tense. "I'm not sure. Come on—let's hurry back. They might need us." Without another word, he turned and set off at a quick pace towards the village.

Chapter Thirteen

The village came into view, and I immediately noticed a shift in the air. The usual hum of daily life was gone, the villagers hurried past with tense faces, their voices low. The hairs on the back of my neck prickled with unease, and a knot formed in my stomach.

"What do you think has happened?" I asked, glancing at Eirik.

His expression darkened as he swept his gaze over the village. "I don't know. But whatever it is, it isn't good."

We quickened our pace, weaving through the snow-covered streets until we reached the central meeting hall. Cora and Theron stood outside, their faces etched with worry. At their feet, slumped against the stone steps, was a man wrapped in tattered furs. His breaths came in shallow gasps, and dark, frostbitten fingers clutched desperately at a wound on his side.

Theron looked up as we approached, his expression turning grim. "He just arrived. A villager from Drusia. Says he barely escaped an attack."

"An attack?" I echoed nervously, rubbing my hands together. Cora was mumbling about bad omens and needing to let Lydia know.

Theron nodded, his voice somber—his eyes traveled from the man to us. "Creatures—dark, unnatural things. He says they came from the foothills of Mt. Psophis. The whole village was destroyed."

I caught Eirik's eyes narrowing as he studied the wounded stranger, his arms crossing tightly across his chest.

The traveler's eyes fluttered open, his voice a hoarse rasp. "Shadows...monsters...they—" He broke off, coughing violently. Theron knelt beside him, trying to calm him, but the man slumped forward, unconscious from pain and exhaustion.

A cold wave washed over me, and I felt Skadi's presence stir. Her voice whispered urgently through my mind. *This feeling is dark, Ravena. This is a form of magic I have not seen used in ages.*

My pulse jumped. *What does it mean?* I shot back, gripping the sleeve of my cloak tight enough for my knuckles to ache.

It means something has been unleashed. And you must prepare yourself. This is only the beginning. She responded before going silent once more.

I turned to Eirik, who was already watching me with worry in his eyes. I swallowed hard, looking down at the wounded man again. "We need to get him inside—tend to his wounds and warm him up." My word spurred the two men into action.

Theron and Eirik moved quickly, lifting the traveler and carrying him into the hall, where a fire already burned in the hearth. I stayed near the doorway, my gaze darting between the stranger and the two men, my thoughts racing.

Eirik knelt beside the man, inspecting his wound. "He's lucky to be alive," he muttered. "But this wasn't caused by any ordinary weapon."

I hesitated, stepping closer. "What do you mean?"

Eirik didn't look up, his brow furrowed. "The edges are blackened, like a burn—but there's cold in it too. It's unnatural."

Dark magic, Skadi whispered through my mind. *There are very few magics that can do this, Ravena. If it's what I fear, we must prepare.*

The traveler stirred, eyes fluttering open. He tried to sit up, but Theron pressed a hand to his shoulder. "Easy, friend. You're safe now."

"Safe?" the man rasped, voice trembling. "Nowhere is safe. They—they came from the shadows of the mountain. They destroyed everything. Nothing stood a chance."

At that moment, Lydia came flying through the door and to the man's side. "What kind of monsters?" she asked, her tone urgent.

The man shook his head weakly. "I—I don't know. They weren't…human. They weren't anything I've ever seen. The cold…just…" His voice cracked, and he slumped back, his strength spent.

Theron's face grew grim. "If what he says is true, something terrible has been set loose. Could this be allies of Agnar?"

Eirik rose, his jaw tight. "We can't wait any longer. We need answers. If these creatures attacked one village, they'll move to the next before anyone can warn them. We have to prepare for a fight."

My heart pounded as I took a step closer to him. "But how? We don't even know what we're up against."

Eirik's gaze met mine, his brow furrowing with thought. "We start by figuring out what they are—and how to fight them." He paused, studying my face. I could already guess what was coming.

"You mean we have to go investigate the village, right?" I muttered, and he nodded as we stepped back out into the cold. The midday sun brought rare warmth for late winter, but I wrapped my arms around myself, trying to process everything I'd just heard. "You kept looking at me back there—like you were worried," I said quietly, glancing at him. "What is it?"

Eirik stopped, his breath curling in the frigid air. He didn't answer right away. His gaze was distant, like he was wrestling with what to say. Finally, he spoke, voice low. "Come on. Let's talk somewhere else." He motioned for us to head towards the training field closer to the village. "It's best to be cautious right now."

The way he said it made a knot form in my stomach. We walked in silence until we reached the edge of the smaller field, the ground frozen beneath our boots. I stole a glance at him—he looked tense, almost uncertain, like he was bracing for something.

At last, he spoke. "I wasn't just chosen because I'm a warrior." His words hung in the air. "I was chosen because of my bloodline." He paused, searching my face.

I blinked, trying to understand why his bloodline had anything to do with me. "Your bloodline?"

He rubbed the back of his neck, letting out a short, humorless laugh. "Yeah. My family... it goes back further than most realize."

Before I could respond, Eirik's keen eyes shifted past me. His shoulders stiffened, attention drawn to something behind me. I turned, following his line of sight, and saw several villagers gathering in the field—mostly younger men and women, armed with wooden staffs, crude blades, and hunting bows.

Eirik let out a low grunt, clearly thinking things over. "Seems they wish to train," he said, his accent thickening.

"They must've heard about...the traveler," I murmured, eyeing the group as the older scout addressed them. "Do you think this is a good idea?" My gaze drifted across each person, some were anxious, some determined.

Eirik tilted his head as he studied the villagers. "Courage is good," he said at last, his voice rough. "But courage alone won't stop what's coming. They need skill, discipline...and more time than they've got."

His bluntness landed harder than I wanted to admit. I crossed my arms, uneasy. "So, what do we do? We can't just stand here and watch."

Eirik glanced over, catching my eye with a look that pinned me in place. For a second, I caught a flicker of something—resolve, maybe, or just the stubbornness I'd probably regret.

"You," he said, his accent drawing out the word. "You must train harder. Show them what it means to fight. If they watch you improve, they'll start believing they can too."

"Me?" I nearly choked, taking an awkward step back. "I can barely keep my feet under me, much less—"

He cut me off, his tone resolute. "Whether you want it or not, they're watching you, Ravena. You're the one the stories are about." His gaze met mine, undaunted. "Your progress gives them hope. If you give up, so will they."

My mouth went dry. "No pressure, huh," I muttered, trying to hide my panic behind a weak smile.

Eirik's mouth curved into the faintest smile, but he didn't look away. Then he gestured us forward, motioning toward the gathering crowd.

The villagers' eyes followed Eirik and me as we approached, curiosity and uncertainty plain in their faces. My heart sank as I took in their appearance, these weren't soldiers. They were farmers, tradesfolk, parents. Maybe a few scouts looked like they'd seen a fight, but most looked more ready to mend fences than wield swords. Still, here they stood, all determined to learn to fight because of a prophecy.

Eirik, however, seemed undeterred. He paused at the edge of the group, surveying them with a practiced gaze. "Is it true what we've heard?" a young woman near the front called out, her voice quivering. "Will you teach us to fight?"

Eirik nodded once. "If you want to defend your home, I'll teach you what I can. Strength, skill, and resilience. The first two I can help with. The last, you'll have to find in yourselves."

A murmur of uneasy agreement passed through the crowd. Eirik raised a hand, silencing the murmurs. "This won't be easy. There will be blood, sweat, and—" his gaze flicked to me, "probably a few tears. But remember, every role matters. Whether you're wielding a blade or tending the wounded, your contribution matters."

He gestured for them to spread out and copy his movements, walking among them, correcting stances with a gentle firmness. "Keep your feet apart, you'll tip over if the enemy has a chance to get near you," he chided, but there was humor beneath his words. "Strength means nothing if you can't keep your balance."

He picked up a staff, demonstrating. "Grip it firmly, but not so tight you lose feeling. Think like a river—strong, but able to bend and flow around what stands in your way."

He stopped in front of a young man who looked barely old enough to be there. "What's your name?" he asked.

"Nikos," the boy replied, trying to stand taller.

"Nikos, your grip is too stiff. Relax your shoulders—let the weapon become an extension of you," Eirik instructed, placing a guiding hand on the boy's arm.

As he moved on, he continued offering corrections and encouragement, his tone level. "Each of you has the potential to be a warrior. It's not about the strength of your body, but the strength of your heart. Fight for your families, fight for your home, and above all, fight for each other."

He returned to his place at the front, his expression diligent. "Now—continue your practice." Then he made his way back to where I stood at the edge of the field.

I watched as the group fumbled with their makeshift weapons. They were determined—some clutching wooden staffs, others holding old, rusted swords with white-knuckled grips. A few of the younger villagers had bows, their arrows trembling in unsteady hands.

"They're trying," I murmured, mostly to myself. "That has to count for something."

Eirik's gray eyes darted to mine, "Aye. They're trying. But trying doesn't win wars." He motioned for me to step forward, his mouth twitching with the beginnings of a sly grin. "Come. We spar in front of them."

"I'm sorry? What?!" My voice cracked as panic tore through my composure. "You want me to fight you? Here? Now? With everyone watching? I just learned about my magic abilities!" I hissed.

Eirik's grin widened, clearly enjoying himself. "Best get used to it," he said, his accent roughening the words. "Battle does not wait for comfort." Without another word, he strode towards the crowd.

Be careful, Ravena... I know the situation has changed, but you've just awakened your magic. Be cautious of your emotions around so many others. Skadi's voice warned.

I hesitated, rooted to the snow, before forcing my feet to move as I heeded Skadi's words. "I don't think this is such a good idea Eirik," I muttered as I caught up to him.

He glanced over, his smirk lingering. "Perhaps not, it's a toss-up. Let's go."

"Are you sure about this?" I asked, my voice uncertain.

"No" Eirik quipped, shrugging as he bent down to retrieve the wooden poles we had been training with. "But they need to see what you're learning. It'll give them hope."

Swallowing my nerves, I stepped into the makeshift circle where the villagers had gathered. The cold breeze stung my cheeks as I raised the wooden staff Eirik handed me. He squared off in front of me, his own staff balanced effortlessly in his hands.

"Ready?" he asked, voice low enough that only I could hear.

"Nope," I muttered under my breath, earning a quiet chuckle from him.

"Good. Let's begin."

The clash of wood echoed sharply as our weapons collided, sending a shiver up my arms. Eirik moved with a speed and precision that made my head spin—his strikes were different than normal. I managed to block a few, though my grip faltered each time our weapons met. *Is he trying to embarrass me!?* I thought, mortified.

"Focus, Ravena," Eirik called out. "Your footing is weak."

"Yeah, I know!" I snapped back, frustration bubbling over. My muscles burned, my breath coming in short, visible puffs in the icy air. His strikes kept coming, forcing me to retreat step by step. The villagers murmured among themselves, their unease obvious.

Suddenly, Eirik's staff came down hard, knocking mine from my grasp. I stumbled back, landing on the ground with a thud. my frustration boiling over as I hit the ground with a thud. Humiliation burned through me as I caught the uncertain faces of the villagers watching.

"Enough," I muttered, my voice trembling as I scrambled to my feet, embarrassed tears prickling at the corner of my eyes. "I can't do this."

Eirik stepped back, his brow furrowing. "Ravena—" he started, trying to encourage me.

"No!" The word shot out, raw and louder than I intended. Suddenly, a burst of cold magic flooded my veins, igniting a chill so strong it made me gasp. The ground at my feet froze instantly, white tendrils of frost racing outward in jagged lines.

Gasps broke out among the villagers. I froze in place—truly frozen, panic locking up my limbs. The only sound was the crackle of ice spreading in all directions. My heart hammered in my chest as I stared at what I'd done.

"Ravena," Eirik said quietly, lowering his weapon. "Ravena. Breathe," he urged, probably realizing his mistake of pushing me.

I tried to focus, but the power wouldn't subside. It churned beneath my skin, feeding off my frustration and embarrassment. My hands trembled, and so the frost continued to spread, climbing the nearest tree in jagged, glittering patterns.

Then, I felt it—a sudden jolt of energy, unlike anything I'd ever felt. The ground trembled faintly, and a distant howl echoed across the mountains, carried on the icy wind. It was a sound that froze the blood in my veins.

"What was that?" one of the villagers whispered, their voice tinged with fear.

Eirik's eyes narrowed, his attention snapping toward the horizon. "I... am not sure."

Before I could process what was happening, the air seemed to shift again, colder than before. The howl rose again, louder this time, and the ground shuddered below our feet. I felt it—a tug deep within my chest, as if some invisible thread had been pulled.

Skadi's voice slid through my mind, awe and pride lacing her words. *Runar. He has awakened.*

I tensed up, "What does that mean?" I whispered aloud, barely audible. The frost at my feet glimmered faintly, as if in response.

"It means your magic is awakening quicker than I expected. And he has sensed it—your magic called to him" Skadi reply came softly.

Chapter Fourteen

The villagers had fallen silent, their eyes wide with a mixture of awe and apprehension. Eirik stepped closer, his hand resting lightly on my shoulder. "Ravena," he said, quietly. "You need to rein it in."

This snapped me back to reality, and to my magic currently creeping across the ground. I shut my eyes, forcing myself to focus on my breathing. Slowly, the icy tendrils receded, the energy dying down at last. Exhaustion washed over me, and I nearly collapsed; Eirik caught my arm, as we both dropped to our knees.

"You all right?" he asked, his voice gentler now.

I nodded weakly, though my thoughts churned. Leaning into him, I couldn't help but notice how strangely warm he was—way too warm for a man standing out in the cold.

"Strange..." I murmured, barely loud enough for him to hear.

Eirik glanced down, concern lining his features. "What's strange? Are you feeling faint?"

I hesitated, struggling to put it into words. *It didn't just feel like normal body heat... I felt like it was something else, something deeper.* I just couldn't place it yet.

"It's not just body heat," I whispered, my fingers pressing lightly into his arm, testing the warmth beneath his skin. "You feel like there's a constant fire burning under your skin... why?"

Eirik stiffened. The reaction was subtle, but I had caught it—the way his jaw tightened, and the flicker of something unreadable in his expression before he looked away. "It's nothing," he said gruffly. "Adrenaline, maybe.

Let's focus on you. You nearly turned the clearing and its spectators into frozen statues."

"Eirik…" I tried to keep question, to ask more, but exhaustion had begun to settle over me. "I didn't mean to…let my magic out like that."

He sighed, his tone softening. "You're still learning, Ravena. It's going to happen. I knew the risk of pushing you like this and I shouldn't have."

At least he has some sense…now, I heard Skadi mutter, clearly annoyed.

I glanced at the frost still shimmering faintly on the ground and buried my face in my hands, embarrassment bubbling up again. "Skadi warned me," I admitted. "She said my emotions effect my powers. And what do I do? I let my frustration get the better of me."

He placed his other hand lightly on my arm. "Ravena, no one master's this overnight—even gods make mistakes."

I couldn't help but let out a long sigh, his words mingling with my own self-doubt as I stared down at my trembling hands.

"I just… need a second," I muttered, glancing at the retreating villagers as they whispered about what had happened.

Eirik's brows drew together curious. "Of course, what can I do to help?"

A little embarrassed, "Could you help me to the house? I could use a change of clothes. Maybe escape to the springs if Cora allows it." I said, struggling to get to my feet.

Eirik nodded, then in one swift motion picked me up bridal style.

My face went red instantly, "H-hey, I can walk!" I yelped.

He just raised an eyebrow, clearly unimpressed with my protest. "You're shaking like a leaf, Ravena. Let me help." he said.

I folded my arms awkwardly, trying to ignore the warmth of his chest against my side. "This is humiliating," I muttered, avoiding his gaze.

His deep chuckle vibrated in his chest. "Humiliating would be you collapsing halfway to the house and me having to explain to the villagers."

I glared at him, but I admit, it lacked any real conviction. "I'm perfectly capable of walking."

He flashed a crooked grin, already striding towards the house. "Of course you are. That's why you're not even fighting me."

The snow crunched beneath his boots, the wind dying down as we near houses. I tried to ignore the steady sound of his breath and the way his arms held me as if I weighed nothing.

As we reached the house, I squirmed in his grip. "You can put me down now," I muttered, the blush on my cheeks refusing to fade.

Eirik paused just before the door, a teasing grin spreading across his face. "You sure? I could carry you all the way to the hot spring."

My eyes widened in horror, and I smacked his shoulder lightly—it was like hitting solid stone. "Don't you dare. I am *not* letting you see me like that again!"

He choked, turning red as he stumbled over his words. "I—you—?" He cleared his throat, glancing away. "That was an accident. Not something I planned." he insisted.

I arch a brow. "Mm-hmm. Sure, Eirik maybe next time, check your surroundings?"

He looked even more flustered; his jaw worked for a moment before he let out a resigned breath. "Lesson learned," he said, finally setting me down. "Believe me, I'll be more careful."

I rolled my eyes, but a small smile tugged at my lips. "Good," I muttered, brushing past him.

Cora appeared in the hallway, her expression shifting from concern to relief. "Oh, thank the gods. You're back," she said, rushing over. "What happened? Are you alright?"

I held up a hand to stop her. "I'm fine, Cora. Just tired. I was hoping to grab some dry clothes and head to the hot spring for a bit."

Her brow furrowed as she took in my disheveled appearance, but she nodded. "Of course, Lady Ravena."

"Thank you," I said, offering her a faint smile before heading to my room.

Behind me, I heard Eirik mutter something to Cora about making sure I didn't pass out on the way, followed by her exasperated response. I shook my head, shutting the door behind me. Grabbing a new set of clothes, choosing to not change right away and heading out again.

Eirik was waiting for me, leaning against the wall. His gaze flicked over me briefly. "Ready?" he asked.

I nodded, pulling my cloak tighter. "Let's go."

As we started down the path, Eirik shot me a sidelong glance. "Want a lift? I could carry you—"

I shook my head, throwing what I hope was a believable glare. "Absolutely not. I have enough dignity left, thank you."

He shrugged, a ghost of a smile on his lips, and offered me his arm instead. I took it, silently grateful for the support, even if I'd never admit it out loud.

The path to the hot spring wound through the trees, the air warming up the closer we got. Despite my exhaustion, the thought of sinking into that warm water was enough to keep me moving.

Eirik walked at my side, matching my pace. "You're really not going to let me go alone, are you?" I asked, arching an eyebrow.

He snorted. "After that ice display earlier, forgive me for thinking you might pass out and drown."

I hesitated, suddenly self-conscious. "It's fine... just, you don't have to wait around if you don't want to. I can manage." My tone was softer, a little embarrassed.

He smirked, but there was reassurance lacing his voice. "Relax, I'll be out of sight. I know how to respect a lady's privacy—" he paused, a small sheepishness flickering across his face, "well, aside from that one accident." His eyes glinted with humor. "You have my word, Ravena. I'll just make sure you don't need help."

He turned and headed back up the path, his footsteps crunching softly through the snow until he found a spot just out of sight but still within earshot. I watched him go, then sighed and shook my head as I stepped toward the steaming pool. The heat rose in curling tendrils, melting the tension in my shoulders before I even touched the water. I quickly undressed—my muscles aching as I did—and slowly I sank in, the warmth enveloping me and easing the stiffness from my limbs.

A deep exhale slipped from my lips as the cold finally retreated. My thoughts, however, refused to quiet.

Skadi's words echoed in my mind: *You can't focus on controlling it. Your magic is part of you.*

My fingers trailed through the water, watching the ripples distort the reflection of the sky. I wanted to believe her. I wanted to trust that I could wield this magic without losing myself to it.

A faint crunch of snow signaled Eirik shifting his stance nearby—not too close, not too far. And for that I was truly grateful.

A tired smile tugged at my lips for now, at least, I wasn't alone.

Chapter Fifteen

The next morning arrived far sooner than I was ready for. The soft gray of dawn crept through the cracks of the shutters as I quickly dressed, careful not to disturb anyone in the house. My movements were quiet as I slipped out into the morning air, determined to find a moment to seek answers. After everything that had happened yesterday, I couldn't shake the fear of losing control over my magic and harming someone. I needed to try and speak to Skadi again, privately.

As I hurried through the slumbering village, the world around me was still and untouched, the sky just beginning to blush with hints of pale orange and soft lavender. The air was frigid, brushing against my skin, and the fresh scent of snow clung to the ground. Not a single soul stirred, and the peaceful silence was a welcome relief after the chaos and tension of the day before.

When the familiar overlook came into view, I felt a sense of relief. I climbed onto the smooth, time-worn rocks and sat, the cold stone seeping through my cloak. "Skadi?" I called softly, my voice trembling just enough to betray the anxiety under my words.

Ravena... you are up early. What troubles you? came her quiet response.

I exhaled slowly, my breath forming a thin white mist in the air. "I think you already know," I murmured. "Yesterday... I let my magic get out of hand. I was pushed harder than I was ready for, and I—" My voice faltered. I stared out at the rising sun, before letting my head hang in defeat. The anxiety I'd tried to ignore crept back in, tightening in my chest and making it hard to breath.

Easy, Ravena, Skadi reminded. *Emotions are powerful, and they will fuel your magic whether you intend them to or not. Your guardian was in the wrong, yes. But we move forward from this. Dwelling on it serves no purpose. You must learn to handle your magic through action, not fear."*

I drew in a slow breath, trying to let the tightness in my shoulders fade. The morning air stung my lungs and made it easier to focus on the present. Skadi's words made sense but doubt still lingered in the back of my mind.

"I'm sorry," I whispered, barely audible. "I know I'm supposed to embrace my magic, but everyone keeps pushing me to *control* it." My words hung between us, uncertain—I was afraid of Skadi's response.

For a moment, there was only silence, broken by the soft rustling of leaves in the faint breeze. Then Skadi's voice came back, calm but level. *They mean well, Ravena, but they don't understand what lies within you. Control isn't about shutting off your abilities. It's about learning to work with your emotions and magic—letting them move together, not against each other. Your power isn't a wild animal to be broken. It's a part of you.*

I hesitated. "But how? Every time I feel something too strongly, it's like... it takes over. I'm scared, Skadi. What if I hurt someone? What if I can't stop it?" My voice cracked, and I clenched my fists, digging my nails into my palms to keep my nerves in check.

You won't lose yourself, child, she answered, her voice softening. *I'll be here to guide you. We'll figure this out together. You'll learn how to live with your magic—not by fighting it, but by trusting it. Your emotions aren't the enemy; they're your strength. But strength takes practice, patience, and trust.*

Her words stuck with me. I swallowed hard and nodded, though she couldn't see it. "So... what do I do? Where do I even start?"

You start by breathing, Ravena. Breathe deeply and let yourself feel. Don't fight the magic within you—stand at its center and let it move through you.

I closed my eyes, drawing in a slow breath as the cold morning air filled my lungs. For a moment, the anxious hum faded, replaced by the steady rhythm of my heartbeat.

Skadi's voice returned, softer now, almost a whisper. *Trust in yourself. We'll walk this path together as long as we can.*

The breeze carried the scent of pine and earth. Sunlight crested the horizon, casting golden light across the overlook. The air was brisk and cool against my skin as I stood at the edge of the rocks, eyes closed, simply breathing.

Begin by focusing inward, Skadi instructed. *Feel the magic—not as something separate, but as part of your very being. It lives in your blood, your breath, your heartbeat.*

I inhaled, trying to follow her lead. At first, I only felt the cold and the nervous tension coiling in my chest. My hands flexed at my sides, searching for something just out of reach.

Don't force it," Skadi murmured, her voice soft. *Your magic is like water. It flows when you call it. Call to it gently.*

With another breath, I tried to let go. My fingers tingled, a subtle warmth blooming and spreading outward. like the first flickers of a flame. It was surreal, as if the magic had waited for me to accept it.

"Good," Skadi said, a note of pride in her voice. *Now, guide it outward. Picture your energy moving past your skin, like frost spreading over glass.*

Opening my eyes, I focused on a small patch of grass growing between the cracks in the stone. Slowly, I extended my hand, envisioning the frost Skadi had described—delicate tendrils unfurling and branching outward. My pulse quickened as a faint shimmer of cold air coiled around my palm. A crackle broke the morning stillness as tiny crystals began to form on the blades of grass, their intricate patterns catching the light.

A smile tugged at my lips, but the moment faltered as a surge of excitement rushed through me. The frost shot forward, jagged and uncontrolled, encasing a larger patch of grass in hard ice before I could stop it. I stumbled back, panic rising as my pulse thundered in my ears.

Steady yourself, Ravena, Skadi said, her voice firmer now. *Don't fear it. Magic reacts to your emotions—breathe, focus, reclaim your calm.*

I clenched my fists and squeezed my eyes shut, nearly holding my breath. The jagged edges of my panic dulled, softening into something quieter. As I exhaled, I felt the frost respond, and when I looked again, the patch of ice shimmered in the sunlight, a tapestry of stars spread across the stone. The tightness in my chest eased, replaced by a cautious pride.

You, see? Skadi said, her voice lighter now, almost playful. *You are far from losing control. You simply need time to learn how to guide it.*

I nodded, my hands trembling slightly as I steadied my breath. "It's... not as scary as I thought," I admitted softly.

No, Skadi agreed, her words laced with assurance. *Because it is not your enemy. Your power is a gift, Ravena—one you'll wield with grace in time. Now, let's try again.*

Chapter Sixteen

I followed Eirik through the quiet halls of the healer's quarters, the scent of dried herbs and burning tallow thick in the air. The traveler—the man found near the valley's edge—was finally awake. When I laid eyes on him his skin still looked pallid, stretched too thin over the sharp angles of his face.

I caught sight of house workers tending to his wounds, their hands methodical yet kind. He barely reacted to their touch, his gaze fixed on something distant, something only he could see. A hollow look lingered in his eyes—a ghost of whatever horror had followed him here.

At the sound of our approach, he turned his head. His expression shifted just slightly, as if part of him had expected someone—*or something*—else to enter.

Eirik spoke first. "You were found just outside the village no more than two days ago. Barely alive. The scouts were able to drag you here." His voice was cautious. "Do you remember what happened?"

The man's lips parted, but for a moment, he only exhaled—the words he wanted to say were seemingly too hard to speak.

Then, in a rough voice, he murmured, "They didn't just spare me." He swallowed hard, his fingers trembling where they rested on the furs draped over him. "I believe I was meant to escape them."

A chill crept over my skin—a quiet, creeping dread settling in my bones. His voice was sullen, raw, and his red-rimmed eyes shone with unshed tears.

I furrowed my brows, glancing at Eirik, who appeared deep in thought, before shifting my gaze back to the man. "What... what do you mean, you think you were meant to escape?" I asked hesitantly.

The man's dark eyes met mine. Pain radiated off him in waves. "They didn't give chase," he whispered. "Just stood there in the shadows of the burning village... watching me crawl away."

Eirik grunted, "Unless they have a dark sense of humor, I fear you were sent as a warning." His voice deepened, edged with something grim. "Meaning they know Ravena is here... or they're trying to find her."

The traveler had already begun to drift again, his eyes unfocused, his mind slipping back into the nightmare he'd barely escaped. I sighed, exchanging a brief glance with Eirik before stepping forward, gripping his forearm.

"Please excuse us, sir," I said quickly, before pulling Eirik from the room.

The cold air hit my skin as we stepped outside, the tension of the conversation looming over me. I exhaled slowly, trying to push away the unease curling in my chest.

Eirik's silence spoke louder than any words could.

I glanced at him. "You think he's right?"

Eirik let out a slow breath, his gaze sweeping over the village before settling on me. "Yes. If they wanted him dead, he wouldn't be here." His voice low, making sure no one besides us could overhear. "They let him go for a reason."

A shiver ran down my spine. I didn't know what was worse—the idea that they had spared him, or that they had wanted him to carry their warning.

I wrapped my arms around myself, shifting my weight from foot to foot. "We should go," I muttered. "If I'm supposed to be ready for whatever this is, I need to keep training."

Eirik nodded, adjusting the strap of his sword. "I agree. But first, let's get your weapon."

I blinked. "My what?"

His lips twitched, a shadow of amusement breaking through. "Your sword, Ravena. You don't plan on fighting with your bare hands, do you?"

I sighed, shaking my head as we started our walk towards the black-smith's forge. "Well, no. I just didn't realize I'd get an actual weapon so soon."

"I had Elder Theron convince the blacksmith to forge it after our first meeting. I would have liked for you to get more practice before putting steel in your hand, but as I've said from the beginning—time is not on our side."

We reached the blacksmith's forge just as the last embers of the morning fire smoldered beneath the anvil. The scent of scorched metal and oil filled the air.

The blacksmith, a broad-shouldered man with arms like tree trunks, gave us a curt nod before retrieving something wrapped in thick cloth. "Been waiting for you, outsider," he grunted, handing it over to Eirik—who bless him ignored the remark about being an outsider.

Eirik unwrapped the bundle with practiced ease, revealing the sword beneath. Even in the muted daylight, the polished steel gleamed like fresh ice. He turned it toward me, offering the hilt. "Go on," he said.

I hesitated only a moment before wrapping my fingers around the grip. The weight was heavier than I expected, yet strangely familiar— as if some part of me had been waiting for this moment.

The blacksmith watched me, with a sharp eye. "Balance is good. Blade's been tempered well; it'll hold, as long as you wield it properly."

I swallowed hard, my grip tightening. This wasn't just a practice staff anymore. I adjusted my grip on the hilt, the sword's heavier than I'd expect-ed yet oddly satisfying. The blacksmith had done a fine job—its polished surface caught the pale winter sun, reflecting my hesitant expression back at me.

I ran my fingers along the hilt, testing the balance. The leather grip felt stiff beneath my palm, and a fresh wave anxiety rolled through me. What if I can't handle this? What if I mess up in front of everyone? Even with Skadi's words echoing in my head, the sword itself felt like a big responsibility.

Eirik watched me closely, observing. "No second thoughts?"

I exhaled slowly, tightening my grip. "No. Just... trying to not run away."

A flicker of approval passed across his face before he nodded toward the open field. "Good. Then let's begin."

"Keep your stance steady," Eirik's instructed firmly. He stood a few paces away, his own sword resting in his hand. "You're still leaving your left side wide open, Ravena. That's an easy kill."

I swallowed hard, shifting my feet. My shoulder ached from yesterday's training, and nerves gnawed at my concentration. *How does he make this look so easy?* "If this blade's so heavy, how do you make it look effortless?" I muttered, trying to shake off the doubt.

Eirik's lips twitched, a ghost of amusement in his eyes. "Years of practice. Now quit stalling—raise your sword and come at me."

I scowled, raising the blade on what I hoped was a proper guard position. My heart thumped as I moved forward, aiming for a careful strike at his side. Steel rang out as our swords clashed; the jolt rattled up my arm. I barely had time to brace before Eirik twisted his blade, knocking me off balance and forcing me back a step.

"Better," he admitted, stepping away. "But your swings are hesitant. You're afraid to hit me. Stop holding back."

I tried again—this time a quicker jab, then a clumsy parry. Eirik batted my blade aside, stepping in close. "Again. This time, put your weight behind it."

My arms trembled from the effort, but I lunged. He deflected with ease, forcing me to try again. Each mistake burned, feeding the knot of anxiety growing in my chest.

"Still hesitating," he pressed, not letting up. "You're thinking too much, and your grips too tight. Trust your instincts, Ravena. If this was a real fight, you'd be dead already."

That was it. I snapped, frustration spilling out before I could stop myself. "I *get it!*" I shouted, louder than I intended. "I'm not some hardened shield-bearer. I'm a historian who got dropped into this mess. So, forgive me if I don't magically know how to fight like you!"

Eirik's expression hardened, his jaw tightening as he lowered his blade. "You think I didn't have to learn too? That I wasn't beaten into the ground over and over until I earned the right to carry this?" He gestured sharply to his sword, his gray eyes cold. "No one's born a fighter, Ravena. You fight to survive, or you don't. Simple as that."

His words stung, and something inside me twisted—anger, shame, exhaustion. I could feel the heat behind my eyes, my hands aching from how tightly I gripped the sword. *You can't lose it,* I told myself. *Not here, not right now.*

The air around us grew heavy—a subtle shift electric and unmistakable. A biting chill seeped into the training field, cutting through my cloak like icy needles. Frost prickled along the ground beneath my boots. Eirik's frown deepened as his eyes flicked to my hand. "Ravena," he said carefully, his voice edged with tension.

The magic beneath my skin surged, razor-edged and cold, fighting for release. My chest tightened, and the sword in my hand seemed to grow heavier with each passing second. Frost crept up the blade in delicate, curling tendrils, its crystalline patterns glinting in the sun's light.

"Ravena," Eirik urged again, stepping forward cautiously, his sword lowered. "You need to get a grip on this. It seems this magic responds to your emotions."

"I'm trying!" The words came out harsher than I meant, frustration boiling over. The frost responded, spreading faster—spiraling down to the ground in jagged, branching patterns that mirrored the chaos building inside me. My breath hitched, every exhale a pale cloud in the frigid air.

Before I could speak again, the ground beneath us trembled a deep, resonant rumble that sent a shockwave through the field. My heart leapt into my throat as the frost around me surged outward, cracks spiderwebbing through the earth as the tremor grew stronger.

"What the—" Eirik started, his head snapping toward the tree line.

A low, guttural growl echoed from the woods, vibrating through my chest like thunder. My grip on the sword faltered, and I turned toward the sound, every nerve in my body screaming to run—yet my feet stayed rooted in place. The growl came again, louder, accompanied by the crunch of heavy footsteps through the snow.

The trees parted, shadows peeling back, and out stepped a creature unlike anything I had ever seen. Massive, towering over even Eirik, its white fur shimmered with an unnatural aura, as if it absorbed the very light around it. Its eyes glowed molten gold, locking onto me with an intensity that made my breath catch. With every measured breath, a plume of icy smoke curled from its nostrils—cold, not heat, warning me of power I didn't understand.

"Runar..." I said the name without thinking, but somehow, it felt right. My chest tightened as realization struck—Skadi's wolf. Or... was he mine now?

Eirik moved in front of me, blade raised on instinct. The wolf let out a warning snarl, the sound rumbling through the clearing.

"Ravena..." Eirik's voice was taut, his grip tightening on his sword. "Who... *is* that?"

"Runar. My wolf—Skadi's wolf. I think." The words tumbled out uncertain. Runar's glowing gaze never left mine, holding a mix of challenge and recognition. His massive paws crunched though the snow as he stepped closer.

The frost pulsed at my feet, drawn to him by some invisible thread, as if our magic was connecting us.

Eirik shot me a look, disbelief and wariness etched into his face. "Yours? You're saying that thing is—?"

Runar stopped a few feet away, lowering his enormous head until his eyes were level with mine. The world seemed to hold its breath as I reached out, my hand trembling. When his nose brushed my palm, a sense of calm washed over me. In that instant, I could feel the connection between us.

"I... I guess so," I whispered, my voice barely audible above my pounding of my heart.

Runar let out a low rumble, something between a warning and a greeting, before turning his golden gaze on Eirik. He made no move to attack—instead, he shifted, settling back on his haunches, posture no longer aggressive.

Eirik let out a breath, lowering his sword as he eyed Runar warily. "By the gods," he muttered, a mixture of awe and exasperation in his tone. "If this is the path fates laid out, the Norns must be laughing."

I let out a shaky laugh, unable to help myself. "Yeah—welcome to my life, Eirik."

Eirik muttered something under his breath, his gaze lingering on Runar. "If this is what fate brings to your side, Ravena, I hope the gods are more kind than they are clever."

Runar's molten eyes held mine, as if waiting for something. My thoughts scattered—caught between awe and unease. Skadi's voice echoed faintly in my mind, her words from days before woven into the moment.

You are not alone, Ravena. Not anymore.

The frost around us stilled completely, and the Runars gaze softened, though his stance remained unflinching. Eirik's voice broke the silence.

"He's a distraction," he said quietly, watching me closely. "And for now, it seems you needed one."

I didn't argue. The magic inside me had gone quiet. With Runar here —everything had changed again.

I sighed, then hauled the frozen blade off the ground. "Should we continue training? We can't stop for every inconvenience that happens."

Eirik didn't answer immediately. He was studying Runar, eyes narrowed with wary suspicion. For a moment, Runar's attention was still on me, golden gaze calm and almost curious. Then, as if sensing Eirik's scrutiny, he turned—locking eyes with him in an unspoken standoff.

I nudged Eirik's boot with mine, pulling his focus. His gray eyes finally met mine, his grip relaxing ever so slightly.

"Are you sure? We could take a short break," he said, the faintest trace of concern in his voice as he fully turned his attention to me.

I shrugged, adjusting my stance. "We don't have that luxury." My gaze flickered toward Runar. "Though... I have no idea what to do now that he's here." Runar was still watching Eirik—studying him. I couldn't shake the sense that he was far more intelligent than he let on. Whatever he saw in Eirik, he clearly didn't trust.

A deep, resonant voice cut through the air, carrying years of wisdom. *"You could just ask, young frostling. I would gladly answer."*

I snapped my gaze up, heart pounding. The voice hadn't come from the trees or the wind—it came from right beside me.

Eirik tensed, his fingers brushing the hilt of his sword as he shifted, poised for danger.

I swallowed hard, meeting Runar's eyes "Did you just...?"

He let out a breath, his gaze steady on mine. "Speak?" His voice rumbled through the quiet space. "Yes, young frostling. I did."

The silence that followed was thick. No one seemed to know what to say. Finally, a grunt from Eirik broke the tension—he let his head fall back in exasperation.

"Well, I shouldn't' be surprised. The only other talking wolf I've ever heard of was Fenrir..." he muttered.

But me? Yeah, I had no words. My brain was still trying to catch up.

Runar tilted his head, clearly unimpressed. "I was expecting more of a reaction"

I blinked, still at a loss. "I–".

Chapter Seventeen

Runar huffed, golden eyes sharp with amusement. "Come now, frostling. Surely you did not think the gods would send you just a mere wolf?"

I just stared at him, my brain still trying to catch up with the fact that a massive, talking wolf was standing in front of me like this was normal.

Eirik, on the other hand, let out a long, suffering sigh beside me. "Well, I've seen some things in my life but this?" he muttered, running a hand through his hair. "Talking wolves. No."

Runar's ears twitched. "Is that irritation I hear, fire blood?"

Eirik's went completely still. The air between them shifted; it was subtle but heated. My stomach twisted at the sudden tension in the space.

Eirik's voice came out slow, controlled. "What did you just call me?"

Runar's golden eyes gleamed, unbothered by the cold edge in Eirik's tone. "I call you what you are. You carry the heat of Muspelheim in your veins. Even if you try to hide it."

The temperature around us felt different now; the winter air still lingered, but now warmth seemed to be filling the air.

I glanced at Eirik, unsure. "What does he mean by that? I asked, searching his face for any hint of an answer.

His jaw locked, and his grip tightened around his sword. But instead of answering me, he kept his glare locked on Runar. "And how do you know that?" he demanded, his voice low.

Runar let out a sound somewhere between a sigh and a growl. "I've seen more centuries than you've seen winters, boy."

Eirik's stance shifted, something guarded flickering in his expression. "You know nothing of my life or my upbringing, wolf. Best keep your nose out of my affairs."

Runar curled his lip in clear irritation. "You may regret this later, young shield bearer."

I looked as the two squared off with one another, Eirik's body tense. The air between them was thick, neither one ready to back down. I hovered uncertainly, hoping this wouldn't turn into a fight.

"Can you both calm down? If you want to have a testosterone contest, can you not do it while I'm standing here?" My voice came out snappier than I intended, and the air around me dropped a few degrees. A sheen of frost shimmered on the ground, catching both their attention.

Runar let out a low grumble, tilting his head at the ice spreading from my fingertips. "The frost my old friend once wielded." His voice carried evident approval. "Good, I'm glad to see your magic awakened."

Eirik, less impressed, shot me an unamused look. "You two are going to be the death of me."

I rolled my eyes at him, feigning hurt. "You have no faith in me, do you?"

Runar rumbled a chuckle before rising to his full height. "You'll thank me later, frostling. For now, focus. That frost isn't going to summon itself."

I groaned, shaking out my hands. "Fine. But if you keep calling me frostling, I'm going to start calling you 'Wolfie.'"

His ears flattened, and a low growl vibrated in his throat. "Do that and see how far you get without my help."

Eirik, clearly wanting to get back at Runar, smirked. "Seems fitting, doesn't it."

"Don't encourage her," Runar growled.

As the frost melted beneath my boots and the last of our banter faded, I found myself lingering. The other two drifted off—Eirik grumbling something under his breath about needing a break and turned away, busying himself with his gear. Runar padded a few steps off, and laid down near the trees, watching us. The silence that settled over me felt heavy, like everyone had something they weren't saying just yet.

Fire-blood. The word echoed in my mind. I wasn't sure why it bothered me. Maybe because Eirik had ignored my question all together. Maybe because it felt like everyone already knew what I didn't.

I looked down at my hands. The frost that had crept out earlier was gone, but my fingers still tingled with its remnants. Skadi's power—or mine now? I didn't know where the line was. I'd joked and smiled like it didn't matter, like I'd just accepted everything. But the truth was, I hadn't.

I was changing, and I didn't know where I fit anymore. I stood there a moment longer, then finally headed into the village for a while, not wanting to sit in silence of the house just yet. The streets were quieter than usual, but the occasional child running by, giggling, made me smile softly. Smoke drifted from the chimneys, and the air carried the faint scent of baked goods and burning wood. A handful of villagers moved about their afternoon duties—repairing tools, hauling buckets of water, and selling what produce they had.

As I walked, I caught a few wary glances. Whispers passed between neighbors, their eyes darting from the frost covered ground to me and back again. A young woman clutching a basket of cabbages pulled her child a little closer as I passed, though she offered a quick, polite nod.

I tried to ignore the hurt that flared through me, and forced myself to keep moving, letting my feet carry me toward the communal ovens. A few women were gossiping as they waited for their bread and pies to finish baking. It seemed more people were here, stocking up after the scare with the stranger.

The smoke curled from the low clay ovens. As I stepped forward, the baker—a round, middle-aged man with flour on his arms—stared at me, uncertain, but then offered a careful smile. "Fresh melitouta, miss," he said, gesturing to a tray of golden cakes.

"Thank you," I managed, my voice soft, almost timid. I paid quickly and found a quiet spot just outside, tearing off a corner of the still-warm cake and savoring the flavors. My thoughts kept circling back—Runar's sudden arrival, Eirik's stony words, the tension that seemed to hang in the air now every time someone was near me. And it was all thanks to my slip up yesterday.

I wasn't sure if I'd ever get used to this: the stare, the whispered prayers, the feeling of not belonging in my own skin. I'd been pulled from my world, from the judgement there—the abandonment, the being used—only to be dropped into a place where it followed me. Maybe Eirik was right, that strength had to be learned the hard way. Either way, right now, I was just a woman with horrible anxiety, no handle on her magic, and half the village terrified of her.

After a while, I finished the last bite, brushing the crumbs from my cloak. With a final glance around—at the half-welcoming, half-wary faces—I stood and started back towards the training grounds. If I planned to survive here, I had to keep going.

Runar was waiting just outside the training field, lounging in a patch of sunlight like he owned the place. His golden eyes were half-lidded, but the moment I approached, he became alert.

"You look troubled," he said, his voice rumbling low.

I just shrugged, arms wrapped tight around myself. "Lot on my mind."

He titled his head, studying me with those ancient eyes. "Would you like to talk about it?"

An unladylike snort escaped me. "You seem a little too serious for heart-to-heart talks, aren't you?"

Runar only huffed, gesturing with his massive head for me to sit. "Better here than hiding what troubles you. And before your guardian starts barking orders."

I settled down beside him, the ground cold even with the sun, but Runar's presence was oddly reassuring. We sat in silence for a moment before he shifted.

"What troubles you, young frostling?" He tried, once again.

I took a shaky breath. "Just everything with my abilities, and emotions. Not to mention how the villagers seem more wary about me now more than ever."

Runar looked off towards the village, "You will learn eventually how to properly use your magic without your emotions hindering you." he paused, "And do not let the opinion of others bring you down, it is their fear of the unknown that makes them that way."

I paused, surprised by his comforting words. I contemplated my next words carefully, "Runar...I can still hear Skadi sometimes. Not always. She just... fades in and out most of the time."

Runar didn't speak at first, but kept his gaze on me, unblinking.

"You aren't weirded out by that?"

"No." He shifted, resting his chin on his paws. "She gave up a great deal to protect you and what she left behind. It doesn't surprise me that part of her lingers. If only to guide you... but."

"But?" I pressed.

"But you are not her. And I can sense your worry that you are not yourself. You aren't a vessel. Her essence lingers, but your strength is yours alone. It'll grow as you do."

I sat back, letting that settle. For a moment, the only sound was the wind stirring the branches, snow dusting the air.

A set of footsteps pulled our attention to the far side of the grounds as Eirik reappeared and exhaled. "Are we ready for another go?"

I stood, glancing back at Runar as I stepped toward Eirik. "Will you be training with us, or just napping there?"

He cracked an eye open before letting out a huff. "You work with him right now. Once you're warmed up, then I'll step in—make sure you don't fall on your face." He grinned as much as a wolf could.

My eye twitched at his quip. "Very encouraging, thanks..." I said quietly, then walked to stand across from Eirik but in front of Runar. Some of the villagers had come to watch, and once again my nerves started creeping in.

"Breath, young frostling. Don't let your nerves best you," Runar's voice rumbled out.

I took a deep breath and pulled my sword from its sheath; the steel glistened in the light. The weight was still an adjustment, but I handled it a lot better than I had earlier.

"Now we continue our work on your stance and balance. Then we'll work on helping you with those abilities of yours," Eirik said, lifting his axe to his shoulder, and his sword firmly in his other hand.

I glanced up at the axe, worry etched on my face. "Thinking of double attacking me this time?" I asked.

He shrugged. "The enemy may have two weapons, Ravena, and it would be good practice for you."

I glanced back at Runar over my shoulder, who was watching intently but offered no suggestions, and I sagged in defeat. "Okay, Mr. Guardian, you're the boss. Please make me a spectacle in front of these people."

I braced myself as Eirik move forward. The strike was quick; I barely had time to bring my blade up to block before the force shot down my arm, making my teeth clench. I held steady, then felt the air change and jumped back, dodging his axe as it swung in close.

Eirik paused, an impressed look in his eyes. "That... was the best I've seen you move since we started training."

I was at a loss for words, surprised by the way my instincts had kicked in. The villagers were murmuring in awe—it actually boosted my confidence, if only a little. The next second, Eirik was moving again and our training continued. An intricate dance, blades and clashing and both of us dodging and weaving.

Time passed, and my body protested more with every doge. The villagers had gone back to their own practice but kept glancing at us, picking up whatever moves they could.

As I slid back from a blow dealt by his axe, my back met Runar's thick fur.

"Enough for now, shield-bearer. Let her rest. Then we'll both train with her," his low voice ordered.

I internally cried at the thought of having to dodge them both. Eirik smirked at the look on my face and gave a short nod, sheathing his sword and axe.

"Drink some water and walk around. We'll train again soon."

I nodded, reaching for my water skin and shakily going over to watch some of the other villagers, Runar right at my back.

"You did well. Next, we work on us fighting as a team—so you don't get ambushed or accidentally freeze us," he said, sitting next to me as I lightly stretched.

He is correct, young one. You have done exceptionally well, even if you doubt yourself. And now with Runar here, your fighting will improve—and he will always be here to fight as your companion when needed. Skadi's voice was there again, her tone carrying a thread of sadness. Maybe from not being able to be with him anymore.

I wanted comment, but nothing I could say felt right, so I gave a soft hum of agreement and placed a hand gently on his neck. "Thank you, all three of you, for helping me learn and survive in this place."

He leaned into my hand a little. "Of course. I don't want you completely lost, and your guardian and I can't scrape you off the ground all the time."

I let my head fall in exasperation at his sarcasm. "Yeah, thanks Runar. I love the faith you have in me." I turned back to Eirik. "Let's get this over with."

Chapter Eighteen

The day had come—we were finally leaving for Drusia, a village nestled at the foothills of Mt. Psophis. Only a day by foot, Cora had reassured me. It wasn't far, but distance wasn't what worried me.

My stomach twisted as I packed, my fingers working nervously as I stuffed small meals Cora had wrapped, extra layers, and a change of clothes into my bag with more force than necessary. No amount of reassurance—not even from Skadi herself—could shake the uneasiness settling over me. I wasn't ready. Not really. My training was improving, yes, but I knew this journey wouldn't be without danger.

Bandits. Bears. Soldiers. This era was far from kind, and even less forgiving to those who let their guard down.

Gods, please let this go uneventfully. I've got a weird feeling about this.

A low hum echoed through my mind, the cool brush of Skadi's presence washing over me. *Listen to these instincts, young one. They will not lead you astray. But do not let them push you to fear.*

I sighed, tightening the straps of my bag. Easier said than done. "I know," I muttered aloud. "Runar made sure I didn't forget my instincts. And my bruises and sore muscles from training are proof.

Adjusting to the weight of my newly crafted armor, I shifted, feeling the leather and reinforced plates settle against my body. "He and Eirik just love to surprise attack me any chance they get."

Skadi's laughter rang through my thoughts, warmly. Yes, *they do. But for good reason. Runar has always been keen on keeping me on my toes ever since my youth.*

That caught my attention. Ever since her youth? The way she said it made my thoughts pause, questions rising before I could stop them. I barely had time to ponder it before a gust of morning air greeted me as I stepped outside, the muted sunlight struggling to pierce through the low, rolling clouds. The crisp scent of damp earth and snow clung to the village, the quiet hum of early activity stirring in the distance. I made it two steps before the sound of approaching footsteps had me glancing to my right.

Eirik and Runar.

Runar approached, eyes meeting mine—golden, and all too knowing. There was something in his look—almost relief, like he'd been waiting on me. Eirik look less impressed, dragging his feet like he'd rather be anywhere but here, especially with a wolf at his side.

A smirk tugged at my lips. "You haven't been making Eirik's life miserable, have you?"

Runar's mouth curled, entirely too pleased. "I don't know what you mean, Ravena."

I rolled my eyes. "uh-huh sure you don't. Just try not to stress my only mostly-human ally, okay?"

He tilted his head, huffing in mock offense. "He'll survive, frostling. I'm sure he isn't as incompetent as he seems."

Eirik shot the wolf a glare, muttering something in Norse I didn't catch. But judging by his face, it wasn't exactly friendly. He set off toward the village gate, scowling at both of us. "Come on. We travel on foot. The horses we were supposed to take were too afraid of him to be of any use." He jabbed a finger back in Runar's direction.

I groaned, resisting the urge to throw my head back in frustration. "Of course. Because walking through ancient Greece during wartime and mythical creatures being around has always been on my to-do list."

Runar let out a low huff of amusement behind me, clearly enjoying my torture.

We made our way down the mountain path, the snow thinning with every step. The further we descended, the thick frost of the high slopes slowly gave way to patches of damp earth and scattered ice. The pines loomed tall, their branches heavy with snow, dripping as the air grew warmer. Now and then, a gust of wind would shake loose a dusting of frost, sending it tumbling in shimmering waves to the ground. The uneven terrain kept me on edge—slick ice and puddles making every step a gamble.

I nearly lost my footing on a particularly treacherous patch and quickly steadied myself. *Great. That would've been humiliating.*

A quiet, knowing laugh echoed in my head—clearly amused. *Ravena... you are a demi-goddess of winter,* Skadi's voice murmured, far too entertained for my liking. *You could melt the ice from your path, if you wished, little one.*

I paused mid-step, her words settling in. "Oh..." I whispered, realization dawning.

Beside me, Runar's ears flicked toward me, in curiosity.

I refused to look him in the eyes and swallowed the embarrassment burning at the edges of my pride. How had I not realized something so simple? I drew in a breath and tried to let my magic respond, focusing on the frozen path. The ice in front of me shimmered and slowly melted away, clearing a path.

"Good job, you have improved." Runar said, nudging me lightly with his massive frame.

I let out a nervous sigh and folded my arms across my chest. "Yea I suppose so."

Ahead, Eirik kept a regular pace, scanning the tree line—clearly on alert now, more so than usual. Even if it seemed he was lost in his own thoughts. I was thankful he didn't seem to notice my little moment.

I adjusted my cloak tighter, bracing against the breeze that sifted through the trees. The air carried the crisp scent of earth and pine, mingling with the faintest traces of morning frost. Overhead, birds stirred, their songs rising with the sun, while unseen creatures rustled through the undergrowth, shaking off the last remnants of slumber. I let my gaze drift across the landscape, mindful of Eirik's training—always watch, always be aware. It was hard to imagine that one day, this untouched land in my realm would be carved apart by roads, stripped of its wild beauty in the name of progress and tourism.

A firm nudge at my shoulder pulled me from my thoughts. I turned, meeting Runar's gaze as he halted beside me. One massive paw pressed into the earth as he lowered himself slightly as an invitation.

"Come, young one," he rumbled, his tone edged with amusement. "Your curiosity is that of a pup, and we are falling behind. I shall grant you a ride."

I blinked. "Are you serious?" My voice wavered somewhere between excitement and nervousness.

Runar gave a short nod, his golden eyes gleaming.

I didn't hesitate. I hurried toward his massive frame, hesitating only a moment before grabbing onto the thick fur at his shoulders. With an easy motion, he shifted beneath me, lowering himself so I could climb onto his back without making a complete fool of myself.

"Hold on, young one," he rumbled. "We need to keep pace."

I barely had time to adjust before he started forward, his massive paws crunching over the frozen ground. It wasn't a full sprint, but the powerful strides beneath me made the world move faster than I was used to. The wind bit at my cheeks, strands of my hair escaping my hood as Runar navigated the uneven terrain with ease.

Ahead of us, Eirik moved steadily through the thinning snow, glancing back every so often to make sure we weren't lagging behind.

"I could go faster," Runar mused, his voice laced with amusement, startling me.

"I'm fine with the speed we're at," I shot back quickly, gripping his fur a little tighter.

"Are you sure?" His tone was all mischief.

"I swear, if you throw me off, I'll make sure you wake up frozen solid." I glared.

Runar rumbled a deep chuckle, clearly amused.

Eirik, clearly catching parts of our conversation, decided to chime in. "If you fall, I'm not carrying you the rest of the way."

I shot him a look. "Please. You'd probably laugh, then *offer* to carry me so you could gloat the whole way." Turning my head signaling the end of our conversation.

For the next few hours, we pressed forward at a brisk but manageable pace.

The trail dipped and rose, winding through frozen thickets and stretches of untouched snow. The only footprints belonged to passing deer and unseen creatures. The land was still, waiting beneath the frost, holding its breath for the turn of the seasons. The birds stirred in the treetops, wings rustling against brittle branches. A lone raven cawed, its dark shape cutting across the dull sky before vanishing beyond the trees.

"We should reach the valley by midday," Eirik called over his shoulder. His gaze scanned the trees, the ridgelines, and stretches of open land—a constant sweep, never lingering for long.

I hummed, silently agreeing, but kept my attention was on my surroundings, hoping for a glimpse of hidden temples or some mythological creature.

Runar padded quietly beneath me, his massive paws barely leaving a trace in the hardened soil. "Keep your senses open," he murmured. "Silence does not always mean safety."

I nodded, gripping the fur of his neck easier now. This land was still unfamiliar. It was one thing to read about history, another to walk through it, knowing every shadow could be watching. For now, the only sounds were the crunch of boots against frozen ground, the occasional snap of twigs, and the wind swirling through the trees. The sun climbed higher, stretching golden rays across the peaks behind us. Shadows stretched long across the valley ahead. By midday, we would stop to rest. For now, we pressed forward, deeper into the waiting land.

By noon, the sunlight had risen higher, filtering through the canopy in soft golden shafts. We had covered far more ground than I could've on foot, but the strain of holding myself steady on Runar's back was starting to settle deep in my muscles.

"We should rest," Eirik finally announced, slowing his steps as he glanced at the narrow clearing ahead.

Runar came to a smooth stop, lowering himself just enough for me to slide off.

I tried to be graceful. Really, I did.

But the moment my feet touched the ground, my legs turned to jelly, and I stumbled. Before I could even think of gasping or falling, two strong arms caught me.

Eirik's grip was firm, his warmth seeping through my cloak as he steadied me against himself. "Easy there," he chuckled, his voice laced with amusement.

Heat rushed to my face for the second time that day, embarrassment prickling at the back of my neck along with feeling uncomfortable. I never liked being touched; it always reminded me of old memories that I didn't wish to relive. It made my skin itch with awareness, like I needed just a little more space to breathe to keep my peace.

But Eirik's grip was steady, firm without any ulterior motive, and for once, I didn't pull away. Well, not right away, at least.

I quickly came to my senses and pulled back, leaning into Runar's fur, clearing my throat. "I had it under control..."

Eirik's brow lifted. "Very well, if by control, you mean almost falling flat on your face."

Runar let out a huff, clearly enjoying this scene. "A fine warrior you are, Raven. Felled by your own legs."

I groaned. "Now you're on his side? I hate you both."

Eirik chuckled, stepping back and making his way toward the stream. He didn't answer, only settling himself by the water with a thoughtful look.

I leaned back, feeling the rough bark press against my spine, grounding me. The stream that wound through our stop was strikingly clear, the water so pure I could see every rock beneath its surface. Even in the grip of winter, it still flowed, the ice creeping along its edges like silver veins, never quite claiming it completely.

"Hmm," Runar rumbled, his voice deep. "Have you always been so curious, young Ravena? I have not seen one with that much wonder in many moons."

I shrugged, absently plucking at the fur on my cloak. "I have... ever since I was little. My parents could never keep me out of the library—I loved history." I caught the confused looks on both their faces. "Oh, right. That word doesn't exist yet. In this place, it would be called a bibliotheca, or... in Norse terms, a place where the records of the old ones were kept."

My fingers curled slightly as I stared at my hands. The warmth of my cloak couldn't quite chase away the doubt creeping up my spine, the old doubt settling in my chest. Was I truly meant to be here? How could I be Skadi's successor when I still felt so... vulnerable?

A soft thump against my shoulder made me jolt. I turned, finding Runar's massive tail resting against me—his version of comfort I suppose. No words were needed. I exhaled slowly, my shoulders easing just enough to keep my anxious thoughts at bay.

Eirik cleared his throat. "You might want to eat what you can, before we continue. We've still got a stretch ahead before we reach Drusia." His gaze flickered toward the path; his usual teasing edge replaced with something more serious. "And with any luck, we won't find trouble waiting for us there."

Our meal—if I could call it that—was quick. There was no small talk, and the atmosphere, though relaxed, held an edge of tension. I was sure each of us had our own thoughts of what lay ahead in the village. Even Skadi was quiet, her presence feeling farther away this day than it ever had been. As we made our way through the shallow creek and pressed on, the silence was almost deafening. Winter had muted not just the sounds of nature, but the sense of what loomed ahead.

I wasn't sure if I liked it or not; it gave me too much time to think—and overthink everything. I glanced down at the scattered, ice-crusted dirt road, my abilities making it easier not to fall flat on my face. The air was thick with the scent of Greek firs, snow clinging to their limbs, and the smell of dirt was rich. We broke out of the tree line; clouds covered the sun, but faint streams of light still trickled through. It cast a somber glow on the surrounding fields, and in the distance, we could see what appeared to be a village at the foothills of the mountain. What was startling about it was the black smoke that still rose—even after days. I froze in my tracks, staring as Eirik and Runar walked ahead, their pace picking up. A lump formed in my throat as I forced myself to keep moving, the village growing nearer as we crossed the dead crops.

Tears stung my eyes as we reached the outskirts—the village was destroyed. Everywhere I looked, there were burned houses, the mudbrick scorched and iced over in some places, the roofs completely burned away. It was a terrible site. For someone like me, I'd only ever seen this kind of destruction on the news—never in person. Eirik branched off with a silent look to Runar, and I raised an eyebrow as he fell in at my side.

"He's going to check for threats before we look around further, and to ensure your safety," Runar rumbled out.

I bit back a response and leaned against him instead, studying the burns on the nearest house. The blackened marks mixed with ice looked wrong—even from here, it felt cold and dark. My stomach churned. The sensation reminded me of the wounded traveler's injuries. I could feel the dark magic seeping from the ice, and to my horror, I gasped, catching Runar's attention.

He followed my line of sight and let out a low rumble of disapproval. Farther down, next to the house, frozen forms of the villagers stood out—captured in the act of fleeing, frozen in time by whatever had caused this destruction. Nausea rolled in my stomach, bile rising as I took in all the different shapes and faces of these poor people. They didn't deserve this. Not for the sick games these creatures were trying to play.

Footsteps snapped my attention to the right as Eirik returned, a grim expression set on his face. "There's no one else here. No new tracks in or out. Even the animals seem to be staying away."

Runar let out a growl angrily. "They destroyed everything and left it to ruin. The smoke still fills the air from the fires that refuse to die."

I let out an unsettled hum. "What do we do now?" I asked, anxiously shoving my hands in the cloak's pockets.

Eirik relaxed only a little, his shoulders slumping forward "We can look around; it seems safe enough for you to split off for now," he said. "But don't stray too far. Things can change quickly." His voice tried for reassurance, but there was caution beneath it.

We went our separate ways, and I stayed mindful of where Eirik and Runar wandered off to. The village was larger than I expected, but every street, every doorway, was scarred—burns and ice tangled together, it swallowed everything within its reach. That sick feeling from earlier still hadn't left me. Seeing the frozen villagers—caught mid-run, some reaching, some turned as if to run—only made it worse. I stopped near one of the bodies and took a shaky breath, forcing myself to step closer. *C'mon, Ravena, you can do this. You can't be scared of everything all your life.*

My gaze drifted over the villager's frozen face, and the energy radiating from the dark blue ice made the hairs on my arm stand on end. The ice wasn't melting, not even where sunlight touched it; the cold seeping off it was so harsh it made the air feel suffocating. *I wonder if they're still alive under the ice—or if they're already gone.* My thoughts were somber, and I hesitated, lifting my hand to touch the frozen surface.

I wouldn't do that young one, Skadi's voice chided, startling me. I pulled my hand back at once. *We know not what this dark magic will do if touched.* She continued, I glanced around and caught Runar watching me from a distance.

That wasn't a smart idea. My curiosity got the better of me, I admitted, embarrassed.

We *all learn. These poor mortals... they're trapped. Unable to pass peacefully, unable to escape this prison.* Sadness lingered in her tone, and it confirmed what I feared.

I turned away, scanning the street for anything that might give us a clue. The silence was heavy, only broken by the wing tugging at burned banners and the distance call of a bird. "You've been quiet lately, Skadi," I said, circling around a smashed wagon. "Is something wrong?"

I could feel her hesitation. *Not at all, Ravena. Since the incident with your abilities, I've been trying to give you space. I'm here to guide, not interfere.*

I frowned but nodded. It wasn't what I wanted to hear, but maybe it was what I needed. "So I'm on my own now?" I whispered, trying not to let my anxiety appear once more.

Not on your own, she said gently. *You're stronger now than you were days ago. I'm with you—for as long as I can be. But you have to trust yourself, too.*

Her words faded as the sight before me stole my breath. That dark energy was back—a suffocating mix of the evil magic and overwhelming sense of sadness and resentment. It permeated into the air, casting an unnerving feel.

"What is this feeling... why is this area so different from the rest?" I asked Skadi in a whisper, hoping she would answer.

Look and listen, Ravena. Open your senses to the things around you. That was all she gave me, her voice fading out once more.

I let out a frustrated huff at her cryptic answer but tried to follow it, forcing myself to really take in the area. I glanced back over my shoulder, checking if Eirik or Runar were nearby, but they were a good distance off, near another ruined house.

A cold breeze swept through, and suddenly—*They destroyed us!* A deep, weak voice rumbled out of nowhere.

My head snapped around, heart pounding. There was no one there. Just the scorched ruins, burned and broken trees—except for two, barely standing, with ice creeping up their bark, flames still eating slowly at the wood.

"H-hello?" I called out, my voice shaky, half convinced I was finally losing it. Gods, please don't let me actually be hearing voices now...

Dead beings walking, burning our sacred trees... another weak voice trembled, this one distinctly feminine.

I blinked hard. The voices were coming from the trees—or at least near them. Cautiously, I stepped closer, my hand resting on the hilt of my blade.

"Who's there?" I questioned, my voice stronger this time, but I could almost feel the air shift around me, like something had been startled.

"You can hear us, mortal?" The feminine voice said again, closer this time.

A moment later, a wispy figure floated out from behind the larger tree. She was nothing like I'd seen before: hair a deep brown tangled with blackened vines and wilted leaves, dull dark-green eyes, and pointed, elf-like ears set into a small, transparent face. She couldn't have been taller than my shin—and the most unsettling part was how she looked almost ghostly, like she was barely clinging to the world.

I was at a loss for words. The things that kept happening to me shouldn't have surprised me anymore, but here we were. "What are you?" I asked, sounding dumb even to myself. In hindsight, I should have known what this creature was.

The spirit—though faint and weak—regarded me with a look of curiosity, as if my question was new to her. "We are called many things, but here, in this once-sacred grove, we are Alseides. Spirits who live with the trees," she said softly, her voice almost carried away by the wind as I knelt to her height.

"I apologize for my intruding. My name is Ravena." My heart ached for these beings. "Can you tell me what happened here—to the village, and to all of you?"

A cough drew my attention left, toward the other tree. A male tree spirit slowly appeared from its trunk. "There were at least ten of them," he said, voice ragged. "Soldiers made of ice. Once living, it seemed. And the Nychtari—most call them Shadow Stalkers. They came from south, through the mountains. They were searching for something."

"They had no mercy for what they did. When they reached our grove, the other spirits fled, abandoning their trees to survive." The female weakly recounted the events of days prior.

I looked over my shoulder, searching for Runar—and thankfully, he was already heading my way, hackles raised. I turned back to the spirits, noting their fading forms and the pure resentment in their eyes, directed at the ones who destroyed their home.

I glanced at the fallen trees and frowned. "What will you do now? It doesn't seem like these trees will ever stand again..." I trailed off, not wanting to offend the spirits.

"We had hoped that by staying, we could help them survive, but this fire does not leave—the snow even avoids it. We will go and find new ones. We were about to leave when we noticed you from a distance. We're surprised you can communicate with us," the male rumbled, studying me for a long moment. Then a spark flickered in his eyes. "Ah you're a demi-goddess—not fully human. It's natural you'd be able to hear us."

He looked up at something behind me, and I felt a warm breath brush the back of my head.

"You seem to have found something, young frostling," Runar's voice sounded right next to my ear.

I jumped, startled by how close he was. "Y-yeah. Tree nymphs—don't hurt them, they're not doing any harm. I found them here." Glancing at his settling hackles, I gave a wry smile. "This sacred grove was destroyed by soldiers made of ice. The strange part is, the nymphs think they were human once, too." I licked my lips; the cold had long since cracked the surface, making them sting. I looked back at the two nymphs, who were staring at Runar with open curiosity. "Don't worry about him. He's mostly bark, no bite," I tried to reassure them, ignoring Runar's annoyed rumble.

"It is alright, young goddess; we will take our leave. It saddens us to abandon our trees, but we would surely perish if we stayed here. One day we will seek revenge for what was done," the female nymph spoke with lividity. She and the male gave a short bow, their forms flitting away toward the mountains.

I let out a long breath, standing up and brushing the dirt from my knees. My mind spun with what the nymphs had described. None of it sounded Greek in origin—except for the Nychtari, which were controlled by The Mormo if I recalled correctly.

"Hmm. The Nalren," Runar said quietly.

I turned to him, glancing around for Eirik. "The what?" I asked, recognizing the word.

"The Naldrengir—corpse warriors made with dark magic by the dark elves. If Agnar has these allies, Ravena, we're facing more trouble than we know." His eyes held worry and something else I couldn't quite name.

A chill crept down my spine, fur cloak or not. "Great... What about the Nychtari? In my understanding, they're shadow stalkers—drawn to places where despair is most potent. But how would Agnar summon them?" I asked, finally spotting Eirik approaching with a troubled looked that mirrored our own.

"I am not familiar with those creatures. The Elder in your village may have the answers we need," Runar rumbled.

I sighed and started toward Eirik.

"Did you find anything?" he asked meeting up with us, shoulders tense, his eyes scanning Runar. "The Nalren are here—but I take it you figured that out?"

Runar nodded, coming to stand closer to me, as if danger could be hiding nearby. "Yes. Our young warrior here has managed to befriend a couple of tree nymphs, who were... not pleased with their grove being destroyed."

Eirik studied the burned and fallen trees, then sighed. "We need to return to the village. It's not safe here. The Nalren... they left a message." He hesitated, the temperature seemingly dropping with the severity of his words. "There were inscriptions left near a house. They're searching for you, Ravena."

My blood ran cold, nausea rolling through me all over again.

"Hop on, frostling. We'll discuss more once we're back with the others," Runar ordered, kneeling down so I could climb on. I nodded, doing my best to mount gracefully—then we were off.

Runar's pace was faster than before, and my grip on his fur tightened until my knuckles turned white. My thoughts spiraled: those corpse warriors wanted me. Not the village or its people. Me.

The journey back to Kyllini passed quickly. The sun dipped behind us, casting long shadows ahead as the temperature dropped. We moved in near silence; the only sounds were the steady thud of Runar's paws and the crunch of Eirik's boots over old snow and exposed earth. My fingers curled even tighter into Runar's fur—not for stability, but to keep the nausea and intrusive thoughts from swallowing me whole.

We veered left, ascending the steep path that led toward the village. My breath caught as my body shifted with the incline, threatening my balance. Being back should've eased the weight in my chest but it didn't. If anything, the unease dug deeper.

As we passed the worn stones marking the village perimeter, the gates came into view—Theron waiting beside them with Cora, who was rubbing her hands nervously. I dismounted stiffly, my legs aching and unsteady.

Cora rushed to me, her hands landing gently on my shoulders. "You're back," she said, searching my face. "But something's happened."

Eirik cleared his throat, drawing her attention. "That it has. We need to speak. Now." His tone left no room for argument. Theron gave a solemn nod and turned to lead the way toward the main house.

Cora shot Runar a tight-lipped glance, then took my hand, guiding me away. "Come, Ravena. Let's get you cleaned up before you talk with the others." I couldn't find it in me to argue; my whole body felt worn out.

We left the group and made our way to my room. My thoughts kept drifting back to the poor tree nymphs and the villagers—the haunting images flashing behind my eyes.

Once inside, the fire was already lit with fresh logs, and when the warm air hit my face, I felt the tears building. I barely made it to the bed before stumbling to my knees.

"Ravena!" Cora's voice gasped as she dropped beside me. I didn't turn my head...I couldn't catch my breath. It hitched in my throat, somewhere between a sob and a gasp. My hands shook and felt numb. I pressed them against the floor, trying to keep my body upright. The images came back even stronger—burned homes, frozen bodies, the nymphs' voices whispering their grief and rage.

I tried to suck in air, but it felt too thick, too painful. Cora cupped my face in her calloused hands. Her touch was warm and safe, but it did little to settle the panic clawing at my chest. My anxiety attacks were never easy. It always felt like I couldn't breathe and every muscle in my body ached, my mind racing through every awful possibility.

"Hey, look at me Ravena," she said gently, her motherly tone more prominent than ever. I forced my eyes open and met her dark eyes. "You're safe right now. Right here with us. Take a deep breath for me." She inhaled slowly, exaggerating it so I could follow. I felt embarrassed, letting her see me like this, but she didn't look away. She gave me a pointed look, so I obeyed. "Good. Now again. In... now out."

My chest still hurt, but the air finally started to move. My hands kept trembling, but the world didn't feel like it was collapsing anymore.

Cora slowly let go of my face as I sat up, turning to rest my back against the lowered frame of my bed. She sat beside me, keeping her hand on my arm.

"You're not alone, you know. Tell me what you found. It might help to talk about it," she said gently.

I let out a shaky sigh. "The village... it was destroyed. Houses burned, and dark ice coated everything..." I paused, pulling my knees to my chest. "The villagers...they were frozen trying to escape." I swallowed, feeling her grip tighten in silent comfort.

"I see. You've seen something no one your age should ever have to see. I'm here for you, so please—don't carry it all by yourself, understand?"

I nodded, barely. My voice came out smaller than I intended. "They weren't after the village. They were after me."

Cora's expression darkened, but her voice stayed calm. "Then they'll have to go through all of us first."

That made a shaky laugh escape me. "You've got some fight in you, huh?"

Her words eased some of the tension in my shoulders. "Of course. I may be old, but no one will hurt someone dear to me," she said, reaching up to brush the hair from my face.

I closed my eyes, wiping away the last of my tears. "Thank you, Cora. I really appreciate everything you've done for me."

She let out a small smile before standing up and holding out her hand. "Come on, let's fix up your hair and face before we go meet the others."

I took her hand, always surprised by her strength as she helped me to my feet.

Chapter Nineteen

The horses shifted anxiously as we prepped their saddles and bags for the trip ahead. I fiddled with straps absently, my thoughts drifting back to last night. We'd gone to meet Theron and Lydia, where I relayed everything—the words of the nymphs, the destruction in Drusia. The words of it all had settled over the room like smoke, making the air feel hot despite it being cold outside. The house attendants had long since been dismissed at Cora's firm insistence, leaving her to serve tea.

The emotions in the room had been stifling, and my stomach had twisted with anxiety, just like it did now.

I sighed, leaning my head against the blanket draped over the horse's back. My gloved fingers fumbled with the unfamiliar straps, frustration building. This wasn't the kind of saddle I was used to—just a curved leather pad molded by years of use, tied tightly around the horse's middle. No stirrups, no pommel, no neat buckles. *Gods. Why would anything be easy?* My thoughts were a jumbled mess. The sun had barely risen over the mountainside, but my companions were ready. Eirik was already finishing up, loading what he needed, and Runar had taken to the tree line, so as not to scare the horses any further.

"Here, let me help. No need to get upset so early in the morn," Eirik's voice rumbled from behind me.

I sagged in defeat. "I feel helpless, Eirik. I swear I'm not incompetent." My voice came out low, tight with embarrassment.

He stepped beside me, his hands already working the stubborn straps with practiced ease. "It's alright, Ravena. Everything here is different for you. It takes practice and time." His voice, still rough from sleep, was oddly reassuring.

I glanced down, ashamed. "I know the general idea from my studies, but actually *doing* all this..." I muttered, trailing off. "I haven't ridden a horse since I was little."

Eirik chuckled under his breath. "That, I can tell. Worry not, you did well up to this part here."

With a final tug of the leather, he secured the bags properly and handed me the reins. His gaze was unjudging and for that I was thankful.

"Come, Ravena," he said, voice lighter now. "We have a long road ahead."

He was right. The journey itself might not be long, but what we were looking for—and where it would lead us after—would take time. I sighed and silently slipped the reins over the horse's head, following Eirik to the village entrance. We were making our way to Korinthos, a port city, hoping to find answers about the creatures we'd heard about. Theron had never heard of such things, only tales passed down in his family. He'd suggested again we try to find Hermes.

The very same in my time's history—the famous Greek god women swoon over and write books about. And trust me, some of those stories don't end well. This god was multifaceted, and that made me nervous. If he didn't want to be found, he wouldn't be. And even if we managed it, would he even give us information? Gods were tricky that way.

I was pulled from my thoughts as Eirik knelt to help me on the horse. My face flushed in embarrassment. "I could have tried to do this on my own, you know," I mumbled.

"But would you be successful or fall flat off the other side?" he mused, patting his knee.

I rolled my eyes. *Stupid shield-bearer always has to be right.* I hesitantly stepped onto his knee and swung myself onto the horse's back. The horse shifted with a snort as I adjusted my weight. I scrambled to gather the reins and find my center before I slid right back off. *I can do this. Just like riding a bike... right?*

Eirik stood and patted the horse's neck. "Let's be off then. Theron says the city is a day's trip at least, and we shouldn't run into any trouble," he said, expertly swinging himself onto his mount.

I looked out toward the decline of the mountain and the brightening scenery, knowing Runar was just off in the distance. I gave a short nod and nudged my mount after Eirik. The trip down the mountainside was quicker this time, the horse's hooves thudding softly against the damp earth. Patches of snow clung stubbornly to the shadowed side of the trail, where the peeking sun couldn't reach—but where it could, thin rivulets of melted water trickled down the rocks, carving narrow paths into the mud.

My breath fogged in the chilly air, mixing with the deep, crisp scent of pine trees and damp soil. The higher altitude was always colder than the lower canopy, so it was nice to see a change. I glanced down as my horse's ears flicked, listening to sounds I couldn't catch. It picked its way carefully over slick patches of stone and muddy ruts.

I tried to sit relaxed, not stiff, knowing the last thing I wanted was to throw it off balance. I heard Eirik let out a chuckle, and I snapped my gaze up to him.

"Ease up, Ravena. You're sitting stiffer than a newly dried hide," he joked.

I glared at him, debating whether to ice him over or just hit him with a sarcastic remark—but decided to ignore him and relaxed my posture, just a bit. My horse let out a huff, possibly as a thank you. In the distance, I could feel the strong presence of Runar as he trailed us, and that eased the nerves in my chest.

Hitting the bottom of the trail was a welcome relief. I picked up the reins lightly and nudged my horse into a trot, drawing up alongside Eirik. The sun barely filtered through the trees at this hour, casting everything in a dim, silvered light.

"I might regret this," I said, "but if we want to make it to the city before nightfall, shouldn't we pick up the pace?"

Eirik glanced at me from the corner of his eye. "Yes, we could. Can you handle that? We've still time before the sun breaks through properly."

I shrugged, already knowing my thighs would pay for it later. "Mmh-mm. Might as well. But if I fall and you laugh..." I let the threat hang, flashing him a grin. "I'll freeze you where you stand."

He let out a loud laugh that echoed through the trees, startling a few birds from their branches. The horses' ears flicked at the noise. "Noted, oh fierce one. I wouldn't dream of such a callous thing," Eirik said, inclining his head as if to say let's go before trotting off.

My eye twitched as I scrambled to nudge my horse forward again, tightening my thighs to keep my balance.

The scenery blurred by at a steady pace, the cold air stinging my cheeks. The steady sound of hooves, horses breathing, and the faint clatter of our equipment were the only noises that filled the otherwise still morning.

It might have been relaxing—if I wasn't focusing so hard on not falling off.

Time passed. As the sun rose higher, we finally broke through the tree line. On one side, the path opened into a field, and the air shifted—no longer just cold soil and pine, but something stronger...salt. Like the ocean waited just a few hours ahead.

Eirik slowed his mount to a stop, and I tugged my reins to stop behind him. "We'll take a break here," he said, swinging easily off his horse and walking back toward me. "Horses need rest—and we can't have you not being able to walk."

I managed to swing my leg over the saddle, but the moment my feet hit the ground, they gave out. I would've eaten dirt if Eirik hadn't caught me by the elbow.

"There it is," he jested, grinning. "First ride will break you in ways you soon won't forget."

I muttered something unflattering under my breath and tried not to lean on him longer than necessary. Straightening as best I could, I stiffly made my way to a huge pine tree and collapsed onto my cloak, not caring if it got wet. Eirik chuckled as he grabbed the horses, tying them up just off the trail.

I laid there; my eyes trailed the clouds as the wind moved them along. It was nice to not be in a constant snowscape. The temperatures were still cold but not numbly so. With a sigh, my gaze shifted to the horses—and I was positive my horse was judging me. Fair enough.

A subtle shift behind me before a black snout settled next to my head. My hand reached up and threaded through thick fur. "Hello, Runar. You have fun running behind us?" I mumbled.

A huff. "Wasn't much of a run for me, little frostling, but indeed it was a decent stretch of my legs," his voice rumbled low as he shifted to lay down. The horses shifted uneasily but settled a moment later.

I sighed, closing my eyes, listening as the wind rustled through the pine needles. Far off, I could hear birds singing and fluttering between the branches. It was peaceful—the kind of peace I knew wouldn't last, no matter how much I wished it would.

It made me miss home....

I hadn't thought about home in a while. Or... not really. Not in a way that hurts. I guess I'd been too busy trying to survive, too focused on whatever came next. But now—here, quiet, still—it crept in. That old ache I'd buried deep.

I shifted on the cloak, tugging it tighter around my shoulders. It wasn't the cold that got to me—it was that hollow space in my chest. That reminder that no matter how far I'd come, this wasn't my world. Not really. It never had been.

Where's Skadi when I need her?

I'd gotten used to her voice in the back of my mind. Always calm, always sure. It wasn't constant, but it was something. And now it was just... quiet.

My breath shook a little, and I hated how fast that emptiness crept back. It hadn't hit like this in a while.

A soft nudge broke the spiral—Runar. His snout pressed against my shoulder gently, and I managed a weak smile.

"What troubles you, Ravena?" he asked, his voice low and rumbling.

I exhaled slowly, staring ahead at the dark water before glancing up at him.

"It's probably stupid," I said, "but... I miss Skadi's voice."

He didn't say anything, just waited.

"Even though I don't know her like you did, I'd gotten used to having her there. And now she's just... absent. She told me back in Drusia that I need to start making my own path. That she's holding on to what little she has left, only stepping in when it's absolutely necessary."

I paused. "I get it. I do. But... I still feel like I'm not enough. Like I'm already letting her down. Letting everyone down."

My throat burned and I bit the inside of my cheek. The tears didn't fall—but they wanted to.

Runar gave a small huff of air. It was a very human gesture, but somehow it seemed normal for him. "You only let yourself down by doubting how far you've come. The fates deemed you the next Goddess of Winter. That path isn't meant to be easy—every soul carries doubt with them. It's how you choose to move forward that matters." His eyes never leaving my face. "Skadi could have left you alone and not helped at all, but she saw the potential in you."

I sighed, looking away as I sniffed quietly.

"For an ancient being that doesn't talk much, you sure do know how to make someone feel better," I said quietly, blinking away the tears that had gathered.

Sitting up, I took a breath. "You're right. I don't need to rely on her for everything if I want to survive here."

❧ ❧

The hour had passed faster than I'd expected, and we were back on the road. Runar had returned to the tree line, and we'd mounted our horses again, much to my legs' protest. Eirik let out a deep laugh at my pain.

"I'm glad I can bring you humor," I muttered, nudging my horse forward.

"I apologize; it just reminds me of the young warriors when they first learn. You're doing far better than they did," he mused.

I rolled my eyes, keeping my gaze forward, focused on weaving through a patch of rough terrain. The mountains rose up on both sides of us again, blocking what little sun had peeked through the clouds. The trade city of Korinthos waited ahead, but we still had a way to go—probably not arriving until late this evening.

I wonder if we'll find Hermes there, or the answers we seek... knowing my luck, we'll be running in circles. My eyes scanned my surroundings as the path grew rockier before evening out.

My brows furrowed. The area had gone quiet—even the wind had stilled. The air felt strange now, almost like—

I pulled my reins back, slowing my horse to a halt. She shifted under me, tense, as if she sensed something I couldn't see.

"Eirik..." I called quietly as he stopped beside me.

"I know, I feel it too. We aren't alone," he said, his hand drifting to his axe.

"An intuitive man, I see. But you, young goddess, have grown remarkably," a beautifully feminine voice spoke.

My head snapped to my left as a woman stepped out of the tree line shadows, and my eyes widened. She was beautiful, and immediately I knew she wasn't mortal—she radiated divinity. She stood between two cypresses, golden armor glinting in the low light. Her long black hair was braided low down her back, and her eyes were a striking purple. The bottom of her outfit was a flowing skirt, a golden metal belt hung low on her hips.

I moved my right hand to my sword, keeping a firm grip on the reins with my left. She smiled— a small, knowing smile.

"Easy, young one. I'm an ally, not an enemy. I am Hecate, Goddess of Crossroads, and I'm pleased to be in your presence—finally," she said.

Eirik stepped slightly ahead of me, protective as always. "What's your business with us?" he challenged her.

She inclined her head. "As I said, Norseman, I'm not an enemy. I've come to see the person I saw in my vision many years ago, and to bring her a message about the roads ahead."

My eyes narrowed. "You saw me? Or Skadi?" I asked, watching her face.

"I saw you," Hecate said simply. "Long before you stepped into this realm. Before Skadi's fall... before any of this truly began."

My breath caught as she continued.

"The Norns—as your guardian know them, for me it's the Fates—they all choose you. Your destiny was written the moment Skadi pleaded to be saved."

She stepped closer, her expression calm but watchful.

"I'm sure you know the path won't be easy, but I'm here to warn you. The enemy of Skadi is on the move, and he knows you're here—just not where." Hecate's gaze didn't change.

I swallowed the lump in my throat. "You mean Agnar?" I asked.

She nodded. "You're the threat now," she said. "Whether you believe it or not."

The temperature around me seemed to plummet, and a cold sweat broke out along the back of my neck. That familiar, heavy feeling settled in my stomach as I tried to keep my hands from shaking.

I forced myself to meet her eyes. It wasn't easy. Something about her gaze made me feel like she could see everything—every doubt, every failure I kept locked away.

But I didn't look away. I wouldn't, not this time.

Hecate's expression shifted, just slightly. It wasn't pity—but something else. Understanding, maybe.

"Fear doesn't make you weak, Ravena," she said, her voice calm. "It means you have respect for the forces of nature beyond your control, and an instinct to keep yourself safe."

She reached beneath her cloak and pulled something from a pouch at her hip—a small object, wrapped in deep violet cloth and tied with black rope. She stepped forward and held it up to me.

"Keep this with you. When the time comes, it will help open what was once destroyed."

I hesitated, then took it carefully. The cloth was cool to the touch, and something about it buzzed faintly against my skin... like it recognized me.

"You won't always have someone to guide you," she added, her voice low. "But you'll have this. And if you ever stand at a true crossroads—just call my name." she finished with a nod.

I blinked, and in the next breath, she was gone.

The area was quiet. Not a word was spoken as I examined the small pouch. Eirik shifted to face me, his gaze focused, studying the cloth as if he could see through it. Runar emerged from the trees, his ears pricked, his golden gaze locked on the pouch. I tilted my head at him, frowning—he looked like he recognized whatever was inside.

"What is it?" I asked, searching his face for a hint.

He looked up at me, eyes narrowing in thought before glancing back to the pouch. "The energy coming from that feels familiar, but not from this realm." He paused, ears twitching. "It feels like something from Jotunheim."

I looked back down; the buzz hadn't faded, but it didn't feel malicious. "We seem to get more questions than answers, don't we? Think Skadi would know anything? She is from Jotunheim, after all."

Runar gave a short nod and backed up once more to the trees. "We won't find answers sitting here. You could try reaching out to her again," he rumbled, but he seemed almost uncomfortable.

I tucked the pouch into one of my belt satchels, then glanced at Eirik, who was watching me closely. Without another word, we rode on in silence. The sun dipped lower, casting gold across the mountain range and through the trees. In the distance, I could just make out the beginnings of a wall that I remembered circled Korinthos.

"You alright?" Eirik's finally asked, riding up beside me. He was relaxed now, but I knew he was still watching for any more surprises.

I nodded, though not very convincingly. "Yeah... I'm just still trying to process that an actual goddess just appeared in front of us."

He gave a wry smile. "From my experience, gods and goddesses never show up when you want them—only when it suits them." he said.

I let go of one rein and rubbed my face. "No, I meant, for me they were never 'real' before—all of this was just mythology. For you, it's just normal life." I looked over at him, and he nodded, as if he understood.

"I try to remember you're not from here," he said. "You've grown a lot since we first met. You're handling everything quite well."

I let out a dry chuckle. "Is that what you see? Because trust me, I'm *not* handling it well inside. And as for me growing... that's still up for debate."

My smile faded a bit. "You don't trust her—Hecate?" I asked, recounting his words.

"Didn't that say," he muttered. "But my trust isn't given easily. Even to those who call themselves allies."

I glanced down at my satchel, running a thumb over the shape of the object inside. "She didn't seem like she was lying," I said quietly. *Though that's gotten me in trouble before... damn, I need to read people better.*

"She may not be," Eirik said with a shrug. "But truth and motives aren't always traveling the same path."

I didn't answer, just stared ahead as the walls of Korinthos came into focus, the buildings inside catching the remaining rays of light.

<h1 style="text-align:center">Chapter Twenty</h1>

We slowed to a stop just outside the western walls of the city. My horse shifted beneath me, hooves crunching against the stone path, but I barely noticed. Korinthos. It was surreal to even say the name, but there it was—looming ahead of us. The walls were aging but sturdy, bleached by sun and crusted by the salt in the air. Here and there, fresh stone patched over old breaks. Tall Doric columns flanked the western gates, simple but imposing.

I leaned forward in the saddle, squinting up at the inscription carved above the arch. "'Towards freedom,'" I translated aloud, before I could stop myself.

Eirik made a sound of surprise, turning in his saddle. "You can read their tongue now?"

I felt my face warm. "Bits and pieces," I muttered, still studying the words. "I studied ancient Greek, remember? So I picked up some of the writing... but this feels different." I glanced at him. "Lately, I'm understanding more and more, almost without thinking."

He didn't reply immediately, but there was a contemplative look on his face. "Maybe a gift from whatever force brought you here. To help you survive?"

I shrugged, looking back at the city.

The air smelled like sea salt, smoke, and all the usual scents of a crowded city. *Ugh, I sure do miss proper sanitation...* The sound of distant music drifted through the walls—soft but melodic. From here, I could see the spires of the temples peeking over the rooftops, and farther off, the homes of the wealthier class perched on a small mountain. It was all beautiful and intimidating.

I turned to Eirik. "Will we leave the horses here? I think it'd be easier to blend in... maybe."

He swung his leg over and hopped off, answering my question without a word. "Yes, but I do believe you're forgetting something?" he mused.

I frowned, then realization dawned. I glanced over my shoulder, catching the shimmer of Runar's white fur where he waited just inside the tree line. He hadn't moved—just sat there, calm, enormous and *extremely* conspicuous.

Damn it, I thought, before looking down at Eirik.

"How exactly am I supposed to walk through a crowded city with a wolf the size of a warhorse?"

Eirik snorted. "You asking me? You're the one whose power surge brought him here."

"That's not helping, Eirik," I muttered, glancing between the two of them. "Do you think they'll panic?"

"Wouldn't you?"

I sighed in defeat. "...Yes."

"Then yes, they'll panic." He shrugged.

"But... this might be normal for them? I mean, gods and goddesses walk around here." I tried.

Eirik just shook his head, not offering an answer.

I muttered under my breath, then looked back at the gate. I didn't want to leave Runar behind, but I also didn't want to give half the city a heart attack or announce that outsiders were here.

"I'll talk to him," I said finally, sliding off my horse and wincing as my legs protested.

"Good luck," Eirik said, clearly amused by the situation.

"Yeah, yeah," I grumbled, tugging my cloak tighter as the wind shifted. The trees rustled as I neared the tree line, where Runar sat—silent and brooding.

"You know you're going to scare the hell out of every citizen, right?" I called softly, nerves bubbling to the surface.

His ears twitched, but he didn't move—nor did he speak, not yet.

I slowed as I approached, glancing back toward the city gates. "You're not exactly inconspicuous," I added, waving my hands in a sweeping gesture to emphasize his size.

"I am aware," he rumbled, voice deep and composed. "I was not made to blend in."

"Yeah, no kidding," I muttered, planting my hands on my hips. "You look like you walked straight out of an ancient tale."

"I did."

"...Okay, fair." I hung my head, trying to figure out what to say next.

He tilted his head, gold eyes narrowing just a little. "You do not wish to leave me behind."

"No. I don't." I exhaled. "But I also don't want to cause mass hysteria and get us thrown in a dungeon before dinner."

He was quiet for a moment. Then his voice came again. "I can shift."

I blinked. "You can do what?"

"I can take on a smaller form. It is not my preference, but I understand... discretion."

Before I could say anything, the air around him shimmered and the temperature dropped. His body compressed inward, fur rippling, bones shifting in a way that wasn't painful—but definitely wasn't natural. When it stopped, he stood just under knee-high. Still brooding, still Runar—just compact. Like a pup. A slightly grumpy, yet proud pup.

I stared at him. "You've been able to do that this whole time?" I nearly shouted.

He let out a breath—definitely a sigh. "You did not ask." If he could have shrugged, I was sure he would have.

I groaned, rubbing a hand over my face.

Behind me, Eirik snorted as he walked over, reins in hand. "Gods above, he's smug even when he's small," he smirked.

Runar flicked his tail and padded past us like royalty. I stared down at him, still half in shock, my eyes tracking his every step.

"I swear, if Agnar or some other crazy god doesn't kill me first, *you two* will be the death of me," I muttered, tossing my hands up.

Eirik, clearly enjoying every second, guided both our horses forward, grinning as he passed me. "We'll stable the horses, grab what gear we can, and move on. I think we're on foot from here."

I didn't answer. I was too busy trying to act normal when my giant death-wolf had just turned into something I kind of wanted to scoop up and carry around like a spoiled pet.

I followed silently behind them back to the main gate, our presence definitely noted by the soldiers who cast us side-eyes as we entered. I sucked in a breath—the city was amazing. Houses lined the walls, and even this poorer part of the city was intriguing to look at.

Eirik stopped at a stable near the exit, and the poor stable boy looked like he'd never seen a man like Eirik before—and honestly, maybe he hadn't. He was gawking, mouth slightly open, hands frozen halfway through taking the reins.

Eirik handed over the coin without a word, his gaze already flicking to the streets beyond. I gave the boy a polite but awkward nod, trying not to make it worse, but I caught the way his eyes jumped between us. *Yeah, we were the outsiders here.*

Behind me, Runar sat like a statue, in his smaller form, which didn't stop him from looking like he belonged to some ancient being out of legend.

A pair of women walking past the stable slowed down—way down—as their eyes locked on Eirik. One of them didn't even try to be subtle. I swear she bit her lip.

Runar gave a low huff. "Even here, the wiles of certain women persist."

I glanced sideways. "Seriously?" Then I looked again. *Oh... seriously.*

They were full-on staring now and one even giggled.

My eye twitched. "Huh. I see now—but why?"

"You can pretend to be blind, young one," he muttered, "but your earlier reactions to him speak otherwise."

My face went hot. "I have no idea what you're talking about," I said quickly, arms crossing on instinct.

Runar didn't bother to respond, just kept watching the crowd like this was his entertainment for the day.

My thoughts started to spiral. I pretended not to notice Runar's words, but of course, my eyes betrayed me, trailing over Eirik's form before I could stop myself. I flushed as I caught the subtle flex of his muscles, visible even from across the stable yard.

Stupid men and their ability to be handsome.

He was annoyingly good-looking, which—naturally, made my brain malfunction. But as always, the moment that thought formed, the familiar discomfort returned. Like he wasn't mine to admire.

Before I could think up a good retort, Eirik had walked back to us. "I asked the boy where we could find a place to eat and rest. He said to follow the main path to the markets—we'll find what we need there."

"That's good, right?" I asked, tying for optimism.

Eirik nodded, glancing at the streets. "He said the inns and taverns are clustered just below the markets. But he warned us to steer clear of the alleys by the docks—unless we're looking for trouble."

"Oh, we definitely radiate 'not from here,' don't we?" I muttered, pulling my cloak tighter.

"We do," Eirik said simply, already starting down the street. "But sometimes the best way to blend in is just to keep moving."

I fell into step behind him, Runar padding at my side. The streets widened as the houses gradually shifted to better quality—aged stone and clay walls, thick wooden beams for the roofs, and climbing vines hanging off balconies. Families lounged outside while the older adults stoked evening fires, the temperature already starting to drop. It was surprising to see so much life after dark. I'd expected the shops to close up early, but the sounds of the Lower and Middle City buzzed around us—vendors shouting, children darting between carts, and wheels creaking over uneven stones.

We reached the market square, and the aromas of spices and unfamiliar food set my stomach to rumbling. I shifted closer to Eirik as the crowd thickened. Our arms nearly touched before I jumped at the feeling of his hand resting on my lower back.

"I've got you. Just stay close—we don't know who might be hiding in these crowds," he murmured near my ear.

My brain short-circuited, flashing back to Runar's teasing. Heat crept up my neck—*gods help me.* All I could do was nod, hyper aware of his hand. Runar padded alongside, and I swear he was smirking.

I forced myself to focus, keeping my eyes moving as we wove through the rush of people and vendor stalls. Near the far side, I spotted a stand that looked promising and tapped Eirik lightly. "That one—it looks like they have parchment. Maybe we can find a map?"

He nodded, guiding me in that direction. "Sharp eye," he commented, navigating us through the press of the crowd.

Many vendors tried to catch our attention, calling out as they displayed their wares. Some gave us wary glances, and I didn't show it, but something about this place unsettled me—as if something dark was slithering through the city. Neither Eirik nor Runar seemed to sense it the way I did, and that alone left fear curling in my stomach.

The stall we stopped at was plain, with parchment stacked neatly and scrolls and papyrus strewn about. The vendor gave a slight bow, his gaze nervous as he took in our weapons—and the obviously not-ordinary wolf at my side.

"Welcome, travelers. What can I do for you this evening?" he asked, speaking mainly to Eirik and barely glancing my way. *Right. I keep forgetting women here are lower on the societal ladder...*

"Heill, we're seeking a map of the city. And maybe one of the greater regions?" Eirik's accent coming through strong.

The man's brows furrowed. "You're not from here, are you? I haven't heard that accent since I was a boy, sailing with my pater." I blinked at him in surprise as Eirik gave a short nod.

"You're right, but our origins aren't your concern," Eirik replied, bluntly but—shockingly— polite. "We're searching for something important, and don't know these lands well enough.

The man nodded and ducked away to fetch two scrolls, returning after a moment. "Here—a map of Korinthos, and another that covers as far as Sparta." He hesitated, finally meeting my eyes as well. "You must be careful. Outsiders are watched more closely here—and the Gods watch also."

"That is what we're hoping for. Do you have any information if Hermes wanders around this city much?" Eirik asked.

The man blinked, rubbing his hands together. "You seek counsel with Hermes—the messenger God?" He shook his head. "He doesn't frequent here as much as he does Athenae. War between Sparta and the Athenians has caused most of the gods to return to their realms."

My shoulders sagged at his words. That meant Hermes could be in Athenae, or worse, Olympus—where no mortal would dare step foot. Lydia had told me stories of smug humans who thought they could enter without permission. Those humans had a one-way ticket to Tartarus.

I let my head fall back and sighed quietly. The sun had dropped lower, night settling in as fires and lanterns flickered to life all around us.

"This is great," I mumbled, mostly to myself—but both men caught it. The vendor did a double take, his face draining of color.

He quickly bowed his head, voice trembling. "I apologize," he stammered. "I wasn't aware a goddess stood in my presence. Please forgive me."

We all blinked. Slowly.

"How?" I asked, stepping back a little, my voice lowering with unease.

"The air around you... it's heavy," the man said, his tone careful. "I may be old, but I remember what it feels like to stand near something divine. Your presence—it feels like the air wavers around you." He glanced at Runar, still calmly sitting at my side. "And the wolf... no wild animal would stay so still unless it knew who it served."

I settled back, Eirik's hand still hovered near but no longer touching. Runar narrowed his eyes at the man and bared his teeth slightly.

"You seem to have had more encounters with gods and goddesses than most," Eirik said curiosity etched across his face.

The man nodded, eyes still lowered. "Yes. My mater worked for an oracle who served at the Temple of Dionysus when I was just a boy. That god's aura alone made the air ripple."

He paused before glancing up at me briefly. "Yours is lighter. A faint outline... but it's there."

He motioned toward the maps. "Please, take them. A gift for your journey." He handed them to Eirik nervously.

I felt bad, noticing his hands trembled slightly. *His experience with past Gods must not have been fun.*

"I must warn you—stay away from the docks," he added, voice low. "The people there... their obsession with the divine has caused trouble in this city before."

I stood there trying to process everything he said, my thoughts lingered to the god Dionysus. If I thought Hecate's presence was powerful, would he be on the same level? And now cultists that worship divine beings to the point people avoid being near them.

"Cultists?" I questioned, and he gave a slight nod, warily glancing around as if the very streets could send whispers.

"Yes, milady. You'll find many worshippers... but not all worship is pure. Their obsession turns to madness, and madness to blood." If possible, he lowered his voice further. "The ones by the docks—they don't just pray to the gods. They try to call them, to bind their souls to them in the name of reverence. There have been talks lately of The Mormo wandering, but no one has seen her, she commands hooded beings that travel in shadows. Not something you want to encounter."

My stomach tightened. Of course, it couldn't just be wine and music in the lower seaside districts. "That's wonderful," I muttered.

Eirik pocketed the maps, giving the man a curt nod. "We'll keep that in mind. Thank you."

The vendor bowed again, quick and low. "Safe travels, may the gods protect you."

We stepped away from the stall, weaving back into the crowd. Runar kept close to my side, his fur brushing my cloak.

"So," I said quietly, still digesting what we'd just heard, "remind me again why we're going to a tavern after a warning like that?"

Eirik didn't break stride. "Because I'm starving, and danger or not, I need something warm and strong before I let myself worry about crazy cultists."

"Okay, but shouldn't we find somewhere different?" The anxious feeling returned.

Eirik turned his face toward me before smirking "Why? Are you already scared, Lady Ravena" he drawled, and my eye twitched. I hated when he called me 'Lady Ravena' because I knew he was mocking me—if only playfully.

"No! I just take people's warnings to heart; it keeps you from getting killed, you know." I huffed.

Runar gave a faint grunt, his tail swishing to hit my leg. "Food first. Doom later, little one."

I let out a long sigh, letting my shoulders sag as I followed them. *They sure do have faith that I'll be able to fight without panicking.*

The scent of roasting meat and spiced wine thickened as we descended the sloping path toward what locals called thed drinking district—though "tavern" felt too generous for what we were seeing. Clay buildings clustered tightly together, low and worn by traffic. Most had open courtyards behind stone archways, where groups of people gathered on benches or floor cushions around low wooden tables. Terracotta lamps flickered in the dark, casting uneven light across the faces of drunk men and women. Laughter spilled into the streets, followed by sharp arguments and the occasional smashing of pottery.

This place was loud, messy and very much alive. It reminded me of my college days, watching my old peers party all night and somehow manage to pass exams.

"This place reeks of indulgence," Runar muttered, his golden eyes sweeping the surroundings.

"Indeed," Eirik agreed, taking it all in. "And danger."

I rolled my eyes. "Told you, but nope—no one listens to the woman with anxiety about walking straight into danger."

A few of the courtyards looked almost ritualistic—bronze masks hanging on walls, grapes strung up like offerings, a few drunkards toasting to gods they likely didn't understand. This part of the city worshiped chaos in its own way. And something told me Dionysus would be right at home here.

Ahead, a narrower stone arch caught my eye—less crowded but not entirely abandoned. The sound of a flute drifted from within, soft and melodic. A carved olive branch marked the entrance. It was simple but decorative in its own way.

"That one?" I asked, pointing toward the least intimidating of our options.

Eirik glanced at it. "Good as any."

We stepped through the arch into the small courtyard at the kapeleion. A few patrons sat hunched over an amphora of wine, their voices low. Clay lanterns hung from thin ropes overhead, giving everything a subdued light. No formal hearth—just a fire pit in the corner, smoke curling into the open sky above. We chose a spot near the back wall, sitting on cushions at a chipped table. Runar curled at my side in a way that ensure no one would bother me.

A woman approached—a server or owner, maybe—her expression wary but polite. "Evening. Bread, lamb, and watered wine?" she offered. I noticed her eyes drifted to Runar and Eirik mainly before shyly glancing at me.

Eirik gave a small nod. "That'll do."

She bowed, her attention back on Eirik. "Of course, I will return shortly." With those words, she scurried off, leaving us to our own silence. Eirik, though alert, had relaxed slightly, leaning back against the wall. I sat tense, my hand running through Runar's soft fur.

"Relax, you act as if a kraken will appear and swallow you whole," Eirik jested, but his brows were furrowed in concern.

I scowled. "I don't enjoy places like this, okay? In my realm, past experiences with drunken men and women were not great. I highly doubt here is any better..."

Eirik crossed his arms, a curious expression on his face "Do you believe I'd honestly let anything happen to you? Any man or woman would be foolish to approach us."

I flushed at his words. "Well, no... I've just lived most of my life looking out for myself." Shrugging awkwardly, I let my gaze drift along the patrons.

"I–uh..." clearing my throat nervously, "I haven't had the best luck with people, so I prefer to stick to myself..." I muttered.

The lady returned with a big tray of water, wine, and food. I sighed internally with relief at the interruption.

As she began setting everything down, I caught Eirik's eyes—his gaze hadn't left mine, even as the woman moved around us. It was a look that made my heart flutter... but also left me with a feeling of wistfulness. I swallowed and looked away, my thoughts swirling with an ache I couldn't describe.

For a long time, I'd dreamt of someone looking at me the way he was... as if I actually mattered. As if my well-being mattered.

Back in my realm, people treated my kindness and anxieties like something to step on, never really hearing me—only themselves. It made for a lonely life, which is why, when I graduated college, I took a traveling job to Norway to study ancient times. Far from home, and far from the people who never cared.

A gentle nudge broke me from my thoughts. I looked down to see Runar watching me in quiet question. I gave him a tight smile. "I'm alright... sorry, I spaced out for a second," I whispered. He nodded, inclining his head slightly toward the food the woman had left. Only then did I realize I'd been lost in my head longer than I thought. My ears burned with embarrassment.

I picked up the skyphos, a simple cup for everyday use in this time. The clay was smooth and cool against my fingers; its edges worn from years of hands. I drank slowly, letting the cold water slide down my throat. It tasted faintly of earth, but it was clean and refreshing. Across from me, Eirik raised an eyebrow. He'd opted for wine, of course. It was the kind you carefully mixed in a krater—but he just poured it straight from the oinochoe, unmixed and bold, as if he were daring it to knock him over.

"You know you're supposed to add water to that," I said, setting my cup down gently and raising an eyebrow at him.

He lifted it in salute, the looped handles framing his calloused fingers. "What's the point in drinking if it doesn't set your chest on fire?"

Runar gave a low huff beside me—either disapproving or amused, I couldn't quite tell.

I glanced between the two of them. "Pretty sure drinking wine like that is considered barbaric here."

Eirik smirked, taking a slow, deliberate sip. "Good thing I'm not Greek."

I shook my head, biting back a smile. Somehow, he always had a way of lightening the atmosphere with his subtle humor.

The rest of our meal had been uneventful. I watched as people left and the darkness of the night had settled over us. I could feel the temperature dropping outside, my skin tingling—as if my body was *relishing* in the colder air, amplifying my abilities.

"I suppose we should find somewhere to rest, right?" I asked, glancing around before looking at Eirik.

Surprisingly, he wasn't even drunk despite all the wine.

"Aye," he said, standing. "There should be some... *pandokeions...*" He tried the word carefully, his brow pinching in slight concentration. "They're marked on the map. We'll head to one near the middle district."

I snorted. "It's *pan-do-kay-on*," I said, sounding it out slowly for him. "It's basically their version of a longhouse or mead hall—meant to welcome anyone who needs it."

Eirik tilted his head, thoughtful. "Interesting. You surprise me every day with your knowledge." He stood fully, stretching with a quiet grunt, and I followed after, brushing my fingers over Runar's fur as we started for the door.

We wove our way through the narrow, stone-paved roads. In many places, holes stood out—puddled with water, and worn grooves marred the terrain from years of carts rolling through. There were still a fair number of people out, so we stuck close together. I could faintly hear Runar grumbling about humans coming near him. I kept my eyes alert, even as some gave us weird looks… which, honestly, were mostly directed at Eirik; his clothes were far different than anything here.

We passed the street that led down in the direction of the docks, and I side-eyed it, shivering. There was an unsettling feeling—like a hum of dark magic bleeding from the area. I could hear faint whispers of people huddled together, voices low as they talked about shadowed creatures roaming about.

Just like the old shopkeeper had said. My thoughts flashed back to what the nymphs had told me: about the Nychtari…could these be the creatures everyone was whispering about?

"Make haste, Ravena. We don't want to linger," Eirik urged, his tone tense.

I sped up to match his pace. "Do you think these shadow stalkers are searching for their next place to attack, or are they playing games with us?" I asked quietly.

"I am unsure, but my instinct tells me we should watch our behinds. It is no coincidence we've heard of them more than once," he said, glancing down at the map before making a sharp right turn that nearly caused me to trip—and almost bump into Runar.

"This way, only a few more paces," he continued.

I immediately noticed the change in architecture. The roads were cleaner, and the people lingering here were dressed much nicer than the lower districts. The streets were free of holes and paved with large flat stones, a beautiful change to the stone and gravel of the lower streets. Small, narrow alleys with cobblestones peeked out from between houses.

I would have loved to stop and marvel at all this—I truly did. The beauty was unmatched by the ruins I studied back home. But I couldn't. Eirik made sure of that with his quick stride, and not a few minutes later, we stopped in front of a decent-sized pandokeion: its clay-tiled roof sloping low, the walls a mix of pale limestone and sunbaked mudbrick, barely cracked with age. A wooden sign hung above the entrance—barely legible in the low light—but the symbol of a krater was carved into its face. That marked it as a place for both rest and drinking.

It wasn't extravagant, but it was something for the night.

We made our way inside, the warmth hitting me immediately. The air was heavy with the scent of olive oil, smoke, and spices roasting. Firelight danced across the walls from the main hearth, casting shadows that moved with the people settled around the low wooden tables. Their conversations carried through the small space, I couldn't make out their words, but the hum of activity was almost calming. The floors, I noticed as we made our way to a worn counter, was stone—uneven in places, worn smooth by countless footsteps and wine spills. Conversations hushed slightly as some people noticed our presence, but no one stared for long. Travelers were common here, it seemed.

Runar's ears were flicking around listening and his nose raised as he sniffed the air with faint interest. I stayed close to Eirik, letting him take the lead.

At the counter stood an older gentleman, polishing worn cups with a rag. I was almost positive the cups were older than he was. His robes were simple but well-kept, dark curls streaked with gray beneath a worn head wrap. He glanced up as we stopped in front of him.

"Evening, travelers," he said, his voice gravely with age. "Looking for a room?"

Eirik gave a curt nod, "Aye, two if you have them?"

The man—the pandokeus, I reminded myself—clicked his tongue softly and shook his head. "Afraid not. Busy week with grain merchant ships arriving at the port. I've only one left upstairs. It's small, but has two beds." he offered.

I felt Eirik turn to look at me, and I blushed. "I don't mind," I said quickly, waving it off before it could get awkward. "We're not exactly in a position to be picky."

The owner grunted, then gestured toward the stairs. "Second floor. Last door on the right."

"Thank you," Eirik nodded, and we made our way upstairs.

The stairs groaned in protest with every step, and the owner side-eyed Runar as we passed. I sighed, laid a hand on his head, and—much to his visible displeasure—quickly scooped him up.

"I am not a pup you carry around, little frostling," he grumbled, his voice low and gravelly.

"Yeah, well, for now just deal with it," I whispered back. "You're getting weird looks."

"I'm a wolf... following you two around. Of course people will stare," he deadpanned.

I rolled my eyes, hugging him a bit closer before we made it to the top landing. Honestly, I was just glad he let me get away with it without losing a finger.

Chapter Twenty-One

I jostled awake, my heart pounding, pins and needles prickling my fingertips. The room was still dim—early morning light filtering through cracks in the shutters. I sat up slowly and rubbed a hand down my face. Whatever I'd been dreaming about, it was gone now. No matter how hard I tried to reach for it, it slipped away, leaving only a bitter taste in my mouth.

Runar was still curled up at my feet, his tail twitching now and then. My gaze swept the room—and I froze.

Eirik was already up, sitting on the edge of his bed with his axe across his lap. He was running a whetstone along the blade with rhythmic precision, only glancing up once to meet my eyes.

"You talk in your sleep," he said casually.

I went pale. *Oh gods.*

"Don't worry," he added after a beat, voice quieter now. "Couldn't make out most of it. But you sounded... afraid. Not like yourself." He kept sharpening, his movements never changing.

I stared at him, completely at a loss. What was I even supposed to say to that? It was so damn embarrassing, I picked at my fingers absently. "I can't remember what it was—just that it was cold, and I could hear roars from far away," I mumbled.

Runar's ears flicked. He lifted his head, giving me a thoughtful look before hopping off the bed with a grunt.

"What?" I asked, my stomach knotting as he stretched.

Runar's tail flicked as he considered. "I am uncertain just yet, young one. But it seems an old memory of Skadi's has surfaced"

"A memory? Of what?" I was only slightly weirded out—mostly because it was Runar telling me, not Skadi herself. I pressed a hand to my chest, feeling her absence more than ever.

He watched me for a long moment, settling himself by the door, eyes fixed on mine. "From the place we called home. Where I traveled from once your magic surged." His gaze stayed on mine, but it was distant—like he was caught on a memory he clearly wasn't eager to share.

Eirik lets out a grunt. "Care to share the name of this place, wolf? Or shall we be guessing?" He asked sarcastically, a shrill shriek sounding from the whetstone as it slid up the axe one last time.

Runar cut his eyes to Eirik before grunting, "It is a matter for another time." His voice rough, his posture defensive—it was obvious he wanted to avoid the subject.

"But if it's important, shouldn't we know about it now?" I asked.

He turned to me again. "No, it can be discussed another time. When you're ready," he said, adamantly. Deep in those golden eyes, I saw something I hadn't expected—worry. Not for me, but for Skadi. It was like he looked past me for a heartbeat, as if searching for someone else.

I swallowed the lump rising in my throat and forced myself out of the bed. My fingers trembled slightly as I fastened the cloak at my neck, leaving the hood down. I didn't dare meet either of their eyes.

"I'm going to look for breakfast... maybe a bath. Alone," I muttered. The door clicked louder than I intended when I shut it behind me.

Thankfully, the hallway was empty. Cold air nipped at my cheeks, and I realized I'd left a thin sheen of frost on the door handle. I clenched my fist open and closed, willing the sensation away.

My heart clenched as that familiar pit hollowed in my stomach again—a loneliness that didn't just sting, but left a cold, sharp ache in my chest. It was the kind of feeling that comes from being useful, but never truly wanted.

I was tired of being someone people looked at for what I could become, or as a reflection from the past, but never for who I was right now. Was that all I ever was? A vessel? Just a second-best shadow of someone Runar actually cared about?

I groaned, shaking my hands out, blinking quickly to clear the sting from my eyes. I forced my legs to keep moving toward the stairs, gripping the wooden railing a bit too tightly as I started down the narrow steps. Frost crept beneath my touch—thin streaks of ice tracing the edge of the railing as my fingers slid over it. I yanked my hand back with a sharp inhale.

Great. Just what I needed—another reminder that I didn't have a handle on anything.

The main floor was quiet. A few attendants moved around absently, carrying fresh linens or sweeping out last night's soot from the hearth. I ignored their curious glances and made my way to the front desk, where the same old man from yesterday sat thumbing through a weathered scroll.

He looked up as I approached, eyes narrowing slightly before his tone softened. "Looking a bit lost this morning, miss."

"Just hungry," I replied, my voice flat. I immediately cringed—hating the way it sounded. I hated being unkind or even seeming that way. "I apologize... Is there a balaneion nearby?"

He nodded, gesturing lazily toward the front doors. "Down two streets, past the olive vendor. You'll smell lavender and steam before you see it. Tell them Leo sent you—they'll treat you decent." A small, understanding smile ghosted over his lips.

I gave a polite nod. "Thanks."

Without waiting for more conversation, I slipped out into the morning crispness. The wind stung my cheeks, but I welcomed it—it kept the heat of frustration in check. Maybe a bath, then some food would help. Maybe it would make me feel normal, if only for a little while.

Because right now... I felt like nothing. Not a demi-goddess. Not a warrior. Just a woman who everyone was keeping something from.

The scent of lavender hit me before I even saw the door, just like the old man said. Steam curled out from the cracks of an arched stone entryway, where ivy climbed lazily up the outer walls. A beautifully carved wooden sign swung overhead, creaking softly in the morning breeze. I stepped through hesitantly, my boots echoing on the uneven stone floors as the warmth of the baths enveloped me.

I looked around in muted awe. The inside of the bathhouse was quiet, relaxed, and filled with warm mist drifting from the bathing areas. Different oils mingled with the lavender scent, creating a layered, soothing scent. I glanced to my right, studying the bathing pools that peeked through gaps in the wooden dividers—each one cut from stone, surprisingly clean. I could hear a few women whispering, their laughter low and unbothered in this space.

A woman near the entrance looked up from a table where she was stacking towels. Her eyes were sharp, but there was a softness in them. "Morning," she said. "You seem new here." It wasn't a question so much as a statement.

I gave a light nod "Uh—Leo sent me," I said, fidgeting with the sleeve of my cloak. "Said you'd treat me decent."

That earned a grin. "Ah, Leo. He can't help himself—especially around a pretty lady. Thinks it'll help him win favors with the gods." She waved a hand toward a far corner, away from where the women were giggling. "You'll have privacy back there. It's a quieter corner and private. Soaps, oils, whatever you need are in the baskets. There's a bench for your clothes and, uh... gear." She trailed off, only now noticing the weapon at my side.

I gave a small bow. "Thank you," I said quietly.

She nodded, still eyeing my sword, but turned away as other patrons called for her attention.

I followed the direction she'd pointed out, slipping behind a divider into a room where a small pool of hot water waited. The space was simple—a stone bath filled with lavender-scented water, petals floating on top.

The walls were decently tall, with small rectangular openings for ventilation, covered in latticework to keep the area private. It was serene. I wasted no time undressing, setting my things where she'd instructed, but kept my sword close, within reach.

The moment I lowered myself into the deep pool, a shaky breath left my lips.

The heat curled around my body, and I felt myself finally relax. It was a strange sensation—ever since I'd awakened these abilities, my body was always cold, but not so much that it bothered me. But the chance for a hot bath was always a welcome relief. I sank deeper until the water covered my shoulders, letting my head rest against the smooth stone edge. My muscles ached; my thoughts were louder than ever. The voice in my head wasn't Skadi's this time. It was my own.

You're not her. You're just a placeholder. A shell to be filled, just a shadow of someone who was once stronger.

The worst part? I didn't even know if those darker thoughts were wrong. And Skadi's voice was nowhere to be found to tell me otherwise.

⁘ ⁙

The wind hit my face the moment I stepped outside crisp and biting, but not unbearable. The lingering heat from the bath clung to my skin like a fading memory, quickly chased off by the morning air. The sky was clear, the low sun peeked over the rooftops, casting long shadows through the winding streets. Somewhere nearby, the scent of fresh bread and citrus drifted on the air, but I wasn't hungry. Not yet.

I needed to walk. To figure things out without leaning on anyone else. I could do this—I just needed to try. Maybe I could even find a clue about Hermes, see if he had knowledge of what was happening. I sighed, tugging a strand of damp hair out of my face as the wind picked up.

I wandered with no real direction (Eirik still had the map), my boots crunching on the iced over stones. People were beginning their work for the day—merchants lifting stall covers, older women sweeping doorsteps, a child chasing a stray chicken through the street.

A small temple sat tucked at the edge of the road, its marble shining in the morning light. Deep green vines climbed its base, stubborn against the cold. I hadn't planned to stop, but something pulled me in. The inside looked quiet—a single oil lantern flickered just past the arched doorway, and soft murmurs floated out. The voices were gentle, layered, a low chant like distant music.

I stepped inside and felt the difference immediately. The energy here wasn't dark, but bright and open—almost inviting. Strange, how I could feel it now, even if it was just from ordinary people. They didn't know they had this kind of power—just by simply speaking prayers.

The air was warmer, thick with old smoke and dried herbs. Statues lined the walls. A single robed figure knelt in the center, her back to me. The moment I entered, her voice fell silent. The others—maybe two or three—looked up as well, pausing their prayers.

I hesitated, feeling nerves starting to coil in my stomach. I hadn't meant to disrupt anything.

She turned slowly. Her face was lined with age, but her eyes were sharp, pale like fog. She said nothing at first—just stared. I realized she might be blind, but somehow, I felt like she could see more than most.

"I'm not here to pray," I blurted, just to break the silence. *Way to be awkward Ravena.*

"No," she agreed softly. "You're not."

I shifted uncomfortably. "I'll just, uh... be on my way."

"You're looking for the one with winged feet." Her gaze held mine—knowing. "He doesn't stay in one place long. He's drawn to the higher places, where marble can meet the sky." She folded her arms, turning back to kneel before the altar. "He is rarely here in Korinthos. Only when new stories are brought in on the sails of the ships."

"What's that supposed to mean?" I asked, already regretting it. Even in my studies, I hated riddles. Could I solve them? Yes. Did I want to? Absolutely not.

But the woman only smiled faintly, as if that was all I'd get. Her attention returned back to the statue, and her gentle voice resumed its prayer.

I let out a sharp breath through my nose and turned to leave, brushing past the faded fabric hanging over the doorway. "Thanks for the riddle, I guess."

The chill bit deeper the moment I stepped outside. Not just cold; edged, like the air itself was watching me. I'd barely made it a few paces down the street before the hairs on my arms to stood up. Someone was following me. Watching. Not just with idle curiosity, but with that skin-prickling, silent focus—the kind that makes you certain there are eyes in the shadows.

I didn't turn around. I kept walking, my boots scuffing the stones as I pushed further into the city. I wasn't going back to the inn. Not just because I was stubborn—though, gods, I was. But because going back meant retreating. Hiding. And I wasn't that woman anymore, or at least, I was trying not to be.

I didn't need protection—I needed answers.

So I kept moving.

The sun had climbed higher, casting a warmer hue on the marble streets, but the feeling never left. Whoever followed me was patient. I tried to look like any traveler—stopping at stalls, asking questions, pretending I was just another visitor with nothing to hide.

By late morning, I found myself at an incense stall near a weathered statue of Hermes. The man tending laughed at my question about the god, shaking his head. "No one important visits the Lower District anymore, not even the gods. Try the marble spires," he said, smirking. "That's where the rich pretend they're closer to Olympus."

So I did.

I wound my way up the sloping streets, past buildings that grew cleaner and brighter the higher I climbed. The grit of the docks faded, replaced by sunlight on painted shutters and crisp linens flapping from balconies. The people up here gave me different looks—measured, suspicious, like I was a stray dog out of place. Still, I kept asking: old men hunched over tile games, a woman sweeping beside a shrine, and a young girl perched at a fountain.

"Have you ever seen the god with winged feet?" I asked a man half-asleep under an olive tree. He just waved me off with a lazy grunt.

I sighed, rubbing my arms as the wind picked up again.

The further I wandered into the upper district, the clearer it became—no one had seen Hermes lately. Some shared rumors, some said he only visited where excitement thrived, where stories sparked. No one offered anything solid.

But they all stared a little too long at the sword on my back.

By noon, I'd reached the base of a massive marble stairway that overlooked the eastern side of the city. It led to a quiet garden plaza—temples scattered between sculpted trees, bare branches tangled above, the ground swept clean. Statues of the gods lined the perimeter. I approached one, my boots echoing against the stone, searching for anyone who might finally give me more than another riddle.

An older woman feeding birds looked up as I stepped closer.

"Excuse me," I said. "I'm looking for someone—well, not *someone*. A god."

Her brow lifted. "Aren't we all?"

"Hermes," I clarified. "Has he ever appeared here?"

She paused, tossing a handful of seeds toward the pigeons. "Here? No. He doesn't linger. Not in places so polished. He prefers places with *movement*—stories on the wind." Her voice lowered. "And when he *does* appear... it's never when you expect him."

I frowned. "So what, I'm just supposed to wait around until he decides to drop in?"

The woman smiled softly, but said nothing more.

I stepped back and exhaled slowly, frustrated. All morning wasted chasing riddles.

Except... the presence behind me hadn't left.

I cut sharply down a narrow path near a stall stacked with jugs of wine, trying to throw off whatever was lingering behind me. I refused to look over my shoulder. I didn't want to give it the satisfaction of knowing they'd gotten in my head.

I hoped that by not stopping, by not changing my pace, I might lose whatever was following me—but they were like the very shadows themselves.

I was nearing the edge of the city now, where the stone roads gave way to dirt, where a low tree line hugged the outer eastern wall. There was a faint path ahead, probably used by travelers and supply carts, winding toward the woodlands outside the city.

I paused, just briefly, in the shadow of an old archway—my breath catching. It was quiet here. Too quiet. That was enough for me to not stop walking. I didn't run, either. I just kept a slightly faster pace, staying close to the backs of homes and the trees. My hand stayed firm on my sword's hilt, my grip tight enough that my knuckles were white.

The moment I felt the movement change—whatever this thing was—I drew my sword. It was close now, too close. The steel hissed as it left the sheath and I spun on instinct, slashing toward the presence. For once, my reaction surprised me. That glint of pride vanished as reality snapped back in.

A hiss split the air, low and inhuman.

Something flinched back—too fast to fully see. But before it could retreat, another shadow slammed into it from the side. The sound muted, almost ghostly. Both shapes twisted together, tangled in motion that didn't make sense—one lashing out, the other forcing it away. The shadows melted into the trees, gone as quickly as they'd come.

I stumbled, breath catching as a sudden sting cut across the top of my wrist—the one holding my sword. I looked down. A thin line of red welled just beneath my palm.

"Shit," I muttered, pressing the heel of my other hand against it. It wasn't deep, but it burned colder than it should have. Almost as cold as the magic that flowed through me.

Before I could think twice, a low growl sounded behind me.

I turned, startled, dropping my blade—only to find a pair of bright, familiar eyes glaring from the tree line. Runar.

He stalked forward, no longer in his smaller form. The air around him was tense, bristling with that ancient energy that always made the hairs on my arms stand up. His focus wasn't on me, but on where the shadows had vanished.

"How did you find—" I started, but the look he gave me shut me up.

Blood. He smelled my blood.

I barely had a second to process the look in Runar's eyes before the crunch of boots over branches and leaves slammed into my ears—fast, heavy, and oh so furious.

"Ravena!"

Eirik's voice tore through the trees, ragged and too loud in the quiet.

I turned just as he reached me, and in the next breath, I was pinned—his right arm slammed into the tree beside my head, his chest rising and falling as he boxed me in.

"What in Hel were you thinking?" he growled, his voice low and edged with restraint.

I froze under the intensity of his expression—wild, shaken. He wasn't just angry. He was scared. His eyes flicked down to the blood at my wrist, and his tone dropped, rougher now. "You left us. Didn't even tell us you were going out into the main city. Do you even realize what could've happened?"

"I can handle myself," I snapped, heart pounding. "I didn't need anyone holding my hand."

"Apparently, you did," he shot back, eyes hard. "You were followed by something that reeks of death! You think that happens to ordinary girls out for a morning walk?"

I flinched, mouth parting. He didn't stop.

"You're not just *you* anymore. Like it or not, that means you don't get to make reckless choices without consequence. You're—"

"No," I cut him off, voice rising. "Don't say it. Don't you dare act like I'm just someone else in a new skin."

He hesitated, but I was already going.

"I know what I am, Eirik. I know I'm the reincarnation of a goddess. I know the magic in my vein's draws attention—beings, people, all of it. But I am me. I'm not Skadi. I'm not some figure for you or Runar or anyone else to shape. I'm Ravena."

The words came out like they'd been clawing to be said for days. "I'm not just your mission." I turned, eyes finding Runar. "I'm not your memory of her, and I am not someone else's second chance at being at her side."

Eirik didn't say anything. His jaw worked, his breath still harsh, but he didn't move away.

I stepped out from beneath his arm, quickly—before my nerves could make an appearance. I didn't care that the cold wind had picked up harsher, or that the blood still beaded along my wrist. I walked over to my sword, picked it up, and sheathed it ignoring the sting of pain as I did.

"I didn't run off to be reckless," I said more quietly. "I needed to *breathe*. To feel like I wasn't just a walking prophecy—and to remind myself that I am my own person."

Runar padded up beside me, silent but close. There was something new in his eyes—regret, most of all. Eirik still hadn't moved, not even a step.

"You want to protect me?" I said, not coldly, just tired. "Then start by seeing *me*." With that, I started my way back toward the city, frost spiraling lightly from where my boots touched the soil and broken branches.

"Wait."

The word was quiet—barely above the wind—but I heard it.

I paused, my back still to him, but I waited.

Eirik stepped up behind me, his hand brushing mine gently as he reached for my wrist. I flinched but didn't pull away.

He pulled a strip of cloth from his belt and began wrapping the cut with steady fingers. No snark. No lecture. Just care.

"You should've said something," he muttered finally, voice lower now "I would've helped you figure it out... on your own terms."

I didn't answer. I couldn't, not yet. But I let him finish tying the knot.

The walk back toward the city was quiet. And tense as hell. Runar had shifted down into his smaller form, padding close like he wasn't sure where he stood with me. Occasionally, I'd catch Eirik watching me out of the corner of his eye, but he stayed quiet. Maybe even he knew not to push it.

The sun was at its highest now, peeking through the clouds—it cast a soft golden light across the upper district. People were more active now—merchants calling out their deals, children running through the narrow alleys with laughter trailing behind them.

Of course, that was the exact moment my stomach growled—loud enough for Eirik to raise an eyebrow. I rolled my eyes, heat creeping up my neck. "Don't start."

He just smirked and nodded toward a shaded corner where a small open-air vendor sat beside what looked like a community oven. Its awning was crooked but inviting. A few stools circled a clay oven, with the smell of fresh flatbread and roasted lamb drifting in the air.

We settled in quietly. The older man behind the stall eyed Runar skeptically until he tucked himself under the bench, curling into a white-furred lump. I nearly let a laugh slip, but the glare Runar shot me had me biting it back. The vendor shrugged and handed us warm food wrapped in thick leaves—roasted lamb and vegetables stuffed into soft flatbread.

I chewed slowly, the warmth helping settle my nerves.

"I did find something," I said after a minute. "A priestess in one of the temples. She mentioned... Hermes." I didn't bother explaining the whole cryptic riddle. It still annoyed me. "She said he only comes here when ships bring new stories. That he prefers... higher places. Somewhere with marble that meets the sky."

Eirik wiped his mouth with the back of his hand, brow furrowed. "That could be a lot of places."

The vendor—who had been quietly humming to himself—suddenly snorted. "You mean Athenae?"

I blinked. "What?"

"Marble and sky, eh? You're describing the Acropolis of Athenae, girl." He pointed vaguely east with his thumb. "If your god with winged shoes is listening for new stories, he's probably doing it from the top of Athena's hill."

I stared at him, then let out a sigh. "Of course." I felt oddly dumb. I should have known—if only it had been said normally and not riddles!

Eirik chuckled. "Don't look so offended. At least now we know where to go." He glanced east. "We'll need to secure a ride—preferably by ship. Our horses wouldn't make that trip."

I let out a low groan, catching both their attention. "I hate boats—ships, anything that floats really."

The vendor nodded sagely. "Then you're going to hate getting to Athenae. You'll need to head down to Isthmia—merchant ships leave for Athenae a few times a week. You'll want to go before the weather shifts again. Storms have been rolling up the coast."

"Perfect," I muttered, dragging a hand down my face. "Because why not? Poseidon having a bad day?"

Eirik clapped his hands together once. "Then it's settled. We restock, head for the docks by nightfall. Camp near the port if needed, then catch the next ship out."

Runar gave a small, half-hearted grunt from underneath the table.

I looked to the vendor "Any help on who to ask in Isthmia?"

He stoked the fire as the wind blew through, sending embers swirling away. "Ask for Dimitrios. If he's still at port, he'll leave first thing tomorrow afternoon." With that, he turned away to help other patrons.

I leaned back, finishing the last bite of bread. "Well. That's about as clear as it gets," I murmured, rubbing at my wrist. "I'm starting to think they all talk in riddles here."

Eirik's mouth twitched as he stood, brushing crumbs off his hands. "Then we head out before sunset. Get as close to the port as we can."

I gave him a long look. "No lectures this time?"

He shrugged. "Figured I'd let you stew in your own brilliance a bit longer. Marble touching the sky, hm?"

I groaned under my breath. "Alright, alright. You made your point. Besides, you weren't any brighter."

Runar huffed, clearly agreeing with him—the traitor.

I stood, brushing my cloak straight as Runar hopped to his feet with a shake of his fur. "Let's just find somewhere to grab a few supplies," I muttered, "and maybe something for seasickness." I was already dreading the next day. *Why couldn't we just stay on land?*

Eirik laughed. "Already planning to be miserable, are we?" He made his way to stand by my side as we started putting our plan into motion.

I shot him a look. "I'm planning to not lose every meal I've eaten since being here."

❧⸙❧

We gathered what we needed quickly—dried fruit, water skins, travel bread, a few new bandages. I slipped an herbal vial into my satchel—something for nausea the vendor claimed sailors swore by. I wasn't convinced, but I wasn't about to argue.

The stable hand had already prepped our horses by the time we returned. Eirik tossed him a few coins with a nod, then helped hoist our packs up onto the saddles. I mounted up quickly, and for once, with surprising grace. Then we headed off.

The sun began to dip lower, brushing the tops of the buildings in gold as we rode out of Korinthos through the east gate. The road toward Isthmia curved along the cliffs before winding through open stretch of wilderness. A colder wind picked up as we rode, but it wasn't horrible—just sharp enough to remind me we weren't far from the sea and that winter was still very present.

We made camp just before full dark, tucked up on a ridge overlooking the valley below. In the far distance, barely visible through the haze and the gathering snow, Athenae rose. Its marble glinted faintly in the dying light, just enough to make out the ridges of temples and columns reaching toward the sky.

I stood at the edge of the overlook for a long moment, arms crossed, my breath misting in the air. Eirik and Runar, sat around a small fire they had going. The horses grazed a short distance away, unfazed by the dropping temperatures.

I sat down carefully at the edge of the overlook, brushing aside a few bent winter blooms to make room. I yanked my cloak closer—not for warmth, but for a sense of security. The flowers here had no business still being alive—thin-stemmed, pale blue things peeking through snow-covered grass. But they were. Stubborn, quiet, still reaching for the fading light.

The wind stirred again, colder now that the sun had dropped behind the hills. It tugged at the edge of my cloak, curled around my fingers, and moved through the flowers beside me. They swayed—not just from the breeze, but like something unseen was moving through them with intent. Gentle. Curious. Almost respectful.

A few petals loosened and lifted, carried off on the wind without resistance. The rest stilled slowly, as if the moment had passed.

I stayed quiet, my gaze fixed on the ocean below, but my mind was somewhere else entirely.

Golden Vines

High on a cliffside that hung over the ocean, the temple remained hidden from the world below—untouched by unwanted visitors. Only those meant to find it ever did.

The temple pulsed with music—soft drums, layered flutes, the hum of voices caught between laughter and song. Wine poured freely. Silk danced across polished marble. A fire roared in the open hearth, its heat casting flickers across the floor and up the columns. Outside, the pool rippled beneath a breeze, its surface disturbed by the slow, steady fall of snow. The flakes didn't stick to the stone—only to the high arches and tiled roofs, where the cold seemed to only linger.

The music drifted through the air, slow and hypnotic. Bodies moved with it—some clothed in silks that barely clung to skin, others bare beneath painted gold and strands of ivy. Maenads spun barefoot across the marble, laughing softly, lost in whatever trance held them—if it was even a trance at all. They danced in circles and swayed between pillars, skin glowing in the firelight. None of them noticed the snow. None of them noticed the difference in the breeze.

But he did.

He sat at the edge of it all—reclined, relaxed, a figure half-wrapped in golden light and ivy-draped columns that rose behind him. Deep crimson robes hung loose over his frame, stitched with gold thread that caught the fires light as it shifted. The front of his robe remained open, exposing the line of his chest and the carved shape of someone too perfect to be mortal. His head tilted back slightly, as if lost in the sound. One hand rested beneath his chin, unmoving. The other hung over the side of the chair, fingers relaxed, a single vine curling lazily around his wrist, dancing to the low music.

The spirits arrived quietly, carried in by the wind. They fluttered through his hair, whispering in his ear as they circled. These most devoted spirits communicated only to him.

"A woman, beautiful. And she commands the cold," one whispered, lowly.

His eyes remained closed, but he listened.

"Chione?" he murmured, almost bored. While Chione was beautiful and could captivate many, she never caught his attention—and besides, she was very much attached to Hermes.

The spirits circled once more, a soft shift in the air around him, as if sighing.

"No," they whispered. "A woman, not of this realm. Not of our world's magic," the first voice sang airily.

One vine tightened gently around his wrist—the only subtle gesture that she had his attention.

"This girl carries hair darker than the soil... eyes such a dark blue, like they were carved from the very depths of a glacier... and freckles, scattered across her nose like the cosmos."

He breathed in, deeply, just once. Then, slowly, he opened his eyes. They burned molten gold, and they held an emotion he hadn't felt in quite some time—fascination.

The music played on. The dancers spun. But the god didn't look away, he inclined his head back to gaze at the falling snow.

"Show me."

Chapter Twenty-Three

There were many things I didn't like—or maybe it's better to say there were certain things I *hated* to face. People, public speaking, and most certainly this massive thing called a ship. It rocked noisily at the docks.

We had arrived shortly after sunrise and, thankfully, made quick work of asking around for Dimitrios. We found him in a merchant area, laughing loudly as he watched his crew haul wares for the day back to the ship. Eirik had barely needed to ask; most of the patrons just threw their thumbs toward the loud, dramatic man.

It was almost comical, the way my companions turned their heads and realized this was who we were looking for.

He was loud, way too chipper, and didn't exactly like to keep his hands to himself—much to Eirik's and Runar's discontent, which was obvious in the way Runar would growl low any time the man tried to get close to me on the way to the ship.

The dock groaned beneath the weight of crates, shouting men, and one very uneasy passenger.

I stood stiff at the edge of the ramp, arms crossed and shoulders set, as if a creature of the sea might hop out and drag me under at any moment. The ship rocked gently in the harbor, its wood dark and salt-worn. It wasn't the worst vessel in the port—but it wasn't exactly reassuring, either.

"I don't like this," I muttered.

Eirik, behind me, gave a low chuckle. "Aye, I gathered that from the ten minutes you've stood there scowling at it."

"I'm not scowling," I snapped, already feeling the ice form at my feet as if to anchor me to the docks.

"You are." Runar sneezed from somewhere near my feet, entirely unbothered. I could only glare, still adamant about not speaking to the white fur ball.

I exhaled through my nose, muttering something that would have made my mother blush, before taking one reluctant step forward. The ship shifted and I froze. *For fuck's sake.*

Eirik grinned, leaning his weight onto one leg like he had all the time in the world. "Should I carry you over the plank, Ravena?"

"I will throw you into the sea," I said—and I meant it.

The moment my foot touched the deck, I knew this was a mistake.

The ship lurched—not violently, but enough to make my stomach pitch, and I just knew breakfast would be coming to visit. I stopped mid-step, one hand flying out to grip the nearest rail, and I swore I felt my soul rise halfway to Olympus. *Why me? Why not some other poor human from my realm!*

"Gods, this is awful," I muttered, certain my face had to be paler than usual.

Eirik stepped up behind me, far too sure on his feet. "We've not even left the dock yet."

"Exactly," I snapped, clutching the rail tighter as the ship groaned and shifted. "If it's this bad now, what the hell is it going to feel like *out there?*" I gestured weakly toward the open seas.

Runar strutted past me like he owned the place, tail flicking. He jumped up onto a crate near the bow and promptly laid down like we weren't floating toward death.

The crew yelled something about pulling the lines, and a moment later, the ship jolted forward. I slammed my other hand on the railing, knuckles white. Then came the cold. A thin frost spread under my fingertips, trailing along the wooden rail before I yanked my hands back. *Dammit.* My breath hitched—I hadn't meant to do that.

Eirik noticed. He stepped closer, voice low so only I could hear. "You alright?"

"Fine," I muttered. "Just... hate ships. And movement. And the possibility of drowning."

His brow arched. "So just the entire thing, then."

"Yes." I curtly nodded, making my way to Runar.

He didn't laugh—credit to him—but I could see it in the corners of his mouth.

I turned to face the sea—and regretted it immediately. The horizon shifted. The wind picked up. And I had no idea where to put my focus without feeling like the world was tilting sideways. *Oh, good gods, this is going to be a long ride...* I heard a strangled noise—someone was definitely holding back a laugh.

"Don't say it," I warned, glaring over my shoulder at my guardian, who leaned calmly against a stack of crates.

"I wasn't," he mused.

"You were thinking about it."

"I was," he admitted.

I scowled and turned away, bracing myself against the nearest support beam as the ship picked up speed. Salt sprayed up from the bow, and the sails snapped above like thunderclaps. The farther we moved from the harbor, the more I regretted every single decision the Fates had made to bring me here.

The nausea crept in slow, cruel waves. I tried breathing through it—short, controlled inhales—but my stomach had other plans. At some point, I stopped responding to anything Eirik said and just glared weakly at the sea like I could convince it to stop moving.

By midmorning, I gave up pretending to be strong. I found a narrow stairwell leading below deck and all but collapsed on a pile of old fish-ing nets in the corner. The smell wasn't helping—salt, damp wood, and something that might've once been fish. At this point, I just didn't care. I reached into my belt pouch and pulled out the small vial the merchant had given me. *If this doesn't work, I am coming back to find him.* I unwrapped the cloth and choked down the bitter mix, trying not to gag on the taste alone.

It didn't help right away, but at least I felt like I was doing something instead of standing around useless. The sway of the ship made everything worse, but at least it was darker down here. I curled in on myself, arms wrapped around my knees, and closed my eyes. The cold inside me flickered—unsettled, irritated, maybe just as seasick as I was.

I let my breathing slow and the ship groan around me, letting the nausea fade to the background. I let the cold inside me rise—not forcefully, just enough to pull me away from the sickness and everything else.

❧ ☙

Snow. Not a storm—just steady, slow snowfall. It melted across my skin and clung to my hair. The same field stretched endlessly, quiet and untouched. And she was there—as she had been the first time I'd mediated and saw her.

Skadi. She stood not far off, wrapped in fur, her armor now gone, arms crossed as she watched me approach. Her expression was the usual firm gaze, but I caught the flicker of something else in her eyes—something gentler.

"You look pale," she said, her tone low.

"It's the ship," I muttered. "And this cursed sea. I hate it."

Her lips lifted in the smallest hint of a smile. "I never liked it either."

I blinked, searching her face. "Really?"

"Remember, I married Njord. That didn't last." She shrugged, letting her arms fall to her sides.

"…oh? But I thought it was because you preferred the snow and mountains instead of the sun and sea…" I furrowed my brow, trying to remember the myths my realm taught us.

"Yes, that too. I wasn't built for the heat." She looked at me directly. "But also, the seasickness."

I snorted.

It was quiet for a moment before I looked away. "You've been gone for a while," I murmured, sitting down on one of the many stones. She walked forward and sat beside me. The energy between us always hummed when we were near.

"I've been here," she said. "But as I have said, this is your path to take—to live and grow into your own abilities yourself."

I didn't answer. My face fell, and I fought to keep my emotions from showing.

Skadi shifted closer, her shoulder barely touching mine. "You feel abandoned."

I looked up quickly to meet her gaze. "I didn't say that." My words stuttered, but the truth lingered heavily.

"You didn't have to. I can feel your emotions, remember?" she said.

I clenched my jaw.

After a moment, her voice lowered. "You need to understand—what I am now is not a soul, not fully. I'm what remains. A final strand left behind before the shift. Once your soul and abilities ascend, I will be gone."

I felt that like a crack through my ribs. "So, this… this is it?"

"No," she said gently. "This is what's left. But I'm not afraid. You shouldn't be either."

"I don't want to lose you," I muttered, tears pricking at the corner of my eyes.

"I know. In this short time we've communicated, I've grown rather fond of you. But for now, don't let this hinder your journey—you must be ready for whatever lies ahead." Her tone wasn't cold—it was quiet, and final, and unbearably kind. She reached out then, resting a hand on my shoulder.

"We're both stubborn," she added. "That much, you've already inherited. Maybe more than I meant to give to you."

"It'll keep my companions on their toes, hmm?" I tried to joke.

She gave a small smile in reply, before we both turned to look out at the snow as it thickened, and the cold wind blew through my mindscape gently.

"I'm proud of you," Skadi said softly.

I didn't have time to reply.

The world tilted, and I opened my eyes below deck, the ship creaking around me. My throat was tight. I sat up slowly, blinking through the dim light. The nausea was still there, but dulled now.

I rose, stepped toward the stairwell, and made my way up shakily.

Raising my hand to shield my eyes, I squinted into the sun as it started to peek through the clouds, casting a warmer light across the water. The wind had picked up, and salty spray hit the deck. It was bitter cold, and I could see it freezing slightly where it touched the wood.

My gaze drifted over everything—Eirik sat his axe over his lap, appearing to sleep—though I knew better—and then my eyes landed on my wolf companion.

Runar was stretched out across the same crates near the bow, ears twitching lazily in the breeze. I hadn't spoken to him properly since the inn, after storming out of the room.

I hesitated, then crossed the deck and sat beside him.

He shifted his head to glance at me but didn't speak.

"I've been ignoring you," I said quietly.

Runar only offered a slow blink, waiting.

"I was angry, but not just at you. I think I was hurt more than any-thing." I looked out at the water. "You looked at me like... like I was her."

He didn't deny it.

"And I think that's what got to me. That maybe you weren't protect-ing me... you were protecting her."

He shifted, curling his front paws beneath him.

"I'm not her," I said. "I'm me. And I need you to see that. She's..." I swallowed the lump in my throat, "she's no longer here, and I am my own person."

Runar's gaze turned back to the sea. He was silent for a long time before he huffed out a sigh. "I followed her because I was made to, even though I grew close to her. I follow you because I choose to."

I didn't answer. I just sat there with him as the sky turned orange and the sails snapped above us. There was still so much I didn't know—about myself, about my dream, and why he refused to speak about it yet.

For now, I just had to listen to Skadi's words. Don't let it distract me. Focus on what we were doing.

Shouts from the crew pulled me from my thoughts. I looked up to see men rushing across the deck, tightening ropes and shouting orders as the sails shifted overhead. The wind from the north carried a stronger scent now—salt, smoke, and something else I couldn't place.

I turned toward the horizon, squinting.

The sea had thinned, and in the distance, I could just make out the edge of land. Pale stone walls climbed the shoreline, interrupted by red-tiled roofs and clusters of rising buildings. The details were too far off to make out, but the shape of the city was unmistakable—a port, bigger than the last.

This had to be Piraeus, and we were most likely headed for Kantharos, the main port city.

A low whistle startled me. I turned as Eirik made his way next to us. "Now, they don't have many villages this big where I'm from. The Greeks sure do love fancy things, no?"

I rolled my eyes. "It's a form of art and pride in their way of living." I paused, looking back to the city growing closer. "They have that in Norway too—longhouses and your traditions. Though not like this... would still be extravagant to others."

Eirik gave a low hum. "Calm down, young scholar. I was only jesting."

I gave him a sidelong look, my eye twitching.

He grinned, nudging me. "Besides, you've got enough color back in your face to lecture a stone wall."

I glared at him, crossing my arms. "Thanks? Though I'm offended."

He just gave his usual smirk. "Means the nausea passed, right?" He leaned on the railing beside me, casually watching the port come into view. "I'd hate to see all that wit wasted over the side of the ship hurling."

I didn't reply, just exhaled slowly and focused on the horizon. The closer we came, the louder the city became—even from this distance.

The ship groaned as it pulled into the port, bumping harshly against the stone quay. Crew members scrambled to tie off the lines, shouting to one another as the sails were pulled tight overhead. The cold wind whipped through the harbor, sharp with salt and smoke. My fingers curled into the railing on instinct.

And then—

"Ah! There they are!"

A too-familiar voice boomed through the din. I turned just in time to see Dimitrios striding down the ship's upper stairs toward us, arms wide, a grin stretched across his weathered face like he was greeting old friends.

"Welcome to glorious, frigid Piraeus!" he called. "Where the wine is cheap, the gods are always watching, and the carts never stop trying to run you over!"

"God's help me," I muttered.

Dimitrios waved again, clearly spotting me. "Ravena! You look less pale than usual! Excellent!"

Runar let out a low, unimpressed noise beside me.

"Now, now," Eirik murmured, stepping up behind me. "Play nice."

I gave him a glare that could've frozen seawater.

We stepped onto the docks, and the city hit me all at once.

Cold stone beneath my boots. Voices layered over one another in at least three different dialects. Merchants barking over prices, wheels creaking, gulls screaming. The smell of fish, roasted nuts, spices, seaweed, and smoke tangled in the air until I couldn't separate one from the other. Color and motion flooded the space—vibrant robes, rough leathers, metal armor clanking down the alleys.

Temples rose behind the rows of buildings, their columns reaching for the clouds, and further inland—half-shrouded in winter mist—the Acropolis climbed above the skyline like a crown. Even from this distance, I could feel the divine energy pressing down from that direction.

A priest in white robes passed close enough to graze my arm, murmuring something under his breath.

A fishmonger shouted something obscene at a cart driver.

And in the middle of it all, Dimitrios was still grinning.

"Let's get you somewhere warm!" he declared. "Before you freeze to death or get trampled by a mule!"

"Charming place," I muttered, pulling my cloak tighter.

Eirik gave a low chuckle beside me. "Aye. Feels like home already."

Dimitrios was still talking as he walked ahead. "You'll love this place," he said, gesturing toward the narrow streets ahead. "I know these roads like the back of my left cheek. If you need a map or directions, I can grab something for you—Athenae can be a maze if you don't know it."

I gave a small smile, shaking my head at his words. "I appreciate it, but I'm familiar with the area. I know the layout."

Dimitrios blinked, surprised, but nodded. "Well then—good to know I'm in capable company."

He turned and kept walking, still rambling on about drinking places, fireplaces, and the right ratio of wine to conversation. The streets curved uphill in a tangle of stone and sounds—clattering carts, overlapping voices, distant temple bells. I kept my eyes ahead, taking in the rooftops and the way the columns of distant temples rose above them, just visible through the pale winter haze.

Then, true to form, Dimitrios edged closer, his arm starting to lift—like he meant to steer me along by the shoulders.

It never landed.

Eirik stepped in without a word, his arm sliding across the small of my back, firm and easy like it belonged there. His hand rested lightly at my waist as he glanced sideways at Dimitrios.

"Careful," Eirik said calmly. "She's still recovering. Sea travel makes her... unpredictable."

I froze.

Dimitrios blinked, clearly reading the message but keeping his grin. "Ah, of course. My mistake."

"Mm," Eirik murmured, as if that settled it.

I didn't look at either of them—I was too busy trying to remember how to walk properly with Eirik's hand resting on my waist. My stomach was no longer upset, but my face was another story.

We reached the kapeleion a moment later, and I was still warm with embarrassment—but not from Dimitrios.

From the fact that I hadn't wanted Eirik to let go. I'm doomed...

The kapeleion was tucked off a side street, half-shielded by weather-worn stone and a low awning draped with faded fabric. Smoke curled from the chimney, and the door creaked as Dimitrios shoved it open ahead of us like he owned the place.

Warmth hit instantly—dry air, firelight, and the sharp scent of wine.

The room wasn't crowded, but voices echoed off the low-beamed ceiling. A few men sat hunched at tables playing dice. A woman in a heavy cloak stirred a pot behind the bar. No one looked up when we entered.

Dimitrios swept his arms toward a round table near the hearth. "Sit, sit! You've all been tossed around by the sea—this is the cure."

We followed without protest. Runar curled up beneath the table, resting his head on his paws. I sank into the nearest seat—next to Eirik, of course, because the other options weren't appealing—and tried not to visibly decompress.

Eirik didn't sit close, but I could still feel the heat radiating from his side. Dimitrios dropped into the seat across from us and immediately launched into a story about how he once drank with a man who claimed to be the half-brother of Ares. *"Big scar across his back, horrible singing voice, but decent with a sword."*

I barely heard the rest. My eyes drifted to the fire, the way the light flickered against the walls and caught in the folds of Eirik's cloak. My body had finally stopped swaying like the ship, but my mind hadn't quite let go of that moment on the street. That warmth. That ridiculous arm around my waist.

Even now, sitting beside him, I could still feel it—that heat. Not just from the fire, but from him. It had been there before, I realized. More than once. I just hadn't really thought about it.

I frowned slightly—not at him, but at the realization. How could someone who walked through snow without it bothering him give off that much warmth? I shook the thought away or tried to. There were bigger things to worry about, than some one's body temperature. Dimitrios was still talking—now something about a haunted vineyard and a runaway goat. This man sure has some interesting stories, even if some were preposterous.

Eirik leaned forward, resting his forearms on the table, his tone dry. "You have a story for every city, don't you?"

"Oh, several," Dimitrios grinned, unfazed. "Though some are more factual than others. Depends on how much wine I've had."

I let a giggle slip before I could stop myself, my hand flying to cover my mouth.

Eirik glanced at me out of the corner of his eye, brow raised, but said nothing.

"What? I found that funny." I shrugged, cradling the warm cup of tea I was given.

Dimitrios raised his small cup as if to toast. "Laughter keeps us alive, you know. Especially with the wars going on right now."

My smile dropped. The remembrance of the Athenian and Spartan wars happening right now had my gaze dropping to the steam rising from my cup; it swirled like mist above the surface. "I forget that this time had wars often..." I trailed off, and I could almost feel Dimitrios' questioning gaze.

"You sound as if you're not of this time?" he asked, uncertain, and my group tensed up slightly. I really didn't want to discuss something like this to a total stranger—if word spread, I'd become more of a spectacle than the gods.

I gave a careful smile and rubbed the back of my neck. "Ah, I'm not from these parts—foreigner here. Guilty."

Dimitrios seemed to consider that, then nodded like it was enough. "You do have that exotic air about you! Must be why myself and this handsome lad here are drawn to you!" he boasted playfully.

And there it goes—my eye twitching again, at the audacity of this man. But the heat that crawled up my neck had me glancing at Eirik out of the corner of my eye. He sat reclined, eyes closed as if he were ignoring the world around him... or just Dimitrios.

"Speaking of exotic! You'd fit well here with the gods. Athenae is crawling with them. Some walk openly; others prefer their own domains over our city. If you're lucky, you might even catch wind of Hermes."

My eyes brightened and Eirik sat up immediately. "Have you seen him before?"

"Once." Dimitrios held up one finger, as if to amplify how many times he'd seen him. "He didn't speak much, just pointed at something in the distance and disappeared before I could ask. He probably thought he was funny, trying to give me a heart attack."

Eirik's brow furrowed. "You didn't follow to ask?"

Dimitrios laughed. "Gods, no! I'm not that brave—or that stupid. Following a god, I could end up trapped somewhere." His tone held a slight tremble.

I raised a brow—the poor guy seemed afraid. "Surely the gods or goddess wouldn't trap anyone..."

"You've got a lot to learn about Greek gods and goddesses here, young lady," he said, lowering his voice as if the divine beings themselves could hear us over all the noise. "There have been plenty who've disappeared to the temptation of the more mischievous-natured ones."

The words hung heavy in the warm air. Before Dimitrios clapped his hands and leaned forward, grinning again.

"But if you're really hoping to catch a glimpse of him, you'll want to start higher up in the city." He motioned loosely toward the open windows.

"Hermes is drawn to places that are busy—trade routes, ports, temples... but the locals always chatter, saying he shows up near the Acropolis. Tallest place around. I've heard of him slipping in and out of the Temple of Hephaestus too—likes to eavesdrop, maybe."

I leaned forward. "So, there's no pattern?"

Dimitrios shrugged, unbothered. "It's Hermes. You'll find him when he wants to be found—but asking around the city might help. Priests, travelers, market folk. Just... don't ask the drunk ones. They'll tell you he's a goat."

I blinked. "A goat?" my mind trying to picture Hermes flaunting around as a little goat.

He raised a brow. "Don't ask." As if that answered everything.

Runar snorted somewhere near the hearth, earning a raised brow from Dimitrios—as if he was seeing him for the first time. "Is that a wolf?"

"No," I said flatly. "That's our goat." A nip on my ankle had me jerking my leg back.

The tavern emptied way faster than I expected. Apparently, the sun settling just above the rooftops was signal enough for most to return home—or wherever they laid their heads in this city. We stepped outside not long after, the air brisk with sea wind and the promise of a colder night.

The streets were louder than before—merchants packing up, lanterns being lit, and the distant echo of someone playing a stringed instrument. I walked just behind Eirik, shoulder brushing his cloak every so often as I glanced around. The stone roads stretched ahead in sloping curves, some leading uphill toward more refined buildings, others dipping down into darker, noisier alleys.

It was overwhelming, but familiar.

Piraeus had always been one of the great ports of the classical world. Even back in my realm, I studied it—its role as Athens' lifeline, its bustling trade, the way it was fortified like a stubborn gate between sea and city. To walk it now, like this, was... surreal.

"Which way?" Eirik asked over his shoulder.

I blinked, then pointed toward the rising path. "We follow the main road north and cut through the upper districts. We'll reach the outskirts of Athenae by nightfall if we're quick."

Runar padded ahead, ignoring the murmured stares and the occasional flinch from a passerby who clearly wasn't used to seeing a wolf this calm wandering through their city.

We veered toward the quieter route, following the rise of the road as it wound upward. A few lanterns swung from iron hooks, their flames dancing in the breeze. The light wasn't strong, but it was enough to catch the marble outlines of shrines tucked between homes, the curve of a statue's shoulder, the shimmer of coins left at a small offering bowl near a stairwell.

We passed statues draped in vines creeping up columns, and beautiful murals of gods painted in blues and golds. The further we went, the more the city thinned, giving way to wider streets with fewer vendors and more temples—the forest surrounding them lining the roadways. The winter's chill danced through the roadway, but people still lingered, dressed in heavy wool cloaks and huddled in groups, enjoying the coming nightlife.

It wasn't loud either—less shouting, more murmurs and ritual songs coming from gatherings tucked behind stone walls.

I paused near the steps of a small shrine to Hestia, my fingers brushing the cold marble edge as I glanced upward, and there it was in the distance–small but unmistakable. Far beyond the rooftops, I could just make out the shape of the Acropolis. The Parthenon loomed like a watchful giant, flanked by smaller temples and columns that caught the last glint of sun before dusk pulled it all into shadow.

I exhaled slowly. Even knowing what it was, even having seen what remained in person, to see it now in full—untouched—was a feeling like no other.

A bump on my shoulder shook me from my awe, and I apologized quietly to the patron trying to walk past. I hurried to catch up with Eirik, who was only a few paces ahead, and we carried forward up the road, my attention narrowing back to the climb ahead. The outer edge of the city was quieter than I expected. The buildings spread out more, with a few scattered shrines and flickering lanterns lighting the road. It wasn't silent—far from it—but the noise felt... lively.

We found the inn tucked between a tall cypress and a weather-worn statue of Hermes that had definitely seen better days—simple stone walls, a wooden sign painted blue, and light glowing behind thick curtains.

Inside, I spotted the innkeeper right away. She was older, heavyset, tired eyes but a kind voice. "Evening. Only two rooms left. Down the hall, if sleep is what you're after." She held my gaze kindly, which surprised me; most here would've looked straight at the man.

"We'll take it," I said with a quick nod in thanks, grabbing coins from my pouch before Eirik could. The woman smiled and pointed us down the hall.

Our rooms were right across from each other. Honestly, I was just grateful not to have to share again.

I let out a sigh of relief and turned to my companions. "So, will you be staying with Eirik tonight, Runar?"

Runar looked at me like I'd grown two heads. "I will not leave you alone, even if it's only a door apart. I do not trust the nature of any beings," he said, with finality.

I sighed and opened my door, gesturing him through. He padded inside, his tail hitting my leg on his way past.

The room was small but clean. One clay oil lamp sat on the table under the window, which overlooked the city's edge.

"I'm going to clean up," I said, heading for the basin behind a draped cloth hung on a rope anchored to the wall. It offered a bit of privacy from the rest of the room. "Try to scrub the sea spray off."

Runar had already wedged himself in front of the door, back in his massive form—barely fitting in the space. I shot him a look.

"I feel like you're overdoing it, Runar." My tone was exasperated as I tugged the curtain closed.

"And you trust far too easily, young one. Anyone meaning you harm could break that door down." He paused. "After that encounter today, whatever those creatures were, I'm not taking any chances with your life, Ravena."

His tone left no room for argument.

I paused, pouring clean water into the basin and stared at my reflection in the ripples.

My gaze traveled to my wrist, the mark had long since faded, but the sensation of that shadow slicing through my skin hadn't left me. Whatever it was, it had followed us all this way. Hecate's words echoed through my mind. *You're either the threat, or the potential now.*

If this was Agnar's doing, had his creatures been trailing us the entire time? Since Korinthos? Since the mountains? Was it only a matter of time before they decided to attack us directly. I clenched the edge of the basin, fighting to keep it together. If I was the reason Runar and Eirik—hell, everyone—were in danger, what was I supposed to do?

Chapter Twenty-Four

Are you sure you know where we're going?" Eirik's voice rang from my right side. It was barely a few minutes after sunrise, and I was already irritated at my human companion.

"Yes, Eirik. I swear—it's this path," I pointed up the small incline that veered left. "That way leads to the Acropolis." I gestured toward the huge Parthenon perched on the mountain. The roads looked only slightly different from modern times, but a rising doubt was creeping into my gut. Maybe I'd gotten us lost.

The streets were starting to crowd, citizens hustling off to work, temples, markets—wherever their lives pulled them. The weather was cold, but not as bitter as it had been the past few days. Flakes of snow dusted the trees, the temples, and the city walls. It was light, the air still carrying that Mediterranean wetness, but something itched my brain. I didn't know what, until a group of farmers jostled past, their conversation drifting my way.

"This weather's been strange, no?" One man's eyes were tired as he looked around. "It's been cold before, but never like this."

His companion nodded, "Yes, I wonder if a god or goddess is angered... this surely won't be good for the crops."

I slowed, thoughtful. *Could this be Agnar's doing? Or something else?*

"Tch, I bet it's Chione. That woman's always flaunting her abilities for Hermes—anything to make him visit." An older farmer hobbled behind the rest.

They moved on, their conversation fading as they turned down a smaller path, to the fields.

"I was beginning to wonder if this weather was normal," Eirik said.

I glanced at him, pressing my lips into a line before sighing. "The weather here is usually pretty mild," I said. "It gets cold, but for snow to stick around this long—and not just up in the mountains—that's weird."

We went around the slight curve in the road, and I stopped, my face dropping. "I swear only I could get us completely turned around in a place I'm supposed to know." I leant back on my heels, frustrated. In front of us stood the Temple of Hephaestus, and not far from it, the Agora. There was a road that did lead up toward the Parthenon, but it was definitely the long route.

"So... I feel obligated to say," Eirik started.

I pivoted around to face him, only a few paces ahead, and stabbed him in the chest with my finger.

"Don't. It's way too early for your snarky comments," I huffed.

He chuckled, gently batting my hand away. "Aye, but it seems your expert knowledge, young scholar, ends with us wandering in circles."

I shot him a withering look. "I said it was this way. And technically, we're still going uphill—in the direction of the Acropolis."

He didn't respond right away, but the amusement dancing in his eyes made the ice in my veins prickle to the surface in sheer annoyance.

"We're not lost," I grunted, turning and starting forward again. "We're just taking the scenic route," I muttered over my shoulder.

"Whatever you say, all-knowing one," he grinned, falling into step beside me—his gaze drifting back to the city around us.

The road curved, and we stepped into the outskirts of the Agora, the city slowly beginning to stir. Sunlight crept higher over the rooftops, casting soft gold across marble and clay. Not quite noon, but already the crowds had thickened—priests passing by in pairs, shopkeepers unloading goods, and voices rising in low chatter as citizens bartered or gossiped about the strange snowfall and whatever deals they would be making today.

We moved toward the Temple of Hephaestus, its stone steps slick with frost that hadn't yet melted under the day's weak sun. The chill hung oddly here—more than just the season, more than just weather. My thoughts flicked back to the farmers' words from earlier. Something about this felt off. I flexed my fingers as the cold bit at my skin, slowing my steps before I even realized it.

Eirik noticed it too. "It's colder here," he muttered, scanning the temple's perimeter. He was used to *my* abilities—this felt like someone showing off.

I nodded, trying to stay focused. "Feels... weird."

And then—

"Looking for someone?"

The voice cut through the air like clean ice, carrying a trill that made my nerves crackle with irritation.

A figure stood atop the temple stairs: a woman—tall, poised, draped in white and silver layers that shimmered faintly in the rising daylight. Her long white hair was untouched by the breeze, and her expression was calm... too calm. Like still water hiding jagged rocks beneath.

I stopped walking, my magic rippling under my skin at her presence, ready to defend myself.

She smiled—just barely. "You seem lost."

"Not lost," I said, lifting my chin. "Just trying to find someone." I glanced around the area, already thinking through exit strategies if this conversation went sideways.

"Hermes?" Her tone made it sound like a joke, but something in it—something jealous—made me snap my gaze back to her.

"Yes," I said carefully. "Know him?"

"Who doesn't?" she replied smoothly, stepping down a few steps. "But he doesn't show up for just anyone."

Eirik shifted beside me, his voice level. "We heard he sometimes appears around here."

She crossed her arms and nodded once. "He does," she said. "And then disappears just as easily. Always chasing a new story or delivering a message."

Her gaze slid back to mine, and I crossed my arms in return. That look in her eyes was too curious for my liking. I bit the inside of my cheek and drew a slow breath.

"And you are?"

"Chione." She offered it like it meant something. "Daughter of Boreas. Perhaps you've heard of me?" She grinned, and gave a little curtsy like she was royalty.

Eirik shot me a worried glance. He hadn't seen my attitude yet—boy, was he in for surprises. I didn't break eye contact with her, deep blue to ice blue, locked on one another.

"Sure," I said, voice even. "Arrogant minor deities who think their little frost tricks make them special? I've heard of a few."

Chione's smile didn't waver, but something flickered behind her eyes. She stepped down another stair, her boots light against the stone. "That temper," she said smoothly, "will get you in trouble one day. I can tell you're new to all this." Her gaze dipped briefly to my hands—probably sensing the magic beneath my skin. "You don't even realize what's spilling off you, do you?"

I didn't respond, but my heart rate fluttered a bit.

She tilted her head, almost like she pitied me. "There are beings who would kill to steal a power like yours. Or worse...use it, use you. For their own games." Her words were meant as a warning, but the tone was too bland to be sincere. She wasn't concerned. Or maybe she was, but I wasn't about to ask her for help.

Eirik tensed beside me, picking up on it too. His hand hovered near the hilt of his blade.

"I'm doing fine," I said coolly. "But thanks for the unsolicited advice."

Chione gave a soft laugh and turned just enough to glance over her shoulder at the temple. "He comes here," she said, her voice slipping into something more casual now, like we were old acquaintances. "Usually when I'm around. Or when he's bored."

She looked back at me, smiling. "But for no one else. Besides Hephaestus, of course."

I raised a brow. "Right. Of course."

Her expression didn't shift. She was too practiced. Too used to being the center of whatever pedestal she put herself on. Her gaze dropped down my form like she was still trying to figure out what I was or what I wasn't. She clicked her tongue against her teeth.

"I wouldn't get your hopes up though," she added, turning back toward the temple steps. "Hermes isn't known for interest in uncontrollable demi-goddesses." Without waiting for a goodbye, she walked back to the pillars slowly, gracefully, and fully aware of the agitation she left in her wake.

I turned on my heel and headed straight for the Agora, not saying a word.

Eirik let a few steps pass before falling in beside me. "So... what in the nine realms was that?" His hand relaxing from the hilt of his sword.

I didn't look at him. "A very tense conversation?" I didn't have a reason for my sudden attitude.

"Mmhmm," he hummed. "She seemed interesting..."

I shot him a look of annoyance. Only he would find what happened interesting.

He raised a brow. "I'm just saying, I've met Jarls of neighboring villages with better social skills. And less ego."

Runar's claws tapped against the stone behind us, his voice gruff. "She reeks of jealousy. I don't like her."

"Yeah, no kidding," I muttered, pushing past a few people lingering near a merchant stand. "She acted like Hermes is her possession. I mean, they could be together, but to show that much distaste towards us right away?"

Eirik exhaled through his nose with a chuckle. "So, she's the clingy deity type."

"She's the I-think-I'm-above-everyone type," I bit out. "And I'm not in the mood to play along. She was flexing her abilities like it was some show."

Runar kept pace beside me, his tone flat. "Next time, I'll just bite her, if you want." A hint of a wolf's smile on his snout.

"No," I said, dragging a hand through my hair. "She wants a reaction, I bet. I'm not giving her one."

Eirik smirked. "Little late for that, Ravena."

I didn't reply. I was too focused on shaking off the tension in my chest, and the strange pull of power still lingering in the cold air behind us. It was like our magic was fluctuating against each other unconsciously, trying to prove the other was the strongest.

I shook my head and shoved the encounter to the back of my mind as we stepped into the bustling Agora. The Agora opened up ahead of us wide and structured, with polished stone walkways cutting through rows of market stalls and shaded columns. It wasn't the crumbling site I remembered from books and old photos. This place was alive and still very much standing.

Vendors called out in bursts of Greek, voices sharp but not aggressive. Clay pots, dyed fabrics, scrolls, and fresh produce were stacked neatly under linen canopies. Bronze and silver glinted under the sun from a jeweler's table, and a scribe was already at work near one of the benches, pen scratching across parchment.

Temples framed the perimeter, small shrines tucked between stone arches, while larger structures sat at the far edges— towering, with carved columns and painted friezes. Everything here felt orderly but lived in, like it pulsed with routine and ritual. Locals moved between the stalls and steps with practiced ease. A priest offered a quiet blessing near a small altar where offerings of bread and oil sat, already half-gone.

Even in winter, the air buzzed with warmth—conversation, footsteps, the hum of people who had places to be. I observed Athenian soldiers riding through on the roadways; we had to step out of the way more than once as they galloped through. We only got a few wayward glances from people and random soldiers as we stopped by stalls.

Eirik lingered at a table displaying old coinage and polished weapons, lifting one bronze dagger with a faint smirk. "They don't make them like this in my village; the craftsmanship is impressive."

"That's because yours are built to kill, not to show off." I muttered, scanning a table of small jewelry and woven trinkets. A pair of simple earrings caught my eye—nothing extravagant, but delicately made, with a deep blue stone set in the center. I remembered the small pouch of coin Cora had given me before we left Kyllini. I could still hear her voice: *Just in case you see something pretty, dear.*

I handed over a few drachmae without a second thought. Something about having a small, personal thing from this time...made me giddy.

Eirik grunted, eyeing the dagger then looking at me. "I feel that is a challenge. No weapon is too much for this warrior." He puffed out his chest comically.

Runar huffed near the back of the stall, his eyes watching everyone pass. "You humans and your objects."

"Let me enjoy something, for once, while we search for this elusive god," I muttered, slipping the earrings into the side pouch of my cloak.

We made our way along the inner arc of the Agora, weaving between stands and the small shrines nestled beneath tiled awnings. The scent of roasted meat and herbs drifted through the square, mixing with the cooler sea breeze that funneled up the streets.

At one of the temples, a priest glanced up as we approached—then quickly looked away. Another whispered something to a fellow priestess as we passed. It wasn't fear. But it wasn't welcome either.

"They're wary," Eirik muttered, his eyes following a priest who quickly turned away.

"Yeah, I noticed," I said, keeping my voice low. "Maybe they can sense we're not exactly ordinary travelers." I shrugged.

He raised a brow. "You mean because we've got a small wolf trailing us and you keep radiating magic like it's no big deal?"

I rolled my eyes. "Not my fault, I'm still learning to control it. And Chione's attitude didn't help any."

Runar snorted from behind us. "They should be wary. At least one of us actually bites." I rolled my eyes at his comment; he was full of himself sometimes.

We didn't stay long near the temples—no one seemed eager to talk. The few questions we did ask were met with vague nods or polite misdirection. But I caught a slip from one temple servant—something about a divine presence being felt recently near the Acropolis. It wasn't much, but it was enough to push us onward. It could be Hermes, or it could be any other god or goddess visiting the area.

By midday, we found ourselves partway up the incline that led to the higher grounds. The road wound through olive trees and patches of rough rock, where travelers rested or picnicked along the way. I was sweating now, my boots scuffed and legs sore. I had long since stripped off my cloak and carried it on my arm.

"If I were in my true form," Runar said, not for the first time, "this hike would be done in minutes. I could carry you both."

Eirik grunted, pulling off his cloak now. "If you were in your true form, we'd have the entire city panicking on our hands, wolf."

Runar gave a wolfish grin. "Details." He wandered ahead of us slightly, parting foot traffic for us.

The Acropolis finally came into view—looming above us in sunlit stone, its sacred walls rising behind long marble steps. I slowed down as we neared it, my breath catching.

It wasn't just the scale; it was the power. The way it seemed to emanate beneath the surface, as if the gods really had laid every stone themselves.

Eirik stepped up beside me, gaze tracing the columns. "Makes you feel small, doesn't it? I have never seen such huge structures before."

"Yeah," I murmured. "But in a good way."

The crowds thinned the higher we went. By the time we reached a more secluded terrace overlooking the city, the noise had faded. The soft murmurs of distant groups drifted through the air—it seemed most had gathered near the front of the temple. So just the sound of wind, the distant murmur of footsteps, and the clink of armor far below were our only company.

We paused to breathe, the three of us standing in quiet defeat. We hadn't gotten any closer to finding the messenger god.

A change in the air, a subtle shift in the wind, had me stiffening. And then—

"I heard from the chatter of these mortals that you were looking for me?" a deep, playful voice spoke.

Chapter Twenty-Five

I whirled around–and froze. He was sprawled across one of the many marble benches, as if it were his own private stage. Deep bronze cuffs caught the light at his wrists, a scroll tube rested against his hip, half-tucked beneath the loose folds of his white robes. I glanced down—his winged sandals hovered just above the ground, faintly fluttering, like they deemed themselves too grand to touch earthen soil.

But his face was what stopped me. Striking features framed by dark, loose curls and—surprisingly—a well-kept beard, not too wild but enough to give him that rugged look. But gods, his eyes were interesting: hazel that seemed like they would shift with his mood. They remained sharp and calculating, but underneath I could see the slightest glimmer of mischief hiding.

This was Hermes, the messenger of the gods, and he was staring right into my eyes like I'd just become his next story.

I glanced to his right and there stood Chione, now looking more composed and less hostile—and maybe a little apologetic?

Her posture was still graceful, chin up, hands lightly folded at her waist. "I didn't know," she said, the words quiet but clear. "Who you were, I mean."

I blinked, caught off guard. "Yeah, well, most don't know. I'm still trying to figure it out," I muttered.

Her gaze flicked to Hermes, then back to me. "I don't usually get it wrong."

Eirik stepped forward slightly, arms crossed, eyeing the two like they were a potential threat. "So now what?" he asked flatly.

Hermes sat up straighter, elbows on his knees, fingers loosely laced. "Now," he said, glancing between us, "you tell me why the winds are shifting in cities that haven't seen snow in decades... and why the reincarnation of Jotunheim's daughter is walking around Athenae with a wolf and a shield-bearer. Looking for me, of all gods."

Runar growled under his breath. I reached over and tapped his ear once, and he settled with an annoyed huff.

"We need answers," I said, keeping my voice kind. "Or at least a direction—to help with the threat of what's coming." I finished.

Chione nodded once curious, her attention sliding back to Hermes. "Then maybe it's good you kept looking."

Hermes raised a brow. "Maybe," he echoed, amused. "Or maybe it's the beginning of something far more complicated. Maybe Hecate was right all those years ago." He stood in one fluid motion from the bench, then motioned for us to follow. "Come. We will speak somewhere without mortal ears present."

I hesitated, watching them walk away. Chione had looped her arm around Hermes elbow. I glanced at Eirik, his arms were crossed, and he wore a skeptical expression.

"Well, we found him... and now we're all on edge" I muttered.

He looked at me and exhaled "It is not in my nature to trust someone who isn't my brethren. We just have to stay heedful." He started forward, Runar following as I looked up to the sky before falling in last.

❧❧❧ ❧❧❧

We followed at a slight distance. The people of Athenae who lingered around the Acropolis would stop and bow to Hermes, but he only offered a small smile in return, never stopping. We made our way down the northern side of the mountain, following a path hidden by thin trees. It seemed no mortals had ever ventured this way.

"Do not worry—normal mortals cannot see this path. It is hidden from their eyes." Hermes's voice floated back toward us, his tone cheery as we wrapped around the bend of the mountain's east side. And there, jutting out from the rocks, was... a small house?

I slowed as we neared it. It wasn't anything like I'd expected a god—or goddess—to hang around in. The house was tucked away into the stone, vines and ivy curling over a veranda, and a stretch of cypress and wild olive branches hugging the slope's edge, obscuring it from view below.

"Wow..." I whispered. *Won't find this in any history book.*

Chione twirled around and grinned. "Hermes and Athena had this constructed—a place for any visiting god to rest, should they want to linger in the city."

"Not many stay here, though. They prefer the comforts of their own realms. So, we'll be safe to discuss what is needed—and you may use it to rest." Hermes spoke as he opened the door, gesturing us inside.

Once I stepped inside, my mouth opened in awe. Smooth limestone walls curved gently around the space, catching the midday light in soft, golden streaks. The floors were a blend of polished stone and inlaid marble, cool underfoot but warmed by a flickering hearth set into the far wall. The scent of herbs—bay, thyme, maybe mint—hung in the air, tucked into small bundles near the windows and woven into the braziers' smoke.

Wooden beams ran overhead, carved with protective runes and symbols of rest: the winged caduceus of Hermes, the owl of Athena, and the sigils of peace. The furniture was minimal but very well-crafted—low tables, sturdy benches softened with thick woven cushions, a few tall-backed chairs with subtle detailing along the arms. It was all so beautifully made that I immediately took back what I'd said about it not looking the part.

I looked toward a dining area where scrolls and clay pots lined a shelf in the far corner, and glass decanters of wine sat untouched beside a small tray of dried figs and olives. It wasn't flashy; there was no gold, no divine glow. Just a sense of comfort and quiet. It felt as if this place existed outside the noise of the city above and below.

A hallway to my right led to what I guessed were separate sleeping quarters. Another passage cut into the rock led deeper into the mountain—the scent of saltwater and lavender drifting up to my nose... a bathing room built right into the stone?

A rustle of fabric had me turning. I watched as Hermes flopped down on the cushions on the floor, facing a patio that looked out toward the city, ivy vines hanging over the roof. He held a cup of wine in one hand and looked at us in contemplation. Chione had chosen to settle herself in one of the many high-back chairs nearby.

"Tell me young demi-goddess, what has caused you and your guardian here to seek me out? Answers? A story?" he asked, running his fingers through his beard.

I swallowed, glancing at Eirik—who was still looking around—and at Runar who sat stiffly near the hallway. I turned back to Hermes, who waved to another cushion across from him. "Come, sit. I promise I don't bite. I'm one of the nicer gods," he joked.

I slowly sat down, setting my cloak next to me. "I—uh, no, we were hoping to find an answer. The elder in the village we traveled from said you were the most likely to listen to us. Though, we should expect to give something in return."

Hermes let out a deep laugh and grinned playfully. "Silly mortals! Always assuming all of us prefer to barter. I do love a good game once in a while, but no, I don't expect anything in return for this"—he waved his hand between us—"little meeting." He paused, the mischievous light returning to his eyes. "But if you're set in your endeavor to offer an excha nge..."

This earned a raised brow from Chione, her mouth setting into a thin line.

"There is a festival tomorrow. The mortals are celebrating winter," he said, a grin tugging at his mouth. "How fitting to have the soon-to-be goddess of winter present—even if she hails from the Norse pantheon."

I blinked. "How—?"

He chuckled, setting his wine down. "Come now, did you really think I wasn't aware of who you were, Ravena?" He glanced at Eirik, who was now tense. "Easy warrior. I mean no harm. A message was sent the moment you arrived in this realm, preparing for her arrival." He looked back at me.

"So, what do you say, young goddess? Does this seem like a decent exchange?"

I nodded with no hesitation. "Yes, I accept. We just want any help we can get. You must know about Agnar... Hecate seemed to know," I mumbled.

He nodded. "Yes, she would know. Years ago, she told me what was coming." Hand resting on his chin now, he looked like he didn't carry a sliver of concern about it.

He must have caught the look on my face, because he sighed. "I did not believe her at first, and didn't for many years, until I laid eyes on you at the Parthenon. The happenings around Greece were starting to make myself and other gods alert, but we have no desire to interfere. Call us selfish, but even we do not mess with fates. Until the time comes when something threatens us directly."

I sat there, lost in thought—and an emotion I quickly recognized as anger bubbling to the surface. Ice began to coat my fingers.

Hermes's eyes flicked down, curious. "That lack of control will get you killed."

I gritted my teeth. "You're saying you won't interfere? An entire village was wiped out—by corpse warriors, shadow stalkers, things from this *realm* causing chaos. Your followers and others are gone, and you all still won't fight?" I forced myself to focus, reigning in my magic.

"If we helped with everything, the balance would be thrown off," he said evenly. "War happens. Creatures cause destruction. The events in that village did raise alarms for some of us—but we're bound by rules. We'll gather answers, find out Agnar's motives, and which one of us let him into our realm."

I sighed, a headache forming at how things were seen here. "That's what we want to know too—what was spoken all those years ago, when the prophecy was given: *'He will build an army and have an ally who betrays their kind for the freedom they seek.'* Those were the words spoken by the voices. That's our main concern, because whatever this means, it's already in motion. Any ideas?"

Hermes's face turned contemplative; a flicker of emotion crossed his features before vanishing just as quickly. "A speculation," he said slowly, "but that's a huge assumption. One I'll be keeping to myself."

"So, essentially—trust no one?" I muttered, picking at a loose thread on my satchel. "Can you at least give us something useful? Anything?" So far, it seemed what we know, he knew—or he was only telling us what he wanted to.

Hermes's expression shifted; a smirk tugged at his mouth. "You remind me of someone..." he trailed off, then suddenly grinned. "Oh, by Zues, this just made my day. Don't get excited—I'm definitely not sharing." He stood quicky, energy shifting.

"There were murmurs among the fisherman—the island of Thera has grown cold, its volcano going silent. Quite odd, no? The Nychtari, usually linger around battlefields, so for them to be hunting you down... someone, or something, is using the Mormo and her abilities to find you." He rocked back on his heels, wings fluttering slightly. "Also, that little display of your ice—you need to train and find clarity quickly if you want to survive whatever's coming."

I glanced down at my hands, embarrassment rising in my chest. I had trained—though not much—and even the smallest emotional outburst made me lose control.

Someone cleared their throat, making me look up. Chione was standing now too. Her expression was serious as she stepped up beside Hermes. "I can train you. Your abilities are far beyond mine, but I can at least help you learn to wield them better—so you can give these poor mortals a break from the weather. That is, if you'll allow me." She inclined her head slightly.

I stared, surprised. The same woman who'd been so rude was actually offering to help—and she had magic close to mine. Finally, some real help. *Wait...was I the reason the weather had been so cold?*

I realized she was still waiting for a response, and I blushed.

"O-of course! I'd really appreciate the help. I do get tired of accidentally freezing things... like ships," I muttered.

"It's settled then. I'll return this evening to train," she said, offering a tight smile.

Just like Skadi during meditation, she vanished in a flurry of frost. Where she'd stood, a light sheen marked the floor.

"She's always been such a show-off," Hermes joked. "I'll leave you to relax. No one will bother you here—you're protected."

And then, he was gone. I stared at the spot where he'd been—he disappeared like he'd never even been there.

"Wha—?" I turned to my companions, pointing at the empty spot "Can I do that?" The awe in my voice didn't fade—in fact, I got more excited at the thought of being able to teleport.

"It takes years of practice—and you have to know exactly where you want to go, young one," Runar's voice rumbled.

I deflated at his answer. "Of course it takes years. Never get the badass powers right away, huh?"

I turned to Eirik, who was still quiet. "So, what are your thoughts?"

He locked eyes with me and frowned. "I still don't trust him."

I rolled my eyes. "Yeah. Didn't think you would—as always."

Chapter Twenty-Six

I stretched my arms overhead as I stood, letting out a soft groan as the stress of the day pressed into my shoulders.

"Well," I said, turning toward the hallway, "I'm going to find that bath. If I die to a hidden monster in there, please just let it."

"That... is awfully dark," Eirik muttered behind me.

I gave a crooked grin but didn't reply. The smell of saltwater and lavender intensified as I made my way through the hall. The stone shifted beneath my feet, turning smoother, cooler, until the corridor opened into a sunken bath chamber carved straight into the mountain.

It was... beautiful.

A deep pool reflected under soft torchlight, steam rising in lazy curls. The water seemed warmed by something beneath the stone itself, and small alcoves lined the walls, holding linens, woven robes, and polished basins. A fire crackled quietly in one corner, heat drifting up to the ceiling in thin ribbons. I exhaled, easing off my outer layers and setting them on the rack near the fire. The robe I pulled on was surprisingly soft, but not scratchy like the ones I'd used at the bathhouse. Once I stepped into the pool, I let out a real groan. The heat hit every sore muscle from the day's travel. I sank down slowly, closing my eyes, letting the silence stretch.

Maybe the gods didn't intervene much... but at least they built good bathhouses. I blew out a breath, sending ripples across the water's surface. I leaned forward, resting my arms on the stone edge and laying my head down. I tried to relax, tried not to think about everything that had happened so far—the words from Hermes about how the other gods and goddesses wouldn't help. I tried not to dwell on how he'd said my lack of control would get me killed, like I wasn't already aware of my shortcomings. I was carrying a dead goddess's legacy on my shoulders, and it was starting to sink into my heart.

Great, so much for relaxing. As my thoughts drifted to training, it wasn't that I minded training—especially with someone who might actually understand what I was dealing with. Or maybe I was just the different one. That thought formed a knot in my chest, that pressure of knowing everyone was watching, waiting, expecting more from me. They knew I was coming—the gods knew—and that made me even more nervous than before.

I looked up as a soft scuff of claws on stone echoed into the room. Runar padded in, his fur slightly puffed from the moisture in the air. He sniffed once, then let out a huff as settled on the smooth floor beside the pool.

"Tired of Eirik's company already?" I asked, eyes still half-closed.

I only got a low grunt from Runar in response, which made me chuckle. *Glad my company's at least tolerable.*

After a while, I looked over at him. He was already napping, stretched out quite comfortably.

"You know… I never actually asked you," I said quietly. "Do you have any abilities?"

He lifted his head, up, giving me a long, knowing look.

I pressed on. "I mean, you can't just be some ancient wolf that's massive for no reason. I feel like you're not exactly powerless."

He huffed softly through his nose, the sound almost like a laugh. His golden eyes caught the firelight, warm and amused, before his voice rumbled out amused.

"You are correct, you never asked. Or at least you never asked the right questions."

I squinted at him. "That's cheating, Runar."

He straightened up in his smaller form. "Think of it as a lesson. You should learn to ask questions about your companions better. Did you really believe I was just a regular wolf?"

I stared at him, then let out a groan. "Of course you'd turn this into some smug learning moment…"

"I feel you're just slow to catch on," he yawned.

I gasped. "Okay, that was rude." I flicked water at him.

He didn't flinch or seem bothered. He just stared, then let a small curl of frost lace along the edge of the bath where his paw rested. It snaked across the stone, its icy pattern beautiful before melting away.

I stared, wide-eyed. "Seriously, Runar?"

"Seriously."

"…So, I'm behind in my magic compared to the talking wolf. Amazing." I sank deeper into the water with a groan.

"I'm ancient," he said idly. "You're still learning. I'd say you're doing well enough—aside from your temper and anxiety… almost freezing ships."

I let out a defeated groan and splashed water in his direction again.

I resigned myself to finishing my bath quickly. I made sure to clean my hair thoroughly and quietly wished I had a razor. Once done, I stood to dry off. Runar, to his credit, had turned to face the door a while ago.

After drying off, I wrapped a new robe around myself. Its surprising softness was a small comfort. I gathered my old clothes before stepping carefully into the hallway. The stone was cool beneath my feet; the air from the bath spilled out into the hall, carrying the lingering scent of lavender and the wet stone. I peeked around the corner, cautious.

"He's outside, frostling," came Runar's voice from behind me.

I relaxed. "Oh, thank you—now I don't have to try and sneak to a room."

A huff. "This is you being sneaky? You age me quicker each day."

I turned sharply to him and glared "I am *not* that bad."

Facing forward again, I started walking. "Let's claim a room before Eirik takes the good one."

I moved fast—honestly, it was a power-walk down the hall, Runar trailing behind with an amused snort. I didn't stop until I found a room tucked near the far end.

And gods, it was breathtaking.

A round bed stood at the center, draped in soft blue linens and sheer curtains that spilled from a gold-framed canopy. The base was etched in delicate swirling metalwork shaped like owls, and the entire thing was slightly elevated on a polished marble platform. It faced a wide arched window to the south, carved to frame the distant mountains. Light pooled across the floor in soft streaks, catching the gold threads stitched into the edges of the cushions.

I walked around slowly, marveling at everything. The rest of the room was equally elegant: blue and ivory fabrics with intricate Greek patterns lined the walls, draping between marble columns and over medium sized windows. Vases painted with owls and mythic symbols were scattered throughout. A low table with fruit and a pitcher of wine rested beside a seating area of velvet-cushioned benches, all lit by soft-glow lanterns built into the walls.

Do I want to know how the fruit and wine just appeared there?

A shuffle had me turning as Runar padded in and immediately claimed a cool patch of floor near the far column. I smiled and walked straight to the heavy curtain near the back, dragging it closed as I ducked behind to dress. The area was cut into the rocks of the mountain—a small space for privacy. My clothes were dry now, and I tugged them on fast before wrapping my damp hair into a loose knot at the base of my neck, leaving my armor off for now.

When I emerged, Runar lifted his head lazily. "Ah, and she wears clothes once more," he muttered.

"We are guests in a divine rest house," I shot back. "I'd rather not nearly flash Eirik twice in one lifetime."

Runar yawned, showing a row of sharp teeth. "Ah yes, mortals and their dignity," he said lazily. "Though somehow, I doubt he'd mind."

I froze mid-step, heat rushing to my face. "Wha—Runar!" I hissed, mortified. "That's—no! Absolutely not!"

Flustered, I hurried from the room. *Nope, not a mental image I needed. At all.* The scent of roasted herbs and bread grew stronger as I followed the hall. I didn't make it far before I found Eirik in the lounge area, already into the wine and looking entirely too happy about it.

I raised a brow. "Why do I smell food?" I glanced toward the kitchen area and spotted warm food sitting out.

"Seems the messenger god is quite hospitable. Left us fresh meat and bread while you were bathing," Eirik grinned, gulping down another swig of wine.

"Was that before or after you decided to drink half the amphora?"

He shrugged, unapologetic. "Hard to say. Time moves differently when you're relaxed."

I made my way over, snatching a piece of bread before settling onto one of the cushioned benches. The moment I sat, I caught his eyes flicking to my head, his expression shifting ever so slightly.

"What?" I muttered around a bite of bread.

"Nothing," he hummed, lifting his wine up to his mouth.

"No, you did that thing. That's your judging face, Eirik." My mouth was full of bread, but the frown was clear on my face.

"You have a lot of hair," he said plainly, gaze lingering. "And it's a mess... and damp still."

I gave him a flat look. "I didn't exactly have time to braid it like some royal. Or do you have a spare brush in your pouch I don't know about?" I reached up, suddenly self-conscious, touching the bun I'd twisted together—it was already falling apart.

His grin tugged wider. "No, but it's amusing to see you try to be intimidating with half your hair spilling everywhere."

I rolled my eyes and stuffed a grape into my mouth in retaliation. "Glad my suffering's a form of entertainment."

He leaned back in his seat and pointed to his hair, eyebrow raised. "I also have long hair, my kaerr. But as warriors, we must keep ourselves ready for battle."

I stared. His hair was always neatly braided down his back, the sides shaved. It was your typical warrior hairstyle.

I looked up to his eyes. "Yeah," I said, pointed to the braid. "I have never been good at braiding my own hair." I paused, blinking slowly. "What did you just call me?" I tried to rack my brain for old Norse, but I was drawing a blank.

Eirik froze, then shifted—suddenly more interested in the wine than before. "It's just...a word," he muttered, so quietly I almost couldn't hear him.

I narrowed my eyes at him. "A word that sounds suspiciously soft coming from someone who usually calls me *Lady Ravena* for his own amusement."

He didn't look at me—flat-out refused to. His response was a shrug. "You misunderstood."

"Pretty sure I didn't" I blinked at him, gaping slightly before setting my bread down and leaning forward.

"No, you surely did," he insisted, clearing his throat before standing abruptly. "I am going to go check the perimeter."

I rolled my eyes. "The perimeter? You just came from outside. Runar gave you away."

"Well..." he was already halfway to the door. "I'm going again—to make sure we stay safe."

I opened my mouth to protest, but he was gone before I could say a word. *Didn't Hermes say we'd be safe here?*

I stared at the door for a long second after Eirik left.

"What the hell just happened?" I muttered, still processing that little moment.

The silence that followed made it worse. I glanced at the food again and sighed, grabbing a slice of meat this time and tearing into it. I sank deeper into the cushions, chewing slower now, letting myself try and relax while I ate. Whatever Eirik's little word slip was, I wasn't sure I wanted to unpack it right now.

Eventually, I pulled my legs up on the bench and stared out the nearby window. The light outside was starting to fade, painting the walls with softer tones. *Chione would be here soon enough. I guessed I should get ready and wake Runar.* Now I just had to figure out where the hell one trained on the side of a mountain.

I took one more bite of the food before pushing myself up with a grunt and straightening my clothes out. I made my way back down the hallway to my room, my bare feet sliding slightly on the slick marble. The door was still ajar, and as I nudged it open, I quickly noted Runar had moved. I stopped, hands on my hip. Runar had decided to make his new resting spot the bed.

One ear flicked toward me, but he didn't move. That was the only indication he'd heard me enter. "Okay, you bed-stealer, it's time to get up. You're going to come sit and watch training, at least." I grabbed my armor, quickly put on what I had, and tied my sword back to my side. Sitting down on the edge of the bed, I slid my boots back on—the dark leather now cool to the touch.

"Come on, you lazy wolf. You haven't even moved." I crossed my arms in judgment as he let out a huff and stretched.

"Why must I come watch you and that snow nymph likely destroy half the mountain? I am tired, and the bed is open," was his bland reply.

"Emotional support, Runar. Emotional support. I need someone I'm familiar with there, and Eirik is currently being weird," I muttered.

That caused him to raise his head. "What did you do to the poor boy?" he rumbled.

"I did nothing! He muttered a word—kaerr. Then got all jumpy and left." I crossed my arms defensively.

Runar laughed—an actual bark of laughter that made me jump. "Oh, and did the fire-blood deny this word?" His tone was mischievous.

"He told me I misunderstood, then left, saying he needed to check the perimeter. I can't remember what that word means right now." I let my hair down all the way and ran my fingers through it, wincing at the knots. *I really needed to buy a brush from one of the markets.*

Runar jumped down from the bed "This is an extremely amusing situation, young frostling. Who knew your guardian would feel such a way?" he said, making his way out of the room and leaving me standing there, confused.

I quickly followed after him, my cheeks flushing. *What does he mean? Eirik feels what way?*

I rushed to catch up, nearly slipping on the floor as I did.

"Wait! Runar, you can't just leave it at that and walk off!"

He didn't stop, just kept going as the entrance to the main hall came into view.

"Hey, I'm serious, what does it mean—"

I skidded to a halt, nearly tripping over Runar when he stopped short. I glanced up—and there she was.

Chione stood in the center of the room as if she never left, her hands folded neatly in front of her.

Chione tilted her head. "You look decently rested, Ravena, but it seems I've appeared at an inopportune moment?"

"Uh—no, just a stubborn wolf who won't answer any of my questions." I muttered, embarrassed.

"Good, then we can train if no further distractions are present. Follow me," she said, making her way through the door onto the veranda and turning to the right, her shimmering robes flowing behind her.

To the right of the house, hidden by trees on the cliff's edge, a circular area had been cleared—the dirt holding old grooves in multiple places. I could feel this area was no stranger to fighting. It was darker here; the sun had lowered on the western side of the mountain, so our only lighting came from braziers around the area, their flames glowing an unnerving light blue. Chione must have caught me eyeing the flames.

"They're not normal flames, as you've gathered. Hestia added this to the training grounds after she finished with the house. Have you not noticed yet the fires never dwindle inside?" she stated.

I stood there, feeling like an idiot. But could you blame me? Since the beginning, we'd been staying with humans, not gods. So yeah, I was a little amazed at seeing their powers up close.

"I wasn't really paying attention—though some things made me wonder," I answered, reaching up to rub the back of my neck.

Her mouth set into a frown. "Hmm. Hopefully in a fight you're more skilled at picking up signals of what's mortal and what's not. The energy is there; you just have to sense it."

"I can feel when energy is off, but I can't yet pinpoint the direction or what the energy is...exactly," I stated.

She let out a long exhale—one that clearly showed she was judging me. "Your guardian has failed you, then."

My right eye twitched, but I said nothing in response.

"Let's get started then—see if your Norseman has shown you anything in combat." She drew her own sword from a sheath I hadn't seen until now.

The blade caught my eye immediately: a leaf-shaped xiphos, but not like any I'd seen before. Pale blue-silver steel glinted in the light, etched with swirling designs that resembled frozen rivers. The guard flared outward, shaped like frostbitten leaves, icy blue against the pale leather-wrapped hilt. But it was the pommel that held my attention the longest—an intricate snowflake, artfully carved.

"Are you going to draw your blade, or just stand there and stare at my mine?" Her tone reached my ears—taunting, almost bored.

I snapped my gaze back to hers, jaw tightening. I settled my hand on the handle of my sword and pulled it from its sheath.

In a blink—before I could even raise my sword properly—Chione was gone.

"What..." I mumbled, just as the air shifted. I dodged sideways. Where I'd been standing, a deep gouge tore through the ground, ice spiderwebbing up the sides in intricate, sharp patterns. The air around us was bitingly cold.

"Hm. Your reaction time is decent. Still slow. Is that guardian of yours teaching you anything, really?" Her voice ghosted behind me. I spun fast, parrying on instinct. Sparks flew between us at the sheer force of our blades colliding.

Sweat gathered at the back of my neck, my ice prickling at my fingertips. I clenched my teeth and pushed back with everything I had, my arms trembling under the strain. The ground beneath my feet cracked, magic slipping loose, snaking upward through the stone.

Push now, Ravena. Jump backwards.

I did as told—pushed, leapt, my sword scraping the ground in front of me, leaving a razor-thin line of frost.

"Oh, so you do have some fight in you, girl... or are you only able to evade?" Chione taunted, then launched at me, her weapon raised for an attack. For once, I lunged forward without hesitation and met her halfway, our swords clashing in a shower of sparks. Ice built across the ground, creeping up both our blades.

"A warning before we started fighting would've been nice..."

I gasped, pulling back just in time to dodge a slash that would've carved my side open. I slid on my feet, catching my balance—barely.

"An enemy will give no warning. You'd be dead. Your reaction time's good, I'll give you that. But you're still fighting like a mortal." Her blade raised again. "Fight like the goddess you're meant to become. Right now, you disgrace her magic. Her name."

My jaw locked. From the corner of my eye, I saw Runar—ears pinned flat, breath curling frost.

I raised my blade—the stance Eirik drilled into me burned into my bones.

Don't let her words get to you. Focus, or you'll fail. Skadi's voice was firm. I tried to listen.

But her words were muffled in my ear. I was angry. Skadi didn't care if someone was sullying her name, but I did. This woman had no right to speak of things she didn't know.

"Come on, young goddess—is that all you've got, or are you done?" Chione jabbed again.

I grunted and surged forward with a speed even I hadn't expected. I locked swords with her in a rush of wind, ice crackling where our blades met. Chione's hair blew back from her face, her eyes went wide—then she smirked, matching me step for step.

My temper rose, and my hold over my ice slipped. Frost snaked up my blade, spreading with rapid speed.

Then—a horrible groaning sound split the air, and a crack shot up my blade.

"Ravena!" Runar yelled. But it was too late. Before I could move, my blade shattered as my ice exploded outward, shaking the area. Chione's' blade narrowly missed my arm before she leapt back. I dropped to one knee, out of breath, heart racing.

The area fell silent before a voice broke through, lightly amused.

"My, my, that was impressive." Hermes voice sounded from my right. "Your little power outburst nearly caused the barrier around this place to waver."

I stayed kneeling, staring at the shattered remains of the sword I'd gotten not long ago. Ice spread along the ground and wove its way around the forest trees. The air had grown drastically cooler, but none of us seemed to care.

Chione knelt down and picked up a piece of the blade. "This is a mortal-made sword…" She looked quickly up at Hermes.

He reached my side, placing a gentle hand on my shoulder. "You might want to recall your ice, unless you wish to freeze the poor trees any further."

I snapped my head up and saw the ice creeping higher up the trees. *Dammit.* My mind flashed back to the poor tree spirits. I quickly worked to rein in my ice and watched as it slowly retreated back toward me.

A massive, furry body settled on my other side. I glanced up to see Runar glaring at both Chione and Hermes.

"It's okay, Runar. It was my fault for losing control."

"No, young one. This woman should not have provoked you," he growled, hackles raised even as he sat.

Hermes removed his hand from my shoulder in a surrendering motion to Runar. "You and I both know, wolf, that an opponent will taunt to gain the upper hand. In battle, there's no time for breaks or loss of control," he said calmly, moving to Chione's side.

Runar exhaled, his hackles easing. "Then it's time for Ravena and me to discuss Skadi's old home—and how we can secure passage there. It seems she needs space to better understand her power, away from so many eyes."

"Skadi's' home?" I slowly stood, my legs still shaking as I asked the question.

"Yes, Thyraheim is the fortress she grew up in and lived through her years," he replied.

Before I could reply, Hermes stepped forward. "You said you required passage? We don't usually travel between pantheons, but for our future goddess here, I believe I can help you out." He winked.

I rolled my eyes before turning to Runar.

"If we have to secure passage—through portals, I'm assuming—how did you get here?"

All eyes turned to my wolf.

"Every god or goddess has the ability to form ripples for travel, as you saw Hermes and Chione do. It is not the same as the guarded portals," he said, looking up at the night sky. "When you lost control of your powers the first time, you released a surge that created a ripple right in front of me. It was only for a moment, but it was enough."

I thought back to that day—the embarrassment I'd felt in front of the villagers, and the anger at Eirik's words. A familiar uncertainty crept in again; I still couldn't find balance between my emotions and my ice.

Chione let out a thoughtful sigh before sheathing her blade, and Hermes offered a small smile.

"We'll discuss getting you and your group to Thyraheim tomorrow, after the celebration, yes? Relax tonight—or train, whichever you choose—but don't let yourself dwell on that slip-up. We all mess up at some point in our existence. Divine or mortal, everyone has their flaws," Hermes said, wrapping an arm around Chione.

"Meet us at the Acropolis before midday. We'll enjoy the festivities first—then get you out of here."

One moment they were there—the next, the space was empty.

Chapter Twenty-Seven

I don't think I will get used to that. My shoulders slumped once they were gone. The night had turned cold; part of it was the air, but most of it was me. My gaze swept the surrounding trees, a flicker of concern rising—Eirik hadn't come to watch, especially since he wasn't the one leading the training this time. Maybe I'd been too intrusive earlier and made him upset.

"Are you alright?" Runar's deep voice cut through my thoughts as he settled beside me. His eyes were softer than usual—gentler than their typical stern look.

Despite the cold and half-frozen soil beneath me, I slumped down on my backside. The familiar ache of training starting to settle in. "To be honest? No. Something new always comes up. If it's not me losing control of my emotions, it's finding out mortal weapons are useless—or that I apparently have a fortress now." I wrapped my arms around my knees and looked up at the stars.

"I apologize for not mentioning it earlier," he rumbled. "Back at the pandokeion, I felt it wasn't the right time. I was mistaken."

His left ear twitched at a distant sound, but he stayed relaxed, so I ignored it. If we were in danger, Runar wouldn't look so at ease.

"Skadi's home in Thyraheim was where she trained and performed her duties. It's also where Odin decided to imprison those who betrayed the gods. Think of her as a warden," he paused, then huffed. "I told her it was a mistake to keep that giant locked up there."

"Because he's an ice giant?" I asked.

He nodded, "Correct. Even with all the wards, locked away where the cold couldn't reach him, I wouldn't put it past him to gather his strength by leeching whatever chill he could from the earth."

Runar stood and inclined his head for me to follow. "Thyraheim is like any other fortress, but her father also built deep into the mountain. There are floors even Skadi never accessed—most of them are sealed with old magic."

I dusted off my clothes as I followed, glancing down at the remains of my shattered sword for only a breath.

"How hard would it be for someone, or even something, to break in there and release him?" I asked.

We wove our way down the lighted path back to the house; the only sound was our light footfalls on the ground.

"Very," Runar said. "Someone like Eirik—or any lesser being—would die by the magic surrounding it if they even tried to break through. Even higher divines would struggle," he paused, "unless they had help and specific knowledge of the wards." His voice was tense, hackles raised as he relived those old memories.

"The prophecy, or warning, that someone would betray their pantheon to gain the freedom they seek, but it didn't specify Norse or Greek. So how did this individual even meet Agnar?" I pondered aloud.

As we stepped inside the house, I glanced around and realized Eirik was nowhere to be seen—a small frown settled on my face.

A nudge to my back made me stumble; Runar had shifted down in size once more was back and padded toward our room.

"Let's rest, Ravena. Tomorrow will be busy, and I'm not looking forward to it," he grumbled, probably already dreading being around so many humans.

The room was warm when we stepped inside, a bigger fire now burning. I quickly ducked behind the changing curtain to peel off my dirty clothes.

At this rate, I was going to need to do laundry again. Strangely enough, and randomly, I'd kept my sleepwear from my own time. It was my one chance to wear something actually comfortable and not just another robe.

I slid into bed and pulled the covers over me, letting out a deep exhale out. Runar jumped up at the end of the bed and sprawled out, earning only a raised brow from me.

"What? I also prefer to be comfortable, so why should I sleep on the cold floor?" he muttered.

"I didn't say anything, just seeing an ancient being laying at the foot of the bed like a dog is amusing" I grinned, and he raised his upper lip at me in annoyance.

I looked up at the ceiling, the intricate designs capturing my attention. "Do you think we'll find any answers at the fortress?"

"Finding answers to who did this won't be possible. Any traces of magic are long gone. It's been two years since he broke free, and I couldn't detect whose magic it was when I investigated. This person is strong—to be able to hide their presence like that. But we will be able to get you proper battle armor—and a weapon that won't shatter with your ice." He laid his head down and relaxed.

"Well, at least part of that was reassuring." I shifted under the covers, pulling them closer. "I forget it's only been a short amount of time since Skadi had passed. I apologize for being insensitive sometimes."

Runar cracked one eye open. "No apologies needed, young one. For you, twenty-three years have passed. Your realm's time runs differently than ours, so for us, Skadi's death was recent."

I closed my eyes, letting his words sink in. I had lived for twenty-three years—grew up, made connections, enjoyed life... but for them, Skadi had only just died.

Sleep that night was not peaceful. One moment I was closing my eyes, the next I was standing in a massive room so cold I could feel it.

The area was covered in ice, like it lived there—it didn't crowd the spaces or take over anything, it shimmered like decorations. I could feel myself wandering forward in a rush, down hallways with so many twists and turns, my heart racing as the building shook from a force below. A horrid growl rang up from the lower levels, and as I breached the last door, there at the bottom of the stairs, free from a cell, stood an impossibly tall figure covered in gashes, his skin a pale blue. This had to be Agnar; the unease that snaked through me had to be from Skadi, as dream-me drew my sword defensively.

"Skadi, you betray your own kin! You and your pathetic father are siding with the All Father!" Agnar spat, standing to his full height—over seven feet.

"The giant's way of thinking wasn't what my father and I aligned with. The war against the gods was pointless," my voice—no, her voice—carried through the cavern. Shifting in anticipation, none the sooner before Agnar, despite his injury, leapt forward with a stolen blade from a fallen guard and clashed with Skadi. We danced in a heated sword fight around each other. Skadi's strength in this moment was powerful, but Agnar was gaining strength as the wards keeping the snow and cold out had broken.

"You allowed Odin to name you a goddess? Pfft. You were a giantess of the highest honor here in Jotunheim, but went for revenge for your father and came back married to a god!" Agnar taunted.

"I have no interest in explaining my life to you. You broke laws and tried to disrupt our realms barriers. Surrender, and stop this unnecessary chaos, Agnar."

He snarled, feinting left before driving his blade forward. Skadi tried to block, but the impact knocked her off balance—then came the searing pain.

A sharp gasp rang through the air. My eyes slid slowly down to my—wait, her—midsection. There, a blade made of ice pierced through Skadi's stomach. I could feel the amount of pain she was in, and my horror actually mixed with hers.

He leant forward. "The gods don't deserve to be the only powers out there, and I plan to succeed in my goals—not that you will be around to stop me." He wrenched the blade free, and I watched as we fell to the ground.

Before his sword could come down again, my vision tore away. I was running, holding my side, weaving in and out of the hallways and trying to make it outside. The dread and nauseous feeling was creeping into me; I slid around the corner, breaking through big double doors and into the barren ice lands below.

Slipping down the side of the mountain, I crashed into the snow below, but still those footsteps followed. I could hear the ring of metal slice through the air as his sword narrowly missed my head.

"This will be your end, Skadi of Jotunheim! Where is your precious Odin now?" He jeered.

A white blur came out of nowhere, barreling into Agnar and throwing him away from me. I ran and didn't stop until my body could no longer go on.

I realized I had seen this part before, when I was in my time. I could only observe as Skadi pleaded for saving once again.

Chapter Twenty-Eight

"Ravena!" a sharp voice yelled out. Warm hands were shaking me roughly. I sat up with a strangled gasp, my vision blurry.

"Breathe—breathe, Ravena. It was just a dream," Eirik's voice rang out, his hands still gripping my shoulders.

Tears welled up in my eyes as I finally made out his face, and before I could second-guess myself, I collapsed into his chest. His arms immediately, instinctively, wrapped around me—holding me close.

"It wasn't just a... dream, Eirik," I strained to get out. I kept seeing her blood seeping from the wound on her stomach, Agnar's roar, and the dread she felt as it all happened. "It was her memory—the night Agnar escaped."

"Talking about her last night must have triggered the memory. I'm sorry you had to relive that," Runar's deep voice echoed from somewhere on my right.

I couldn't respond, and I didn't want to. I kept my face firmly planted in Eirik's tunic. His warmth was the only thing keeping me from fully panicking, and it chased away the cold left from the dream. His muscles were tense, but he held me securely, as if his body alone could drive off what I'd seen.

I stayed there for who knows how long—my tears dried, and my embarrassing sniffling had finally stopped.

"Are you alright, Ravena?" Eirik asked, leaning back slightly to study my face.

I straightened, flushing as I realized I was still collapsed against him. I looked down and shrugged, "I—uh, can't answer that. Not right now, at least."

Eirik nodded, a frown crossing his face in understanding.

Runar came to my side and nudged me. "Why don't you get cleaned up for the day? We spent quite a while trying to wake you. We leave soon for the top of this mountain."

I snapped my head toward the window and froze—the sun was already climbing toward midday. I scrambled shakily out of bed and away from Eirik's arms to stand on the cold floor.

"Thank you... for waking me. And for the emotional support," I mumbled, managing a small smile.

He only tipped his head in acknowledgement before standing to straighten his clothes and leave the room.

I quickly grabbed my clean tunic, pants, and armor before following Runar down the hall to the baths.

The water warmed away whatever extra cold clung to my body, and I relaxed against the stones. Runar had settled with his back to me, guarding the door. I took a deep breath and closed my eyes.

"You know, I saw you in the memory. You were fully ready to sacrifice yourself so Skadi could escape," I murmured.

Runar's ears perked, and his body shifted. "Yes. She was my friend. I knew the chances of losing her to her injuries were great, but I'd rather see her escape than be finished off by something she couldn't fight." He turned his head, his right meeting mine. "I'd do the very same for you, you know. You're my friend—not just someone I follow."

Tears pricked at my eyes again and I quickly wiped them away, a watery smile finding its way onto my face.

"Thank you."

I felt lighter as we stepped out of the house and made our way back up the Acropolis. The memory lingered, but I did my best to shove it to the back of my mind. I could hear chatter, laughter, and kids screaming as we got closer to the top. The weather today was mild, crisp, and for once, I didn't need a cloak. We'd left them behind at the rest house. I was honestly shocked; usually, with this much anxiety, I'd have sent the temperature plummeting.

As we reached the steps at the rear of the temple, I saw the area had been decorated with winter flowers and banners, and there were people everywhere.

The energy felt lighter. Everyone was happy, drinking wine, eating food, enjoying each other's company. But I could also feel something heavier in the air, most likely divine. I couldn't see any gods or goddesses yet—not that I'd even know what they look like.

"Ah, there you are! I was hoping you didn't decide to skip out," Hermes's voice floated through the crowd as the humans parted for him and Chione. Some whispered in awe, while others acted as if this were a normal occurrence—being in the presence of the divine.

I gave a tight smile and nodded a greeting. Hermes studied my face, a knowing look passing over his features before it vanished.

"Come, let's enjoy the festivities. No one would dare try anything here," he said, holding out his arm to me. I quirked a brow but accepted, despite Eirik's obvious disapproval.

A small clay cup of wine was pressed into my hand as we walked through the celebration. I glanced up at the marble structure above us, craning my neck to look inside the temple. "It's strange to see them all so relaxed around two divine beings...."

"Hmm. We're not like most of the others who look down on mortals. I find their company fascinating. Besides, how can they pray to us without knowing our true selves?" He smirked. "And you meant three, future goddess."

I rolled my eyes, but listened as he talked about the festival and how it celebrated the coming end of winter. A few elders came up to speak with

Hermes—who knows about what—but I'd already drifted toward the Parthenon, my focus slipping. The building was stunning, but something about the energy here set my nerves on edge.

I gently unwound my arm from Hermes, catching his attention. "I'll be back, if you don't mind? I want to explore the area a little more."

"Of course. Chione and I will be around here somewhere if you seek us out," he said, giving a small bow before turning back to his conversation.

I followed that strange sensation—the closer I got to the Parthenon, the colder and heavier the air became. As I stepped inside, the giant statue of Athena greeted me. Around the base lay coins, flowers, and an overflowing amount of offerings.

A throat cleared behind me. I turned to see Eirik and Runar making their way to stand beside me.

Eirik studied the statue curiously, but I still couldn't shake this feeling.

"Who is this woman?" he asked, gesturing toward the statue.

"Athena—the Goddess of Wisdom, warfare, and handicraft," I mumbled, keeping my voice low so I didn't disturb the area. "Her name is what Athenae is named after, and it's said she's Zeus's favorite of his children."

"Such knowledge coming from a woman... and was the favorite." a deep, rich voice practically purred.

I whirled around, Eirik following suit, his hand going for his blade. I quickly laid a hand on his arm to stop him and shook my head. No—we definitely didn't want to start a fight in a temple.

There, standing no more than sixteen feet from us, was a man with unruly, curly brown hair that swept over his face, lightly shielding molten gold-colored eyes. His jaw was sharp, with barely noticeable stubble along it. He wore the standard Greek robe, but his was a deep wine red that exposed well-muscled arms. The final touch: grapevine leaf wreath woven into his hair, and a wine glass carried lazily in one hand.

His presence hit me like a physical force, the air itself seeming to bend around him. Those golden eyes caught the torchlight inside the temple, glinting with amusement.

"Well, well," he said, "I just had to see who Hermes was talking about." His gaze swept over us, lingering on Eirik for a moment before sliding to me. "A demigoddess, a demigod, and... a wolf?" He gestured lazily.

Eirik shifted in front of me in an instant, his body a wall of heat and muscle. "State your business," he demanded, his hand resting on the hilt of his blade... again.

The man didn't even flinch. Instead, his golden eyes stayed locked on me, his smirk deepening, as though he found the whole situation endlessly amusing.

"Business?" he echoed, his tone light and mocking. "As I said, I am merely indulging my curiosity. And I must say..." He drawled, "You, my dear, are quite the curiosity."

My breath caught in my throat as his gaze bore into mine. It wasn't just his words—it was him. His presence was overwhelming, magnetic in a way I couldn't fully explain. I clenched my fists, forcing myself to hold his gaze.

"Who are you?" I managed, my voice sharp despite the unease clawing at me. I felt like I *should* know him; he reeked of divine energy.

He placed a hand over his heart, his smile playful. "Ah, where are my manners, my *kalos*. I am Dionysus, God of Wine, revelry, and all things delightful." His voice dipped lower, golden eyes gleaming. "And you, it seems, have captured my attention."

Eirik immediately stepped between us, blocking my view. "I sense nothing good from you, God of Wine. Ravena has no need for your attention."

Dionysus tilted his head, that ever present grin never wavering. "Oh, but are you sure?" he murmured, his voice now harboring something darker.

I narrowed my eyes and stepped out from behind Eirik. "I most certainly have no need for your attention. You can answer us by explaining what you meant about Athena—*used to be* the favorite of Zeus?" I demanded.

He only smirked, turning slightly toward the exit, his head cocked as if about to speak. But before he could answer, another voice cut in—and a disappointed look crossed his face.

"Dion, leave this young woman alone. You and her have no business together," Hermes voice ordered as he stepped into the temple tense. Chione at his side was uneasy as well, and I could gather from their postures that this God wasn't someone to trust if even his sibling was wary.

Dionysus rolled his eyes, then smiling playfully. "You are absolutely no fun, brother. I was simply curious." He sauntered toward the exit, stopping next to Hermes, then turned to study Athena's statue.

A wicked smirk crossed his face. "What a shame, isn't it, brother? The great Athena—not even around anymore to enjoy all these offerings, huh?" And just like that, he was gone in a golden ripple.

The temple was oppressively still. I noticed Hermes's jaw was set hard, his face flickering with something—anger, sorrow, fear—I couldn't quite place it. But in the next blink, it was gone, replaced by a subdued smile.

"I apologize for my sibling's behavior, dear friends. He has always been one for theatrics—and it's only worse around new company." Hermes tone was casual, but I could hear the strain. He shifted, draping an arm around Chione's shoulders. Chione's gaze stayed fixed on a spot in front of her, making no eye contact with any of us, which only made me worry there was something more behind the conversation the two siblings had.

Eirik finally let his posture relax and stepped back, still watching Hermes. "That brother of yours seemed rather interested in Ravena—he didn't care that I was in his way."

I crossed my arms. "Like I told him, I do not desire his attention. But I am more curious about his statement about Athena..." I turned to her statue. The air still held a somber feel to it, like there was a story that needed telling but had been buried. "I find it strange we haven't met her—a festival for winter is being thrown directly outside a temple dedicated to her…" I trailed off.

Hermes shrugged. "Our sister prefers to stay away from things such as this. Dionysus just loves to rile me up over past events, nothing more. Nothing to worry your pretty head over."

I narrowed my eyes and opened my mouth to argue, but a nudge at my calf had me glancing down to see Runar shake his head no.

I sighed "So, I assume he's left the festival, correct? We can go back out and not have to worry about him?"

"I am unsure. This type of festival is his favorite—wine, women, you know, all the fun things." Hermes smirked before turning himself and Chione around. "It is unlikely he'll approach you again. He's all about games."

And with that, they were gone, back to mingling with the mortals and whoever else had shown up for the event.

I heard Eirik grunt, and to be fair, I totally understood his reaction—we didn't want to run into some god who scarily seemed to have his eyes set on me. I turned to Eirik. "I think I'm done with people today…. could we sneak away back to the rest house and maybe train?" I asked.

That earned me a smirk and a chuckle before he wrapped an arm around my shoulder. "Let us go train then, but you've shattered your sword. So, hand-to-hand combat it is. Are you up for that?" he teased, pulling me along toward the exit.

I groaned in realization; *I was either going to end up with a broken bone… or just be sore.*

"I have to keep practicing—talking my way out of fights isn't going to happen," I admitted, already regretting asking to train.

His deep laugh echoed up the marble pillars as we walked along the trail to the house. No one stopped us, and thankfully we didn't run into

Dionysus again, but the hairs on the back of my neck prickled before we turned the bend—someone had definitely been watching us walk away.

Chapter Twenty-Nine

Afternoon came faster than I expected, and my hopes of ever winning a spar against Eirik dwindled just as quickly. My behind hit the earth for what had to be the fifth time—though honestly, I'd lost count by now. My guardian had hit his second wind, apparently, because he wasn't holding back.

"Come on, Ravena, I've seen children hold their ground better than this," Eirik teased, holding out a hand to help me up—which I begrudgingly accepted.

I wasn't as worked up as I normally would be, so I was counting that as a win. My ice had stayed steady on my fingertips and hadn't flared once. I stepped back into a neutral stance with a grin. "Let's go again—I want to try working with my magic a bit more."

I slipped off my gloves, earning a raised brow from him, but only smiled before focusing on forming a thin coat of ice around my hands. I clenched my fists as it spread, creating a protective layer.

"Oh, that looks like it won't be painful at all," Eirik muttered dryly.

I giggled, nearly losing concentration. I swear his ears turn red... though what caused it, I wasn't sure.

With a quick shake of my head, I surged forward aiming a punch at his face with my right. Of course, he dodged left, specks of snow left in the air where my hand struck. I steadied myself and lashed out with my left, trying to land a blow to his stomach. His eyes widened in shock, but he still grabbed my wrists. His hands were hot, not normal at all, and to make it worse the ice near my wrist turned watery but didn't melt completely. I furrowed my brow as he released me, stumbling back a step.

"Okay. That…" I pointed to his hand. "Was not normal." I started thinking back to all the times I'd noticed his odd temperature and frowned. I stepped back. I had an idea—it might be stupid and I could hurt him. But something told me to trust my gut on this. *Please don't let me be wrong… if I'm right, I'm going to be pissed.* Those were my final thoughts before lifting my hand, fully committed.

"Ravena? I don't like that look… whatever you're planning, don't" Eirik said, caution in his tone as he shifted into a guarded stance.

I exhaled a deep breath and, in one fluid motion, sent a wave of ice mixed with snow I'd pulled from the cold air around me straight toward him. I watched as it hurtled in his direction—and right before it could make contact, it stopped. No—it didn't stop. It melted, and behind it stood Eirik, a hand raised, palm out, fire dancing dangerously around it.

My mouth dropped open in disbelief as I watched the fire die down, and then that feeling morphed into hurt.

"You… you've had abilities all this time?" I whispered, my hands dangling uselessly at my side, the ice slowly dripping onto the ground.

He's kept that from me all this time? Even as I've struggled…

"Ravena… let me explain," he began, stepping forward, and I immediately stepped back.

I let out a sharp laugh. "Let you explain?! Now? You've known about my abilities—magic, whatever it's called—since day two! You've seen me struggle, cry, feel absolutely helpless with control, and you've been walking around with fire abilities this whole time! And never once offered to help!" My breathing came fast, shoulders shaking. I was pissed, hurt, and betrayed all at once as my brain scrambled to process it.

I held his gaze—his expression was a mess of emotions that, right now, I didn't even want to try to figure out. But guilt stood out the most. He opened his mouth as if to say something, then closed it just as quickly. I clenched my teeth in frustration.

"Even now, you have nothing to say?" I threw my hands up and turned, walking off into the surrounding trees, away from them.

Eirik made no move to follow, or say anything to stop me. He stood frozen to his spot. Runar's words were the last thing I heard before I was out of range.

"I told you, fire blood—this would come back to bite you if you weren't honest from the start."

I stomped my way through the thin trees, swatting branches out of my way and silently thanking the gods I didn't trip. I didn't want to add any more embarrassment to my day. My boots crunched over rocky ground, sharp stones digging into the soles. As I moved, frost spread across bark when my fingers brushed the branches. I quickly pulled my hands back, clenching them into fist and shoving them deep into my cloak.

It wasn't a long trek, and soon I exited the tree line on the east side of the mountain. The sun had already started setting, casting the area in deep shadows. A bitter, chilly wind blew through and hung in the air, and I wasn't sure if it was the weather or my fault.

I dropped down onto a flat rock with a huff, hanging my legs over the edge. The view from here was—ironically—the Theatre of Dionysus. The outer area was already glowing with torchlight, and from this distance, I could make out the small figures of patrons gathered in groups, their laughter barely carrying up the hill. The wards here kept them from seeing me, I assumed—if they even bothered to look up this direction.

More patrons began arriving, and it had me wondering how a god like him could have so many worshippers. His attitude was far from pleasing. Even if they came for the theatre show it still baffled me.

Watching the crowd below, my thoughts refused to settle. I was still angry—hurt, mostly—but underneath it, some annoying voice kept whispering that maybe I'd gone too far. I shoved the thought down. He'd lied.

He'd kept something that big from me, even after knowing about my struggle. Still... maybe there was a reason he hadn't said anything.

This thought process continued for a bit, the sky growing darker, the air colder as dusk settled in. I noticed the laughter from below getting louder, and the theatre was now full of citizens and performers.

Not a care in the world for them—right now, anyways. I rubbed my face with both hands, trying to ease the pressure of a headache forming behind my eyes.

Chapter Thirty

"My Kalos, why the long face?" That same seductive, honeyed voice purred. I'd only just heard that voice a few hours ago, and to hear it again so soon startled me.

I scrambled up so fast my foot slipped and I rocked backwards. I didn't fall—golden grapevines appeared out of nowhere, wrapping around me and pulling me away from the edge. I didn't like the feel of them at all; their energy was suffocating, heat crawling over my skin.

This god's abilities are not honest, Ravena. Stay aware. Skadi's voice echoed sharply through my mind.

I shook my head quickly, narrowing my eyes as I spotted Dionysus lounging in a nearby tree. The top of his robe was even looser now, like it was only a suggestion. I flushed deep red before looking away.

"Remove these from me," I demanded.

A chuckle was my only response as the vines unraveled and disappeared.

"A simple thank you would suffice for not letting you fall to your demise, little goddess. And you never answered my question... was it because of the quarrel with that... friend of yours?" he inquired.

I crossed my arms, frowning. "That really isn't any of your concern. Do you make it a habit of spying on other people's affairs?" I snapped, ignoring his jab about gratitude.

The situation was far more uncomfortable now. Knowing someone had seen and heard the argument made me uneasy. I wasn't sure if Dionysus had seen us use our magic, or just overheard the yelling.

"Such a brazen attitude from someone not of this realm. But do not fret, my kalos, I only heard the words in passing." He jumped from the tree, landing lightly before strolling toward me. "I wanted to speak to you again, without my insufferable brother getting in the way." He circled me, in a slow manner.

Ice crept across my fingers—trepidation settling in my chest. The air felt heavier now, his aura suffocating. My stomach rolled as I remembered the old man's warning in Korinthos about the man before me.

"What could we possibly have to talk about? You're a stranger, and you speak as if you know me." I turned with him, refusing to let him out of my sight.

He stopped, smirking. then stepped even closer—close enough that I had to look up to meet his gaze. His eyes were impossibly golden, and I swear the colors were moving. Every nerve went on alert, and I raised my hand between us in defense. But he didn't even flinch.

"A stranger, maybe... but I've seen you before today. My wind spirits carried your description across the sea days ago. They spoke so beautifully of you—eyes dark blue, like they were carved from the deepest glacier in Poseidon's oceans."

He raised a hand as if to touch my cheek but stopped.

"And freckles like stars scattered across her face," he murmured, "I just had to see you for myself."

I stepped away, face pale and my head suddenly feeling hazy. "Whatever you think will happen between us, it won't." My teeth clenched together as I put more distance between us.

He followed my movement, a mischievous glint sparking in his eyes. "You fascinate me, little goddess. Tell me, what would it take to make you mine, then?"

I blinked, my mouth dropping open at the boldness of his words. "You're being serious, aren't you?" I whispered, though I knew he could hear me.

Before he could respond, a deep snarl broke through the trees, and I nearly sighed in relief.

Runar's massive frame stalked through the trees to stand next to me, a rumbling growl vibrating in his throat. He stopped on my right side, so close I could feel his fur brushing my arm, his eyes locked onto Dionysus.

The air around us lifted immediately, as if Dionysus withdrawn his aura, and my mind cleared. A disappointed expression flashed across his face before settling into a nonchalant grin.

"It would seem our conversation is over—for now. The pleasure was mine." With that, he turned, dissolving into a golden ripple that shimmered in the night—and then he was gone.

Runar's head shifted toward me after a moment. "Why is it that when you go off on your own, trouble seems to find you?" His tone carried pure resignation.

I glanced up at the stars, then at the spot where Dionysus had vanished, shaking my head as I turned for the house. Runar fell into step beside me.

"Your guess is as good as mine," I muttered. "I never had the best luck, but lately? This is just getting ridiculous,"

We passed through the training area. My eyes lingered on the place I had stood—ice still coated the ground there. In Eirik's spot, the earth was scorched black. I clenched my fists and walked faster, Runar keeping pace.

As we neared the house, nerves knotted in my stomach. I didn't want to run into Eirik—not yet, at least.

"Do you think I overreacted, Runar?" I asked, slowing to a stop just outside the door.

"I believe your frustrations were valid. Could you have found out in a better way? Possibly..." he surmised, nudging me forward with his head and shifting back down to a medium size.

"If I'd asked normally, he would've deflected like usual. He's not exactly the most open when it comes to sharing..." I mumbled, kicking off my boots just inside the door.

Runar cocked his head, giving me a *really?* kind of look. "And you are no different. We have seen you withdraw yourself on many occasions."

I opened my mouth, but closed it just as quickly—because he was right.

Pushing open the door to my room, I finally let my shoulders relax and dropped onto my bed with a groan. The blankets were cool and soft, so much that I could have fallen asleep right then.

Runar grunted before sprawling out at the foot of the bed.

"I think you and the young warrior have much to discuss when you are ready. I won't say he was either right or wrong in his decision to keep this from you." He finished with a huff before closing his eyes.

I mulled over his words as I reluctantly pushed myself up to change. I know I'm not always open about my past, about my family or my experiences, but it still stung. I pulled a clean tunic over my head and collapsed back onto the bed with a thud.

My mind circled back to Kyllini, to the moment I'd asked Eirik what Skadi had meant when she told me, *I believe you should talk with that guardian of yours; he can help more than you think. I feel he may understand your situation.*

That really should have clicked with me then—but it didn't. And now, here we are.

Part of me wanted to forgive him, but the hurt lingered. Did he still not trust me enough, even after everything? If he understood my situation, wouldn't it have helped to tell me sooner?

My thoughts kept spinning as my eyes grew heavy. Slowly, my body relaxed, and sleep finally pulled me under.

⊰•————•⊱

I was the last to wake. Runar had slipped out of the room without waking me.

I hurriedly dressed, fastening my light armor for the first time in a day. The weight of it felt heavier today; I hadn't realized how much I'd gotten used to it over the weeks.

I ran my fingers through my hair and decided today it would be braided. Weaving my fingers through the strands, I worked them into a fishtail braid, leaving a few pieces out to frame my face. I paused, my eyes widening, breath catching in my throat at what I was seeing.

At the end of the braid, when I tied it off, a small section of hair was white—white, weaving up through the rest of the braid.

I rushed to grab the polished silver katoptron. Light from outside reflected off the mirror, and my face grew pale.

Why is my hair white!? What is happening now?

Setting the mirror down, I grabbed my things and bolted out of the room into the common area, where Runar and Eirik were already waiting.

"Runar!" I shouted, skidding to a halt in front of him.

His ears flicked forward as he sat up straighter, confusion on his face. Eirik, too, looked startled—he'd never seen me react this way before.

"Why the yelling, young one? I can hear you just fine at a normal tone," he grumbled.

I turned, showing him the braid and pointing at the white streak weaving through my brown hair. "What is happening?" I demanded.

Both of their expressions turned thoughtful. Runar's face quickly shifted back to calm.

"You had me thinking something horrible had happened," he sighed, standing up. "No need to panic. With your magic becoming more powerful, your resemblance to Skadi grows." His gaze lingered on my hair.

I slumped forward. "Great! Let's add to my already brewing identity crisis. Isn't it *enough* that I'm her reincarnation... now I have to fully look like her, too?" I exclaimed.

To Runar, it seemed like it wasn't a big deal. If he could, I think he would have shrugged.

I could feel tears burning as the temperature in the room dropped. Anxiety hurled back into my chest—something else about me was changing, and I wasn't sure if I could handle that right now. Skadi's presence was nowhere, and it hit me that her essence was fading faster now.

I clenched my fists, glaring at the floor as a couple tears escaped. I couldn't let my ice destroy anything here.

I didn't hear him approach, but suddenly two warm hands wrapped around mine and squeezed. I looked up, meeting Eirik's dark grey eyes.

"Hey, hey... do not let this ail you." He paused, his eyes softening—a surprise to see. "This change does not mean you're her. You're Ravena, and no one can take that from you." His grip tightened, as if he was uncertain of what to do or say next.

I let my gaze drop to the ground. "I want to believe that... but my appearance is what makes me... *me*." I trailed off. "Who am I if I look completely like someone else?"

Eirik released my hands, then lifted one to my chin, tilting my face up to meet his gaze. I flushed at the contact, unable to speak. The way he looked at me was unlike anything I'd ever seen from him, and a lump formed in my throat. The warmth of his hand stood out against the coolness of my skin—it startled me.

"I can't answer that for you. You'll have to decide who you are in all this. But know this—it doesn't change the person I see standing in front of me." His thumb brushed lightly against my cheek before he pulled back.

The warmth lingered, leaving my chest tight. I wanted to reach for it again—to cling to the comfort he gave me, to the way he looked at me as a person, not some prophecy. But that moment was gone, and all I was left with were echoes of it.

Runar huffed, side-eyeing Eirik. "He is correct. You may resemble Skadi, but you are not her. Your personality is refreshing to see, and your soul's energy is far different from hers."

Their words should have comforted me. Instead, they only scraped against the doubt I was already drowning in. I forced myself to nod, because that was easier than explaining the mess of thoughts inside me. I'd just endure this conflict internally, and maybe later I could find some reprieve.

A knock on the door interrupted the silence, and then Hermes stepped in, a wide grin on his face.

"Greetings, friends! Are you ready to depart to the Norse realm?" he exclaimed, and I swear I saw Eirik's eye twitch. It was far too early for me to deal with his playful attitude.

I noticed Chione wasn't with him today—or maybe she was just waiting wherever the portal was located.

Hermes's eyes scanned the room, and he raised a brow. "Oh? Have I interrupted something?" he asked, clearly picking up on the tension.

Runar pushed his way past him and out the door without a word.

"Nothing," I said quickly. "Just an internal... or maybe external crisis about my hair changing color." I adjusted my satchel, avoiding Hermes's amused stare.

Hermes gave my hair a glance and shrugged. "I see no reason for a crisis, young goddess."

I groaned softly and facepalmed. *Of course, another person would not see the issue.*

Hermes smirked before gesturing towards the door. "Let's get you all to Thyraheim, yes? The day is still young, and you've quite the journey ahead. The portal is only a short walk from here—behind the training grounds in the mountain."

I raised a brow, intrigued, and stepped forward with Eirik close behind. Together, we followed Hermes toward the training grounds.

The sun had risen over the horizon, our breaths puffing white in the chilly morning air. Moisture clung to the branches, dripping to the ground as the rays of sunlight warmed the area.

I noticed the tension from earlier had melted away, replaced by a new feeling in my chest... apprehension. We were about to travel through a divine portal to another realm—to the very fortress of the one I'd been reincarnated from.

Our boots crunched against the soil as we trekked through the woods and training area, following an unseen path in the tree line. It opened up at the side of the mountain, where a beautiful marble archway marked the entry inside.

Torches lined the path, leading—I hoped—to the portal, and not some trap. Eirik nudged to keep pace with Hermes, and we entered the tunnel, Hermes humming a tune that bounced off the rock walls.

Yeah, that doesn't make this anymore nerve-racking.

The tunnel was short. At the end stood another magnificent archway, flanked by statues of Athena standing guard on either side. Inscriptions were chiseled into the marble, with words I couldn't read.

I shot Hermes a questioning look. "Are all portal locations guarded by certain gods or goddesses?"

"Yes. There are only so many portals, and since Athena is worshipped in this city, it made sense to put her statues here as a symbol. If you had stayed in Kyllini, there is a portal there with my statues as well." He walked to an altar, mumbling words too quickly for me to catch.

A pressure started building in the cavern—not oppressive, but almost electric. Then, before my eyes, the portal lit up a mesmerizing blue, rippling from an unseen wind.

I gasped in awe, stepping backwards at the sight, my hands tightening around the strap of my satchel.

"This will take you to Heimdall at the entry to Asgard. Law bans travel from here to other private portals without first seeing the watchman," Hermes said, turning to face us with a small smile.

I mulled over his words, then frowned. "If that the case, wouldn't whoever freed Agnar... have been caught?"

Hermes shifted and, for the first time since the run-in with Dionysus, he looked uneasy. "In theory, yes. But someone with ill or ambitious intentions would find a way to sneak around—law or no law," he said.

I narrowed my eyes. His shoulders had tensed, and his usual playful attitude had diminished.

Could he know something we didn't? Or was I just overthinking again?

I glanced at Eirik, who was locked on the portal, his face clouded with apprehension.

Runar's ears were pinned back, suggesting he sensed something off in Hermes's words.

Hermes gestured toward the portal, pointedly ignoring our looks. "Good luck on your journey, young goddess. I do hope you find the answers you all seek—for everyone's sake."

Those cryptic words were his last as he stepped aside. The motion seemed to snap Eirik out of his thoughts.

He moved forward, walking past me, and I nervously followed behind. My head tilted up as we neared the rippling blue portal. Runar stuck close to my side.

"It'll be alright, Ravena. Just stay close and don't hesitate," he said, his tone serious, his shoulder bumping me so I wouldn't stop.

With a nervous exhale, I watched Eirik step through and disappear. I squared my shoulders and, with renewed determination, stepped through as well. Blinding white light greeted me—the sensation like passing through a curtain.

Golden Desires

She had left—the little goddess. Hermes had opened a portal to another realm, granting them passage away from here. That supposed guardian of hers led the way, and she—every bit as beautiful as the night before—looked uncertain to follow. They hadn't noticed me, but I knew Hermes had, he let his gaze travel to me more than once. I listened as she questioned Hermes about the statues guarding our portals, and I smirked. Athena was always such a sore topic for my dear brother. It had been years, but even now, he lingered on trivial things that no longer mattered.

I toyed with a golden vine curling lazily around my wrist, watching with disappointment as they finally disappeared and the portal closed.

"You can come out now, Dion," Hermes called, his tone weary. He turned to where I was lounging in the shadows, narrowing his eyes.

I smirked, sauntering out and circling the pedestal beneath the portal. "You sure are playing the hospitable messenger god, Hermes. Have you grown tired of Chione already? I mean, I can't blame you—Ravena is delicious to look at, no?"

"You will leave her be, Dionysus. This goddess does not belong to you, nor will she ever," Hermes bit out, arms crossed tight over his chest, his expression stony.

"Oh? And what makes you so certain those are my intentions?" I rolled my shoulders, letting the sleeves of my robes slip farther down. Hermes rolled his eyes in agitation—which only served to amuse me.

"I know you, Dionysus. Someone new comes around and you think you can play your games, keep them like some toy. Ravena is not fated to you; her thread is elsewhere."

His words dragged the corners of my mouth downward.

What an unfortunate circumstance.

I started toward the exit. "Once again, dear brother, you have knowledge of events to come... and yet,"—I gestured at the archway—"you chose to keep silent."

I stopped by his shoulder, lifting a hand to pat it.

"This has nothing to do with the past. I cannot mess with threads of fate—you know that," Hermes snapped, shrugging my hand away.

"You can't, but I have no issues cutting those very threads to get what I want."

I looked up as the temperature in the cavern dropped—and there stood Chione, an uneasy look plastered on her face.

"Goodbye, brother. It seems our conversation is finished... for now." I smirked, walking out past Chione, who refused to meet my gaze.

Chapter Thirty-Two

I stumbled forward out of the portal and carefully peeked my eyes open. I hadn't realized I had closed them—the light had been so bright. Moving through the portal felt like passing through rippling water, only you could breathe, and you didn't get soaked.

I looked up slowly, and my breath caught. Spread out below us were magnificent stone-mason walls, so high that no mortal could have built them from bottom to edge. Water cascaded into an endless void below...

Behind those walls, citadel peaks towered, their surfaces shining gold and silver, rainbow hues shimmering in the air.

This was Asgard—the home of the Aesir and Vanir gods. Here was where the gods and goddesses dwelled, Alfheim with its light elves, fallen warriors in Valhalla, and in the far distance, Yggdrasill, the tree of life, rising above it all. There was even more, but a nudge at my side snapped me out of my trance. Runar stood grinning at me, his wolfish teeth gleaming in the light.

"You will catch flies, young one. Isn't that what Midgard-born say?" a deep, resonant voice spoke with humor.

That's when I noticed the man waiting for us in front an imposing golden structure. Middle-aged and tall, he wore armor—but not ordinary armor; its golden color glowed and rippled as if the very sun's rays were trapped inside. A long, billowing deep-crimson cape hung down his back. His dark-blonde hair was braided in a typical warrior's style, and what really caught my gaze were his eyes—iridescent, shining just like the Bifrost itself.

"You—you're Heimdall…" I sputtered, in awe at the sight of the Norse watchman of the gods.

"That I am, Lady Ravena," he stated with a small bow. "Welcome to my dwelling, Himinbjörg. I have waited quite a while to meet you."

"You know my name? You knew we were coming?" I asked, nerves prickling under the presence of this god.

"Why, of course. I am the watchman of the gods and goddesses, and I have been following your journey since before you arrived here. You seek passage back to Midgard—to Jotunheim, to Skadi's old fortress, yes?"

I stood speechless, my thoughts flying in every direction. Runar took my silence as a sign I needed help and stepped forward.

"That is correct. We hope to find answers there about the incident two years ago. Also, to retrieve better armor and weapons that won't shatter from her usage of magic," he grumbled.

"I see. And the fire demi-god here?" Heimdall's gaze swept over Eirik, who stood tense under the god's look.

I glanced at Eirik. He looked more uncomfortable than I'd ever seen him, his jaw tight.

I cleared my throat, finally finding my voice. "He is my guardian. His words were that Odin, long ago, assigned him to me."

Heimdall studied Eirik for a moment, then nodded. "Ah yes, he was but a young boy then. A child of a shield-maiden and a fire giant of Muspell. I'm glad to see you have grown into a fine warrior."

Eirik only gave a short nod and kept his eyes trained on the Bifrost behind Heimdall's structure. Honestly, this was the first time I'd ever seen him be rude. I elbowed him in the ribs, and he grunted, finally glancing my way.

"It is alright, young one. His experience with the gods has not always been the best in this pantheon, if I remember," Heimdall said, stepping closer. "Let's get another portal open so you may get to Thyraheim. I shall not keep you waiting any longer."

He walked past us to the pedestal, and the portal lit up once more—this time, white, a cool breeze slipping through as we turned.

"This will take you to the outer portal of the fortress. I apologize—the one inside was destroyed when the battle happened." He stepped aside, gesturing toward the glow.

I drew in a deep breath before stepping forward first this time. *Here we go again.* Pausing at Heimdall's side, I managed a small smile.

"Thank you. We really appreciate the help."

"Of course," he said, inclining his head. "Anything to aid a fellow Aesir."

My eyes widened, my stomach tightening with nerves at the word. But Heimdall only smiled and turned back to the portal. Runar nudged me forward, and with a stumbling step, I tumbled into the light.

Chapter Thirty-Three

A bitter cold greeted me as I fell through the portal—and almost landed face-first, but warm hands caught me.

This is becoming a habit.

Runar padded past me with a wolfish smirk and shifted back to his massive form. As Eirik steadied me, I wanted to huff. Despite his comfort earlier, I was still mad at him, so I shook off his grasp and followed Runar, who was already heading down a snowy path.

"Ravena, can I try to explain?" Eirik called out. He hadn't said much since the house. I yanked my cloak closer and turned my head just enough to see him trailing behind.

"No, not right now. You could have explained weeks ago—or last night. Not kept it a secret. What other things about you don't I know?" I shot back with a scowl.

I heard him exhale behind me, but didn't say anything more—just kept following. I could feel the warmth radiating from him, as if he raised his body temperature to help keep the cold away. I didn't mind the cold. Here, it felt like my magic thrived. I felt rejuvenated and strong; the cold here wasn't like back in Greece it was like the ice and snow lived on its own.

The walk to the bottom wasn't anything extraordinary, but soon we were surrounded by tall mountain peaks. And in front of us, a massive stone stairway waited. I raised my head, eyes wide. At the top of the spiraling stairs, a fortress rested on the mountainside—made entirely of ice. Towers spiraled upward, their edges sharp and glimmering in the pale sunlight. Behind a huge wall and gate, windows arched and they seemed to glow from within, icicles hanging from every frames. The whole structure seemed to hum with energy I couldn't explain; frost clung to the stairs leading up to the gate and seemed to hang in the air itself.

I started up the stairs, Runar allowing me to go first. As I stood at the gate, the carved runes glowed faintly. I looked at Runar, confused. "It feels... alive. Like it's waiting for me."

"It is, young one. You are the rightful owner of this place now. Your home," he said.

The word home felt hollow right now. My home was in another realm... this wasn't home, not yet. "I feel like I'm trespassing. This doesn't feel right," I muttered.

"You're not trespassing, Ravena," Runar said. "Go on. Lift your hand to open the gates."

Eirik huffed from behind. "Then why do I feel like it's watching us? Judging us?" He crossed his arms.

I looked up at the walls. I didn't feel any negative energy—only a strange sense of welcome. I turned to Eirik.

"Because I think it is. This place doesn't trust you, Eirik. But it trusts me and Runar."

I slowly placed my hand on the gate. The runes burned to life, and a surge of energy swept through the area as they lit up. I stepped back, staring in awe as the massive gates opened.

I wasn't sure what I expected once the gates fully opened, but it definitely wasn't a courtyard garden. There were actual ice flowers, their petals translucent and blue, mixed with winter blooms that somehow thrived together. In the center stood a giant fountain—frost spilling from the spout instead of water.

This place is beautiful. For war giants, they sure had good taste.

We were not savages, Ravena... I did enjoy decorating the place. Skadi's exasperated voice echoed through my head.

I jumped. *Oh, now you appear again. And yes, I was just surprised. It's all very beautiful here.* I answered her as I walked up a short stairway to the main door.

This place gives me more power to speak through to you. The magic settled here is replenishing your magic. I won't be leaving you alone again. I deeply apologize if it seemed I had abandoned you. Her voice was earnest.

I pushed the door open with ease and stepped inside. *No need to apologize. You've explained it before*—my words trailed off as the sight of the interior stole them from me.

The walls stretched high, smooth in some places, rough in others where frost gathered thicker in the corners. The floor was a mix of pale marble and frozen patches, streaked like veins through the stone. Every step I took echoed, hollow and crisp against the cold.

Tall pillars lined the hall, carved from solid ice and catching the blue glow of torches set into the walls. The light danced across every surface, making it seem as if the whole place was shifting, even when it wasn't. My breath fogged in the air as I continued down a short hallway, guided almost by instinct.

At the end, the space opened into a throne room. More columns lined the sides, carved in such detail it was hard to believe they were solid ice. The walls held frozen figures locked in motion, their features so sharp and lifelike it seemed they might step out any moment and become real.

A sprawling chandelier hung from the ceiling, scattering rainbows across a deep blue floor that shimmered with crystal-like patterns. Each step echoed, the sound carrying all the way to the dais at the far end.

The throne sat centered beneath a towering window, framed by the pale silhouette of a frozen tree etched into the wall behind it. Its branches stretched upward like veins of light, casting a faint luminescence that made the whole chamber feel alive.

I was so lost in my surroundings that I almost forgot Runar and Eirik were behind me—until Eirik let out a curse and I heard a crash. I whirled around to find him flat on his back. I raised a brow as he scrambled up.

"Did you seriously just fall? Oh, great warrior," I teased.

He glared, brushing frost from his cloak. "It's not my fault there are random ice patches where you're supposed to walk."

Runar rolled his eyes before nudging to me. "Let me show you your room. You'll see it's not all ice here." He pushed open a side door.

I followed, at a slower pace, still taking in the details. The walls shifted from ice to pale blue stone, with the frost tapering off near the windows.

Runar stopped at a door at the hall's end. "This is your room now. I'll take Eirik to his while you settle in," he said, leading Eirik away.

I opened the door slowly. The chamber inside was vast, just like the rest of this place. A chandelier of icicles hung from the ceiling, glowing blue flames flickering as lights. Sunlight from outside traced delicate patterns across the stone floor.

A grand hearth sat on the right, empty for now but clearly meant to warm even this space. On the left stood a bed, its oak frame carved with wolves in mid-stride. The bedding was plush and cool to the touch—luxurious, not at all what I'd expected. My head tilted in confusion; the walls were stone and ice, yet nothing had melted—not even near the hearth.

Do not think too hard, young one, Skadi laughed. *Remember, magic exists. This very castle holds ancient enchantments to keep things as they are—to preserve what must remain frozen.*

I straightened, a flush heating my cheeks. "Right, I forgot." My gaze landed on two doors on either side of the hearth.

Those lead to the bathing chambers and the wardrobe, Skadi answered before I could ask. *You will be able to wear proper armor from now on.*

I gave a slow nod, then frowned. "Wouldn't the armor and clothes not fit properly?" I looked down at my height. At five-foot-seven, I was nowhere near a giantess's height.

The bed is a normal size, isn't it? She countered.

I glanced back, realizing much of the room was scaled to mortal size.

While yes, we are giants, like Runar we can shift down to a more man-ageable height—though taller than most mortals. I stood at what you'd call seven feet, she explained calmly.

I sighed, feeling like an idiot. "So the armor can magically shrink to fit me?"

Correct. Divine armor is far superior to anything a mortal could make, she replied with pride.

I opened my mouth, but a sudden knock startled me. Assuming it was either Runar or Eirik, I called, "Come in."

The doors opened—and it was definitely not my companions. My hand dropped to the dagger at my side before Skadi's urgent voice stopped me.

Wait! It is alright, Ravena. They won't harm you.

I relaxed slightly but stayed tense. "Who are they?" I whispered.

Two females knelt down on one knee—the sight made me step back.

They are snow elves, Skadi said, her tone heavy. *Only a handful of their kind remain. My father cursed them long ago to serve this fortress. No matter how strong I became—even after his death—I could not break the bind. They must remain here, whether anyone lives in the castle or not.*

I frowned. The thought of being bound to this place forever made my chest ache. "So... they do everything here?" I shifted uneasily as the two remained absolutely silent and still. They weren't looking at me, and their heads were bowed, but I could feel their curiosity.

No. These two were my personal handmaids—Azhrina and Prymsdora. Others serve as guards, cooks, cleaners, healers, seamstresses. Your return has alerted them someone once again resides here.

My thoughts spun. We'd seen no one on the grounds, but perhaps they'd known we weren't a threat. Their kneeling was starting to creep me out.

"Uh—you two can stand. No need to kneel," I stammered, fiddling with a loose thread on my sleeve.

They rose gracefully and met my eyes. Both were stunning. The one on the left had dark blue hair, silver eyes, and pointed ears peeking through. The other had softer features, light blue hair in a braid, and brilliant blue eyes.

The darker-haired one stepped forward. "Welcome, milady. We sensed energy like Skadi's, but you are not her?" Her voice was soft, despite her stern posture.

"No, I'm not. My name is Ravena." My stomach twisted with nerves. "I am... her reincarnation."

Their brows shot upward. The lighter-haired one folded her arms. "Her reincarnation... you mean Skadi has died?" Her voice wavered, eyes shining with unshed tears.

I looked away, throat dry. "I'm sorry. She passed two years ago. No one came to tell you?"

They shook their heads, heartbreak evident on their faces. Azhrina straightened, lips pressed tight. "I'm Azhrina, Skadi's eldest handmaid. I look forward to serving you, Lady Ravena. Your resemblance is remarkable."

The younger one stepped forward. "I'm Prymsdora. It is a pleasure to meet you, though I wish it were under better circumstances. I am saddened by our friend's passing." Her voice faltered. "We all grew wary after she didn't return the night of the prisoner's escape. But no word ever came."

Their eyes studied me carefully, respectfully. Nothing I could say would take away their pain.

Do you wish to tell them anything, Skadi? I asked silently.

No. They are not mine to lead anymore, they are yours. Forge your own bonds. Her presence faded once more.

I sighed, cheeks warming as the elves watched me in confusion. "Sorry. I get lost in thought. My companions and I came for answers—and for weapons that won't break when I use my ice."

"Are you not staying?" Prymsdora asked timidly. I could tell she was upset at the notion we'd be leaving so soon.

I shook my head. "A day or two at most. I need to train, handle my emotions better, and find out how Agnar escaped—and who helped him."

Azhrina's eyes widened slightly, surprise flickering before her expression hardened. "No one here would betray Lady Skadi," she said firmly. "She was far kinder than her father—kinder than most giants. She gave us freedoms we never thought possible."

Her tone had sharpened, almost defensive, and then she seemed to realize who she was speaking to. Her shoulders tensed, gaze dropping instantly. "Forgive me, my lady. I spoke out of turn."

"Hey, no need to apologize. We don't believe it was anyone here. There are whispers that a divine being from another pantheon was involved." I unclasped my cloak—only for Prymsdora to dart forward.

"Let me help you, Lady Ravena. We haven't had anyone here in so long, we've forgotten our duties." She gently folded the cloak, as Azhrina lit the hearth. My stomach decided at that moment to growl loudly.

Prymsdora's eyes widened. "Oh! I'll see to the kitchens. It will be a joy to serve company again." She set the cloak down and scampered out.

A laugh slipped from me at her bubbly energy, so unlike my brooding guardian.

"She is the most energetic among us," Azhrina said from the hearth.

"No, it's fine. Kinda helps, actually. I'm the outsider here, and there's... a lot to live up to."

"Nonsense," she said firmly. "Getting into the fortress unscathed proves you're no stranger here. Anyone can see your resemblance to Skadi. But if I may be blunt, milady, you don't need to live up to someone else's image. Build your own."

I exhaled slowly, trying not to let her words sink in too deep. She was one of many who told me not to compare myself to Skadi. Everyone seemed to believe I was capable of more. But my doubts still clung to me. My fate had been woven, long before I was even born.

"You know she is right, frostling," Runar's deep voice echoed, making us both whirl around as he walked through the door.

"Runar!" Azhrina exclaimed, bowing at the waist. "It's good to see you once more. We wondered why you just took off." She turned to me with a grin. "And now we see why."

He nodded. "Had to stop this one from freezing a poor village over."

I glared at him. "That seems far-fetched—it was only Eirik. Besides, where is he? I thought he'd stick close, being in a new place." My arms crossed.

Azhrina's gaze turned curious. "There is another here?"

Runar settled near me. "Yes, a young warrior of fire blood. He is her guardian by the All-Father's orders." He turned his head toward me. "He decided to stay in his quarters—said he would meet us for lunch."

Azhrina nodded in understanding. "I take it you ran into Prymsdora, then?"

He nodded before nudging me. "You should go tidy up before lunch, and Azhrina here will gather you new clothes and armor." He pointed his head towards the bathing chambers.

I let out a sigh, still unsure of even *using* anything here. Azhrina was at my side in a second, already guiding me toward the room. "I'll get it all set up for you. You'd be surprised by the warmth of the water here—it comes from an aquifer deep in the mountain, warmed by magic."

She rambled on as we entered the room, my backwards glance at Runar's face the last thing I saw before the doors closed.

"There is a changing screen over there," I heard Azhrina say.

I turned back and stopped walking. *Okay, why is everything here so grand!*

The right wall was made of deep blue ice, light bouncing from it to cast a low glow across the room. To the left, massive frosted windows stretched tall, their stained glass patterned with snowflakes. The rest of the walls were mountain stone.

A marbled tub sat directly in front of the windows—so huge I could practically swim in it. One side of the wall held a spout capped over in ice. The floor beneath my feet was smooth stone, and a giant white rug softened the center of the chamber.

Azhrina was kind enough to let me take it all in.

To the right stood a changing screen with benches and shelves. Beside it, another door caught my eye.

I glanced at Azhrina. "Another door?"

"Yes, milady. It leads behind the hearth to your wardrobe. It allows us to be quick in getting you ready," she explained.

She moved toward the tub—if I could even call it that—and waved her hand over the spout. The ice melted, releasing steaming water that rushed into the basin.

As she prepared oils, I shifted nervously.

She stopped and looked at me. "Is everything alright?"

Before I could answer, an understanding look crossed her face. "Oh, I apologize if this all seems too forward. If you wish, I can step out once I finish putting the oils in." She pointed towards the screen. "You can leave your clothes there, and as I go through the wardrobe, I'll take those with me. I assure you, your privacy will be maintained." She smiled

I cringed. It wasn't so much my privacy... okay, that did play a huge part—but it was overwhelming to use these items that had once belonged to someone else.

I quickly nodded, realizing I'd just been staring at her. "Thank you. I'm sorry for all the trouble. I really appreciate you being so kind, having just met me."

I shuffled behind the wooden partition and sighed in relief—a brief break from being seen. I quickly undressed, placing my things neatly by another divider that blocked the door. My toes dug into the fur rug as I stood there awkwardly.

A shadow that I recognized as Azhrina appeared on the other side by the door, and a robe was gently draped over the top. "The bath is ready, milady. I'll be going to look for clothes."

"Thank you, Azhrina," I said earnestly, grabbing the robe and quickly tying it.

I stepped around the screen and padded my way to the bath. A sharp breath escaped me as the cold stone sent a jolt up my body. With renewed speed, I slipped into the bath and immediately relaxed.

The water was hot, but not so much that it was unpleasant. The oils carried the scent of rose and mint, the blend both refreshing and soothing.

I quite literally swam to the window, leaning my elbows against the cool stone sill to peer outside through one of the clear panes. The mountains beyond were blanketed in snow, and far below, trees dotted the canyons.

This place felt surreal, and I couldn't shake the feeling that it was all one big dream.

A soft creak of a door made me sink lower into the water, and Azhrina's voice carried through the room. "I have returned with some clothes. I'll set them on the bench for when you're ready. Is there anything else I can get you, milady?"

A thought hit me, and my hopes grew that maybe they had the item I needed. "Would you happen to have a *shaving knife*... for my body? I'm not used to having hair everywhere," I asked meekly.

"Oh, of course! Is it alright if I bring it out to you?" She asked.

I nodded before realizing she couldn't see me. "Yes, that's fine," I called out.

"Alright, I shall return quickly." The door closed behind her.

Oh, thank gods, I can finally shave and feel somewhat normal for once.

I closed my eyes and ducked under the water. Coming up, I carefully washed my hair and wrung it out. Opening my eyes, I studied the white strands that were appearing more and more, and sighed.

It'll be okay, Ravena. Deal with it later and worry about more important issues right now. Your anxiety can wait.

Another creak sounded, followed by light footsteps approaching the side of the tub.

I looked up to see Azhrina, who was holding out a small shaving knife, her eyes carefully averted in respect. I took it gently and smiled.

"Thank you! I'm so relieved to finally get this," I chuckled.

She smiled and bowed before retreating behind the screen. "I'll wait here until you are finished—no rush. Prymsdora has said lunch is nearly ready, and Runar has already made his way to the dining area."

"Oh, okay. It shouldn't take long," I replied quickly, tackling what I needed to.

Not a few minutes later, I pulled the robe back on and stepped carefully out of the tub. Back behind the screen, a new set of clothes lay neatly folded on the bench.

The first thing I picked up was a deep blue linen underlayer with silver stitching along the hem. I used the robe to dry off a bit more and wrapped my hair with a towel from one of the shelves. Slipping the underlayer over my head, I found that it ended just above my upper thighs.

I leaned over and pulled a spare *perizoma* from my satchel—my only form of underwear besides the one I had arrived here in. I quickly wrapped myself in it, and to my surprise, beside the tunic lay a full Norse outfit:

A long-sleeved wool tunic, meant to be worn over a light linen underlayer. A pair of sturdy wool trousers. And boots lined with fur, warm enough to endure the cold outside.

I dressed quickly, layering the soft linen beneath the heavier wool tunic. The trousers were snug but comfortable, and the fur-lined boots fit as though they'd been made just for me. For a moment, I simply stared down at myself. They didn't feel borrowed—they felt as if they were made for me.

Before I could overthink, a knock sounded at the main door. Eirik's voice carried through, rough but hesitant. "Lunch awaits, Ravena. Are you ready?"

I opted to leave my satchel tucked carefully under the bench, and Azhrina and I made our way out the door. Eirik stood just outside, studying my room. He turned to me as we stepped through and held out his arm, catching me off guard.

I sighed and looped my arm through his as Azhrina led the way down the corridor, opposite the direction we'd come. This part of the fortress was quieter; the muffled crackle of a distant hearth reached us. The halls no longer screamed of abandonment—the fortress felt alive now, and the stray ice patches that had once covered the floor had been cleared away.

We wove through the halls and down a flight of stairs until we reached a long hallway that opened onto a landing. A beautiful staircase curved downward into a wide foyer, where another set of massive doors stood. My curiosity slowed my pace, and Eirik adjusted his stride so he wouldn't pull me along.

"This is where the inhabitants of this fortress would enter," Azhrina explained. "Any other would enter through the throne room hall. Lord Thiazi wanted no strangers in his dwelling."

We veered into a short hallway to the left, which opened to a space lined with cushions—clearly used for relaxing. A massive ice wall divided the room, making me wonder what lay on the other side. A giant hearth dominated the left wall, positioned to warm both spaces.

As we rounded the wall, a dining area revealed itself: crystalline chairs tucked beneath a long oak table. Runar lay sprawled on a pile of furs and straw in the corner. I unwound my arm from Eirik's as Azhrina guided him to a chair, then she led me toward a massive throne-like seat at the end of the table—and I froze.

I was supposed to sit there? My gaze darted to Runar, who offered no help, then to one of the many smaller chairs. "I can sit in one of these. It would be no problem..." I stammered.

Prymsdora entered just as I said it and gasped. "Absolutely not, Lady Ravena! That chair is yours. It would be unsightly for you to be seen sitting in a lower seat." Her hands went straight to her hips.

I'd sit, Ravena, lest you offend the elves... Skadi's voice hummed.

My eyes widened, and I quickly sank into the chair pulled out for me, folding my hands in my lap.

An older female elf emerged from a side door I assumed led to the kitchen. She carried a tray and walked straight toward me, while another headed cautiously toward Eirik.

"My Lady, what a joy it is to meet you. I'm Felydra, the main cook here, and I just had to personally bring the food out to you." Her smile was bright and motherly. It reminded me of Cora—and I realized how much I missed everyone back in Kyllini.

I shook my head and smiled up at her. "Thank you. It's wonderful meeting you all. I'm sorry I'm not who you were expecting..." My words trailed off as I averted my eyes.

"Nonsense. Life happens, and we know Skadi gave her all to protect us and tried to stop that giant from leaving. She would be ashamed if we moped. You are the rightful owner of this place now, and we will grow to love you just as we did her."

She set down the tray, revealing a stew of wild game and root vegetables, a cup of wine, and to top it off, a loaf of bread baked with berries.

"Please let us know if you need anything. We'll leave you to enjoy your meal." Felydra bowed and motioned for the others to go.

I picked up the spoon and stirred the food absentmindedly, glancing at Eirik as he cautiously tasted his portion. I raised a brow but didn't comment, and began eating.

When you finish your meal, young one, I wish to guide you to a place I am sure you'll enjoy, Skadi's voice rang in my head.

I stopped mid-chew. *Oh? What is it?*

You'll just have to wait and see. And bring your guardian as well—I believe you two have much to discuss.

I frowned. Was I ready to talk to him about it all? I sighed, catching Eirik's attention as his gaze snapped to me. I couldn't keep being stubborn. How could we work together if I refused to hear him out? He'd listened to my outburst without judgment once before.

"After we eat... could we talk?" I asked quietly. "Skadi has a place where she says we can speak."

Eirik's expression shifted—hopeful. I returned it with a small smile, hoping it reassured him that I didn't exactly hate his guts.

Chapter Thirty-Four

The rest of our meal was uneventful, and we soon found ourselves wandering a long hallway, Skadi's voice telling us which way to go. Azhrina had look worried when I said I wanted to explore, certain I'd get lost. I had to reassure her and Prymsdora more than once that I'd be fine—and that at least Eirik was with me.

Skadi directed us to make a sharp right toward a tall set of winding stairs.

Really, Skadi... more stairs? I deadpanned before starting my climb, Eirik right behind me.

You're in far better shape than you were in Kyllini, so no complaining. Besides, I promise what waits will be worth it.

I couldn't argue—she was right. But now, my curiosity was eating at me. *What could possibly be behind that door?*

As we reached the top, excitement started to build. Skadi already knew what I loved, and with that realization, my eyes widened in anticipation.

Ah, you've finally guessed it. Go on, then. Second to hunting, this place was my favorite to escape to.

I quickly pushed open the door—and a grin spread across my face.

Inside was a circular library, filled floor to ceiling with books—shelves carved right from the mountain itself protected them from the chill. Wooden chairs sat scattered around the room, topped with cushions. A dark bearskin rug lay stretched out beneath them. I glanced up, and my jaw dropped in awe: on the mountainside, a skylight made purely of ice poured soft, clear light into the room—no torches lit, and even the hearth was cold and dark. Below the skylight, a balcony with giant glass doors stood frosted over, the cold seeping in from outside.

We will be able to meditate out there. No one will bother you here unless you call for them, Skadi said.

I nodded slowly, moving toward one of the shelves, running my fingers along the spines of leather-bound books and scrolls. I took a long breath, relishing the scent of leather, ink and old oak.

I turned, smile ready, wanting to ramble to Eirik about everything—but I stopped short, remembering why we'd come here. The excitement faded a little as I faced the thing between us that still needed to be said.

I watched him move along the shelves, busying himself to give me time to look around. Always the gentleman, even when I was being a pain.

I cleared my throat lightly, catching his attention. His eyes flicked to mine as I sank into one of the deep seats, trying to calm my nervous stomach. Eirik began pacing, arms crossed, his face tight in thought.

"I'm sorry I yelled..." I said first, my voice quieter than I intended as I watched him.

He stopped suddenly, mouth parting as if to answer, then slumped forward. "No, it is I who should apologize. I should have told you about my fire heritage the moment I noticed your ice making itself known."

"We'd only just met," I said with a nervous chuckle. "Not exactly the time to start spilling life stories, right?"

Eirik frowned, then stepped forward and knelt in front of me. His tall frame dwarfed mine, making my breath catch.

"I had other chances," he admitted. "Long after we met. During training, I could have told you. Instead, I pushed you, snapped at you to try harder, and... look what happened." He raked a hand through his hair. "I've grown fond of you—more than I expected."

I blinked, caught off guard. "You're special to me also. You, Runar, everyone—you've all become dear to me." I trailed off, missing the shift in his eyes.

He let out a breathy chuckle, gaze lingering on my face longer than it should have. "I don't think you understand, Ravena. I was trained to guard you, train you, to make sure you survived. That was supposed to be it... not this."

I tilted my head, brow furrowed. "I—I don't... not what? What do you mean?" My confusion was obvious.

Oh, dear child... Skadi's sigh echoed through my mind, only adding to my confusion.

Eirik's mouth opened again, like he was ready to dig down, to explain what *not this* meant. His voice was steady, but there was something in it I hadn't heard before—hesitation, maybe?

"Ravena, what I mean is..." His words trailed, jaw tightening as if he couldn't decide what to tell me. "I never expected to care for you the way I have come to. It isn't just duty anymore, it seems."

I froze, breath catching in my lungs. The shift in his tone, the way his eyes searched mine—it all started to click. My hands clenched with the realization I'd been dancing around since Korinthos.

But then something stirred again. That same faint tug deep within me—like an invisible thread being pulled taut. I had felt this before, back in Kyllini, the day he steadied me during training. His hands had lingered a moment too long, and a strange sensation had sparked inside me. Subtle at first, almost ignorable—but it had urged me to step back even then. Now it returned sharper, and more insistent, until it physically hurt.

I flinched back, as if a little distance might help me escape it.

Eirik's face shifted to concern, his hand reaching out to comfort me. "Ravena?"

That sensation pulsed again, and I quickly shook my head to stop him. He froze in place.

"What is wrong?" he asked, straightening, to give me space.

"I'm not sure…" I trailed off, searching for the words that wouldn't come. I couldn't meet his eyes. He was only trying to help—but after everything he'd just said, I didn't know how to respond. So I fell back on the easiest thing to say.

"I think I'm just tired. It's been a long day." I glanced aside, pretending to study the books instead of him, though I knew he noticed.

He sighed, shoulders sinking in quiet defeat. "Of course. I'll give you some time." Another breath left him, heavy, before he turned and walked out.

The library was quiet once more, the only sound was the wind gliding across the skylights surface. My mind, though, was anything but calm. My thoughts spiraled between Eirik's words and that weird tug I'd felt. I couldn't make sense of it, rubbing my temples as a headache began to form.

Young one, why don't we meditate, clear your mind? Skadi's voice cut through.

I glanced at the balcony, then exhaled sharply through my nose, smacking my hands against my thighs. I stood, heading toward the spiral stairs, my footsteps echoing as I went.

If I get a lecture during meditation, I'm leaving, I muttered under my breath. *I already made a fool of myself.*

Reaching the landing, I grasped the cool metal of the doorknob and yanked it open. The cold wind rushed in, loosening strands from my braid. The balcony was smaller compared to the grandeur of the library—a pallet of cushions sat at its center beneath an awning that shielded it from the elements.

I drew in a deep breath, the cold air burning my lungs—but it helped. The tension began to ease from my body. Walking to the edge, I admired the mountains and the canyon below. Trees streaked the ravine, hiding whatever lay beneath. It should have been peaceful, should have relaxed me, but that faint tug—now ebbing slowly—still nagged at the back of my mind.

Eventually, I made my way to the cushions, turning my back on the scenery as I sank into a comfortable seat. Closing my eyes, I focused on my breath, trying to find my center. The wind and noise faded away. When I opened my eyes, my inner world took shape—trees stretching tall, sunlight dappling the ground. And there, leaning against one of the trunks, was Skadi, a gentle smile on her face.

"Hello Ravena. It is good to see you again." Skadi's voice was light in the quiet space.

I crunched through the snowy ground and headed to the same rock I always sat on during our talks. With a heaviness settling on my shoulders again, I sank down. "It's nice to see someone besides men for once. Will you be alright... appearing like this?" I asked, curiosity coloring my tone.

"My essence is stable here. Being in this place makes me a bit stronger." She stepped forward. "It seems you have much on your mind—the winds here are unsettled, more so than usual."

I sighed in frustration, already sensing where this was headed. "The thing with Eirik, why was I so oblivious? And that painful tug from earlier—I haven't felt anything like that since Kyllini..."

A flicker of emotion passed over Skadi's face, one I recognized but knew better than to question. Everyone always seemed to know more than I did about these things.

"I know that look, but you're not going to tell me, are you?" I muttered, resting my hand on my chin.

"Some things must be learned with time. I do not know for certain, but I have my suspicions—as did the other god who helped you," she said cryptically. "Now, let's train. We should make use of the time we have."

I quirked a brow at her, but relented, rising from the stone. At least this was something other than talking about Eirik—my supposed crush and his apparent feelings, which everyone but me seemed to understand.

"We'll work on your ice wielding. I want you to be able to create weapons, should your sword or other weapons fail." she lifted her arm, and I watched as ice enveloped her right hand, the fingertips extending out into deadly, claw-like shapes.

I stepped back as she smirked. "Runar made sure to teach me this. If your sword fails, claws work just as well."

"He's definitely been holding back on his teachings," I muttered, thinking how useful this would've been during my spar with Chione.

"You've had a lot going on. Training hasn't exactly been plentiful with the time you've had," she replied. "Now, give it a try. Focus on pulling the cold from the air around you."

I exhaled, slowly gathering the ice around my hand and concentrating on forming the sharp, extended tips as she had. It took far more energy than simply coating my hand in ice. As the final point formed, my focus slipped, and the claws shattered into frost with a sigh of defeat.

"That wasn't bad. Your magic is growing, but you still need more practice with your stamina. Soon enough, it'll be second nature to summon ice as you need it." She let the ice from her hand dissipate, and before I could even blink, she was in front of me—a sharp point lightly touching the underside of my chin.

My eyes widened, breath catching as I glanced down. A gleaming dagger made of ice rested comfortably in her grasp.

"In a moment's notice, when your weapons are taken and time is of essence, a dagger is your most reliable asset." Her cool presence radiated over me.

I gulped. "Uh well, that's helpful and all... but you can't actually kill me here, right?" I asked, voice small.

She let out an exasperated sigh and stepped back. "No, young one. You are perfectly safe here. This was only a demonstration of the tactics you could use to your advantage."

I tilted my head in fascination. "What if I'm somewhere it isn't cold?"

"That won't be a concern. Your gift allows you to cool the environment from within—you're never without a means of protection." She circled me, careful not to make me feel cornered.

I marveled at the thought. It made sense, of course.

"Your ice is nearly indestructible, unless parried by another divine being's magic. It requires control and prowess—which you are learning." She came to a stop, her clothes shifting with her movement.

"With the time we have, I'm going to push you—to build the resilience you'll need."

Her words sparked a sense of dread in me. The air around us shifted, heavy, as if a storm were approaching.

"And what exactly are you planning? What do I need to do?" I frowned, both scared and curious.

"Now, form that dagger and attack me," she smirked. "No holding back. Eirik has been coddling you."

I opened my mouth to protest, but she was in front of me almost instantly. I barely dodge back, teeth clenched, rushing to form a dagger—half of one, that's all I could manage before we clashed. The screech of our ice blades grinding together rang out. I gasped at the force behind her blow. Her gaze had changed—gone was the soft eyed goddess I'd come to know. Now a terrifying, cold stare froze me in place, this was a warrior and she wasn't playing.

It was a warning.

To take this seriously or else I'd suffer consequences I didn't want to find out—whether it was here or out in the real world.

I tightened my grip on my poor excuse for a dagger and pushed back, a thin line of sweat forming on my temples. I didn't even think that was possible here.

We were locked in a stalemate, neither of us overpowering the other. Why couldn't I get the upper hand?

And as if she could read my thoughts—which, honestly, she probably could—Skadi smirked.

"I am only as strong as you, Ravena, in here. I have experience, yes, but remember, I am only the essence of what I once was. You hold all of the power now. You're limiting yourself out of fear." she snapped.

"I–I am not scared." I grunted, my arms visibly shaking.

"Then show me!" She bit out. "You always speak of not wanting to disappoint me, then prove it"

My eyes widened, and with newfound determination I pushed myself back and rapidly formed a new dagger, its sharp end catching the pale light.

Underneath it all, I still felt the tremors in my limbs. I was panting for air—this was eerily exhausting, both mentally and physically.

I steadied my stance again and blinked, only to find Skadi moving toward me, but now I could track her movements more easily. I needed to be faster, just like they all seemed to be.

I raised my dagger, blocking yet another blow. But instead of stopping, the hits kept coming. I forced myself to focus, to stay centered. I could feel my counters and dodges improving. Ice shards littered the area as Skadi took to launching them at me.

After what felt like hours, she finally conceded, and I collapsed to the ground, drained. "Why does it feel like I'm going to regret this when I leave? My head feels like it's going to explode," I muttered, messaging my temples.

Skadi approached and knelt beside me, chuckling. "You can't be physically hurt here, but it's still training. You're learning. Your body will carry that exercise and knowledge back to the real world."

I closed my eyes in irritation. "Oh, fun. And yet I still have to train tomorrow while we're here..."

A hand rested on my shoulder, its touch almost ghostly. "Ravena... I know you want to bury what happened with Eirik, but I feel we should discuss what to do from now on," she said gently.

Groaning, I rolled my eyes. "We already talked about it. What more is there to say?" I sat up, her hand sliding from my shoulder. I fiddled with my sleeve, avoiding her gaze.

"He's still your partner in this. Whatever you feel—however confusing—you can't let it fester. If you do, it'll break more than just the bond between you; it'll break your focus in battle."

I let go of my sleeve, biting the inside of my cheek as anxiety curled in my chest. I knew she was right. I knew there were battles ahead.

But I'd never been good at this. I wasn't the type of girl men took an interest in—not really. So to have a man admit his feelings for me? It was strange. And I didn't know what to do with it.

"How do I even begin to say something to him?" My voice cracked slightly. "It's not like we're mad at each other..." I trailed off.

"But the situation is still awkward, don't you think? Especially when things get serious?"

"No... I don't think so," I mumbled.

She crossed her arms, giving me a pointed look. "Yes, Ravena. He has feelings for you. So, anytime you're in danger, he'll be more protective. More observant."

I blinked. "So just because he has a crush on me, that's why he worries so much?"

She sighed in exasperation. "No. He's your guardian and your friend. His concern would exist either way. The feelings just heighten it."

My cheeks warmed and I fidgeted with the hem of my sleeve. "I don't know if that makes it better or worse." I hesitated, then blurted before I could stop myself, "But even if I maybe have feelings for him..."

That same tug flared again, pulling tight in my chest. I winced, pressing a hand there as if I could ease it. "Something about it just doesn't feel right. And you won't tell me your suspicions—like you said, I have to learn over time."

Skadi exhaled, a sound edged with both patience and weariness. "Yes. Some truths must come in their own time. But this much I will say: talk to him, Ravena. You'll train together again tomorrow, and you can't let this rift grow. If you fight at odds—simply because of feelings—you both will fail."

Her words left a knot in my stomach. Of course she was right. The tug had started to fade, thankfully, but we both knew it was still there, waiting.

A soft, ghostly tapping at my arm startled me, and the vision of Skadi and my inner world faded away. My eyes blinked open to the dimming light of the balcony. Azhrina stood beside me, her voice careful.

"Milady, the hour grows late. Dinner is prepared."

I sat up straighter, every muscle aching from training. Skadi had been right—those lessons carried over. With a small groan, I pushed myself up from the cushions.

Azhrina dipped her head politely and offered her arm to guide me. "Runar and your guardian are already waiting."

I nodded, brushing stray strands of hair from my face, and followed her inside. The echo of Skadi's words about Eirik lingered in my chest. I swallowed the lump in my throat. I couldn't ignore this—not anymore.

We walked through the library, down the endless stairs and winding hallways. As we neared the dining hall, I heard the clatter of plates being set down, the sounds echoing toward us. The moment we entered, the movements ceased. The ice elves present bowed their heads.

A male elf in a dark navy tunic straightened and stepped forward. "Lady Ravena! Welcome. Dinner will be brought out fresh for you short-ly," he exclaimed.

My gaze flicked to Eirik. He'd already started eating; my place was still empty. Some of the tension from earlier eased, and I offered the elf a small smile. "Thank you—what is your name?" I asked, curious.

A shocked expression crossed his face, as though no one had ever asked him that before.

I thought they said you were nicer than your father... I would assume you'd have talked to everyone.

I knew my handmaids and a few others, but there are many more you've yet to see. It would be impossible to greet them all, Skadi's voice drifted through my mind.

"My name is Arun, milady!" he said quickly, bowing low.

"No—no need to bow. Please, if you all don't mind," I sputtered, glancing nervously at the room.

Arun bowed again before hurrying toward the kitchen. Azhrina guided me to the same high-back chair from lunch and pulled it out for me. I sat, placing my hands on the armrests. Eirik was halfway down the table, his plate already half-finished. He hadn't looked at me once since I arrived.

The room grew quiet as the food was set down before me—a tray of steaming stew, fresh bread still warm from the oven, and a cup of wine. The elves continued their work, moving with practiced grace, but their presence only made the silence between us linger longer.

I picked up my spoon, stirring the stew without taking a bite. The clink of metal against the bowl echoed louder than it should have.

Runar lifted his head from the furs where he'd sprawled in the corner. His golden eyes shifted between me and Eirik before he offered a wolfish grin.

"Well," he rumbled, voice thick with amusement. "I don't know what weighs heavier in this room—myself or the tension between you two."

Heat rushed to my cheeks, and I ducked my head, wishing the floor would swallow me. I rolled my eyes, too, because once again... here was the topic I wanted to avoid.

Eirik froze with his cup halfway to his mouth. Slowly, he set it down—maybe a little too hard. The thud of clay on wood made me flinch.

"You truly don't know when to hold your tongue, wolf," he snapped, pushing back from his chair.

His tone surprised me. I'd heard them bicker before, but right now he sounded genuinely upset.

Runar only snorted, completely unbothered. "What? I was merely pointing out what even the blind could sense."

Eirik's jaw clenched. He stood abruptly, the chair legs scraping hard against the floor. "I'll see you all here for breakfast tomorrow," he bit out, voice clipped, before striding out of the hall without so much as a backwards glance.

Silence fell again, heavier this time, broken only by the soft crackle of the hearth.

Runar shifted, watching as Eirik exited, then turned his focus back to me. "Did I miss something? He usually isn't so bothered by my jesting."

I scraped my food around the bowl, nerves bunching in my shoulders. "Not really, unless you are interested in semi-human drama."

"Humor me, young frostling." That wolfish grin slid right back into place.

I rolled my eyes and set down the spoon. "Eirik might have admitted he has feelings for me."

Runar's ears twitched, his head tilting with interest. "Oh? And did you admit yours to him?" he rumbled, tone deceptively casual.

I froze. "I do not!" My voice shot up higher than I meant. The look he gave me in return was deadpan—so flat I almost cried.

I slumped forward, lowering my voice so only he could hear. "Even if I possibly did... something feels off about it. Like I'm not meant to." I pressed my hand to my chest. "There's this... pull. The closer I get, the worse it gets. This time, it actually hurt."

Runar's grin faded. His ears flicked back as he studied me. "A tugging thread," he muttered. "That sounds like the work of the Fates."

This was new information, and it made my stomach twist into a knot. The Fates. But Skadi always said I had to find my own destiny—that nothing was written in stone. Yet this felt an awful lot like a path already laid out, dragging me forward whether I wanted it or not.

I clenched my jaw, forcing myself to pick my spoon back up. "I don't like it," I admitted quietly. "I don't like feeling like I don't get a say. It's like I'm being pushed somewhere, not choosing it for myself."

Runar tilted his head, eyes thoughtful but impossible to read. For once, he didn't make a joke. "Threads can be cut—by choice or not, young one. But sometimes... they lead us exactly where we're meant to be."

His words didn't comfort me. If anything, they left me even more unsettled. Because what the hell, to be pulled along by something invisible, some plan I couldn't control?

I toyed with the spoon, appetite long gone, thoughts circling the same pit in my stomach. The lack of choice clung to me, this constant, irritating reminder that I'd been tossed into something I was still trying to figure out.

Runar shifted beside me, his gaze slanting over. "You're dwelling on it too much, young one. Better to put that restless energy towards something useful."

I raised a brow at him. "Like what?"

"Like what we came here for," he said simply, stretching before standing tall. "Clue. Answers. The fortress still holds what happened that night. If we continue sitting here, we'll find nothing."

I sighed, setting my spoon aside.

Right. We came here to find out how Agnar escaped. Not my supposed crush on Eirik.

"Fine. We start with the destroyed portal, then?"

A glimmer of approval flashed in his eyes. "Exactly." He moved to my side as I stood, his fur brushing my face. "Better to uncover what shadows still linger than let them creep closer while our backs are turned."

I took a steadying breath and followed him out of the dining room.

The fortress halls were dimmer now, pools of torchlight our only defense against the shadows. My boots echoed softly, Runar's claws clicking beside me as we wound through stairways and passages I had yet to discover. The lower we descended, the colder it became—and beneath the chill, a sense of emptiness lingered.

"What is this feeling? It's like something is dampening the area," I murmured.

"There are spells—wards, if you prefer—that suppress magic. They keep the creatures contained," Runar explained.

I rubbed my arms, the heaviness in the air twisting a new knot in my stomach. "It's strange... it feels like the walls themselves are holding something back."

Runar flicked an ear, calm as ever. "That's because they are. The wards here don't just keep prisoners in—they keep memories of the past trapped too."

I frowned, slowing as we neared the end of the corridor. "Memories?"

He didn't answer straight away, just gave a small grunt that could've meant yes, or that he didn't feel like explaining. Either way, nausea coiled in my stomach.

The floor sloped lower; the air felt stifling—hot, if that made any sense. The torches burned brighter, chasing away the cold, but everything felt muted and heavy.

"This way leads to the cells," Runar rumbled lowly. "Agnar was kept here. And others like him—those tied to ice."

I swallowed. "So that's why I can feel it so much. Like the walls are sucking the air out of me."

"That's the wards," he nodded. "These cells were built to drain your power. To take everything until nothing is left."

We passed rows of thick iron doors, the bars steaming to the touch, scorched in places. My steps slowed at one, its surface scarred deep, as if claws had raked the stone. For a split second, I thought I heard echoes—screams, chains groaning—but when I blinked, it was gone.

"His cell is—was—at the end."

The final cell loomed larger than the rest, its heavy iron door torn open. Inside, melting frost still coated the wall, thick enough to catch the light and shimmer. This ice shouldn't be here, not in a place so stifling.

A shiver ran through me. "This is where he broke free?"

Runar's gaze hardened. "No. This is where he was freed."

We lingered only a moment longer in the ruined cell before Runar grunted and turned sharply, padding back into the corridor. It hit me then just how massive the cell was—large enough for him to move freely at full height.

"The portal isn't far," he said. "It branches off above us, through a side hallway."

I cast one last look at the frost-scarred walls before hurrying after him. My boots echoed off the stone, the air shifting as we climbed back toward the higher levels—cold now, no longer hot and suffocating.

The corridor split, one path curling back to the main stairs, the other narrowing into a dim passage. Runar took the latter without hesitation.

At the end, a wide chamber opened up. The marbled stone portal stood broken, half-collapsed into rubble, fractured down its center. Ice clung to the ruined frame, scorched ice marks marred the area like old wounds.

I stopped at the bottom of the raised stairs, my heart sinking. A nostalgic feeling making me dizzy. "This is it."

Runar prowled ahead, nose close to the stone. "Here is where he escaped—and where he was guided."

I looked around, nudging rubble with my boot, watching the frost float down. Something reflected out of the corner of my eye. I crouched, brushing frost aside, my breath stilled. A flower—out of place, its petals pale as bone with the faintest blush of blue at the edges. Still fresh, but no sunlight had touched this chamber in years.

"What... is this doing here?" I whispered.

Runar's ears twitched, his head snapping toward me. He padded closer, eyes narrowing at the sight. The low growl that rumbled from his chest vibrated through the stone beneath us.

I swallowed hard, the sound making the tiny hairs at the back of my neck stand on end.

This flower didn't belong here... not in this chamber... it was as if it had fallen from something. And the longer I stared at it, the more certain I became... I wasn't supposed to find it.

Chapter Thirty-Five

Sleep came in fragments that night—scorched ice marks and rubble looping endlessly in my mind. The walls of Agnar's cell, the flower lying in the ruins of the broken portal, the faint echo of screams that weren't really there. Every time I drifted deeper, the images enhanced, pulling me back awake.

By the time pale light filtered through the stained-glass windows, I felt more wrung out than rested. My body ached as if Skadi's training had bled into my dreams, and my head throbbed with the pressure of it all.

A soft knock pulled me upright. The door eased opened and Azhrina slipped through, Prymsdora close behind. Both carried folded stacks of fabric, and between them, I caught the glint of polished metal. Curiosity nudged aside some of the fatigue.

"Good morning, Lady Ravena," Azhrina said gently, setting her bundle across the foot of my bed. "We thought it best to bring something fresh for the day. Runar says you have training."

Prymsdora laid hers down more heavily, with a faint clink. "And this," she added, tone bright. When she pulled back the cloth, the light caught on chain and leather, gleaming faintly.

A chainmail shirt lay beneath reinforced leather plates, the dark hide stitched with silver thread in curling snowflake patterns. A heavy belt and fur-lined shoulder pads gave it a battle-ready feel; it wasn't anything ceremonial. This wasn't for show.

My breath caught as I brushed my fingers over it. The leather was so dark it nearly looked black, but when it caught the light, the faintest shimmer of deep blue appeared. Beneath lay a lighter linen underlayer and a pair of sturdy trousers, folded neatly for ease of movement. At the end of the bench waited a pair of boots, fur trimmed along the tops.

"It is yours now, milady," Prymsdora said proudly, her chin lifted. "Forged for battle, not ceremony. So you carry both strength and presence."

I traced the faint runes etched in random places, almost invisible unless the light hit them just right. I wondered what their purpose was.

Eventually, you can channel your magic through it and the runes will help guide it, Skadi's voice interjected, softer than before.

Azhrina clasped her hands, smiling faintly before I could reply. "Come, let us help you. It was made to fit, though it may feel heavy at first."

Before I could protest (and I really wanted to), Prymsdora was already unfolding the linen underlayer and ushering me from bed toward the screen. "You will need the full outfit, Lady Ravena. This is no time for soft clothes," she said—and I knew she was talking about my modern-day pajamas.

I sighed but obeyed—slipping into the linen first, then the snug trousers. The fabric was warm but breathable, just enough to keep me comfortable. They layered everything with skilled hands—fastening the chains over my shoulders, tugging the leather plates into place, and cinching the belt tight at my waist.

When they stepped back, I caught sight of myself in the polished silver propped against the wall. The chainmail hugged close, but gave me room to move, the leather reinforcing my chest and shoulders. The faint blue shimmer caught in the morning light, silver stitching curling like snow up my sleeves. I looked... different. More confident, somehow.

But Prymsdora wasn't finished. She took a comb to my braid, unraveling it and reworking it into tighter plaits—making me wince—then weaving it all down my back in an intricate pattern, with small strands left to frame my face. By the time she finished, I almost didn't recognize the woman staring back at me.

"Now," she declared, satisfaction clear in her voice. "You look as a Norse warrior should."

I gulped, adjusting the boots hugging my calves. "I look like I'm ready to go to battle. To fight."

Azhrina tilted her head, calm as ever. "Isn't that exactly what you're supposed to look like?" She smoothed one last seam at my shoulder, and Prymsdora clapped her hands, delighted with her work.

"Breakfast is already being set out," Azhrina reminded gently. "Your guardian waits also."

I sighed. Of course he does. My stomach twisted—whether from hunger or nerves, I wasn't sure. The three of us left the room, my boots hitting the stone a little heavier now. I tried not to fidget, but I couldn't shake the imposter syndrome. I didn't feel like a warrior, goddess, or protector—none of it felt like me just yet.

As we entered the dining hall, our footsteps echoed through the entrance. Runar was already sprawled on his usual pile of fur, lifting his head as we walked in. And there at the long table sat Eirik.

His hand stilled halfway to his cup. His eyes dragged over me once, twice, before he looked back down at his meal. It was quick, but not quick enough—I caught the flicker of surprise on his face.

Prymsdora nudged me toward my chair as if nothing was happening. I sat, adjusting the belt at my waist, the silence suddenly loud.

Runar's tail thumped once against the ground, a smirk tugging at his muzzle. "About time," he rumbled. "Your guardian was growing restless."

Eirik shot him a look sharp enough to cut, but said nothing. He went back to his meal, ignoring Runar all together.

Silence held through the rest of the meal, broken only by the clink of cutlery and the low crackle of the hearth.

Runar dozed with his head on his paws, ear twitching at every shift between us. Prymsdora and Azhrina busied themselves with clearing the table, tactfully pretending not to notice the tension.

When the last of the food was gone, Eirik pushed back from the table. "I'll wait in the hall. I don't know where we're meant to train." His voice was even but distant. Without another word, he strode out of the dining room.

Runar gave me a sideways glance, tail flicking. "Best hurry up, young one. He won't wait."

I exhaled, nerves and determination warring in my chest. Rising, I turned to Azhrina. "Where can we train? I need somewhere with space for actual fighting."

Azhrina paused in thought, then nodded. "There is a southern yard outside built from the side of the mountain," she decided. "It was once used for the guards training and weapons practice. There's plenty of space, and no one will disturb you. Just... please take care and not fall over the edge..."

Before I could question her, Prymsdora clapped her hands, already bustling off to fetch cloaks. "I'll have the handmaids keep the area clear—unless you wish for some of the guards to participate?"

Runar stretched, rising with a yawn as he moved toward the entrance. "Not necessary. We will train her. Let's go—the fire-blood can finally work off the storm brewing in his chest."

I winced at his words but force myself to stand straighter. If Skadi was right—and she always was—I couldn't keep avoiding this. Better to face it now than let this rift between us deeper.

The hall outside felt colder without the hearth. Eirik waited at the far end, his back to me, posture rigid and hands clasped behind him as if holding himself together by sheer force.

I swallowed and made myself walk forward, each step echoing too loud in my ears. My palm itched with nerves.

"Eirik," I called, my voice catching.

He turned, face unreadable, eyes searching mine as I stopped a few paces away.

I drew in a breath, steadying myself. "There are things I need to tell you... about what Runar and I found last night. And about..." My fingers clenched at my sides. "About what happened in the library."

His jaw flexed, but he didn't move, didn't push me—just waited.

"The cells," I started, the words barely scraping out. "We went down there looking for answers. I saw Agnar's cell. The wards, the frost still burned to the stones... Runar said Agnar wasn't just escaping—he was freed. And at the portal, we found something else. A flower. It definitely didn't belong there."

Eirik's brows furrowed. "A flower?"

I nodded. "It felt off, like it was left there on purpose... or it fell during the escape. I thought you should know."

For a moment, silence stretched between us, his gaze never leaving mine. I couldn't stand the silence, so I forced the words I'd been avoiding and I glanced away. "In the library... when you said you cared for me. I pretended I was just tired, but that wasn't the truth." Heat prickled my cheeks, but I refused to look up. "I do feel something for you. I can't deny that anymore." Admitting that made me want to throw up.

The air between us tightened, my chest constricting along with that faint tug—harsh enough to make me wince. I pressed a hand to my sternum, breath hitching, but forced myself to keep going. "But it's like... something won't let me go further. The closer I try to step toward it—toward the possibility—the stronger it gets. And I don't know what it means yet."

Eirik's eyes softened, though his jaw stayed tight. He took half a step forward, then stopped, weighing every word and respecting my space. "Then we'll figure it out together," he said quietly. "Whatever that pull is... it won't stop me from being at your side, even if it's only as your guardian."

The sincerity in his voice made my throat tighten, but we couldn't linger. Not now. I gave a small nod, forcing a timid smile, and willed my feet to move.

Runar was already ahead, halfway down the hall, ears flicking back at the sound of our boots. He glanced over his shoulder with a wolfish smirk. "Are we done with the feelings, then? Or should I fetch cushions so you can sit and talk it out longer?"

Heat flared up my neck and I shoved past him, muttering, "We're coming."

Eirik's low grunt of annoyance was the only reply, but the faintest curve of his mouth told me he was fighting a smile.

The training field opened beyond the last set of frost-crusted doors—a wide expanse carved into the mountainside. Dim light poured through arched gaps in the stone walls, casting shifting patterns across packed snow and hardened earth. Wooden dummies stood at odd intervals, their surfaces scarred by slashes, burn marks, and frost—years of practice marked on every inch. It made me wonder what kind of guards they had here... I hadn't seen any since arriving.

Runar padded ahead, tail swishing, clearly at home in this space. Eirik followed, his stride steady but his shoulders tense, and I trailed after, my nerves taut as a bowstring.

I barely had time to take it all in before movement caught my eye. An armored guard approached from the side alcove, head bowed, a bundle cradled in his arms. He stopped a few paces from me and knelt, unwrapping the cloth.

A sword rested within, and in his other hand, a shield—both elegant in their simplicity, yet undeniably divine. The sword was long and narrow, its steel kissed with faint blue light along the edges, as if ice itself had been forged into the blade. The shield was round, rimmed in silver, its face etched with wolves that caught in the mid-morning glow.

"These were once Lady Skadi's," the guard said reverently, holding them out. "Her weapons, kept safe until the day her successor would come."

My throat tightened as I reached forward, fingers brushing the cool hilt. The air around the blade seemed to hum in recognition, frost feathering lightly across the ground at my feet.

I drew in a breath, lifting the sword and testing its weight. It was perfect—balanced, like it had been waiting for me all this time.

Turning to Eirik, I squared my shoulders, pushing aside the doubt buzzing in my chest. "Don't hold back please," I told him firmly. "Not today. I need to see what I can do."

Runar gave a low rumble that might've been a laugh as he stepped into the ring beside me. "Then I'll make this interesting. You'll fight us both."

I shot him a look, but he only bared his teeth in a wolfish grin. Poor Eirik's expression wavered between irritation and focus, his hand flexing around the axe handle.

I raised the shield, Skadi's words echoing in my mind as I called my magic to my fingertips. This was no ordinary spar—this was a test of everything I had learned.

The three of us faced off in the wide circle of snow and stone, our breath clouding white in the cold air. My pulse thundered in my ears, Skadi's blade firm in my hand, the shield snug against my arm. It all felt surreal, but nostalgic—like I'd done this countless times before.

Eirik adjusted his grip on his axe, fire already smoldering along the blade's edge. He wasn't hiding anymore—his eyes locked on mine, steady and sure. "You said not to hold back."

I swallowed and nodded, lifting the shield. "I meant it."

Runar moved fist. His massive form lunged forward with a growl, claws sparking against the packed earth. I braced, raising the shield just in time to block. The impact rattled up my arm. My boots slid back in the snow, but I pushed against it, calling ice to my feet, anchoring myself. Frost splintered in jagged cracks beneath me.

"Good, young frostling" Runar rumbled, retreating only to circle again.

Eirik came next, quick and deliberate, his axe swinging low. I raised my sword, deflecting his strike—sparks bursting as heat surged against the cold of my blade. My breath caught; fire licked across the edge of his weapon, forcing me back.

"Dammit." I gritted my teeth and focused, remembering Skadi's voice: *Pull from the air. Center yourself. Shape it—don't let it shape you.* Ice surged along my arm, reinforcing the shield as his strike landed hard. This time, I didn't yield.

He smirked faintly. "That's better, Ravena."

I lunged, swinging for his side, but Runar intercepted with a swipe of his paw, forcing me to twist and duck. My blade skimmed the fur along his leg before I rolled to the side, snow scattering. My lungs burned, the tug of magic in my chest both exhilarating and exhausting.

They weren't letting up. Nerves fluttered, but I knew I could do this—I had to.

Eirik's fire flared brighter, heat rippling through the frigid air as he pressed forward again. Runar mirrored from the opposite side, their movements coordinated without a word. I realized too late—they were driving me, forcing me to split my attention, to prove I could handle fighting both at once.

Panic threatened, but I shoved it down. I caught another flaming swing, twisting under Runar's paw as they both closed in. Steeling myself, I slammed my shield to the ground, frost exploding outward in a burst that coated the snow in a thick slick sheen. Runar slipped, claws scraping for leverage, and Eirik faltered just long enough for me to strike. My sword arced, ice gleaming, catching the sunlight as I aimed for his shoulder.

Our blades collided—fire and ice meeting. The clash shook through me, but this time I didn't break. I parried his blow, my blade holding firm, the frost along the edge refusing to yield to his fire. Steam hissed dangerously where our powers collided, curling thick and acrid between us.

I stared into Eirik's eyes, breath ragged, chest heaving. His fire burned hotter, mine colder, the air between us trembling.

Then Runar barreled back in, snapping the tension. His massive shoulder slammed into my side and sent me sprawling across the snow, my shield tumbling from my grip.

I gasped as sparks burst behind my eyes—my head hitting the ground. Scrambling, frost raced instinctively from my palms to shield me. My body trembled with the effort, vision blurring at the edges.

Stand, Ravena! Skadi's voice roared in my mind. The Goddess of Winter accepts no defeat!

With a growl of my own, I forced myself to stand. Ice surged at my call, sharper, more controlled this time. A dagger formed in my free hand, my sword secure in the other.

Both of them came at me again, and this time I didn't cower. I met Runar's strike with the dagger, deflecting his claws wide, and swung the sword in a clean arc at Eirik's chest. He barely caught it, flame sparking in protest, but the impact drove him back a step.

Snow sprayed, steam curled, ice cracked. The field echoed with every strike. New gouges marred the training field, and I was sure anyone nearby could feel the tremble of our powers colliding.

My muscles screamed, my swings growing sloppy, each breath ragged as I fought to keep pace. Minutes blurred together in the frenzy until my body simply refused to obey anymore. My knees buckled, sword clattering from my hand. Darkness edged my vision.

The last thing I felt as everything faded was strong arms catching me, heat wrapping around me as my magic dwindled.

Eirik's voice, rough but steady: "I've got you, Ravena."

The world swayed gently, and it took me a moment to realize it wasn't my own steps but Eirik's. My head rested against his chest, the calm rhythm of his heartbeat loud in my ears. Heat radiated from him—comforting, in a way, but I'd grown so used to the cold it almost felt foreign.

"You're safe," he murmured, noticing I was awake. His voice was low enough that I might've thought it a dream if not for the way his arms held me so securely. Then softer, almost regretful: "I should've told you the truth sooner. About my heritage. I'm sorry, Ravena. I'll do better by you."

I wanted to answer, but exhaustion weighed me down. All I could manage was a soft sigh as my eyes drifted shut.

I could hear the door opening, Azhrina's gasp carrying across the room. Prymsdora rushed forward, already ushering Eirik toward the bed. He lowered me gently onto the blankets, his hands lingering at my shoulders before he finally let go and stepped back.

"She overexerted herself, didn't she?" Azhrina muttered, already working at the clasp of my armor. Prymsdora tugged the belt free and unfastened the leather plates with efficient hands.

Azhrina looked at Eirik, brow raised, "Out. Milady doesn't need you seeing her undressed."

I was too tired to flush—honestly, Eirik had nearly seen me naked before—but I heard him grunt before exiting the room. Piece by piece, the weight of armor fell away until I was left in just the linen underlayer, my skin clammy.

"She needs rest, and food," Prymsdora huffed, laying out a clean tunic. They eased me into it with care, and it warmed me how gentle they were being before swiftly tucking me beneath fresh furs.

"We'll fetch dinner," Azhrina whispered, brushing stray hairs from my forehead. "Rest, milady."

I must've drifted, because when the door opened again, the scent of meat and bread roused me. A tray clinked softly at my side, Prymsdora setting it on the small table. "Eat a little. Then sleep more," she urged gently.

By the time I'd eaten half, Runar padded in, his great head lowering until his golden eyes were level with mine. "You did well today, young frostling," he rumbled, his voice full of something that almost sounded like pride—which, for him, was a huge feat. "I've not seen you fight with such fire–even Lydia would have approved."

Despite my weariness, warmth bloomed in my chest. I leaned back, smiling faintly. "Thank you, Runar."

"Don't expect another compliment, young one. I was nice this once." He grunted and went to sprawl by the hearth.

I snorted. Of course he had to have the last word. I glanced toward the window as the sky darkened; night was settling over the fortress, and even though I was tired, I felt wired, like just lying in bed wasn't enough.

A soft creak from the door pulled my attention toward it, and Eirik stepped inside. He hesitated in the doorway until I rolled my eyes and motioned him over. In a few strides, he crossed the room and offered me his hand.

"I figured you wouldn't want to just lie in bed..." he said quietly. "The library's a better place if you want to rest easier."

I blinked—it was like he could read my mind, catching onto my thoughts from just moments ago about not wanting to lie around in this bed all night. I hesitated for only a second before letting him help me up. His grip was strong, guiding me through the winding halls, patient with every stop I needed to catch my breath.

By the time we reached the bottom of the stairs, I cringed. No way was I making it up there. Before I could protest, Eirik swept me up into his arms and started striding upward, all without a word.

Curse him. My face was probably going to stay red forever.

The vast shelves of the library greeted us, the fire crackling low in the hearth, its glow spilling across carved stone and endless rows of books.

Eirik set me gently into one of the deep chairs, and the exhaustion caught up to me all at once. The warmth from the fire and his quiet presence beside me were all it took for my eyes to drift closed—too tired to even read.

I sat up gasping. My vision blurred, the air so cold it burned my lungs—even I could feel it. As the haze cleared, I found myself in the middle of burning trees. Smoke curled up into a blackened sky. With a jolt, I recognized Kyllini—it was burning below me, its streets swallowed in ice and shadows. Screams carried on the wind, distant but clear.

The vision shifted. Athenae shimmered into view—temples cracked, markets torn apart, torches were scattered in chaos. The laughter was gone, replaced by sheer terror.

My stomach churned. What was all this? A rustle made me whirl around.

From the haze stepped Hermes, his form tense, his expression heavy with regret—and was that actual fear?

"I am sorry. This was the only way to contact you," he said, his voice edged with apology. "But I must show you what the winds whisper. They grow darker by the day. I fear Greece will soon meet the darkness that Agnar has planned."

The ground split, and suddenly water churned beneath me—black, thick, endless. The stench of iron and decay twisted my stomach. My breath caught as I stepped back. "Is that... the river they say runs into the Styx?"

Hermes didn't answer. His eyes alone gave me the truth I didn't want to hear.

"Time is running short, kali mou," he warned, his voice sharp as the cold. "Prepare yourself."

The dream fractured—shattering into a million pieces.

I woke with a sharp inhale, sweat slick on my brow. The echo of dark waters still roared in my ears. I didn't know why I was seeing this, but I knew one thing for sure: we had to leave—we had to get back to Greece. Now.

But how? I hadn't even thought to ask before we came here.

A blanket had been draped over me; the library was empty and silent. Anxiety sliced through the lingering haze as I scrambled upright, only to tumble out of the chair and hit the floor with a dull thump. My body ached from the training, making me groan.

Thank the gods someone walked in just then. The door creaked open, footsteps rushed toward me, and a pair of strong arms lifted me gently.

"Ravena, what happened." Eirik's voice was thick with concern.

I clung to his tunic, struggling to steady my breathing, but the words tumbled out anyway. "It was... it was Kyllini—burning with ice, shadows everywhere, people screaming. I saw Athenae too, and then a river—black water. Hermes was there; he showed me all of it. He said the winds are growing darker every day, that time is running short." My voice cracked as I forced the last part out, desperate for him to understand. "We have to get back to Greece. Now."

Chapter Thirty-Six

Eirik carried me back through the fortress halls, his stride calm even as my thoughts reeled. The vision still clung to me—black water, burning trees, and screams that weren't my own but felt like they could be. He lowered me gently onto bed, and only then did I notice my hands trembling.

The door burst open not long after. Azhrina rushed in, Prymsdora at her heels. Both froze at the sight of me—pale and shaking, still tangled in the aftermath.

"What happened?" Azhrina's voice cracked with alarm as she hurried to my side.

"I thought it was a dream at first, but it was Hermes," I managed, retelling the events. "He pulled me into a vision. I saw Kyllini—" My throat closed, but I forced myself to go on. "It was burning, not normal flames... ice-cold fire and shadows everywhere. The villages near it too, shadows and frost tore them apart. Then Athenae: cracked temples, destroyed markets. Hermes said he had to show me what the winds whisper. That time is running short."

Prymsdora's face drained of color, her hand pressed against her chest. "By the gods..." she whispered.

I knew they didn't know about the village back in Greece that had burned, but my other two companions did.

Runar padded in from the hall, ears pinned back, his gaze guarded. "If Hermes risked that much to reach you, then this is no illusion. The danger is real, and it is close."

I pulled the blanket tighter around me, my voice low. "We need to go back. Now. If what I saw is true, then Kyllini... maybe even Athenae... won't survive what's coming."

The room fell into a heavy silence, broken only by the crackle of the hearth. Eirik stood stiff beside me, his jaw set, but his eyes burned with something I couldn't place.

Prymsdora finally lifted her chin, her usual cheer replaced by a hardened expression. "Then you will not go unprepared. Right now, we bathe you, ready you with fresh armor, and gather what is needed. By this afternoon, you all depart."

Azhrina nodded, already moving. "Yes, milady. We'll see to everything."

Runar rumbled his agreement, golden eyes fixed on me. "Prepare now. By this evening, we return to Greece—before nightfall."

Azhrina and Prymsdora didn't waste another moment. They moved with quiet efficiency: one fetching linens and oils, the other gathering fresh armor from the wardrobe.

"Come," Azhrina urged gently, her hand cool against my arm. "The bath will clear your head, milady. Let the water strip away the heaviness before you take on new weight."

Prymsdora muttered under her breath as she tugged at straps and buckles. "New weight is right. You'll need steel, not softness, for what potentially waits back in Greece." Her words were blunt, but the worry behind them was unmistakable.

Eirik lingered only a moment longer before turning toward the door. His voice was quiet, but it reached me. "I'll be outside." He left with Runar at his side, their footsteps echoing into the hall.

The two women guided me to the bath. Steam rolled across the stone as I sank into the heated pool, muscles sighing in relief even as my mind refused to settle. The vision clung to me—Hermes' eyes, the way the black water had churned, the screams that refused to fade. Why was I seeing the river? There was nothing like that in Greece, except in stories. Unless I was wrong...

Azhrina poured warm water over my hair, her voice soft. "Do not let fear dig its claws into you. You saw what you needed to, but fear clouds more than it clears."

I exhaled, closing my eyes as Prymsdora scrubbed the remnants of frost and dirt from my armor plates at the pool's edge. "It wasn't just fear," I murmured. "It was a very loud warning. Like a door opening—and if I don't move fast enough..." I trailed off, shivering though the water was warm.

Neither of them answered. Their silence spoke said more than words.

By the time I stepped out, wrapped in clean linen, the armor gleamed brighter. They dressed me piece by piece—chainmail, leather plates, the belt cinched tight at my waist. My body still trembled faintly from the vision, but their presence steadied me.

When they finished, I hardly recognized myself. The armor sat heavier—not from its make, but from its meaning. The faint runes etched along the plates caught in the torchlight, glowing pale like ice about to crack. My braid was pulled tighter than before, strands pinned firmly back as if even my hair had no room to be unruly.

Prymsdora's usual brightness had dimmed; her eyes held quiet resolve. "There. Not as someone playing at war, but someone preparing to face it head-on."

Azhrina adjusted the clasp at my shoulder, her touch firm. "It suits you, milady. Not because it's beautiful, but because it was meant for you. Only you can wear this with such grace."

I swallowed, my reflection in the polished plate sharper, more unfamiliar than ever. Not just a girl fumbling in a world of gods. For better or worse, I looked like someone ready to fight.

"Ready or not," I whispered to myself, "we're going back."

The chamber was darker than I remembered, the broken portal looming. A faint hum lingered in the air, remnants of power clinging here still—uneasy and restless. Eirik's steps echoed behind me, his presence steady, while Runar paced ahead, claws scraping lightly as though even he didn't trust the silence.

My fingers brushed the cracked arch, frost bleeding at my touch. From my satchel, I pulled out the small obsidian charm Hecate had given me—its center pulsed faintly, like a heartbeat caught between realms.

Skadi's voice stirred in the back of my mind, calm but firm. *Focus on where you wish to go, young one. Picture it—its air, its people, its soil beneath your feet. The magic will answer.*

I exhaled, grounding myself, clutching the charm tight in my palm. "Kyllini," I whispered.

Eirik stepped closer, his hand raising, flame flickering along his palm. "If you're to open it, I'll help anchor it. This is no easy feat." His eyes pierced mine—certain, steady—the kind of look that promised he wouldn't let me face this alone.

I nodded, pressing my other hand to the runes. Frost spread, curling along the cracks like veins of ice. His fire followed, searing across the other side. For a moment, the portal screamed against us, stone groaning, sparks hissing where frost and fire met.

"Hold steady!" Runar barked, planting himself at the center.

I clenched my jaw, pulling harder. The image of Kyllini filled my mind—its streets, its rooftops, the snowy temple. Slowly, almost impossibly, the arch lit up. Pale blue light bled into the cracks until the ruin shone whole again. The portal tore open with a crack that rattled through my bones, frost curling against fire until the stone itself groaned. Runar pushed through first, his fur bristling as he vanished into the glow. Eirik followed, his movements sure and deliberate, before his hand reached back to guide me.

Crossing was like being dragged through ice water and fire all at once, my lungs seizing until—suddenly—air.

I stumbled forward, boots striking stone. The cavern walls loomed around us, smooth, carvings glinting in the low firelight Hermes must have left behind. It was his cave, the one he'd mentioned back in Athenae.

Runar sniffed the air, ears flicking back. "We're close. I smell the village."

Eirik steadied me as I caught my breath, the echo of the crossing still ringing in my ears. Then I turned toward the cave mouth, the first slice of twilight spilling in. My heart lurched.

The village. I sprinted to the opening.

Kyllini stretched out below, nestled into the mountainside—its streets and rooftops intact. No screams. No shadows burning things down. For the first time since the vision, relief broke through the knot in my chest, piercing enough it almost hurt. "It's okay... Kyllini is okay."

But the relief didn't last.

Beyond Kyllini's mountains, further south in the direction of Naxos, smoke smeared the horizon. Black plumes curled upward, black against the starry sky. Villages—smaller, scattered places between here and Drusia—were burning.

Eirik's jaw clenched as he came to stand beside me at the cave's edge, moonlight catching faintly along the edge of his axe. "They're burning."

Runar growled low, the sound rumbling against the stone beneath us. "And it's spreading this way." His golden eyes found mine, knowing. "Your vision wasn't wrong, young frostling. Time is of the essence."

Skadi's voice stirred faintly in my mind, quiet but certain. *You made it back. Now the fight begins. Be cautious, Ravena.*

We descended the narrow mountain paths at a pace that bordered on reckless. The stone steps and winding trails were familiar, but my nerves still pricked with every shadow along the way. Runar led, tail stiff and ears twitching, while Eirik stayed close enough that I felt the heat radiate from his body with every step.

When Kyllini finally appeared, relief hit me so hard my knees nearly buckled. The wooden homes, clustered around the central square, still stood. Lantern smoke curled into the air. Children darted between doorways. No ice, no screams, no ruin. It was still safe—for now.

As we reached the outskirts, the first villagers spotted us. Whispers spread quickly, and soon Lydia, Theron, and Cora pushed their way through the gathering crowd.

"Ravena!" Lydia's cry split the air as she threw her arms around me. "By all the gods, you're alive!" Her eyes searched my face before dropping to the armor I wore, her breath catching. "You've changed."

"It's been... a long journey," I admitted quietly, offering a small smile.

Cora was next, slower, her hand trembling as she reached for mine. Her eyes glossed with tears that she tried to blink away. "You've grown so much," she whispered, her voice breaking. "Skadi would be proud."

My throat tightened—the words were too much, so I only squeezed her hand in return.

Theron clasped Eirik's arm in a firm nod, then gave Runar a respectful glance that earned only a rumbling huff.

That evening, we rested just long enough to eat and gather our bearings. The hearth's warmth felt too gentle compared to what Hermes had shown me. My mind never stopped replaying the images. Kyllini still felt like home, but even here, safety felt like it was on a timer, and we were quickly reaching zero. We all settled in for a restless night of sleep.

At dawn, a scout stumbled into the square, breathless. "A village to the south—ice burning and the village destroyed. Just like Drusia."

Runar's ears pinned back, a low growl rumbling in his chest. "Then we don't delay. We move."

Eirik's gaze met mine. He didn't need to speak; I already knew his answer.

I gave a single, firm nod. "We leave today. I won't let another village fall if we can stop it."

Lydia's jaw tightened, her composure cracking just enough to reveal the worry in her eyes. "Then go," she said quietly. "But understand—what waits for you is far worse than anything you've yet to face."

I nodded solemnly, "I know, but I've been preparing for this."

Cora reached out, her fingers brushing mine, lingering like she didn't want to let go. "Be careful, Ravena. Please."

We resupplied quickly—water, cloaks, food wrapped tight for the journey. I was almost certain we wouldn't even get to the food. Eirik adjusted his axe at his back; Runar padded close to my side.

By the time we set out, the sun had just crested the mountains, pale light falling across Kyllini. I glanced back only once before turning my eyes southward, to the smoke that marked our next step.

Runar knelt down, I swung onto his back, Eirik mounting his horse, and we began our journey.

The smoke thickened as we pressed on, the sky dimming to a bruised gray as snow began to fall. It wasn't heavy—soft, but unnatural—each flake drifting eerily to the ground. It gathered across our cloaks, carrying a darker energy. I reached out, letting one melt against my palm. The air hummed with cold, but... this wasn't mine.

Runar's head lowered, golden eyes narrowing. "Is this you, Ravena?"

I shook my head, stomach dropping. "No. I haven't call to my magic."

His ears flicked back, a warning growl in his chest. "This isn't just snow... something's close."

The trees thinned, opening to cliffs above the village below. From here, we could see everything—homes shattered, not-flames devouring roofs, people fleeing into the snow. But what made my blood run colder were the shapes moving in the smoke.

Shadows given form. Twisted limbs, stretched too far to be human, their bodies flickering like they were made of pure shadows. Their shrieks carried even this far, high and hollow, like laughter warped into terror.

"Mormo's spawn—same as in Drusia," Eirik muttered grimly, his hand already on his axe.

We kept moving. The sound of rushing water grew louder until the cliffs split into a canyon. A waterfall thundered before us, its pool dark at the base. Frost crept along the rocks, defying the rush of water that should've kept the ice at bay.

Something shifted below the surface.

I stumbled a step back, breath catching. The water stilled unnaturally—too smooth, as if the river itself were holding its breath. Then, ice cracked along its edge.

Shapes emerged from the cascade —not stepping, but forming. Cloaked figures bled from the spray, water sheeting off armor black as night. Their swords pulsed with a faint blue light, each movement warping the air with cold.

One landed heavily in the pool, water freezing instantly where its boots touched. Another followed. Then another.

Eirik shifted at my side, fire sparking along his axe. "Nál," he muttered, his voice rough with recognition.

Runar's growl rumbled deep, enough to make the stones underfoot tremble. "Undead ice warriors. Agnar's soldiers."

The closest one lifted its head—no face beneath the hood, only a metal mask—and the blade in its hand hissed, dripping frozen light like venom.

The shadows answered the hiss. From the tree line behind us, the Nychtari slithered forward, their forms shifting between solid and smoke. Dozens, maybe more.

I raised my shield, Skadi's sword trembling in my grip. My breath came fast. "We're surrounded."

"Then we fight," Eirik said, steady as ever.

The Nál struck first. Water surged upward as its blade came down, clashing against mine. Ice screamed, shards scattering across the stones. The impact jolted my arm to the bone. Another closed in, forcing me to twist, barely catching its strike on my shield.

Eirik's fire roared as he met one head-on, flame hissing against frozen steel. Sparks and steam lit the air. Runar lunged at the Nychtari, his massive body tearing through shadow as claws met smoke and shrieks filled the dark.

I swung for the nearest Nál, frost surging along my blade. It connected, ice biting deep into its chest—but the thing didn't fall. It only staggered, void gaping where a wound should have been.

"Ravena!" Eirik barked, catching another's strike before it could land across my back.

We fought back-to-back, our powers colliding with theirs in violent bursts. Fire and frost met shadow and ice, each clash rattling the ground. My lungs burned, magic clawing at my veins. Every swing, every strike drained more from me than the last.

A Nál stepped through the mist, its blade glowing brighter than the rest. It lifted its sword—and the pull of its magic dragged at mine.

Instinct flared. I raised my own, frost spiraling down the steel as power surged.

Our blades collided—and the explosion ripped the world apart.

The ground screamed beneath us, ice and stone shattering in every direction. A fissure split wide, the roar of the waterfall swallowed by the thunder of collapsing earth. The blast tore through me—sharp, searing pain streaking across my side as shards of ice and the Náls blade pierced my shoulder.

"Ravena!" Eirik's voice cut through the chaos.

The world tilted, my grip slipping on the sword as the ground gave way beneath my boots, the fissure yawning open like a hungry maw.

I fell.

The last thing I saw was Runar lunging—Eirik's hand reaching for me, panic and horror blazing in his eyes.

As I plunged through the fissure, a searing pain tore through my shoulder where the soldier's blade had struck. The wound burned fiercely, the ache spreading like wildfire. The light from the surface vanished, leaving me in suffocating blackness. Fear clawed at my chest. Jagged rocks scraped my armor, some sharp enough to pierce through, and shallow cuts burned as I fell.

A shimmer of blue light flickered around me, like a veil stretching as I crossed through. Then the space I was falling through vanished, and I slammed into icy water with a jarring splash.

The current dragged me under, relentless. I kicked, clawed, fought against the cold that bit into my wounds and stole the air from my lungs. When I broke the surface, gasping raggedly, the river slowed—its fury giving way to an unearthly calm. I floated, carried aimlessly through the dark. The black water's chill seeped into my bones, its stillness broken only by the faint splash of water against my skin.

Exhaustion burned at my soul. My thoughts blurred. Where was I now? What happened to Eirik and Runar?

Eirik's face flickered through my mind—panic and horror written across it—before darkness tugged me under again.

That's when I saw it through half lidded eyes—a small ship drifting out of the shadows, ghostly and silent. Before I could comprehend it, strong, pale hands seized me, pulling me from the water.

Cold air slapped my face. A deep voice rumbled, calm yet edged with authority:

"What is a living mortal... no demi-goddess doing here?" A pause followed with a tired sigh, "Do not fret—you are safe."

When my vision cleared again, the ship rested at a shadowed dock. A man knelt beside me, slow in every movement, as if he had eternity to spend. He scooped me up, protective and with a respectful stillness, his pale face framed by black hair, and his faintly glowing eyes were sharp as ice.

"I'm Charon, Ferryman of the Underworld," he said simply. "I'm taking you to the palace. We will seek help for you there."

The word hit like a blow: Underworld. The shimmer I'd seen was the barrier. I had crossed into yet another realm.

Charon carried me onward, each stride steady, unhurried—and so painstakingly calm.

The sky stretched in eternal twilight, drenched in deep blues and purples, and stars scattered thick as snow. A luminous moon hung low, its glow spilling across black grass that rippled in a phantom wind. The air felt ancient, heavy, but not suffocating.

And then I saw it.

The palace. Perched high on a mountain, jagged and dark, its silhouette tore into the star-swept sky like a crown. Its stone gleamed faintly, as if alive with the essence of the Underworld itself.

My breath caught, pain and awe tangling in my chest. A low, creeping fear settled in my stomach.

Do not be scared, Ravena. You are safe here. I sense this is only the beginning of your journey. Skadi's voice whispered in my mind, then faded. As if it was all she could say, her essence dwindling.

Charon walked on in silence, his steps measured, as he carried me further toward the haunting beauty of the Underworld.

Acknowledgements

I'd like to thank my husband and friends for their encouragement and patience as I poured myself into this crazy adventure and world of Greek & Norse Gods. And of course, Ravena's story, because after all it is her adventure.

To the readers who pick up this book—you're the reason these stories come to life. Your support means more than I can ever say.

A huge thank-you to my first ever alpha reader and future indie author, Katarina Vaughn—your honest feedback and support mean the world to me. Also! Her book *Tides of Fate* will be appearing soon.

About the Author

J.D.Victery is an indie author who loves to write mythology, adventure, and personal growth into stories filled with flawed but relatable characters. Her work blends myth and romantasy with a touch of the unexpected. When she isn't writing, she's usually baking something new, homeschooling her kids, caring for her horses, or finding inspiration (and the occasional escape) in video games.

Winter's Awakening: Ravena's Prophecy is her debut novel, and the first in a planned series.

You can connect with her on:
Instagram: @valkyrie_sagas
Facebook: J. Victery-Author